A SECOND LOOK

UPCOMING BY W.S. SIMONS

Losing August

Weeding Out the Lies

Stone by Stone

A SECOND LOOK

A NOVEL

By W.S. Simons

Thank you to all those in
workshops who helped me
find my way with this story.

CHAPTER 1

Weary of being seven, Peter is about to turn eight. He dresses quickly, scarcely having slept, in anticipation of sunrise, of spending the day back at Spirit Lake. The first time he saw her, nearly six months earlier, she had begun to freeze over, boundaries growing vague under snow. On brief visits over the winter, bundled against the cold, he listened to her ice sing. When away from her, usually for an entire week, sometimes two, he yearned for her, for her hypnotic stillness, for the scent of pinewoods skirting her shore. She began to thaw in March, timid ripples lapping his rubber boots.

He steps from the cottage this warm spring morning, each breath taking in the lake's unique aroma, sweet and a little acrid from silt and decaying leaves. He closes his eyes. A robin warbles from above. A tufted titmouse calls from the far woods. The chipping sparrow's unceasing squeaking underlies a field sparrow's mewing trill, and above them all, a jay's mournful pleading.

Opening his eyes slowly, he takes in the fullness of the lake and grins. It is a shallow 200-acres surrounded by a hodgepodge of small cottages. He turns to admire the sun rising behind the woods, bathing the sky in what he will describe in his journal as pale apricot. He turns again toward Spirit Lake and ambles down the slight hill and over the stretch of lawn to a neighbor's dock. He does not hurry, reveling instead in each step he takes on dew-laden grass.

An angular boy, his narrow limbs appear fragile, his neck too thin, his ears protrude a bit too far. He wears a plaid shirt, his favorite, buttoned-up to his neck and tucked into baggy shorts, pockets bulging with small field guides and a spiral-bound notepad.

He pauses mid-dock where shade is not yet overtaken by sunlight, the demarcation of night and day. His shadow casts long and narrow, bisecting the gleaming rectangle at the end. No air stirs. Spirit Lake is a mirror. He leans over the edge struggling to peer past his reflection, past his world and into hers. She rewards this attention with a school of minnows. Smiling, he sits down on the end of the dock, removes his shoes, tucks his socks into them, and dangles his legs. Toes rake the cold water. Behind him stand five modest bungalows. Lots of windows, lots of beds, they comprise an enclave of sorts, sandwiched between a marsh to the north and a narrow channel to the south. Like all cottages on this lake and the next one over and the next one over from that, they are summer places. In 1960, summer in Michigan is measured by the school year. Families arrive in June and leave on Labor Day.

New to the lake, Peter and his parents don't adhere to such constraints. George and Mildred Eastman purchased their cottage late November and spent the winter on renovations. A few more touchups, painting doors and trim, putting up screens, and they'll be finished. It has been a warm spring and they've spent nearly every weekend at the lake enjoying what they worked so hard to create: A sanctuary of calm.

Peter looks at his watch then withdraws his notepad and pencil. Flipping to his last entry, he writes below it: May 7. *6:32 AM - Sun rises over trees. Birdsong: sparrows - field and chipping, robin, jay, titmouse.* He pulls a thermometer from his pocket and lowers it with a string into the water. He counts to thirty, retrieves it and records the reading. *Water 62°.* Having accounted for pertinent information of the moment, he stills his feet and his body, and listens. *Only when one is still can one become one with the natural world.* His father taught him that, taught him how to observe without interruption or interaction.

He hears something behind him, a watery flutter. He waits without turning. He listens. Nothing. Now, dripping. It stops. Turning slowly, he sees a magnificent Sandhill Crane walking shoreline shallows. Its attention fully on the water, it doesn't notice him or hear his gasp. Water drips as one leg folds and unfolds, expanding toes slipping silently into the water. Peter makes mental notes of every detail to write down later: *Massive body, long legs, maybe four feet tall, gentle sloping 'S' neck, gray feathers with blue and brown mixed in, white chin, golden eye, brilliant red patch above the long black beak.* It stops, stands so still there are no ripples. Suddenly it pecks the water, snatching a small perch, its tail flicking. Stretching its long neck out and up the crane takes it in, swallowing it whole. After two more attempts it catches another, downs it, and takes flight in an ungainly display of aerodynamics, a wingspan so wide it seems prehistoric. Peter spins around to watch it, thrilled to hear the whoosh of its feathers.

His heart pounding, Peter jumps to his feet, looks up to the cottage, to his parents in the window, and hollers out. "Did you see it? Did you see the crane?" Mildred waves. George gives two thumbs up.

Peter pulls out his Audubon guide confirming his identification. To this moment, he has only seen cranes soaring high, their distant calls like tree branches creaking against each other. He sits back down to record his sighting, checking his wristwatch. *6:45 AM Sand Hill crane caught 2 fish. Perch and maybe a sunfish.* The remainder of his notes will have to wait as his attention is drawn to a low drone from across the water.

He scans the empty lake. From the far corner, a boat appears, taking its time crossing toward him. As the skiff draws closer, he sees a man. *Black windbreaker, white shirt, wide-brimmed hat, dark glasses.* Details. Always taking note of details.

Pulling up to the dock, the man tosses a rope. "Here," he says, and Peter catches it. "You're the Eastman boy, aren't you?"

"Yes. I'm Peter."

"You remember me?" He shows Peter how to tie the line to the cleat. There's small talk. He says he lives through the woods on the channel, that he brought some firewood over to them last winter when they spent a snowy weekend.

"Walter Stem," Peter interrupts. "Is this your boat, Mr. Stem?"

"Yes. And you can call me Walter."

"I don't think so," Peter says, having learned to treat adults with respect. "I'll have to ask. That's our canoe over there on the rack."

"It's a beaut," Mr. stem says without smiling.

Peter likes this abridgement of beautiful and will use it a lot during the summer ahead. *That hat is a beaut* he will say of a new friend's fraying straw hat. *That skull is a beaut* he will say of the owl skull in this friend's collection of found objects. *It's a beaut.*

Peter takes in the particulars of Mr. Stem, surmising him to be about his father's age. He likes that he wears his shirt tucked in into his trousers. It must have been colder earlier because there's a gray sweatshirt folded on the seat.

Mr. Stem lifts a stringer of fish from the water.

Peter lets go with a barrage of questions. He knows Spirit is one in a chain of interconnected lakes and asks which fish came from which lake. Mr. Stem answers with specifics about location, depth, lure, bait, and snags, one of which is notorious for harboring bass and eating lures. His voice sounds like an educator, confident and comforting.

Mr. Stem says he needs to go clean the fish, that he just stopped to say hello. He says he'll be out again tomorrow. As the skiff disappears around a bend beyond the trees, Peter scribbles everything in his small notepad. The record of his life.

Sunday morning, Peter waits on the dock with a ruler and his big drawing notebook, the one bulging with scraps of birch bark, lichen bits, and taped-on mayfly wings. Mr. Stem arrives with another full stringer. Peter measures each fish, writing everything down, filling the last empty page, spilling over to the inside back cover. He asks to keep a bluegill so he can draw it on the first page of a fresh book. Mr. Stem obliges, filling a bucket from the lake and carefully removing a fish from the stringer, dropping it in.

Peter watches it swim to the bottom, a bit of blood drifting from its yawning gill.

Mr. Stem putters off.

By the time Peter retrieves a new notebook, he finds the fish belly up in the bucket. His drawing of it is labeled DEAD BLUEGILL. At his mother's suggestion, he buries it where they are about to plant a small vegetable garden. It will be good fertilizer.

June brings chaos. The other four families of the enclave arrive with fourteen kids among them. In the second cottage from the marsh are the Hodges with five kids, all born into summers of sunburns and fireflies, squalling, crawling, then learning to ski, running in from the lake, screen door smacking, wet feet slapping linoleum. Tyler is the youngest of them, eight going on nine. He's a beautiful boy with deep dimples and eager grin. He breezes through the day like trouble can't touch him. He is quick-witted. Sure-footed. He loves to waterski, play baseball, and swim. He is a social creature, and like Peter, quite fond of Walter Stem. Walter occasionally lets Ty tag along when he goes across the lake to Anglers Tavern.

On an overcast day in late June Walter collects Ty in the skiff, guns it, and shoots straight across to Anglers, tying up to the dock out front. Cigar smoke hangs heavy as they walk through the door under a large carved bass with a welcome sign hanging below it. Ty strides in, grinning at all the old men on their barstools. The bartender calls out. "With or without the cherry today, Ty?"

"Two cherries today, Tucker. I'm feeling reckless!" Ty loves the laughs he gets almost as much as being known by name in a bar. By the time he and Walter take their stools, there's a fountain Coke, heavy on the syrup, and a cold beer waiting for them.

Walter puts his hat on the bar, revealing a bald head.

Ty listens to Walter and the barflies hash over the latest issue the local paper has everyone stirred up about, talk of bringing in water and sewer. *Don't need it,* one says. *You watch,* another says. *Taxes will shoot up sky high.* An old man, so big the stool disappears under his girth, wonders what the hell they need it for when most folks are only out here for three months. As is their habit, Ty and Walter leave after the second round.

Tyler Hodges belongs smack in the middle of things. Peter Eastman is content on the fringes. They have little more in common than being the youngest kids on Spirit Marsh Road, yet their names will forever be linked as the boys who drowned together on a stormy night in July of 1960.

CHAPTER 2

Forty years later, Penn Hodges-Coburn, Tyler's only sister, still suffers a melancholy that sometimes overtakes her, when her focus is stolen by the days before loss, on memories certainly reimagined, for there is little truth to memory. As to the unresolved circumstances surrounding Tyler and Peter's deaths, there are only so many words to use when old questions have no new answers.

She rises after a restless night, slips into thick socks, lifts her fleece robe off a hook behind the door and wonders how long the summer cotton kimono robe has been there, realizing it never got put away with the summer clothes last fall. She steps around the corner to the tiny half bath cluttered with facial cleansers and creams for daytime hydration and nighttime anti-aging, most of which she forgets to use. There's a tube of cortisone on the sink for the eczema patch on her arm, and a near empty tube of antiseptic that just never made it back into the medicine cabinet. She pees, brushes her teeth and washes her face, but there's no towel. Stepping into the next room, she grabs one off a stack on the hospital bed recently installed there. She pulls on the sweatpants from the floor and a turtleneck sweater off a hook and pads through the cottage, ignoring a large wicker bin overloaded with magazines, mostly unread, and the clean clothes folded and stacked on a chair in the living room. Looking out the bank of windows to the lake, she longs for mornings warm enough to drink coffee on the patio. Downstairs in the kitchen, she wades through dirty dishes looking for yesterday's mug, rinses it out, fills the coffee pot and waits for it to brew. With effort, she can maintain focus on important things. Her daughter is important, as is teaching, the house in town, the cottage, and her research. It's everything else, the minutia of life, that sometimes sifts between floorboards. She is all too aware her surroundings, messy as they are, are in direct conflict with her scientific endeavors, efforts that require detail and clarity.

A tenured professor at the University of Michigan, she's an expert in her field, researching wetlands, examining their morphology, their vulnerabilities. She has authored two books on the sustainability of inland lake ecosystems and publishes annually in several scientific journals. A therapist once suggested the connection between her work and the death of her little brother, but Penn refuses to think of it in such terms, insisting one has nothing to do with the other. Yet every marsh she wades into, every time its pungent aroma hits her, memories swarm of the morning the boys' bodies were pulled from the cattails.

It is May of 2000 and she has just taken leave to tend her dying mother.

Penn calls her oldest brother, someone she hasn't spoken to in close to five years. She tells him their mother is terminally ill and wants to move in with her at the cottage. This pisses him off.

"Don't be stupid," Jim chides. "Just stick her in a goddamn nursing home and forget about it."

"There isn't any money for that."

"What happened to Dad's life insurance?"

"Gone."

"Social security?"

"Not enough."

"The house money?"

"Long gone." By now Penn is annoyed he has so little concept of their mother's situation.

"What do you mean, long gone? How'd she piss it away? That's some of the most expensive real estate in . . ."

Penn cuts him off. "Seriously? It was a dump by the time she sold it."

"It's lakefront."

"It was a shit hole with a lake view."

The house in question was their parents' house. It stood on the bluff in Edgewater overlooking Lake Michigan. It was an inheritance from Evelyn's parents, people who would rather their only daughter had married anyone but Dick Hodges. Had it sold then, as Dick wanted, it would have brought a nice price. But Evelyn wanted to live there and the family of four, soon to be five but not yet their full seven, moved from their cramped two-bedroom bungalow into the stately two-story, four-bedroom, fully furnished home. Over the years, Dick refused to sink any money into a house he resented as much as his in-laws had resented him. He patched the roof when it should have been re-shingled. When the porch needed re-decking, he tore it off, installing a readymade concrete stoop. It needed paint outside and in. The foundation had cracks. After Dick died, Evelyn and the house decayed together. When she needed money, the house was sold "as is," worn out furniture and all, cupboards full, closets crammed. Evelyn walked out with only a suitcase.

"Then what about the cottage?" Jim snipes.

"What about it?"

"It's still hers. Sell it."

"What the hell?" Penn says. "You know damn well Matthew and I bought it from her years ago."

"What did you pay? Not enough, I'm sure."

Penn grinds her teeth. "It was falling apart. We paid her what it was worth."

Jim's silence fills with old arguments not worth resurrecting. "What do you want from me, Penny?"

In the space between his asking and her answer, no longer than it takes to exhale, she wonders what it was she thought she might get out of calling him, if she had deluded herself into thinking there was any love or empathy to be gained by it. "Nothing," she says, and hangs up.

The emptiness of the moment, the sensation of absolute isolation is a feeling she's all too familiar with; a place where nothing matters; a place without past or present; without pain or desire; where nothing exists; a place where life and death do not register; a place where the loss of her own life would make no difference.

She doesn't hear a blue jay scream a warning, or notice it dart by the window. Only when another joins it, screeching, then another, and another is she drawn to watch them, all intent on dislodging something from the huge maple outside the window. She looks within its budding branches to the barred owl perched not ten feet from her, unfazed by the jays' protestations. It does not budge except to scratch at its belly and preen a few feathers. The blue jays move off. The owl closes its eyes. For an instant Penn is ten again, anxious to tell Peter, her best friend for eight weeks and two days forty summers ago, about this owl perched so close to her. But he's dead. Then it occurs to her maybe he is the owl, come to save her from herself. She smiles. She sighs. She dreads her mother's impending intrusion.

History between Evelyn and Penn precludes intimacy. Though Penn has always managed Evelyn's finances, finding her affordable places to live, her mother has not reciprocated with consideration of any kind. She did not attend Penn's wedding or celebrate the birth of Penn and Matthew's daughter Andrea. She did not go to Matthew's funeral. Whenever Penn would go by her apartment without calling first, Evelyn didn't let her in, talking through the door, demanding she leave. In light of this estrangement, Evelyn's request to spend her last days in a place she abandoned decades earlier makes no sense. But dying has a way of changing a person's outlook, and Evelyn Hodges is no exception. Though nothing in her behavior toward her children should have made her think any of them would take her in, she asked Penn, and Penn said yes.

Penn lifts the journal she bought to keep track of medication schedules and pertinent information for the Hospice people. She knows the drill from taking care of Matthew as he died. The mere familiarity of the task makes her long for him, not for when he was ill, but for the quiet times when their life together was certain, when his hand would trace the small of her back. Life before cancer and chemo and pain; before he died with her next to him begging him to hang on one more minute.

She hadn't thought to write anything in this new journal yet, but as is often the case, intentions carry no weight.

May 15, 2000 - I sit here like I used to as a kid and I swear I hear the voices of boys frogging in the marsh, calling out they've got another one. But there is no more marsh. There are no more boys. I get lost in here sometimes, especially now, caught between lives and time. I am my younger self. I am my brothers as children running room to room. I am my parents talking softly on a warm summer evening in darkness, crickets keeping time. I am pain and tears and ache. I am laughter and smiles and the slightest of grins. I am everything and then I am nothing. I want the life I gave my daughter. Her contentment should be my reward, but I crave more. More love. More attention. More assurance when there was little love, no attention - so much doubt. Maybe it was because I grew up in the wake of loss. I don't know that I've ever been more aware of these things until now. Mom arrives tomorrow.

Some time in the night, Penn wakes to darkness except for an amber glow spilling from the living room. She rises from bed and walks naked to the front room to find Matthew sorting through stacks of old mail. He smiles at her, mildly scolding for her messiness. "You've let the place go to hell a bit," he says.

"That's your job," she answers, smiling.

A magazine turns into a dust cloth and he wipes the mantle. The room that was cluttered and dusty only the day before is spotless. The couch pillows are fluffed unusually full, instead of squashed into corners.

"I forgot you were here," she says. "How could I do that?"

He turns to her with his smile, the one that always reassured her. "I'm here," he says. "You're not alone."

Penn wakes on the couch in the clothes from the day before. It's dark except for the glow of moonlight through open windows. The pillows are flat, the coffee table strewn with magazines and yesterday's lunch plate. She goes to her bedroom, takes off her clothes, leaving them on the floor, and crawls into her single bed, imagining it is the old double and Matthew is about to join her. "I'll clean tomorrow," she says quietly. The remaining night is uninterrupted. Rising at dawn, Penn cleans the house before Evelyn's arrival.

Hospice delivers Evelyn to the cottage late afternoon. Penn watches two attendants trample the last of the daffodils out back unloading Evelyn from the van into a wheelchair. Evelyn screeches at them to take her back home. So it is that the day makes its steady decline into regret.

Evelyn takes up residence in the spare room where Matthew died several years earlier. Before that, it was Andi's bedroom. Before that, the four brothers bunked there. As two men plant her withered body in the hospital bed, Evelyn slaps at them and kicks, her scrawny appendages too weak to inflict harm. Evelyn is sick, angry, and at only seventy-eight appears long past her expiration date.

Penn sits in the living room within earshot of Evelyn's cussing. A nurse, an efficient woman in her forties, explains to Penn the med-pack for pain, anxiety, nausea, constipation, and psychosis. Penn shouts to the bedroom.

"Mom! Give those boys a break!"

Evelyn hollers back. "I haven't set foot in this place for thirty years. Don't see why I have to now!" Something falls to the floor.

"You asked to come here, Mother. Behave."

"Don't you tell me to behave!"

Nothing about Evelyn's rambunctiousness seems to indicate a woman with days to live.

"I have plans to travel in August," Penn tells the nurse, looking at her for some kind of assurance. She finds none. "There's a prognosis, isn't there? I was led to understand she was close." Evelyn lets go with a string of obscenities from the next room. "That doesn't sound like a woman close to death."

The nurse feigns a smile. "You'll have to discuss that with a doctor. One will be by tomorrow." She rises to leave.

"Don't judge me," Penn says.

The nurse is quick to respond. "I assure you, I'm not judging. In the best of circumstances, this is not easy." She asks Penn for a water glass. "I'll give her a sedative to settle her."

One of the attendants, a young man whose buttons strain at the belly, steps in to ask Penn where she'd like the wheelchair. He has a compassionate face with an expression that seems to say he'd be happy to take the old lady back where she came from. He stands there, waiting, but when no request is made of him, he nods and leaves.

After convincing Evelyn to take her pill, the nurse leaves and stands in the doorway for a moment, smiling at

Penn, reminding her she is not in it alone. There are resources available to help her as the caregiver. Women would come in to bathe her mother and doctors would stop every few days for evaluations until the end. There would be a steady supply of liquid morphine, Roxanol, presumably for the patient. There are grief counselors and support groups. Penn gives the nurse a dismissive smile. Nothing they can do will be of any real assistance. She's in it alone.

Once Evelyn is asleep, Penn walks around the cottage to the lakefront still piled with docks on shore. Sun warms her face as robins peck in the grass under the pontoon boat. A cardinal calls out. A hatch of mayflies swarm at water's edge as minnows nip the surface, creating tiny concentric ripples expanding through each other.

Had Tyler not died so young, it was conceivable Evelyn might have been a better person, a loving mother, a decent human being. Because of this, Penn has forgiven her mother all the slights and insults, but not her absence. Evelyn's abandonment of her family after Tyler's death is the mortar in the wall between them still. Back inside, she finds her mother out cold, her jaw hanging open, a viscous string of drool dangling. She is still asleep hours later when Penn goes to bed.

It's three in the morning when Penn startles awake. Hearing nothing, she reaches for the bedspread, pulling it up against a chill from the open window. Rain begins to fall, a steady breezeless shower like someone turning on a sprinkler. Rain-drenched air sifts through the screen, a soup of atmospheric chemicals reacting with volatile oils from budding trees, the faintly sour scent of last fall's decaying leaves, the earthy smelling spores of bacteria rising up from the grass, all laced with rust from the old screen. Spring rain. Altogether different from autumn rain. She can tell just by the smell.

She thinks about getting up to check on her mother, but can't muster the energy. She looks over to the baby monitor to make sure it's on. It isn't and she wonders if she'd forgotten on purpose. The transmitter is on her mother's nightstand.

She closes her eyes and hears a scratching somewhere in a wall. She re-sided and re-insulated the cottage the year before; put on a new roof three years before that. Still, they get in. Mice. Squirrels. Having done as much as she can to keep them out, she's accepted there will always be creatures making it their home as much as hers. There will always be squirrels in her attic.

A raspy exclamation of panic comes from the next room. "Where are you, Goddammit!"

Penn rises, grabs her robe from the chair and lifts the Roxanol off the dresser. There is an urgency about night pain invading the already loneliest hours. She flips the hall light on, enough light to see by without flooding tired eyes. She finds her mother wide-eyed, mouth open in silent agony, hands clenching the sheet. Without a word, Penn withdraws a measure of Roxy into the dropper and releases it under her mother's tongue like a bird feeding a chick. She gives her a pill to calm her, and a sip of water to wash it down. Together, they wait. Silently.

Her mother's eyes shift about the small room, landing on everything but her daughter – a door jam, window pane, the gingham curtain – as if searching for the one thing to make it all stop, as if just looking at it could be enough. Penn does not hold her mother's hand to comfort her. She does not offer soothing words. She sits in a straight back chair by the bed looking at the perfect triangle of light on the floor, moving her eyes from dark to light and back, imagining she can feel the expansion and contraction of her pupils.

"Don't let Tyler see me like this," Evelyn says, her words barely audible.

It would serve no purpose to explain that Tyler isn't there, that he died long ago. Evelyn closes her eyes and releases her grip.

This first night sets the pattern for all to come: sleep with expectation of interruption. Back in bed, Penn turns on a small lamp and opens her journal.

> May 16, 2000   3:45 AM - Roxy, Ativan - 10 minutes. Mom is dying. I assume it's cancer. She hasn't said. I'm just expected to ease her path – a hospice term – as if dying is a leisurely stroll through the woods. Why did I agree to this?

She puts the journal on the nightstand, turns off the light and tries to get back to sleep. As she nods off, a chorus of bullfrogs wakes her. Listening for them, she hears only the gnawing in the wall. It was a dream. There are no more frogs. Her eyes well. Croaking frogs always make her think of Tyler and Peter. Over the years, her chosen memories of them have grown into gentle, comforting thoughts. But Evelyn's presence is changing things. This time, thinking about them stings. Like fresh pain.

CHAPTER 3

On a Saturday morning in the spring of 1970, in Doylestown, Pennsylvania, Edith Stem answers a knock on her front door finding two police officers on her porch. Behind them, on the front lawn, a stocky woman in a dark gray skirt and jacket argues with two men. Edith can't make out what they're saying. Out on the street, a swarm of men, some in uniform, some in suits, pour out of cars. Neighbors congregate up and down the lovely tree-lined block.

An officer hands Edith a piece of paper, steps inside, and asks if her husband is home. Walter Stem appears from the hallway, his white shirt tucked into tan chinos, folded over in the back to appear more fitted to his thin frame. His black belt shines. His black shoes gleam. He stands erect, head high as two FBI agents escort him out of the house. He calmly tells Edith everything will be fine. He'll be back soon.

"Your hat!" Edith shouts after him.

"He won't need that," says one of the officers.

"But his head. It'll get sun burned."

Several men from the street enter and spread out into the house. Edith presses against the wall to allow them passage, hands flat to the dark wood paneling, at a loss for what to do next. She hears someone going down the basement steps.

As Walter crosses the lawn toward the cars, the woman in the gray suit, Alberta Higgins, pleads her case to an FBI agent and the sheriff, both of them resistant. As the only female assistant district attorney in Bucks County, she's earned a modicum of respect. "Let me do this," she urges.

The sheriff says she is the last person he'd consider sending in. "Obvious reasons," he says as if that should end it.

"No," Alberta says. "Let me talk to her. She's more likely to respond to another woman." The sheriff relents, urging the FBI agent aside.

Alberta steps to the door offering a warm smile to the woman plastered against the wall. While Walter looked to be in his mid-forties, Edith appears several years older. Her dishevelment seems incongruent with her husband's tidy appearance. A pudgy woman with bulgy eyes and droopy jowls, her bright pink sweater set doesn't go with her blue plaid skirt, the pleats of which are askew. Edith and Walter seem to Alberta an unlikely match.

"You shouldn't wear those pumps in the grass," Edith says in a heavy British accent, not scolding, just deeply concerned. "You'll ruin them."

"I'm sure you're right," Alberta says. "I'll be more careful." She suggests they move into the living room. Edith complies, eyes down, as if accustomed to being told what to do.

The living room is inordinately spare and dark. Wood-paneled walls have no photos or artwork. There are no pillows on either the orange couch or the two green side chairs. An oak coffee table sits empty. Heavy yellow curtains hang alongside the front picture window. Alberta scans a bookcase in the corner finding old college textbooks and two shelves filled with paperbacks, all science fiction.

Edith looks to Alberta for approval before sitting on an edge of the couch.

"Mrs. Stem? My name is Alberta Higgins. I am an assistant district attorney. I have a few questions for you. OK?"

Edith's eyes bounce between the floor and the men heading toward the bedrooms.

"Mrs. Stem?" Alberta asks. "Do you know what's happening here?"

"No." Edith looks at Alberta then quickly away. "You're pretty." It is a simple statement without gesture or smile. "I like your suit."

Alberta smiles at Edith to put her at ease. "Mrs. Stem . . ."

"Call me Edith. You're younger than me, but you can call me Edith. I don't mind. How old are you? I can't tell."

"I'm forty-one."

"I hope your husband is older than you. I'm older than mine. We don't fit. I know people think it. They don't say so. But they think it. I know they think it. Your husband is probably handsome. Is it one of the men out there?"

"No, Mrs. Stem. I'm not married."

"Edith."

"No, Edith, I'm not married."

Edith takes a breath to speak, purses her lips, then says nothing.

"Edith, they're taking Walter in for questioning concerning the disappearance of this boy." Alberta places a newspaper on the coffee table, its headline reading BUCKS COUNTY BOY MISSING.

"That poor boy," Edith says. She takes hold of a stretched-out corner of her sweater and begins mindlessly working it with both thumbs, pressing them back and forth against tight fists. "His poor parents."

"Yes," Alberta says, gently touching Edith's knee.

Edith gasps, her eyes darting down and away.

Alberta withdraws her hand. The fidgeting stops. "Edith, how long have you lived here?"

"Three years. August of '67." Edith glances out the front window, her back to the room. "Never had neighbors before. Not like this."

Alberta hears someone ascending the basement steps. Two men walk through the room. One looks to Alberta shaking his head on his way back outside. The other carries a plastic bag of what looks to be wet clothes.

"What are they doing?" Edith asks.

"Nothing to worry about," Alberta says.

"We heard that poor boy was missing when we were at the cemetery yesterday. Putting Velma in the ground." Edith claps her hands. "Oh, my goodness," she says, her smile exposing a mouthful of crowded teeth, her eyes unnaturally wide, irises surrounded by motes of white. "My manners! Tea! Would you like a pot of tea?"

"No, thank you," Alberta says. "Who was Velma?"

"Walter's mother. Several teachers were there. A sweet bunch. And the principal of the elementary school. Police came to talk to her. That missing boy was one of her students. She lived with us."

The clatter from the kitchen distracts Edith but Alberta waves a hand, catching her attention the way one would a child or a puppy. "Who lived with you? The principal?"

"What? No. Velma." Edith cocks her head and bites her bottom lip, her eyes falling to a corner.

"It's OK," Alberta says, trying to sooth.

"She was sick for weeks before she died. Never let on she had the cancer. I went to see her in hospital every day, I did. Walter couldn't bring himself to go. I don't blame him, really. She was a hard woman, that one."

"How so?"

"Oph!" Edith says, throwing her hands in the air. "Controlling. Mean. Spiteful. Controlled his every move." She pounds her forehead with both index fingers. "Nothing made that woman happy."

"That must have been very difficult for you."

There is a moment of silence as Edith seems to catch herself, her eyes cast downward again in submission. She smooths her skirt with the flat of both hands.

"Tell me about your husband."

Edith does not speak.

"You're from England? Is that where you met Walter? You're a war bride?"

After some hesitation, Edith mumbles an answer, saying she wasn't one of those silly girls trying to hook an American soldier. She stops abruptly.

Alberta smiles. "It's OK, Edith. I'd love to hear your story."

Edith leans forward, glancing down the hall, then toward the kitchen. When she begins speaking, she almost whispers, shoulders hunched, her head tucked down. "I never wanted to leave the Midlands. It just happened. I knew I had no prospects with my looks." She smirks and immediately sits up straight, her expression going flat as if she'd been scolded by some unseen superior.

"It's alright, Edith. Tell me about meeting Walter."

Edith relaxes a little and adjusts a pleat on her skirt. "Our town was overrun with American GIs. All the pretty girls got the attention, which is not to say men did not proposition me. They just had to be pissed first." Her words begin spilling out like an overflowing pitcher. Her gaze drifts about the room but never to Alberta. "I'd still be back home if it wasn't for my girl. A fat lot of good she brought me. I met Walter in my uncle's pub. He was different than the other Americans, he was. Never got drunk. He listened to people. I watched him one night beat the bloody hell out of two airmen bothering a woman in the alley out back. I thanked him and invited him inside. One thing lead to another and I ended up taking him to bed. Wasn't his idea! All Mine!"

Alberta lets her rattle on, words without benefit of filter.

"I didn't know much about doin' the deed, but he didn't know a bloody thing! Didn't know where to put it! I even thought he might be a puff. I told him a few weeks later I was preggers and he said we should get married. Married!" Her eyes open wide again. "I'd have been a lot happier if he'd left me there. I'd have had my family, my friends all these years. And Debra might have turned out better, but how's a person to know that? How's a person to know how things are going to turn out?" Edith finally looks at Alberta, her eyes intense, almost pleading. "How?"

"Debra is your daughter?"

"Yeah. My girl. Haven't seen her in years. Not a word from her. Did you know Walter is the principal of the junior high? Spends all his time at the school helping the coaches after school and other school doings. Then he comes home to me and Velma. Every evening she waits for him and as soon as he steps foot through that door she hounds him. Where have you been? Who did you see? She treats him like a child."

Another silence falls over Edith until she suddenly reaches out as if pushing someone away. "Guess she can't do that anymore."

"Why do you think she did that?"

"She was a one off, that one. Got a bit lairy."

"Lairy?"

"Always pushin' a person around, always bossin' me. Clean off her nut, she was."

"Why would you say that?"

"Her house. Not this one. Hers." Edith scowls. "Every room painted like she was expectin' a circus in there. Colors. Too many colors. You shoulda seen our bedroom. Purple tulips on the bedspread. Red roses on the curtains. My dresser was pink. Walls orange! Orange! She wouldn't let me paint over it. And strict? Dinner was at the same minute every night. And if I didn't set the table just right she'd yell at me. Her house. I wanted to move out but Walter wouldn't.

"Then we moved here," Edith continued, "and Walter put his foot down. No colors. I felt bad cuz the bedrooms were such nice colors, pale blue and light green. The kitchen was a real pretty sunshine yellow but he had it all painted over. White. No color anywhere. Just white.

Velma was so angry with him." Her gaze wandered the ceiling as her thought drifted away.

"Edith? Do you know where Walter was two nights ago? Thursday?"

"Can't say I remember," Edith says as a man in a suit steps into the living room. "Velma died Tuesday night." She watches him take all the books down. "Those need to go back in order."

Alberta motions for him to leave and he disappears down the hall.

"Walter had to take care of things. The funeral. Everyone at the school knew about it, that his mother passed."

"And Thursday night?"

"I remember Walter wasn't home because a neighbor stopped in with a casserole. It's been so lovely to have neighbors close by. They keep bringing food. Would you like a casserole to take home?"

Alberta smiles. "No thanks. Did he say where he went?"

"It was after ten when he came in."

"Did he say anything about giving anyone a ride that night? Anyone caught in the rain? A student maybe?"

"No. He didn't say. But wouldn't surprise me if he did. He's like that. Always looking out for the kids. Not like him to let a child get soaked if he can help it."

"Someone said they saw the missing boy get into Walter's car Thursday night."

Edith shrugs.

"But he didn't say anything to you about it?"

"No. But with his mother dead and all. And her funeral yesterday. I know I should say he was sad about it all, but I think it's a relief. And I'm not ashamed to say it is for me!" She begins picking at the piping of the seat cushion.

"Did Walter change any of his habits lately? Anything different about him?"

Edith shakes her head. "No, no, not that I can say. Even with his mother gone in hospital, he was the same old Walter. Routine. Routine. Mustn't upset the routine!" She crouches a bit, as if anticipating a scolding. "He was fine right up to the day Velma died. But, the night before the funeral, he was off."

"Thursday." Alberta takes a breath, running out of patience.

"Thursday? I suppose it was. He came home late and went straight to the den to polish his shoes like he does every night. Every night! But when I checked on him, well, looked like he was going to rub that leather right off. He was brushing them so hard. I told him things would get better, and he stood up, came real slow across the room, and closed the door on me real quiet like. Men. They never know how to tell you how they feel, do they? He's been gettin' out of bed during the night again. Started a couple weeks ago. I hear him in the bathroom washing his hands over and over, muttering to himself."

"Is that unusual for him? The compulsive behavior?"

"What'd you call it? It comes and goes. His mother was all about keeping things clean. Perfect. She…" Something crashes in the kitchen. Edith runs to the kitchen and Alberta follows. An embarrassed officer picks up fragments of a glass on the otherwise empty counter.

The floor is littered with pots and pans they've emptied from two cupboards. Edith panics at the sight, falling to her knees, grabbing a fry pan, placing it carefully, quietly back where it came from, adjusting and readjusting the angle of its handle. Alberta motions the officers to back off. As Edith urgently returns another pan to its place, Alberta opens a cupboard, startled by the precision of its contents. A tin of pepper, box of salt, a tin of tea, a sack of flour and a bag of sugar occupy one shelf. Two cans of soup and two cans of vegetables sit on another, each equidistant from the next. Labels forward. Nothing askew. She looks to Edith. The rest of the cupboards, doors all open, are empty except for a couple bread pans. She asks one of the men where they put the contents from the other cupboards.

"Empty," Edith says. "Everything in its place and nothing we don't need." Her gaze falls to the back door stairwell and a wall of coat hooks. "Oh, no. That's not right. It's on the wrong hook." She rushes over, still compelled by Velma's directives. "It hasn't moved since the day we moved in. He never wears it." Edith reaches for a jean jacket but Alberta stops her and takes a close look at the jacket, noticing a dark spot on one sleeve. It has metal buttons imprinted with Levi Strauss. Four are sewn on with red thread. One is missing, apparently ripped off, leaving a small tear in the denim.

"He must have worn it," Edith says, puzzled. "Why else would it be on the wrong hook?"

Alberta tells an officer to bag the jacket as well as all of Walter's shoes and his polishing gear. She asks Edith where the clothes Walter had been wearing over the last few days might be.

"SaniDry cleaners on Washington," she says. "He has two suits. Wears one suit a week. Cleaners pick-up on

Saturday, deliver on Tuesday. But this week he dropped it off before the funeral. I wash his shirts and shorts every day . . ."

"On Friday?" Alberta looks to an officer who understands the unspoken directive to get his hands on that suit. He bolts through the house hollering out the front door. "SaniDry over on Washington! Don't let them clean Stem's suit!"

". . . and his weekend clothes on Monday," Edith says. "He can't stand to have dirty clothes around. I wash. Every day. Today's are in the washer. Oh! They need to go into the dryer!" Edith starts downstairs but Alberta grabs her arm and Edith recoils, folding in on herself, arms tight under her chin. "They'll get wrinkled," she mumbles. "I'll have to iron them twice. Walter will be upset and . . ."

"It's OK, Edith. The officers took them. "

"Do they have a dryer?"

"Let's go back to the living room. Let these men do their job. They'll be gone soon." With Edith planted on the couch again, Alberta takes a walk through the house. She sees a photograph of a young boy in Velma's bedroom, probably Walter as a child. Showing it to a sergeant, she takes it from the frame and tucks it in her pocket.

Alberta tells Edith not to expect her husband home tonight and apologizes for the mess the men would leave behind. On her way out the door, she turns. "I never asked where you lived before you moved here."

"We used to live in Michigan," Edith says. "On Spring Lake. Still have the house there. But we never go. Velma wouldn't go."

A commotion in the street draws Alberta's attention, someone on a radio, men gathering. Alberta feels her chest tighten when the sheriff looks at her, averts his eyes, then begins walking slowly toward her. She forces herself off the porch but stops. He does not speak or look her in the eye as he steps to her side. The two walk silently to his car.

Alberta rides with the sheriff out of one neighborhood into another one, bigger houses, bigger yards, then through town, past two women laughing on a street corner, past a woman walking a baby carriage, the infant buried under a cloud of pink blanket, past a man emptying a can of trash into the back of a garbage truck, past a school where children stream out onto a playground. It is a silent drive out of town beyond alfalfa fields sprouting iridescent green, beyond farm houses and outbuildings, beyond rolling hills where cows congregate around big spools of hay. They enter a wooded tract, crossing a bridge, pulling off at an abandoned mill on a river, its weather-worn clapboard curling. They park alongside FBI, state trooper, county sheriff and township police cars. A dozen uniformed men loiter in a cluster, all eyes on Alberta.

When her body refuses to step from the car, the sheriff, a man who has known her since birth, holds out his hand. When she does not take it, he reaches in and touches her shoulder at which point she seems to awaken from a trance. She emerges and follows a path through the woods, her black leather pumps finding unsure footing. A cardinal whistles. A squirrel chutters from a branch overhead.

She is aware of the officers ahead, at the river, but does not look to them, even as they step aside at her approach. In their parting she catches sight of a small tarp-covered mound on the riverbank, and her knees buckle. The sheriff puts his arm around her shoulders for support.

Stepping closer, her mind reels with visions of her brother's boy, Alby, short for Albert, named for his auntie Alberta; his wrinkled face moments after his birth; stumbling through his first steps; splashing through shallows at the beach; his excitement about second grade; the squish of his nose when he smiled. She can't breathe as the man kneeling next to the mound withdraws the covering. She wants to scream at him not to do it because once he does, once she sees it is Albert, it will all be real, there will be no turning back.

Finding Alby's body is the end of hope.

CHAPTER 4

"Steak, charred, and three shots of Rye." Two nights later, Alberta Higgins finds herself in Michigan in a corner booth ordering dinner at Anglers Tavern overlooking Spirit Lake. With knotty pine walls and red vinyl seats, it feels cozy. A haze of smoke hangs over the handful of tables filling the isle between the booths and bar. In her wool slacks, snug camel turtleneck and tailored navy blue jacket, she stands out from the handful of regulars in their flannel and jeans.

Exhausted by grief, the ten-hour drive from Pennsylvania has been grueling. Her brother Michael, who just lost a son and doesn't understand why she left, accused her of running away. Yet, nothing she could do at home could help him or his wife or their only remaining son, so she did what she always does. Like her father before her, she followed her gut.

The case against Stem was thin and DA Groves had people looking for other suspects. "If Walter Stem had anything to do with Albert's death," she told him, "he didn't wake up one day and decide to kill a kid. Something in his history made it inevitable. That history isn't in Pennsylvania. It's in Michigan." He gave her a week to chase it down.

Wanting little more than to eat and get to her tourist cabin and sleep, she lights a cigarette and takes a long drag. She notices a local newspaper on the next table over, its masthead touting a hundred years in print. Alberta snuffs out the cigarette and steps outside, glancing up and down the street, all two blocks of town. There on the corner is the office of the Lake Country Gazette.

The building is dark except for a light upstairs. Alberta knocks. Then she pounds. A woman hollers down to lay off. Alberta asks if she keeps an archive and if she can see it.

"Of course I do," the woman says. "Come back tomorrow."

"It's important. I've come a long way."

"You do know what time it is, right?"

"I know."

The window slams shut. Lights come on one after another.

Lydia Metzger, a bone-thin woman in oversized dungarees opens the door, smoke swirling from her pipe, her sharp eyes sizing up Alberta. Her long white hair is drawn back in a braid. "What's this about that it can't wait till morning?"

Introducing herself as an assistant district attorney without mentioning jurisdiction, Alberta asks about any drownings or deaths of young children in the Spirit Lake area prior to 1967.

Lydia grins at the vague deception. "I know every ADA in four counties. They're all men." She waves Alberta in. "We've had our share of drownings here. Sad stuff. Our entire county is nothing but water. Fifteen lakes. Had one just last year. Water skiing accident. Pulling two kids at a time. Collided. Juliette Shaw cracked her head open and that was that." She takes a moment. "1958 was a bad year. Two toddlers, Um . . ." She closes her eyes to think. "Mary Ellen something and Kay Fanslau. A young girl, Carol Jackson. And a boy in '47."

"How old was the boy?"

"Not sure, nine maybe if I remember right. Todd Anderson. Somebody looked away for a second and he went under. Happens fast sometimes. He was an only child. His folks split up after that. Couldn't take it, I guess. The little Jackson girl would have been old enough now to have kids of her own. Funny how they live on in imagination long after they pass." She ticks off the names of two teenagers who died in water skiing accidents in 1963 and 1964, and a third who ran his boat into a dock in '66.

Alberta stares at this woman who knows all the kids who drowned over two decades. "How . . .?"

"A kid drowns," Lydia says. "You remember. You owe it to them to remember."

"So, nothing in 1967?"

"No, but now you have my curiosity up. What's so special about that year?"

Alberta said nothing prompting Lydia to grin. "Being an ADA, I presume you're more interested in deaths that weren't so tidy. I have a couple of those. From 1960. That one never smelled right to me. Died together in the marsh. The marsh that isn't there anymore. Was over in the northeast corner," she says, her arm swinging up to point in its direction. Lydia disappears into another room, returning shortly with coverage of the story, laying newspapers on a large table. "The drowning of those two boys that July was the last big story my dad covered, and it never did sit right with him. Questions still gnawed at him, but he couldn't get anywhere with it."

A chill shoots up Alberta's spine looking at the photos of the two young boys, one so like her nephew Albert, thin, angular.

"I think if he'd felt better, he might have done some more digging, but he was already in heart failure. Just didn't realize it. Or wouldn't accept it. Was one stubborn shit. And I wasn't about to go stepping on his story. He'd have strung me up!"

Disappearing again, Lydia returns with a large envelope. "Copies of the articles, his notes, all the photos. Just get them back to me when you're finished."

"That's very kind. Thank you. This is it, then? All questionable deaths?"

"There it is," Lydia says, tapping her index finger on the table. "Questionable. OK. How far back do you want to go?"

"I don't know. How long have there been cottages out here?"

Lydia heaves a sigh and relights her pipe. "I suppose it was the twenties when the first summer places were built. After the First World War. Those houses by the marsh, they went in around 1935 or so. A boy drowned back there in Spring Lake. His family built in '36 I think. A hoard of kids. The Carters, or Kitrons. No. Conners."

Placing her pipe in an ashtray, she vanishes again, hollering for Alberta to follow. "Had a six-year-old of my own that year so I remember it all too well." In a room lined with deep shelves labeled by date and piled with newspapers, Lydia goes straight to the year, then to the month. "Here they are." She grabs a stack and leads Alberta back to the table. "My dad ran the paper back in '38. Ran it till he died first of September 1960. Seventy-eight years old. Still sharp as a tack." Lydia sifts through the papers. "His heart gave out sitting at his typewriter. Appropriate for a newspaperman, don't you think? I took it over after that. Here it is," she says, pulling one with the headline: YOUNG BOY DROWNS. "Samuel Conner. Only one ever to die in that spring. A bunch of boys were skinny dipping." She relights her pipe.

Alberta is immediately drawn to the front-page photograph of the Conner boy, so lean, big ears sticking out. Like the other drowned boy, he reminds her a bit of Alby.

Something about Alberta's silence disturbs Lydia. She digs into an old file cabinet and pulls out another package of photos.

Alberta is about to speak but Lydia puts up her hand, says enough for the night, and opens the front door. Alberta is several steps down the street when Lydia says she's interested to know what she finds out. Alberta keeps walking, waving the envelopes, shoulders hunched against the chill.

Back at her corner booth, Tucker, the tavern owner, delivers a plate of food with a look of consternation. "Cold, burned and bloody," he says. With barely a glance at him, Alberta downs the first shot of whiskey, shuddering. Tucker walks away.

She lights up and reads the Lake Country Gazette articles on the drownings of the two boys. The first, from the day after it happened, reported few specifics of the deaths, stating that bodies of two boys were recovered from Spirit Lake Marsh. Undefined injuries appeared consistent with a struggle.

She picks at the green beans and baked potato, too cold to melt the butter.

The follow-up story in Tuesday's paper, made poignant with photographs and names of the boys and their families, used terms that seemed cautious. "The boys *apparently* snuck out to Spirit Lake marsh. A pillowcase and flashlight recovered from the scene *may* be evidence they intended to hunt frogs. It is *presumed* one of the boys got caught up in weeds and the other attempted a rescue." A neighbor at the lake, Bill Fry, was quoted saying the incident was a careless waste of young life, *a tragic miscalculation, just boys being boys*. The article quoted Sheriff Carson Bates as saying *Those roots can be quite a tangle*. His second quote summed up the accident: *Ever try to save someone who's drowning? They're just as likely to take you down with them.*

It seems to Alberta a vague version of heroic tragedy. She wonders if this story might have been a fabrication, something everyone needed to believe if they were to cope with impossible loss. Two boys dead. Two families grieving.

She leaves the uneaten steak and a ten-dollar bill on the table, enough to cover the meal and a tip. Downing one of the two remaining shots, she leaves the tavern.

Returning to her cabin she feels like a wounded animal returning to its den. Dark pine walls, dark furniture, dark green drapes, dark plaid couch. The dull yellow glow of two lamps is all she has to fend off the night. She peruses the bookshelf packed with board games and threadbare books, probably rummage sale finds, picked up for a nickel each, the same time they bought the dresser lamp, the one with the ceramic trout leaping from a stream. A largemouth bass with its yawning gap mounted on the wall seems less a trophy than a reminder of death.

The heater in the corner begins to snap and crack to life, smelling of burnt dust. In a few minutes, the room is too hot. Soon after, it is too cold. These cabins are summer places, not meant for cold spring nights.

The clutter is too much for her. She moves all but a few books, all the knick-knacks, a dragonfly wind chime and a bounty of decorative pillows to the closet shelf, out of sight. She unpacks her clothes, putting them into a drawer next to an extra blanket. She hangs her blouses and suit, her sweater and second blazer in the closet. She drapes two pair of slacks over the back of a chair. The hangers would leave creases.

She moves a large amber glass ashtray from the dresser to the round table by the windows, tossing her red leather cigarette case next to it.

Too tired to sleep, she pours some rye whiskey into a glass she's unwrapped from the bathroom and stares into it as if it could speak. She downs it fast, winces, shudders, and holds the empty glass to her heart.

Out the window, a scant string of lights glimmers across the lake. She wonders what would happen if she just went home, turned it all over to someone else to investigate. But they might not see what she does. Another investigator might give up, seeing her quest only as the desperate attempt of a woman in the thick of grief looking at things that aren't really there to find answers that don't exist.

She lights up and empties Lydia's big manila envelopes onto the chenille bedspread. She moves the ashtray to the nightstand and props pillows against the headboard, kicks off her shoes and climbs onto the bed. Group photos show men and boys standing around two small bodies in the mud at a marsh. On the back, someone has written all the names. Walter Stem hardly stands out as one of three bald men among them. Another photo, a smaller one, shows two teenage boys holding a giant snapping turtle upside down by its tail.

Tucked in the bottom of one envelope are a few pages torn from a notebook. Though the writing is a nearly illegible scrawl, she can make out a few things. *Bates never talked to the kids. One flashlight? Who would cook? Frogging in a storm?*

Alberta shifts her weight causing a slow-motion avalanche. From between pages, a sliver of a face slips out, eyes flashing an invitation. Alberta pulls it free. Tyler Hodges. The smile of a kid who owned the world. Sky blue eyes flirting with a future he would never have. It was a family snapshot taken a month before he died.

She finds Peter's school picture, the one from the front page. Second grade. White shirt. Smart necktie, slightly crooked, ears like budding wings, his head tilted unnaturally to the side, probably a photographer's dictate. He pretends to smile, another dictate, the corners of his mouth lifting slightly, eyes unsure. She studies his face, longing to see it relax, to speak, to smile at her, an honest, reassuring smile.

Like laying out a hand of cards, she places Sammy Conner's picture next to Tyler and Peter. Then she takes out another photo, one she'd brought with her from the Stem house. It's a young boy, thin-faced with pointed features, a black and white head and shoulder portrait taken against a dark curtain, chin high, posture rigid, Walter 1929 written in the border. He has little more than a black stubble for hair. The boy's expression holds no pretense of smile. His eyes are vague, either out of boredom or contempt. She wants to see something in this photo to indicate a predisposition for evil, some indication that he would grow up to be a monster. Instead, she sees a frail young boy's vulnerability. She places it next to the others.

She retrieves Alby's photo from her satchel. He was seven when it was taken, also in uniform, though no tie, just a polo shirt with the emblem of St. Barnabas Academy. In his face, she sees her brother's high cheekbones and her sister-in-law's green eyes. She recognizes the small round ears as her father's. Her throat tightens. She puts Alby's photo next to the rest. She stares at the pictures, waiting, willing the answer to everything to appear before her.

Tyler's round face and impish smile make him odd man out. Setting him aside, the other four could almost be interchangeable, so similar in their gaze, their diminutive stature with thin necks and bony shoulders, and something Alberta finds impossible to describe except that it somehow ties them together across time.

She rakes all the papers together and piles them on a chair, all except for Alby's picture. This she places in front of her, inviting the pain.

Michael's firstborn, Tommy, older than Alby by two years, was a mama's boy when he was young, clinging to Erin whenever Alberta came near. Albert, though, even as a baby, loved his Aunt Alberta. She was there for his birth and held him when he was only a few minutes old. They say newborns can't focus yet, but he looked up at her as if he already knew her, a sensation so powerful she sobbed openly, wiping a fallen tear from his cheek.

Alby was four the first time he asked to spend the night at Alberta's. No one expected him to make it all night, but he did. The next morning he taught her how to make his pancakes. He liked them small, flat and loaded with syrup. She told him to wash his hands before they ate. He refused. "I don't feel like practicing good hygiene today." Alby cried when Michael and Erin came to pick him up later that morning and asked why she didn't love him. She assured him she did.

"Then why make me leave?"

"I have to work today to get ready for work tomorrow."

"No. You should play with me."

That Monday was the first time she went into a meeting unprepared, having spent the rest of her Sunday with Alby, waiting until bedtime to deliver him home.

Alby loved to read and was always asking questions, forever asking questions, like the day he discovered meat came from dead animals.

"Do people eat dogs?"

"No. We don't eat dogs."

"Cats?"

"No. We eat cows and chickens."

"Do they kill them at the store?"

"No."

"Can we just have cereal and bananas for dinner?"

"Great idea."

Now, his voice is forever silenced. Now, the inanimate eyes in his school photo look right past his aunt.

The wind stirs a swing set outside the cabin window, chains scraping metal on metal, and she thinks of the squeaky hamster wheel in Alby's bedroom, how together they applied a squirt of oil to quiet it. A drop fell to the wood shavings below and Alby maneuvered his small hand under the wheel to retrieve the oily bits. These memories, like an oppressive weight, suppress the grief she knows will inevitably rise. She puts his photo back in her satchel and changes into pajamas. Her sleep is shallow, the mere ticking of the heater enough to wake her.

CHAPTER 5

Mildred and George Eastman bought their cottage on Spirit Lake for next to nothing in November of 1959. Neglected for years, some might have torn it down and built new, but George said it had good bones, and a house with good bones was worth the effort to save it. They came out every Saturday they could to renovate it. The hour drive from South Bend was manageable without snow. Sometimes they'd stay the night, sleeping in front of the fireplace, George waking occasionally to stoke the fire. Peter enjoyed peeing outside behind a tree. By December, kitchen cabinets were on order. By January, the new wiring and plumbing was in. New windows arrived the first of March. By Easter they were trimming out and painting. April was warm and dry enough to get a crew out to tear off the old roof and siding and replace it all. By the first of May, it was nearly finished. The little cottage was charming, inviting, peaceful. All through May they came up each weekend to reap the rewards of their labors, taking the canoe out on little trips, walking the woods, bird watching. The three decided it was the best decision they'd ever made.

In early May, they arrived to find a dock had been put in next door, the one Peter will sit on when he sees his first Sand Hill Crane up close. A couple weeks later, Mason, Carl and Danny Vogel, father, son and grandson, put in their dock at the other end of the row. George learned Mason and Carl shared a dental practice, and

Mason was on the verge of retirement. He still went in two days a week, unwilling to turn everything over to his son, something Carl appeared to resent. Once the dock was secured, they left, allowing the Eastmans another two weekends of delusional bliss watching purple lupine and blue forget-me-nots carpet the woods.

The onslaught begins the first weekend in June of 1960. It plays out as have all other arrival days at Spirit Lake, a choreography honed over the years, the only variables being the age of the children and this year, the addition of the Eastmans. Boys too young to help the year before, now stand waist-deep in cold water helping fathers and older brothers put in docks. The faint sound of Connie Francis drifts from a transistor radio somewhere. The season's first powerboat cuts across the lake, its whine the siren of summer.

Arriving late morning with all five kids in tow, Dick and Evelyn Hodges are in the thick of the day's chores. Evelyn stands in the sun shaking a rag rug, watching her husband attempt to put the dock in the water. Jim, Ronny, and Mark, fifteen, thirteen, and twelve, aren't a lot of help. Judging by their expressions, it isn't going well. Tyler, too young to do much but get in the way of such undertakings, watches from the pontoon boat onshore.

For Evelyn's part, the cottage needs airing out. There are beds to make, towels and sheets to put away. Both bathrooms need to be scrubbed, floors swept and washed. The winter's residual mouse droppings in the cupboards have to be swept away, and the cabinets disinfected before groceries can be put away. All the dishes and utensils have to be washed. Curtains need to be taken down and hung to air outside. All Dick and the boys have to do is get the dock in the water and move the boats. Everything else is left to Evelyn and Penny.

Mason and Gert Vogel from next door, the cottage closest to the marsh, holler out to Evelyn, asking if she needs anything from Miller's Bait & Tackle, the lake's only grocery store.

Evelyn shakes her head. "Carl and Marilyn out yet?"

"I'm here!" Marilyn pops up from behind an Adirondack chair she's been wiping down, one of several bright white chairs that are rarely used, their only function being to add character to their little clapboard bungalow. Evelyn can see Marilyn has become even rounder over the winter. She used to look like a pear with toothpick legs but seemed to have turned into an apple. Or a bowling ball. Her hair, entirely too wiry to control, is more orange than ever.

Gert and Mason amble to their dock. Marilyn heads over to Evelyn, a tumbler of wine in hand. "Carl and the kids are coming out next week," she says on the way. "Too busy today. Teenagers. Whatever you do, don't say anything when you see Shelly."

Evelyn picks up another rug.

"Poor girl," Marilyn says. "She got her period this year and her body just took up rebellion. Acne like I've never seen on a girl."

Marilyn takes a gulp of wine, adding to the little triangular stains on either side of her upper lip. Evelyn gives the rug a hard snap, cracking the air. Marilyn rambles on.

"I don't expect her to leave the house much this summer even though the sun would be the best thing for her. Dry that stuff up. The boys came out a couple weeks ago to put the dock in. Danny, now he's a worker. Thirteen this year. Just like your Ronny. God help him, he has such beautiful hair. No telling how long he'll keep it. I mean, just look at that old man down there." She points to Mason in his cotton fishing cap as he unties the aluminum skiff. "Bald. Carl? Bald. Father and son. Maybe Danny will break that mold." Mason and Gert pull away, the drone of the Evinrude fading across the lake.

Angry voices rise from the beach. Steven Fry, a lanky seventeen-year-old, shoves his father, who shoves right back, after which the two go back about the business of putting in their dock.

"Bill should just send that boy away," Marilyn says. "He's a lawyer. I'm sure he can figure out how to do it."

Evelyn picks up another throw rug and whips it, generating a little cloud of dust. She looks next door to the south where Betsy Fry sits on her patio, applying a coat of polish to her nails, oblivious to the scuffle below between her husband and son. A beauty queen before she had three kids – Miss Indiana 1937 – Betsy is perfectly coiffed, full makeup, blouse freshly pressed. On anyone else, the effort would seem ridiculous under the circumstances. The lake is not a place for such vanity, but it suits Betsy.

"Maybe I should go over and see if Betsy's OK." The words aren't out of Marilyn's mouth when she scoots down the steps from the Hodges' patio, walks briskly across the grass and up the steps to Bill and Betsy's patio. Three young boys, one of them Tyler, bolt past her almost knocking her down, but she quickly regains upright mobility and ventures forth. Tyler hollers out *Sorry, Mrs. Vogel* as he leaps from the third step to the grass.

Betsy, without the slightest glance to Marilyn, dips her brush and starts in on a pinky finger just as her daughter saunters out of their cottage. Fifteen going on twenty-one, Laura Fry is a walking Coppertone commercial, slender, graceful, long brown hair that by the end of summer will turn to gold and her skin will be the color of caramel. With a quiet smile to Marilyn, she drifts down to their shore. Sidestepping her brother and dad, Laura Fry stakes her territory on the pontoon boat, still parked on the beach. She spreads her towel and drapes her long limbs ever so alluringly on the cushion in the sun.

The next cottage over is in chaos. Gladys Wagner tries to break up a fight between her two daughters. Previous summers they'd been inseparable, yet the day Linda became a teenager, she disowned her little sister Connie. They'd been in a state of constant bickering ever since. A shrill whistle pierces the air as Al Monroe, Gladys's father, steps outside. This is his cottage. Gladys and her family are welcome but they sometimes overrun the place. The girls stop shouting. Linda charges inside, slamming the door behind her. The door quickly opens again. Linda comes back out escorted by her grandmother Merci who stands silently, arms crossed, watching the girl go back inside, closing the door quietly.

A handsome couple, Al is tall and strong, white-haired with a gate resembling an athlete more than a man pushing seventy. Merci is as lovely as she's ever been with soft features and delicate nose, full lips, gentle eyes, and a figure still worthy of a second glance. By the end of the summer, her crepe paper skin will be the color of a well-roasted chestnut. Though Al opened the cottage in May, this will be the first of the season they spend the night.

A boat speeds across the lake toward Al's dock where his son-in-law Marty, a short, swarthy man gestures manically, yelling unintelligibly. The boat approaches at breakneck speed, turns fast, the driver cutting the engine at the last second, snugging gracefully up to the bumpers of the dock. Waves of wake blast along the shore where Dick and the boys are chest-deep in freezing water, trying to clamp their last sections of dock together. The turbulence causes a clamp to let go. Ronny catches his hand between sections and screams obscenities.

Marty Wagner storms the boat yelling at his son Greg, his voice carrying up and down the shore. "If you want that new boat in July, you damn well better take better care of the old one!" It will be weeks before the new fiberglass Hydrodyne with its Volvo outboard arrives. It will only be days before everyone will be sick of Marty bragging about it.

Greg Wagner, fifteen, a strikingly handsome boy with perfect proportions and generous smile, secures the boat. Marty continues his reprimands, waving his arms in some ancillary language. Greg saunters off the dock ignoring his father, crosses the grass, climbs the steps, smiles to his grandparents, ignores his mother, and disappears into the cottage.

Next door at the Eastmans', their sanctuary of tranquility shattered, George and Mildred look at each other wondering if they've just made the biggest mistake of their lives.

Back at the Hodges's, Evelyn fills a bucket with water in the kitchen sink. The smell of iron rises, mingling with the mustiness from the back room where lifejackets, skis, towels, bathing suits, gas cans, and the mower all find their way every evening throughout the summer. Because the cottage is cut into a hill, the perpetually damp cinderblock wall gives the storeroom and everything in it an ever-present smell of gasoline and mildew. It is the smell of summer.

Laden with an armload of curtains, freshly aired from the line, Penny walks through the open kitchen with its sitting area, past the wicker chaise lounge and the table used mostly for cards, rarely for meals. She glances into the bathroom where spiders still hold dominion in the corners. Cleaning it is somewhere down on her list of tasks for the day. The porcelain tub, sink, and toilet are stained to varying degrees of orange, even after repeated assaults with scouring powder over the years. She heads upstairs, adjusting her load on the first landing, then up to the next, stubbing her toe on a box of food by back door, the door leading to where they park under the trees. Three steps more she lands in the living area. Straight ahead is the boys' room. To her left, the living room. To her right, on the back wall, her sleeping cubby.

It used to be a closet before her dad converted it and installed a set of crank out windows with a view of the parking area and woods beyond. Her small mattress fits edge to edge with a large drawer underneath for her stuff. A jelly jar light with a pull chain allows her to read at night. A shelf over the window holds her books.

After dumping all the curtains on the couch she looks out to see progress on the dock. Ron is shouting at Mark. Her dad is shouting at Ron.

First things first, she wets a towel from the bathroom and knocks away the cobwebs in her cubby, wipes down her walls and under her mattress. Tossing mothball remnants into a wastebasket, she is happy to find no sign of mouse activity. She opens her window and wipes down the sill and panes. Sheets neatly tucked in, she hangs her thick green drape, the one that separates her from the rest of the cottage, from everything she's not part of. The boys. The adults. Closing the drape, she sits for a minute in her sanctuary, smiling, content to be the only girl, allowing her private space.

The front of the cottage is solid windows, the crank out kind, downstairs and up. Upstairs, behind the living room is her parents' tiny bedroom, a miniscule half bath, and the bunkroom for the boys.

Sorting sheets for all the beds, Penny begins in her parents' room with the twin beds positioned perpendicular to each other. In the bunkroom, her father built three bunks and a cupboard along one wall and another narrow bunk under the window where Tyler sleeps. It has two doors creating an alley straight through from the bathroom to the hall by the stairs. Getting sheets on the top bunk is the hardest and it seems to her ludicrous the boys can't make their own beds.

Back in the living room, she throws a curtain over her shoulder and climbs onto a chair, attaching wire hooks one by one to small eyes on the rings.

Downstairs, on hands and knees, Evelyn assaults the linoleum floor with a scrub brush, her face pressed into an expression of raw hostility. With both hands tight on the soaked wood of the brush, she presses on the bristles with all her upper body, pushing it out and back, knocking over a stool in the process. "God fucking damn it!"

A thud comes from above her.

"What the hell are you doing up there?"

"I'm fine, Mom." Penny has fallen off the chair.

Evelyn grits her teeth and throws the scrub brush across the room. Glancing up, she sees her daughter standing on the landing. "Go! Outside! I'll finish up."

Penny doesn't budge. "But I'm not done up there yet."

"Go!"

Penny learned over the winter to steer clear of her mother when she was in one of her moods. And lately, it seemed she was always in one of her moods.

Tyler bounds through the front door past Evelyn, heading straight to the bathroom. "Mommy, Mommy, Mommy! We're back. Isn't it great?" He barely makes it in time, and Evelyn watches him pee, her whole body releasing whatever rage had engulfed it. In an instant, he is on his way out again, his mother laughing, grabbing him by the waist and kissing his cheek. Tyler giggles and flies out the door.

Penny knows the reprieve is likely short-lived. She bolts back upstairs, grabs an old mangled straw hat that once belonged to her grandfather and charges out the back door, stepping back in to grab a small rag rug, then out again, past the cars, across the narrow dirt road, into the woods. Into freedom.

She slows, finding the familiar deer trail of compacted soil meandering through grassy vegetation under a burgeoning canopy of maples, ash, oak and Black Locust. A moist breeze stirs the locust blossoms releasing their thick, sweet scent. She stops and closes her eyes.

"Talk to me," she whispers. "Talk to me. What have I missed all winter? What do you have to show me?" A branch snaps to her right and she opens her eyes.

Following the sound, she discovers at her feet a fairy circle of red toadstools. She shouts out *Thank you!*

She crosses the back path, a well-trodden passage between Spirit Lake marsh and Spring Lake, a path two generations of children have worn clean. From there, her deer trail disappears, but she has other guideposts to lead her way. She gives a wide berth to the gnarly Black Locust wrapped in hairy poison ivy vines. She stops to study the decomposing pine tree she was told had fallen during the big storm of '55. Each year it seems to melt a little deeper into the forest floor. The year before, a fern had taken root in a crack. She looks for it, finding three tightly coiled new fronds. She sees the old fence line with its rusty shards of wire. A catbird sings. On and on he goes. Directly under him, sticking out of a leaning, weathered fence post is a pearl-handled penknife. She yanks it free and puts it in her pocket. The Catbird stops singing and flies away. "Thank you," she calls after it, as if he had led her to the find. The year before, he led her to an owl skull under the dead Elm.

She steps carefully looking for gentle bubbling in the boggy soil. Several small springs seep to the surface there. Finding one, she looks ahead to higher ground and sees her ancient apple tree, still there, still twisted and overgrown, its branches reaching to the ground creating a room underneath. Crawling into this hideout, she lays the rag rug carefully in place and sits down. "I'm back," she says. She puts the penknife next to her, thinking of other gifts she'd been given by the woodland spirits, like the pile of hickory nuts they left in the middle of her rug the summer before, and the apple. She couldn't crack the nuts, but she ate the apple. It was sour, but she ate it. Would have been rude not to.

There, alone, she listens for the creakings of her woods, to birdsong and woodpeckers.

CHAPTER 6

May 22 - You'd think by now I'd understand death but I don't. I don't think anyone can. Not really. Nothing is so final, so absolute as that loss of presence. I suppose to grasp death you have to understand life, to know what it is, that vibration, a person's current. It goes beyond the look in their eyes, beyond the sound of their breathing, far beyond the touch of their fingertips. Life in and of itself is weightless, yet when it ceases, the impact of sudden vacancy is like someone slamming on the breaks, a silent crash. I don't yet know how my mother's death will hit me. I hardly know her. Will I grieve? Will I discover I actually love her and have loved her all these years? Will her death finally fill the hole she carved out of my life? And how much time will her impending death hover here, occupying every hour? Will there be any summer left to enjoy or will I go into Autumn having lost an entire season? A few weeks. Maybe less. And then I'll sweep the remnants of death out the door, the obligations, sleepless nights, regrets, and start anew.

As Penn and Evelyn's first few days unfold, rather than grow weaker and die, Evelyn grows stronger. She eats. She starts walking room to room. She can't, however, seem to manage to always make it to the bathroom in time and pees in the bed and on the floor, cussing as loud as her raspy voice is able. *Penny, get your ass in here! Penny clean up this mess! I'm calling the police to come get me! You can't keep me here! Penny! Penny! PENNY!!*

Day seven. Penn observes her mother sitting on the couch, her lips moving, yet no words spoken. Her fingers appear to turn pages, reading an imaginary book to an imaginary Tyler. Penn lets her be. Later in the day, she walks in from the patio to find Evelyn has made her way downstairs and she's pawing through a stack of papers and folders next to a computer on what was once the table they all played cards on.

"What's all this mess?" Evelyn snipes.

"Don't do that," Penn says.

Evelyn continues, pushing aside books, opening one, leafing through pages.

"Mom. Leave it alone."

"Well, I don't know what your problem is. It's not like you're working on anything." She picks up another book having dropped the first one to the floor. "Who's this P. Hodges?"

"Seriously?"

"Yes, seriously," Evelyn says, sneering.

"Me, Mom. I wrote it."

"I thought you got married."

"I did."

"So why the hell use your maiden name?"

Finding no point in explaining herself, Penn asks if her mother wants breakfast. Evelyn grunts and crosses the room to a stool at the kitchen counter. She rummages through an assortment of cereal boxes aligned like books, grabbing the Rice Chex, demanding a bowl and milk.

Penn obliges without speaking. She pours the cereal and milk.

"Sugar," Evelyn demands.

"Right in front of you."

Evelyn slumps, nearly falling off the stool. Penn catches her and helps her to the old wicker chaise, packing pillows to her hips for support.

Evelyn's gaze rests slightly above her feet as if looking at a small child perched there. A smile slides over her face. She soon dozes off, leaving Penn to ponder the papers her mother has just left in disarray. She's been working on a research paper for nearly a year. With all the data collected and compiled, she is left with writing the final text, no small task, and one that requires complete focus. The editor of the journal *Nature* asked for first crack at it when it was finished. They've published several of her pieces over the course of two decades. This one, however, will have to wait. Evelyn's presence is too big a drain on Penn's mental capacity.

Evelyn wakes demanding to go to bed. Getting her mother back up the steps requires nearly more strength than Penn has.

Day eight. Penn finds Evelyn downstairs again, sitting on a stool at the kitchen counter, engaged in a muttered conversation with no one. Penn watches her slide her cereal bowl to the side. "Silly Rabbit," Evelyn says aloud. When Penn takes the dish away to wash it, Evelyn shouts. "Get your own! That's Ty's!"

As if insanity were contagious, Penn begins to see Tyler out of the corner of her eye. She sometimes thinks she hears his giggle. She entertains the idea that Tyler's spirit is indeed inhabiting the cottage, bridging the gap between life and death, as though the closer one is to death, the thinner the veil between. This brings some measure of sadness. If he is there for Evelyn's transition, once she's gone, he'll be gone as well. How empty will the cottage feel then, absent his presence? Imaginary or not, she will miss him.

> May 23 - Full night sleep last night. Dosed Mom late morning. She ate half a chicken sandwich. Her eyes have a yellow tinge.

Penn is familiar with jaundice. Matthew died of pancreatic cancer. The first sign was jaundice. There were earlier indications, signs they both ignored. They wrote off gut pain as indigestion. The back pain was just a kink. By the time the whites of his eyes turned yellow, it was too late to do anything.

Since Evelyn's symptoms are similar, Penn assumes the cancer is in her pancreas or maybe her liver. She asks one of the Hospice nurses only to be told they have instructions not to disclose her mother's diagnosis. "Per your mother's directive," she is told. It doesn't matter. She's dying, and the only question is how long it will take. What was presumed to be days, possibly a week, now seems grossly inaccurate. Evelyn spends the greater part of each day out of bed, even taking a constitutional down to the lakefront. She doesn't eat much, but enough to sustain her. A Hospice nurse called Evelyn's resilience a miracle. Penn can't put quite so positive a spin on it.

With Matthew, there had been only one nurse, a relationship that proved meaningful and supportive. With Evelyn, it is a different nurse nearly every time, not that it matters to Evelyn. She cusses at them all as they measure her arms, take her vitals, and check her meds. They ask her to judge her pain level between one and ten, and she graces them with 467 or 10,325. Then the nurse, whichever one it is, invariably instructs Penn to be the better judge of when her mother needs Roxy and when she doesn't. "And keep up the Senna pills," they all say, "or she'll get constipated. And make up some Vasoline bombs. They'll come in handy if she can't have a bowl movement." Penn is now responsible for her mother's poop and keeps petroleum jelly pellets coated in sugar in her refrigerator wrapped in wax paper.

Night ten. Penn wakes from a sound sleep by a thunking in the storeroom downstairs. Flipping on the light, she heads down. Expecting to find a raccoon rummaging around, as she had once before, she grabs a broom on the way. Instead, she finds her mother sitting on the floor among overturned boxes, holding one of the old puffy life jackets.

"Dick? Where have you been?"

"It's me, Mom."

"What day is it?"

"Tuesday."

"That explains it," Evelyn says, though it explains nothing.

"Let's get back to bed, Mom. It's late."

Evelyn stands up clenching the life jacket to her chest, muttering. "Goddamned Dick."

"Dad's dead, Mom. Long time now. Long dead. Come on." Penn stares at the four remaining life jackets hanging from hooks on the wall. They are little more than memorabilia. Scattered on the floor are men's shoes and clothes. Her mother had gone looking for her husband in a box, leaving Penn to find all that remained of her own.

Penn gets Evelyn settled back in bed, clutching the musty life jacket. Back downstairs, she repacks Matthew's things. She married Matthew after grad school. They shared an apartment in Ann Arbor while they worked on their doctorates and bought a house. Not long after Matthew got tenure, they bought the cottage from Evelyn. Given the option to buy in, her brothers suggested she let the place rot.

Penn and Matthew repaired, replaced, and redecorated, yet no paint could cover the sorrow embedded in its walls. Like some impervious mold, it would bloom at inopportune moments when better things should have won the day, moments when Penn's laughter would turn to tears for no good reason. Matthew would always cover for her, keeping their daughter Andi occupied while Mommy slept. But Matthew is gone now, and Andi is twenty-five with her own life, a life built on solid footing full of possibility; a life untarnished by exposure to Penn's family, three uncles she's never met, one uncle who died as a child, and a grandmother she'd not seen since she was five and then only by accident. Penn tries to make her daughter's life sweet and healthy and free of loss to honor the life Tyler should have had, the life they all should have had. Though Andi lost her father to cancer, Matthew gave her enough love and honesty to carry her forward. And he gave her the greatest gift of all: time to say goodbye. Nobody had the chance to say goodbye to Tyler.

Back upstairs, Evelyn sleeps the night with the life jacket. In the morning she believes her dead son brought it to her.

> May 26 - I dreamed Mom was weightless. Drifting through the house like an untethered balloon, the helium partially depleted.

Days hold no promise of routine for Penn with everything dependent on how much Roxy is administered and when; on Evelyn's state of awareness or lack of it; on her willingness to tolerate a Hospice aide's presence so Penn can run errands. Daily nurse visits will now be weekly, indicating to Penn that her mother won't be dying any time soon.

Day thirteen. Penn sits on the patio, enjoying a steaming mug of coffee talking with Andi on the cordless. The sun, the first real warmth of the season, soaks into her jeans. It will be short-lived. Storm clouds are building off to the west.

"Mom, I don't understand why you won't let me come relieve you for a couple days. You have to get out of there, don't you? You could spend a night at home in Ann Arbor, garden, drink a few bottles of wine."

"Oh, Andi honey, don't do that. I'm fine, honestly. I appreciate that you want to help. And wine therapy sounds appropriate. But no."

"It's not like I don't know what it's like. We both, I, well, with Dad . . . "

"Oh, no, no, no. Daddy was different. This is nothing like that. Please don't get confused."

"It wasn't too much for me. It was –"

"Your grandmother is nothing like your dad. There are good reasons she hasn't been part of your life."

"But I worry about you."

"No need. You doing what you do is all I need to feel better. So you leave me to this. What are you up to, anyway?"

"A bunch of us are talking about going up north camping, taking our kayaks. Sarah and Eric, maybe Mel and her new boyfriend."

Evelyn hollers something from upstairs.

"Maybe," Andi explains, "do the Tahquamenon and head over to . . ."

Evelyn yells again.

Penn interrupts her daughter. "Andi, I have to go. Sorry. Let me know if you go and be careful on the water."

Evelyn shouts again, swearing this time.

Penn gets up, tells Andi she's sorry again and hangs up on her. Upstairs, Penn finds her mother sitting on the toilet, smiling, letting go an erratic stream of odorous pee.

"This is why you yelled to me?"

"Take me down to the dock."

"We can't, Mom. It's going to storm."

"Fine! I'll get my own ass down there." Evelyn grabs a sheet of toilet paper and yanks, unrolling a vast ribbon of tissue to the floor. She rips off a section leaving the rest. "I can wipe myself without an audience, damn it."

Penn turns her back.

"Well, I can't get off this thing by myself. Help me!"

With barely enough room for one in the tiny bathroom, Penn maneuvers herself to lift her mother by the armpits, telling her to lean on the sink while she pulls up her underwear. "These are wet."

"So they are. So they are."

"Your nightgown is soaked."

"Bed too."

Penn closes her eyes, taking a long deep breath, letting it out slowly. She pulls the nightgown over her mother's shoulders, dropping it to the floor. The smell of old urine permeates the tiny bathroom. The emaciated body leaning on the sink is a fragile collection of bones and sinew, skin smudged with blooming bruises, something the Hospice nurse told her to expect. The nubs of her spine look like they might poke through with the slightest touch. Penn wets a washcloth and wipes down her mother's back.

"It's too cold!"

Penn kneels down and wipes emaciated legs, loose flesh draping over the washcloth. "Here," she says, handing the cloth to her mother. "You can do your front. Sit down if you have to."

Evelyn glares at her daughter and turns the hot water on full blast. She plunges the washcloth in and out of the sink, then swipes it, dripping wet, across her breasts and down to her crotch, giving it a deep dig to the back, dropping it to the floor before pushing past her daughter to the front room. Standing naked at the wall of windows, she yells out that a storm is coming in. Penn takes another deep breath, counting slowly to five, and lets it out like so much steam. She turns off the water and gathers her mother's robe from the next room.

Rain begins pelting the glass. Penn watches the old naked woman standing in the living room. She wonders where her mother has gone; the woman who was ever-present in the beginning; the woman whose movements Penn so carefully observed from her perch in the grocery cart, feet kicking big plastic buttons of her mother's car coat as she talked to the man behind the meat counter, the one who died of cancer. She misses the woman who was always cooking or doing laundry or making beds; the woman who dressed her card tables to the nines for bridge club; the woman she was before she lost her mind and left them all behind. Where was that woman, or more importantly, had she ever really existed?

Sleet pelts the window, yet Evelyn seems to be looking out on an altogether different day. She is peaceful, as if cradling a happy memory. Penn wraps the robe around her mother's shoulders.

"Remember the bonfires," Evelyn says, her voice smooth and sweet. "First thing every summer with all you little Indians dancing around and laughing. Do they still do that?"

As their eyes meet, they share a smile, the first since Evelyn's arrival, possibly since Penn was a child, and in that moment, Penn is a little girl again, remembering a mother's love, before she knew the meaning of loss.

"No, Mom. They don't do that anymore."

"That's a shame."

The moment passes, as does Evelyn's clarity. She steps away from her daughter and charges back to the bedroom, shouting obscenities, demanding to go home. A door slams.

Penn speaks too quietly to be heard. "You're as home as you're ever going to be."

Evelyn yells again from behind the bedroom door. "Somebody call my daughter to come get me out of this dump!"

Penn stares out the window. As whitecaps rake angry waters, she tries for all she's worth to see what her mother must have seen. Was it a summer lake under a full moon, the shore aglow with a dozen or more bonfires? Or maybe sleepy kids in pajamas sitting on laps watching the last of the flames rise from vibrant embers. That was her favorite part of the bonfires, the quiet time after the flames died down, the mood calmed, the boys settled. She remembers the quiet voices and being held in her father's arms as everyone finally wandered back to their cottages, amber house lights going off one by one, a couple of the men staying behind, raking the coals. She thinks how young she must have been and for a moment yearns for that safety, for that love. She suddenly envies her mother's dementia and feels guilty for having interrupted whatever moment she was in.

CHAPTER 7

The day after Alberta gets the photos and clippings from the Lake Country Gazette, she calls her office to get a subpoena for the official police reports. She drives around the lake to get the lay of the land, past the public boat launch and the tavern, over the spit of land between Spirit and another lake, over two bridges, finally to Spirit Marsh Road, a cutoff through a cornfield onto a narrow gravel road until she sees water through the trees. She drives slowly past two huge houses and two small cottages, parking at the end. She walks the shoreline, but nothing looks like the case photos from 1960. A T-shaped dock reaches out into the lake off to the north where the marsh should have been. Behind it stands a pavilion behind which sprawls a high-end housing development with carefully landscaped lawns.

To the south end of a beach, dense woods match the photo enough to get her bearings. Looking out over the lake, Alberta feels a presence, someone watching. She turns, glances up, and sees a curtain close in the second cottage.

Returning to her car, she drives round the bend and catches a glimpse of a yellow structure behind thick pines. She pulls over. Pushing through pine boughs, she finds a large house, yellow with a red door and green window trim. A thick mass of English ivy devours one side and pours through a broken window upstairs. What might have once been open yard is overgrown with sumac and honeysuckle. She wades through knee-high weeds to the back door, stubbing her toe on the stoop buried in leaf litter. She pushes the door open, its hinges catching halfway. Squeezing through, a heavy odor of mold assaults her nose. She has found Walter Stem's old house.

Stepping into the kitchen, she recalls what Edith had said. Thick sheets of taxicab yellow paint hang from the ceiling and a wall revealing gray, warped wainscoting. A blackish mold stains the other walls, all painted dark red. Bright blue plywood counters sit atop a bank of green cabinets. The garish colors make her uneasy, wondering what kind of a mind would choose them. Floorboards feel spongy. Dried raccoon scat litters the counter and floor. It was a lot of decay for only three year's abandonment.

A single dusty dish and cup rest on a towel. Inside a cardboard box on the counter, she finds cans of soup, plastic utensils, and mouse droppings. Aside from that, the counters are empty. She opens cupboards finding them empty except for one, apparently forgotten during the move. Within it, every item is equidistant from the next, labels all forward. Nothing is askew.

She makes her way upstairs down a pale turquoise hall, stopping between a room painted salmon orange and another painted lavender. Windows are broken. Floors are covered with years of leaf debris. The house is empty except for the third bedroom. Painted hot pink with blue trim, it has a yellow dresser, a single red chair, and an unmade bed, its flowered sheets in disarray as if someone had just gotten out of it. She flicks a corner of the coverlet upward, dispatching a cloud of dust. At the end of the hall, she tries to open a closed door. When it won't budge, she kicks it in, its rusty hinges giving way so the door falls inward.

The room is empty, the light dimmed by ivy draping both windows. Its walls and ceiling are dark, unpainted wainscoting. Window trim, dislodged entirely from the wall, hangs suspended in the grip of woody tendrils. New green vines reach into the room across a vast web of dead and dying vines, intertwining with the twisted tangles covering the floor, climbing the walls, insinuating themselves behind baseboards. Already wilting leaves lay limp against paper crisp foliage that seem to have died too fast to let go and fall off.

Alberta's chest tightens, then clenches, the pain radiating up to her jaw. She backs out of the room, down the stairs to the back door, but she can't squeeze through again. Nearly running, she feels a stabbing pain in her chest and charges through the dining room and the living room, dodging busted floorboards. She yanks the front door open, jettisoning herself around the house to the road where she stops and bends over, afraid she might pass out.

With the pain unrelenting, trying to catch her breath, Penn stands erect and rolls her shoulders, straining her neck for some fluidity of motion. It has been a long time since she's had a panic attack. She takes several slow deep breaths until the tightness in her chest releases. It is over as suddenly as it arrived.

It is against Alberta's nature to look at the end of a thing without pondering the beginning, the first thing that made everything to follow inevitable. She'd long believed understanding could be found in the excavated underpinnings of a life, as if there would be one singular moment to define, or maybe defend, what came after. This house was where Walter Stem grew up, where he lived before moving to Bucks County. Whatever happened within those walls, in the only unpainted room where even ivy died, was likely the root of all that followed. If her nephew was the end, she is now certain this house was the beginning.

CHAPTER 8

With docks in the water and their first-day-at-the-lake chores accomplished, Danny Vogel, Jim, Ronny, and Mark Hodges, Steve Fry, and Greg Wagner take a Budweiser each out of the spare fridge on the Frys' back porch and head to the marsh to drink it. A girl from up the road, fifteen that summer, sees them on the road, and calls out. "I'll trade you for one of those beers."

"Trade what?" Jim hollers, laughing.

"You know god damn well what."

Steve holds up his can. "I'm first!"

"It's gunna be two beers to do you, asshole."

"What the hell, Debra?" Steve protests.

Jim tells Mark to go back. Mark argues, but Jim points out the rule. "Not 'til you're thirteen. Her rules."

"Yeah," Ron says. "I waited. You can wait."

Mark begrudgingly walks away.

The troupe move further into the woods, Ron saying he should go first, seeing as how it was his first time.

Debra says he'll be lucky if her hand doesn't cramp up by the time she gets to him. "It might seize up, and I might break your dick. It happens."

Ron looks to Jim and Greg. They nodded. "Happens."

They're far off the path when Debra stops, looks the boys over, her intense eyes peering out from under thick black bangs. She takes Steve's beer and pounds half of it down then grabs Jimmy by the hand. "You first." Steve blocks their way, insisting it was his beer, so he gets to go first. "We both know that's a waste of time," she says.

"C'mon, Mr. Quickie," she says, taking Jim behind a thicket. It's over in a flash. She calls for Greg next but Steve pushes him aside and goes behind the bush. The boys wait, kicking sticks around, sipping beer. After a few minutes, they hear a slap, and Debra starts cussing and storms out past the others, grabbing the beer out of Greg's hand. "No surprise. The dipshit couldn't get it up," she laughs. "Fucking limp dick."

Steve shouts out a loud *Fuck you!* as he steps out from behind the bush. "Fuck you all!"

Greg gives him a mock shoulder punch. "Next time, man. No big deal."

Ron says at least she didn't break it and they all laugh.

The boys emerge from the woods a while later, each hauling a small dead tree that they drag to the beach and work onto a large teepee for the night's bonfire.

Having confirmed her apple tree hideout was still intact, Penny ventures out to explore and comes across a strange boy squatting alone in the woods. He turns to her slowly, and she sees he has something in his hands. She creeps closer and sees he's cradling a small garter snake, all curled up.

"It likes the warmth," he says.

His glance down shows her another small snake stretched out in the leaf litter, its tongue flicking. She kneels down and gently picks it up, cupping her hands around it. It settles in and does not attempt to escape. The two sit quietly, very still, for the longest time.

"I'm Penny," she says.

"Peter Eastman. I'm seven. Almost eight. How old are you?"

She says almost ten.

"We bought the old Conner cottage next to Mr. and Mrs. Monroe. We've been fixing it up all winter." He puts his snake down, and Penny follows suit. Peter tells her the Latin name for garter snake and explains they eat worms, frogs, tadpoles, fish, and even small mammals when they get big enough. These are babies. He takes Penny's hand and smells it, praising her snake handling. "If they feel threatened, they release a musky anal secretion. Your hands don't stink. He wasn't afraid of you." He says he should be getting home and they make a plan to investigate the fence line the next day. When they part ways, he hollers to her. "Your hat's a beaut!"

Afternoon is fading when Marty Wagner finally hollers that the inaugural burgers are ready. He holds court next to a brick monstrosity of a barbeque, arms crossed, spatula erect. Half Italian, Marty is a ruddy-complected man, stocky, with a full head of thick black hair and a mustache. His deep dimples would give his smile an irresistible charm if his eyelids weren't too heavy to open all the way. Hamm's in hand, he proudly scrapes one burger after another off the massive grate. Hungry kids grab them between buns, the older boys taking two at a time. Gladys scoops beans and chips onto their paper plates before exiling them from the patio. The bottom step, a line of demarcation, separates the generations.

Adults congeal around the bar, a teakwood cabinet with two stools. Mason and Gert Vogel. Carl and Marilyn

Vogel. Dick and Evelyn Hodges. Bill and Betsy Fry. Al and Merci Monroe. Marty and Gladys Wagner. They are summer friends having little more in common than proximity. Conversation consists of inconsequential snippets, some humorous, some sarcastic, all drawing patronizing laughter, which grows in frequency and volume with each drink. Betsy, donning her best beauty queen smile, mocks Bill for taking a golf vacation over the winter without her. With a wave of her hand, Merci says she and Al spent February in Florida. The gold charm bracelet tinkles as it slides down her arm. She insists it was a delightful getaway. Al says it rained every day. Mason says he wants to retire. Carl says all Mason has to do is give him the practice. Gert scoffs, saying Mason worked long and hard for it and Carl can buy it any day he likes, but they're not giving it to him. Marilyn says she hopes their son Danny follows his dad into dentistry. Gladys asks who in their right mind would want to be a dentist, that she hates hers, and then says Marty landed a new subdivision contract. Al says Marty underbid the job and was digging himself into a hole. Gert says there it is, proof you should never give your kids anything. Merci reminds Al that Marty runs the business now, and he just has to keep still and enjoy his retirement. As the volley ramps up, Dick tries to manufacture something to say.

In the months since he's seen these people, there were no vacations, no promotions, no exotic purchases. He's a working stiff in charge of cottage cheese at Edgewater Creamery, a job that barely rises to middle management, yet one he's proud of.

He finally says he's thinking of getting a new motor for the Lyman, their old wooden ski boat. "The boys are getting bigger. They need more power." Marty hollers from the grill, citing the top speed of his new Hydrodyne. Dick rolls his eyes and grabs another beer.

Bill gulps the last of his Budweiser, grins at Gladys, and scrunches the can in his hand. Gladys throws her head back laughing, and sweeps her hand along his arm, momentarily pausing on his hand. Bill's wife Betsy watches, seething a bit, and refreshes her Scotch, filling it nearly to the brim. Gladys says it looks like Bill got a little too much sun today and she licks her finger, tapping his arm with a sizzling sound. He's a redhead whose freckled skin is now blooming bright pink.

Carl with his Falstaff, and Marilyn with her tumbler of wine, are first in line for burgers after the kids. Carl steps forward, nudging his wife and she wavers a bit to find equilibrium.

Merci stretches out on a chaise lounge with her tall Tom Collins and waits for Al to bring her a plate. He's good at that, taking care of her. After forty-five years of marriage, they still adore each other.

Gert pours herself another highball, bourbon with 7-Up and lots of ice, and a bourbon neat for her husband. Mason likes things simple.

George and Mildred appear through a gap in the bushes carrying a bowl of dip and a bag of chips. Gladys pounces, her smile a bit too wide, her heavily mascaraed eyes already bloodshot. "Mildred, dear! What can I fix you? We have a full bar. What's your pleasure?"

Mildred smiles and holds up her Coke bottle. When Marty sees George is empty-handed, he directs him to the cooler crammed with beer and ice. "Grab one. Go on. Help yourself." George takes one but only to silence Marty.

As the patio banter grows in volume, Evelyn loiters separate from them all watching the hoard of children careening down below in the dim light of dusk, the younger ones chasing each other, the older ones putting the final touches on the bonfire teepee. Gladys comes up behind her and pours a splash of vodka in Evelyn's glass. "Just a little refresher," she says. "There's more Vernor's in the cooler, too. Just for you."

Evelyn empties her glass in the bushes.

This was their lives. Summer after summer, living unscrutinized lives.

Everyone, adults and kids, gather at the fire pit just before ten o'clock. The dads inspect the pile with flashlights making minor adjustments, stuffing more newspapers into holes. Then comes the sounding out from bonfires firing up one after another all around the lake, children's voices hooting and yipping, one vast primal chorus carrying across the water.

"Al," Mason says. "How about you do the honors this year?" The adults gather to one side. As names are called, each kid comes forward until they encircle the woodpile. "Shelley Vogel. Danny Vogel. Jimmy Hodges. Ron Hodges. Mark Hodges. Penny Hodges. Tyler Hodges. Steve Fry. Laura Fry. Timmy Fry. Greg Wagner. Linda Wagner. Kevin Wagner. Connie Wagner. And last but not least. Peter Eastman. Welcome to summer!"

Al asks Peter if he wants to light the fire, but Steve says it's his turn, and when he tosses in a lit book of matches, the boys all jump back fast. The pile instantaneously explodes into roaring flames sending twigs flying and sparks shooting everywhere. Girls scream. Boys laugh. Mothers shout. Dads ask who the hell put gasoline on the tinder. In the chaos of youth, the kids begin yipping like wild hyenas, dancing frenetically, arms and legs flailing about, running circles around the fire.

Flames rise high, slapping the air, wood within the pyre crackling and snapping, the core shifting as it burns, collapsing a bit, sparks flying high into the sky.

Walter Stem approaches from the shadows with Edith on one side, his mother Velma on the other. Though it is dark, he wears his Panama hat. Edith, dowdy even in yellow polka dots, throws up her hands in excitement. "You're all back! Life has returned!"

Velma, in a red dress and orange sweater, tells Edith to settle down. "You're not a child."

The older boys pretend not to see Debra Stem, their afternoon benefactor. She hangs back in the shadows before disappearing entirely. The Stems stay only long enough to say hello to everyone and complement George and Mildred on how nice the cottage looks. They'd crossed paths a few times over the winter during the renovations. Walter had made sure the road was plowed far enough so they could get in. He'd recommended a local contractor for the roof and siding. He'd taken firewood over so they could keep warm while they worked.

George strikes up a conversation, but Velma cuts it short. "It's time to go" is all she had to say for the Stem contingent to leave.

After the initial roar and spectacle is past its peak, when the fire begins its long steady burn, adults pull chairs around and sit talking and drinking. Greg hollers out *Frogging time!* triggering the seven older lake boys to action, grabbing flashlights, a long-handled net and a pillowcase before taking off on a dead run toward the tall grass past Vogels' dock. Tyler runs after them, running like hell to keep up. Dick calls him back. Ty refuses.

"I'm going with!"

"Ronny!" Dick calls. "Don't you let him follow!"

"Somebody come get him then!" Ronny wrestles Ty, who will not be contained. Dick sends Penny to bring Ty back to the fire. Tyler pitches a fit when she grabs his hand, and Ron runs off into the trees, onto the path skirting the cattails along the edge of the marsh, disappearing into the night.

Tyler cries, but Penny doesn't let go. "Two more years, Ty. You have to wait two more years. Hell, they'll never let me go just cuz I'm a girl." He settles down and she loosens her grip. He grins and yanks away, but she's too fast for him and tackles him, both of them laughing. She gets him back to the fire to roast marshmallows.

Ronny can be heard calling out for the others to wait up. From deep in the marsh, someone hollers, "Got one!"

Shining a light on a fat bullfrog sitting on a log, Greg thrusts the net toward it. The frog jumps and he snares it mid-splash, depositing it into a pillowcase. Mark sees the next one, a beefy thing a few feet from shore, deep in the cattails.

Danny Vogel shoves Mark hard, and he goes flying into the inky black water, disappearing into it, the waves rocking weeds back and forth all around. When he bolts up, water to his waist, he holds the biggest bullfrog of the night, bringing the boys to full froth, howling like a pack of coyotes over a kill.

With half a dozen bullfrogs writhing in the pillowcase, they emerge from the swamp and gather around the kill-stone. Mark pulls a frog from the bag and slams it against the rock. Swift. Violent. He holds it up, its tongue hanging out, blood dripping. He drops it on a wooden board where Danny plunges a knife into its groin, separating its legs from the torso. Steve pushes Mark aside to get into the bag. He pulls one out by the legs and smashes it on the rock with such ferocity its body disintegrates, bits of entrails splattering all of them. He laughs out loud, dangling the bloody ribbons in front of everyone. Dan calls him a shithead and walks away, handing the knife to Jim. Just as Steve tries to grab it, Dick walks up. He'd seen. He takes the bag and empties it into the water. Four frogs would escape the frying pan. He tells his boys to bury the dead ones.

Later on, as Ursa Major rises over the lake, everyone gathers around the roiling bed of coals, their faces aglow, as flaming marshmallows drip from their sticks.

Even parents have quieted, sitting in lawn chairs, weary from the day, mellowed by too much sunshine and work to let the booze rouse them from their stupor.

Penny is the first to leave, to go up to bed. She longs for summer pajamas and night sounds. Cubby curtains pulled tight, she crawls under covers, cranks open her window a little wider and listens. A singular unenthusiastic cricket speaks up, and she hears an errant frog croak. It will be a couple more weeks before the tree peepers sing, even longer before the cicadas fill the air with their whirring. Penny could not have been happier under any circumstance.

Lovely Laura sunbathing. Fathers arguing with sons. Sisters arguing with each other. Little boys running roughshod over adults. Wine before noon. Handjobs. Bonfires on every shore. Summer has officially begun, everyone living a version of the American dream.

CHAPTER 9

MAY 25 - There should be some law against holding anyone accountable for what they do in the face of devastating loss, but I don't think I can forgive her any more than she can forgive him.

"Your father was a heartless, soulless bastard." Like most things Evelyn says, the comment comes out of nowhere. Penny ignores it. The sun is too delightful, the patio too tranquil, the dappled shade too beautiful, the air too sweet to pollute with another of her mother's diatribes.

Evelyn sits watching Penn weed a small flower patch along the patio. She takes a mouthful of rice pudding and spits it back to the bowl. A breeze sets a small stand of monarda to swaying, tall young stalks flowing back and forth. Evelyn tries to say something but can't rally the words. One of her hands begins waving back and forth with the flowers. Struggling to speak, she finally says "those green things" and nothing more. Penn takes the bowl and sets it aside.

Evelyn's next words are crystal clear. "Why did he hate me so much?" Her voice holds no anger. She could just as well have asked why grass is green or why vodka gets you so much more drunk than wine.

"Who, Mom?" Penn sighs. "Nobody hates you."

"You know, you little shit. You were there. You let him. You could have . . ." the words slip away. Her hands make tight fists. "Throwing my boy away."

Penn struggles to understand her mother's disjointed shorthand.

"No body threw him away, Mom."

"What?"

Evelyn's head starts nodding the way it does when her neck forgets its responsibilities. Penn lifts her from the chair and helps her upstairs to bed. No discussion, no resistance.

Penn brings a box up to Evelyn and sets it on the bed. "We didn't throw all of him away." Evelyn looks at it with a hauntingly blank expression. Penn steps away, watching from the hallway as her mother drags the carton closer and opens it. What follows from the bedroom is a low sad yowling, like some wounded animal. Evelyn clutches a small baseball glove to her heart, her body shuddering with sobs.

Penn sits in the hall against the wall and softly cries.

When Tyler died, Evelyn refused to come home from the cottage. Dick tried to make things work on his own with his kids. For the first few weeks, neighbors brought casseroles. Soups. Pies. Cakes and cookies. When that stopped, it was up to Dick to figure out how to run the house, keep track of the kids, and keep his job. He tried to tell them Mom would be fine, that she was just working through her grief. It was easy to see he didn't believe. Then, without discussion or warning, Dick began putting everything that belonged to Tyler into boxes, filling one after another without hesitation or emotion. Jim, Ronny, Mark, and Penny watched from the hall. He said something about putting the memories out of sight so they wouldn't get in the way, to give their mother room to come home. He didn't save anything. It all went to the curb next to the garbage can.

None of the kids said anything. They were confused. They were young. Even Jimmy, who'd just turned sixteen, had no idea what he was supposed to do except lead his siblings downstairs so they wouldn't have to watch. Dick took the bunks apart that day, dismantled Ty's bed. Put the pieces in the garage.

All his son's things, Tyler's ball glove, clothes, his models, even his bedspread and especially his pillow - the one that still smelled of his head, the one Dick buried his face in to drink in the scent of him and then used to muffle his sobs - all of it transported him into that space between life and death where the dead still live, always about to run through a room or laugh or sigh. It was the space his wife willingly inhabited, but one he could not afford to get sucked into. He had responsibilities. All of the responsibilities. His actions were a simple case of self-preservation.

As their father worked upstairs, the kids pulled boxes from the curb to the garage, salvaging what was left of their little brother, an odd collection of things of no particular value. His mitt, a rock with a smile painted on it, a few books, his model of Frankenstein, the clay rabbit he made in school, three dirty socks, his favorite T-shirt, and a pair of ratty shoes. Dick caught them at it, shouting with an anger they couldn't comprehend. When he frantically hauled the boxes back to the curb, Jim took and hid the one they'd just filled.

Dick grabbed a can of paint and went back upstairs. The first push of the roller, the first swipe of color, so reticent it seemed he might change his mind, was followed by another faster swath, then another, the roller pressing hard and fast, splatters flying onto his face, his hair, each subsequent refill leaving trails of paint on the drop cloth, on his pants, his shirt. His arm ached, but he could not stop until it was done. Midnight found him painting the trim, touching up. By the end of the weekend, the erasure of Tyler was complete. Jim moved into that room, and Mark moved in with Ron.

How much of his actions were borne of grief and how much was retaliation for Evelyn leaving everything to him was unclear, even to him. It was his only failing in an otherwise valiant effort to salvage his family.

After staying away for weeks, Evelyn showed up at Penny's school on a Wednesday, waiting in the car, watching for her, waving her over. It would have been an innocuous gesture under any other circumstances, but the situation being what it was, Penny was hesitant to climb in. Driving home, Evelyn said she was going to make a lasagna for dinner as though she'd made dinner all the previous nights, as though she hadn't disappeared from their lives. Penny carried a bag of groceries into the house, hoping her brothers were home, feeling an unreasonable, strange sensation she didn't understand except to know having the boys around would be preferable to being alone with her mother.

Penny stood against the wall watching Evelyn silently unpack the bags, methodically placing the Wonder Bread on the counter, a box of butter next to it, lifting a carton of eggs slowly, setting them to the side, each movement mechanical in nature, not quite normal. Evelyn lifted a can of tomatoes from the sack and hesitated. She stopped moving, like an automaton switched off. When she finally put the can down, she turned, and without even a glance to Penny, walked to the stairs and stood at the bottom, waiting for something. Penny watched her mother take one step at a time, ascending in slow motion. Penny thought she should warn her the rooms were rearranged, that Tyler's bed and all his things were gone, but she froze. Then came the scream from upstairs, and the crashing of things, and the wailing, and the thud to the floor directly above her.

When Jim and Ronny got home from school they found groceries scattered everywhere, a broken bottle of vinegar splattered on the floor, hard lasagna noodles broken to bits and scattered to every corner, melted ice cream oozing from a carton under the table and Penny crying on the floor in a corner, clenching what was left of the loaf of bread. Evelyn had walked out on her daughter, leaving her to process alone.

Penny would not recall tearing into the sacks, throwing cans so hard they dented cabinets. She did not remember Jim taking her to her room. She did not know her brothers took every remnant of the groceries their mother brought out to the trash and that they cleaned the kitchen, erasing all sign of their sister's rage.

They did not however touch anything else in the house, leaving their parents' room a mess where the two dressers had been swiped clean, their contents scattered to the floor, the bed torn apart. They did not pick up the broken lamp in the living room, or the broken vase in the dining room. They left what they presumed was their mother's debris for their father.

Penny would be unable to forgive her mother for that day above all others.

Evelyn would forever hold her husband responsible for erasing her son.

Jim would never get over carrying the burden of everyone's rage.

CHAPTER 10

After leaving Walter Stem's rotting lakeside house on Monday, Alberta retrieves the Hodges/Eastman case files from the county records office. Her boss, District Attorney Benjamin Groves, came through with the subpoena. She reads it cover to cover over a sandwich in her corner booth at the tavern. A quick read. Too quick, she thinks. There are holes. Huge gaping holes.

She heads to South Bend, Indiana, to meet the Eastmans. Both of Peter's parents still teach, George at Notre Dame and Mildred at St. Mary's. They still live in the same house Peter had been born into.

At their front door, Alberta is met by a diminutive girl with eager expression. Without asking her name or giving her own, the child says she is seven and she just helped plant tomatoes in the vegetable garden. "Here, smell my hands," she says, thrusting them upwards. "They smell acerbic, don't they? That's what tomato leaves smell like. They get caterpillars on them and the caterpillars turn into a five-spotted hawk moth of the Sphingidae family. They are brown and gray and quite large." She steps back to let Alberta in. "The caterpillar is sometimes called the tomato hornworm. It's a pest." The girl pulls a small book on butterflies and moths from her back pocket and hands it over. "Page 27. There's a picture of the moth." She instructs Alberta to put the book on a shelf when she was finished. Alberta watches the child bounce out of the room.

"Mama will be out soon!"

Alberta looks at the moth picture, then leafs through well-worn pages, landing on the first. In a child's scrawl is written *Peter Eastman*, below it *April Eastman*. She brushes a finger over the letters feeling the indentations. She'd thought, up to that moment, she could keep a distance, but is beginning to see how impossible it will be.

The bookcase takes up an entire wall, its contents stacked on end and in piles, odd objects tucked here and there, a few geodes, an antique iron, and a darkly tarnished teapot. Alberta sifts through a pile of small nature guidebooks.

"That stack is all Peter's," Mildred says, walking in from the dining room.

According to the file, Mildred was thirty-eight when she lost her boy, making her forty-eight now, but she looks much younger to Alberta. It could be her slender frame, or the way she carries herself, or the fact that she wears a cotton blouse and jeans with knees covered in dirt. Then Alberta thinks maybe it's her voice, so bright and clear, or maybe her fresh face, no makeup. It makes Alberta want to find a mirror, to see how this woman might perceive her.

Mildred reaches her hand out to shake. "Mildred Eastman. You must be Alberta Higgins." Alberta puts down her satchel, and they share a confident handshake.

"Never went in the woods without them," Mildred says, glancing to the guidebooks. "Never went to the marsh without at least one. So much to identify. Bugs. Plants. Critters. He was a very curious boy." She pulls a notebook from the top shelf and hands it to Alberta. "This was Peter's. He wrote down everything."

Alberta takes the spiral bound notebook, the cover creased and dog-eared, pages thick with things stuck within, like a treasure to be unearthed, she thinks, like something Alby would make. She opens it and carefully turns pages, paying great attention to the drawings and scrawls, delighted by feathers and leaves glued and taped to pages. Her mind struggles to stick with the moment, to keep her focus on this boy and not to let her mind wander to Alby.

Mildred smiles. "If you want to know Peter, talk to April, his sister. She's a carbon copy."

Alberta apologizes for her visit and for the things she is about to ask. Mildred, however, appears to welcome the visit. "George will be here in about half an hour," she says. "I presume you'd rather speak with us separately." Mildred directs Alberta to the couch.

Alberta pulls out a small notepad and clicks a pen, making scribbles on a page to get the ink flowing. She takes in the room, a cluttered space with toys and errant stacks of books. Obscure drawings and paintings hang on every wall. There are so many chairs, none of them matching. It's easy to imagine a hoard of college students sitting around having insightful conversations with the professors. There's a deep sense of belonging about the Eastman house, an instant comfort. Love lives there.

"When you called," Mildred says, "you had questions for me. About our son's drowning."

Alberta hadn't expected the topic to come up so abruptly. She looks at Mildred as if looking from a pit of quicksand knowing if she reaches out, she'll probably pull this woman in with her. Mildred urges her on with a faint smile.

"Can you give me your impression of the events surrounding the death of your son?" Alberta asks.

Mildred's face melts into a warm, sad smile. "You're the first to ever ask."

"Say that again?"

"The day it happened, the report said they found a pillowcase in the water and that settled everything though it still didn't make any sense to us. They weren't interested in anything we had to say. They had their idea of what happened. Case closed."

Alberta's whole body clenches.

"Are you feeling all right, Miss Higgins? Would you like some water or tea?"

"Tea," she says. "Hot tea would be nice." Mildred goes to the kitchen. Alberta isn't a tea drinker but needs time to get herself sorted out. So much hinges on finding the facts of these drownings and in unearthing some small detail, some piece of evidence that was missed, that might lead to answers in Alby's death. If she is going to get everyone to cooperate, she's going to have to stay above her own feelings. Objective. It was a challenge in the Eastman household to do that. She looks at Alby's photo to remind her what was at stake, slipping it under some papers when Mildred returns with a tray.

"That was fast," Alberta says.

"A microwave oven. Love it!" When Mildred moves the papers aside, Alby's photograph falls to the floor. She picks it up. "Handsome fellow. About seven or eight?"

"Seven. He's an egghead. I'm sure you know the type. Already knows more than I ever will." The words accidentally fall out of Alberta's mouth as if Alby was still alive.

"Sounds like our Peter. I have three master's degrees and a Ph.D., yet he had a way of – well, he knew just how to get to us. Exactly what to say."

"And patient?"

"With us? Oh, yes."

"That's what got to me most." Alberta catches herself and stops. Mildred hands back the photo. Alberta carefully puts it away.

"You didn't tell me his name."

Alberta wants to tell her everything. She wants to spill her grief onto this woman who alone would know the depth of it. But she fights the feelings, turns them off. Her demeanor shifts to mild detachment.

"What can you tell me about the night Peter died?"

"I can tell you every detail. But I don't understand why you're asking."

Alberta straightens and offers a tight-lipped smile, the kind that implies reluctance. "I'm not at liberty to say."

Mildred nods acceptance. "I put Peter to bed," she says, settling back into the easy chair, drawing the warm mug of tea to her heart. "The barometric pressure was dropping. It looked like a storm might develop so George closed all the windows. We went to bed. I woke up to go to the bathroom at 5:30 and noticed Peter wasn't in bed. I went to see if he was outside. He used to step out at night to watch the stars, but he never left the patio. That was the rule. And if he saw a meteor shower, he was to wake us up." She smiles. "That was the best rule."

Alberta breaks into a broad smile and nods.

"You have some experience with this I think," Mildred says.

It was an invitation Alberta can't accept no matter how comforting it might be to share stories with this woman whose memories were a decade old yet still fresh and fond. She wonders how long her memories of Alby will last. Her chest tightens. "He wasn't on the patio?" she asks, getting back to business.

"No. He wasn't on the patio. When I couldn't find him, I woke George."

"Why did you knock on the Hodges' door that morning?"

"Because of Penny. They were friends. I thought maybe he didn't want to wake us and was with her waiting for the sun to come up. They'd done it before. He liked sunrises and that lovely moment between night and morning when the tree peepers stopped and the birds began. Do you know what I mean? It is a magical time of day."

How this woman who'd lost her only son could still see magic in the world astounds Alberta. "Help me understand," she says. "Penny Hodges was ten. Why would she spend time with a seven-year-old boy?"

Mildred smiles. "He wasn't your normal seven-year-old."

"In the same way April isn't a normal seven-year-old."

Mildred grins. "And he would have turned eight in a week. Penny had only just turned ten. So they weren't that far apart. They were so alike. Interested in nature, in observation. Penny wasn't a frivolous girl like other girls at the lake, flirting, sunning themselves, trying on makeup. Penny had substance. I liked her. Still do."

"You've kept in touch?"

"Yes. It took six years, but she came down to see us her junior year of high school. As soon as she got her license. Her independence."

"That must have been difficult. To see her after all that time."

Mildred's eyes open wide. "No! Not at all. She was just the same, just older. Still curious. Still hungry to learn." Mildred stops short, shakes her head. "That's not true. She wasn't the same at all. I don't know what I expected when she showed up. She called to see if it was alright, to get directions. We hadn't seen her since the funeral, and her dad whisked the kids off so fast we didn't get a chance to talk with her. He didn't bring her to Peter's service. I didn't expect them to come, but it would have been nice." Mildred takes a breath. "It was just the day after Tyler's.

"There was no bounce in the girl anymore. No exuberance. She was proud of her four-point in school, but I had the feeling that was all she had. Studying. No extracurricular activities. No friends that I could tell. Our April was good therapy. She was three. Giddy, cuddly, snippy as hell. We saw a lot of Penny after that. Once or twice a month at first. Before long, she was spending weekends with us. George took her to Notre Dame and introduced her around. Wanted to give her a sense of direction, a sense of possibilities. They tagged along on a field trip with a group of grad students to an abandoned industrial site to study aquatic life. She was hooked."

Alberta is almost envious of Penny. Everyone should have a Mildred and George in their lives. Presumably, as parents.

"Penny's presence brought Peter back into our house, into our lives. We helped her get into the University of Michigan. We get together when we can. Her own family life is tenuous at best. April loves her like a big sister."

"Tenuous?"

"They've had difficulty coping with Tyler's death. They may never recover."

"How so?"

"You'll see when you talk to them. I'd rather not say any more."

Alberta asks about the people at the lake, what Mildred thought of them. The response is abrupt, saying they all drank too much and had virtually no redeeming qualities. "All except for Walter Stem," Mildred says.

Alberta looks up from her notepad. Eager.

"Sometimes I thought Walter was a little too interested in my son."

"How so?"

"Oh, not in a bad way, but it drew Peter away from George, and I think it hurt George's feelings." She explains how Walter took Peter fishing and Peter made him release everything they caught. "Peter only wanted to identify the fish." She opens Peter's journal to the back. This was his Walter schedule. Fishing. Chopping kindling. Finding night crawlers. Something every week. Sometimes three or four times a week. I think maybe Walter needed a son."

Alberta's attention peaks. "Why do you say that?"

"He had a daughter. Odd girl. Didn't particularly trust her. Anyway, it wasn't just Peter. He'd been a mentor of sorts for several of the boys out there."

Alberta reviews the Walter schedule hoping something stands out but sees no references to the marsh. Alberta flips through pages filled with sketches of snakes, turtles, and cattails. "Lovely drawing of a dragonfly here. He was quite the naturalist. Mrs. Eastman . . ."

"Mildred, Alberta. My students don't even call me Mrs. Eastman."

Alberta smiles and takes another draw of tea. "Mildred, I was under the assumption Peter had no experience with the marsh. Yet looking at his drawings . . ."

"Who told you that?"

"It's in the report." She digs some pages from her satchel and reads a passage. "The Eastman boy had no prior interaction with the marsh and was not a strong swimmer."

Mildred gasps. "That's not right. Not at all. I don't know where they got that from. Can I see that?"

Alberta hands it over and asks if she hadn't seen it before.

"They never showed us this." She skims the page. "We certainly never said any of this. And he was a good swimmer."

Alberta watches Mildred read. Mildred's hands begin to shake.

"He loved the marsh," Mildred says, her voice pinched. "George and Peter did nature surveys of it. Here." She turns to journal pages full of lists. "They recorded everything they saw. Plants, insects, animal tracks and amphibian sightings. Look here." She hands the book back to Alberta. "And one more thing. If he was going to spend time in the marsh with Tyler, he'd have put it in his book.

He put everything in there like they were appointments. He wrote things in before he did them. He was organized that way. He wouldn't have left the house in the middle of the night on a whim. He'd have had to plan it. It would have been in his book."

"Except to see a sunrise."

Her words sting. Mildred's eyes well up. Suddenly April comes squealing through the room. George is home.

CHAPTER 11

JUN 4 - I will miss Mildred when she's gone more than I will ever miss my mother.

Evelyn is having a good day. She's gotten herself into her sweatpants and sweater. She's eaten part of an egg for breakfast. She feels so good she demands to go back to her apartment.

"We can't do that, Mom."

"Of course we can. We get in your car and you drive. You drop me off and I go in. Pretty damn simple."

Penn has no idea how to break it to her mother that the apartment is gone. "Not today."

"What if somebody gets in and steals all my stuff? I need to get back over there."

"Somebody else lives there now, Mom."

"With all my stuff? That's nuts! Kick 'em out. Some stranger's ass in my bed!"

"You live here now. Remember? You left your apartment. I had it cleaned and donated everything."

"My things? All crap. Crap apartment . . . " The words disintegrated. "Knit the landing. Before it snows."

Penn picks Evelyn's nightgown and underwear from the floor, tosses them in the clothesbasket with the sheets, and carries it downstairs to do laundry.

Her mother's voice carries behind her. "Thief!"

As the washer fills, Penn brushes her hand across the green underbelly of the canoe hanging from the ceiling. It was handcrafted of wood and canvas, a work of art with ribs and rails varnished to a golden sheen, a gift from George and Mildred when Penn and Matthew bought the cottage from Evelyn. Even though that lake held nothing but tragic memories for them, they found room in their hearts to commemorate Penn's choice to keep her family cottage with the only thing they'd kept from their time there. The canoe.

If not for Mildred, Penny would not have had any birthday celebration in 1960. Penny's dad had said they'd celebrate when he came out over the weekend, but things tended to get away from him at the lake.

The day started when Tyler tried to con her out of the rusty penknife she'd found. He saw her sitting in her cubby trying to pry the pearl bits off it. He climbed in next to her, pulling the curtain closed and asked to hold it. She handed it over.

"I'll trade you an Angler's Tavern coaster for it," he said.

"No way."

"Two coasters."

She said no and he begged for it. "Pleeeeze. Pleeeze."

She grabbed it from him, putting it back in the cigar box, returning the cigar box to the drawer under her bed.

When Penny went downstairs for breakfast, Evelyn gave her a donut from a box, stuck a candle in it, lit it, then pulled a new bathing suit from a variety store bag. Holding it up by the straps, she made it dance before laying it on the counter. "Make a wish and blow it out, Dear." She never actually said happy birthday. Tyler ran through, hollered happy birthday, and ran out the door waving the pearl-handled penknife high.

Peter came knocking, hollering as loud as he could when he caught sight of Penny. "Happy birthday! I have the whole day planned out!" He read from his notepad. "Number one: Discover something wonderful. Number 2: Learn something wonderful. Number 3, 4 and 5 are a surprise! I suggest we start here," showing her the page, "and head toward Spring Lake then take the back path to the apple tree." He'd actually drawn their path with little squares for the cottages and clusters of circles for trees.

Penny tossed the new bathing suit to her bed but missed. It landed on the floor where she left it.

Peter reminded her not to forget her straw hat and she grabbed it from its hook in her nook.

They both knew the best way to discover anything was to walk slowly and look carefully. They were just rounding the bend by Stems' house when they found a dead Cecropia moth on the edge of the road. Both of them shrieked at the thrill. Peter pulled out a small tape measure. "5 3/4 inches!" he said. He looked at his watch so he'd know what time to enter the discovery in his notebook. "Off to the tree," he said. Penny carried the moth while Peter collected lichen and a few wildflowers. Sitting on the rug in their hideout, Peter perused his field guides, reading aloud about their day's haul while Penny drew pictures of it all in his big notebook.

Though nearly two years younger, Peter was bright, inquisitive, a kindred spirit. Age didn't matter.

Peter kept looking at his watch until he finally announced they were going to be late for Number 3. He collected his things and pushed Penny out into daylight, laughing when she stumbled and her hat caught on a branch. He rescued it and gave it to her. "C'mon! No time to dawdle!"

Waiting at the beach next to their canoe were George and Mildred with the standard equipment: Four sets of binoculars, four notepads, a small stack of field guides and four sack lunches. They both gave Penny a big hug and wished her happy birthday. As had become routine over the course of three previous outings, George and Mildred did the paddling while Peter and Penny sat in the bottom, draping arms off the side, streaming fingers through the water. Today they were headed to the farthest lake in the chain, meaning they'd have to maneuver two narrow channels and portage over a sandbar to the last. They spoke quietly as they went, sighting plants and birds along the way. Peter looked up flora and fish while Penny identified birds in Peter's book. Lunch was peanut butter and jelly sandwiches, potato chips and a brownie. The cooler, as always, was full of Orange Crush.

It was late afternoon when they made it back to Eastmans' cottage for Number 4 on Peter's list. He ran ahead to beat Penny to the kitchen and stood in front of the table until everyone was there. Stepping aside, Penny saw the cake Mildred baked for her, frosted in pale green with pink sugar flowers tucked in all around and Happy Birthday Penny written on it in blue frosting. Next to it was Number 5, a package wrapped in pretty paper with watercolors of lily of the valley, tied with a ribbon and bow. Mildred lit candles and the three sang to her while she blew them out. Peter handed her the package, eager for her to open it. It was two field guides, one for birds and the other wildflowers, just like his. George, Mildred and Peter signed them both. It was like no birthday she'd ever had. More love, more cheer.

The Eastmans were a different kind of family from her own. They laughed *with* each other, not at each other. Peter's kindness made the alienation Penn felt from her brothers more evident, their taunting, their indifference. Mildred's calm demeanor made Evelyn's erratic behavior, her outbursts and ambivalence, less tolerable. Until she saw George drive an hour to get to the lake from work each evening, Penn hadn't questioned her father's absence when he stayed in town after work all week just twenty miles away. It was her family. They were all she knew. Knowing Peter and his parents made her more aware of her own family's inadequacies.

Penny loved Mildred for her infectious smile. She was easy to be around. So was George, but he was quieter. Penny used to pretend she was in college when either of them talked, like listening to one of their lectures. It made her feel smart to be spoken to like an adult.

Mildred never fit in at the lake. None of the other women worked. Mildred didn't play bridge or like to drink in the middle of the day. She wasn't much of a cook and only baked for birthdays. She was a reader. None of the other women read anything beyond their magazines and TV guide. She tried to start a book club. Didn't work out. She spent the summer in shorts except for Sundays. She wore a dress to Mass. Eastmans were the only ones who went to church.

George was not a handsome man, and it seemed odd to Penny how a younger woman as pretty as Mildred would end up with him. It eventually dawned on her that Peter wasn't a handsome boy either, and he was too young for her, but she was drawn to him, to his insatiable curiosity and eagerness to share. Appearance meant nothing in the face of those attributes. Had it not been for Peter and George, Penny might not have given Matthew a second look later in life. Like George, Matthew was not a handsome man. He did not have pale blue eyes or cavernous dimples, was not tall or lean or particularly fit. But he was funny and brilliant and loving. Had she not loved an awkward boy when she was a girl, she might not have been drawn to an unusual man as a woman. Mildred and Penn were widowed the same year, further cementing their bond.

The washer signals the first load is done. Penn loads the dryer and fills the washer again. Evelyn hollers through the floor that someone's at the door.

"Nobody's at the door," Penn hollers back but then hears knocking.

Mildred Eastman is the last person Penn expects to see. She had not been to the lake for decades. Yet, there she is with three small casserole dishes stacked one on the other. In her early seventies, Mildred looks no more than sixty, still attractive, still teaching at St. Mary's.

"Andi told me you're not eating," Mildred says, putting the casseroles on the floor, enveloping Penn in a hug as a mother does, wrapping her in unconditional love.

Penn melts into it. "Hm. Not sure how she'd know that."

"Because you never eat." Mildred hands two dishes to Penn and takes the third. "She needed to talk to someone." Mildred looks at Penn in a way that demands attention. "She's worried about you. And she can't tell you that. You need to . . ."

"I know." Penn cuts her off. "I know." Words that deny further discussion.

On the way through, Mildred looks in on Evelyn, shocked to see the emaciated woman sitting up in bed, slack-jawed, one skeletal hand draped over the edge.

"Who the hell are you?" Evelyn grouses.

"Nobody, Mom. It's nobody."

"Well, it's somebody cause she's standing right there looking at me!"

Mildred steps away, observing the exchange.

Penn lies, saying it's somebody from Hospice.

"Well, why the hell didn't you say that?"

Penn motions Mildred to go downstairs.

"Get me out of this bed," Evelyn says.

"In a little while."

"Now, damn it!"

"Not now."

"Abuse! That's what this is. Abuse!"

"If you let me speak to this woman in peace, I'll take you for a boat ride later."

"Bribery."

"Yes."

"OK."

Mildred waits in the kitchen. Penn comes down saying Evelyn would be asleep within minutes and will forget about the boat ride.

"It's worse than I imagined," Mildred says, clearly aggravated. "Put her in a home. Let the professionals take care of her. Why in the hell are you putting yourself through this?"

Feeling like a scolded teenager, Penn rallies a response. "You're right. I know. But she's here." Pawing the casserole dishes, she asks what they hold.

"Chicken with noodles, Shepherd's Pie, and beef stew. And don't just throw them in the freezer and forget about them. Eat. Them."

"Yum," Penn says mockingly, putting them in the fridge, appreciation laced with sarcasm.

Mildred puts water on to boil and pulls a tin of tea from her purse, eliciting a broad smile from Penn.

"I didn't want you to feel obligated to come out here," Penn says. "That's why I didn't tell you. I knew you'd come."

"Andi's worried about you. Frankly, now that I see your mother, so am I."

"You sort of get used to the abuse after a while."

Mildred almost speaks but just shakes her head instead. She looks out over the water. "It isn't as difficult as I thought it would be. Everything has changed so much. Doesn't look like the same place. I think part of me wanted nothing to change. But if it was still here, the cottage, I suppose I'd be expecting to see Peter."

"When was the last time you came out?"

Mildred puts tea bags in two mugs, ignoring the question, retrieving a package of shortbread from her bag.

"It was the spring of '70," Mildred finally says.

Penn stops short. "She made you come all the way out here?"

"I said yes before I even thought about it. We wanted so badly to know what she found out." Pouring from the steaming kettle, Mildred asks about Andi, a clear signal there would be no more talking about Alberta Higgins' investigation.

"We've never talked about it," Penn says. "All these years."

"And we never will."

Mildred's finality draws a line Penn knows not to cross.

Over cups of Earl Grey, Mildred fills Penn in on her daughter April's new job, her two kids, her husband's promotion. "She sends her love, and I'm to tell you the girls were inconsolable when they found out they wouldn't be coming out here this summer."

Penn sighs. "Maybe before school starts."

"They love you. They miss you. They want to see you and Andi."

"Does it bother you they come here?"

Mildred closes the tea tin, setting it on the ledge over the sink. This subject, too, is dropped and another begun, one even more painful except for the sharing of it. They talk about missing their husbands, about how sometimes they wake up expecting to feel them in bed next to them. There are apologies for not being more present for each other during those weeks and months, only to remember they were each occupied with losing at the time, unable to be support for anyone but their daughters. "I think we have to forgive ourselves our heartache sometimes, especially when we see it reflected in our friends. If you were one of my students, I'd give you a reading list on the topic."

"Grief in classic literature," Penn says smiling. "Thanks but no thanks."

"Andi says you may have to cancel the Cambridge study in England. Are you OK with that? Of everyone they could have chosen, they invited you. You'll be staying in the Lake District, in a castle for Chrissake."

Penn shakes her head. "It is a month-long study of the lakes and waterways in association with Cambridge. I gave them another name, someone who will give their students a far better experience."

"So, you've already cancelled?"

"Can't leave them in the lurch if Evelyn decides to take her sweet time dying. Spoke with them a couple days ago."

"I see." It's what Mildred says when she disagrees with a decision but is resigned to accept it. "What makes you think you don't give your students a good experience?"

"Because I don't like them and they know it."

"That's why they try so hard to please you. They want your respect."

Penn laughs. "Maybe teaching the humanities is different, but . . ."

"It's all the same. George was like you. Every year there was a new batch of freshmen looking at him, sizing him up, thinking he was brilliant, fawning all over him. Girls falling in love with him. Boys falling in love with him. He was this unattainable get, the professor they wanted to study under, but eventually they'd discover he was just a man who momentarily knew more than they did."

"He hated office hours, didn't he? I remember him saying that. I hate office hours."

"I know you do."

"They want more than I should ever have to give. We're there to transmit information, to enlighten, to inspire. Period. But some of them, they'll suck you dry if you let them. They need to feel special, to belong in some mysterious inner circle. You're what they all want, someone who invites them into her home for special little readings, someone who makes them feel they could actually attain their aspirations, even though most of them will never even come close."

"Literature is different from the sciences. One can't teach writing from a distance. It's intimate. Subjective. Souls get laid bare."

"I like the initiates, how they fight to get on my research teams as grunts willing to do the schlepping and driving. But by the time they're finishing their post grad degrees, finding their own footing, they either loathe me or admire me. I don't much care which, so long as they leave capable of offering something to the world. All I want for them is to graduate and leave. No looking back."

"It still amazes me sometimes how much you sound like George."

Eventually, Mildred gets Penn to open up about caring for Evelyn and doesn't let her stop talking until she's vented every last humiliation and frustration, the interrupted sleep, meds, yelling, confusion, feeling trapped in her own house. "What aren't you telling me, Penny?" Mildred waits.

Penn takes their cups to the sink. "She sees Tyler."

Mildred laughs. "Of course she does. I see Peter all the time."

Penn looks up, surprised. "No. I mean she *sees* him. She reads to him. Talks to him. Like he's right here next to her."

"He probably is."

"What are you saying?"

Mildred sighs and takes Penn's hands. "George was certain Peter was sitting on the bed with him toward the end. He even told me he was sorry I couldn't see him. It's what parents do, Dear. We love. We hang on. We never truly let go." Both of them begin to tear up a bit. "Let her have him."

Mildred gathers her purse and jacket. "Call your daughter once in a while. She needs to know you're muddling through. Call me if you think it will help. You'll get through this, Penny. Maybe this is a good thing you're doing. Honestly, I can't tell one way or the other. Just remember, you are loved. I love you. Andi loves you. April loves you. Her girls love you. We'll all be there for you on the other side of this mess."

Out at the car, Penn thanks Mildred for not mentioning her brothers. Mildred gives her a quick hug. "No point talking about lost causes."

It takes Penn five days, but she eventually eats her way through the food Mildred left.

CHAPTER 12

Before visiting the Eastmans in South Bend, Alberta made presumptions about what everyone knew, never imagining officials never fully briefed the parents. As soon as Mildred contradicted the official report, it reaffirmed Alberta's commitment to uncovering truth. Whatever it might be.

Alberta watches Mildred wipe tears from her face as George comes through the door. He immediately scoops April in his arms, his jaw clenched. He asks April to show their visitor her tomato plants.

Alberta follows the eager child outside, giving April's parents a moment.

In a few minutes, Mildred appears on the back stoop reaching for April's hand for a walk.

George is situating himself in the armchair when Alberta returns to the couch. His scruffy white hair, short white beard, make him look much older than his sixty years. She watches him pick lint off the chair arm, give his slacks a swipe.

"You're investigating our son's death," George says.

"Yes."

"That must mean you have reason to think what happened was something other than what they cooked up." His eyes drill into hers.

"Possibly," she says, trying to gage emotional his state.

"Have you talked to everyone at the lake yet?" He hesitates. "Because you'll be hearing a great deal of fiction."

"Mr. Eastman, what are you trying to tell me here."

"I'm saying I don't know what happened that night." His breathing grows anxious. "I don't suppose I'll ever know. But I know my son. And believe me, I've imagined a thousand scenarios over the last ten years, trying to imagine what Peter's motivation could have been to walk into the woods in the middle of the night with a storm pending, wind blowing, without telling his mother and me."

"Boys do things like that and . . ."

"Not my boy!" George takes a breath and settles himself. With a hint of resignation, he continues. "You sound like lake people. Peter was different from most kids. I heard what they all said about my son. Wimpy. Scrawny. He was not respected. But he respected all of them. He was a respectful boy." His voice starts to quake. "I see you have his journal there."

"I understand not everything went into his journal schedule. Like watching a sunrise with Penny."

"Some things just happen." George's face relaxes, and a vague smile crosses it. "That morning was spectacular."

"The sunrise morning?"

"When I woke up, the whole sky was the color of muskmelon. I went to wake him, but he wasn't there. I looked out the front window and saw Peter and Penny standing on a dock with their arms out wide, heads facing upward, like they were bathing in the light. It was astounding. They were astounding." George shakes his head and takes a deep breath.

"Mr. Eastman, take your time. I want to get to the bottom of this. To do that, I need your help. I know it's difficult."

"I doubt very much you know how difficult."

Alberta looks down to her notepad.

"He kept that journal so I would know what he'd done on the days I had to be here instead of there. We talked every evening about what he'd learned that day. He wanted to know how to pronounce the Latin names of everything. Rana catesbeiana. Know what that is?" Alberta shakes her head. "Bullfrog. He could recite all the pertinent details of size, mating habits, habitat, and life cycle. He had a half dozen tadpoles in a bowl in his room. The bullfrog fascinated him. He did not want to kill it. He certainly didn't want to eat it. He wanted to study it."

"Why do you think none of this made it into the report?"

George's jaw juts out and back. "Sheriff Bates didn't think it was important. He didn't write it down. He thought I was simply one of those parents who thinks their kid is special. That their kid would never do anything wrong."

"Did you talk with your neighbors?"

"I tried. At the marsh. They were a gang, that lake crowd. They thought like a gang. Drank like a gang. Screwed around on each other. Ignored their children. Buying that cottage was a horrible mistake. Then it became impossible to sell. No one wants a house with the reputation it had. Two little boys drowning."

"Two?" Alberta asked then remembers the Conner boy back in the 1930s. "Not a great reputation for a cottage."

"Yeah. Finally got an offer from Marty Wagner for the land, not the cottage. It wasn't nearly enough to recoup our sweat equity, but it paid off the loan."

"Do you have a theory about the night the boys died, Mr. Eastman?"

George doesn't hesitate. "Peter would never have gone out in the middle of the night unless he thought it was safe. I'm certain he was with people he trusted. I think maybe a bunch of the boys snuck out, a summer kind of thing. I think maybe something went terribly wrong and they were - still are - too afraid to come clean."

George leafs through the autopsy report. Alberta goes to the kitchen for water. George calls out to her. "This isn't right."

Alberta returns to find the diagram of Peter's body lying next to the photo of his naked body on the coroner's slab.

"I don't understand. They're not there," George says. "Look. They didn't mark the bruising on his ankle and wrist." George looks Alberta in the eyes. "Doesn't that seem strange to you? Was the coroner really that inept?"

Alberta hadn't noticed the discrepancy. She leans forward, takes the diagram in hand, studies it, and lifts her eyes to George.

"What aren't you telling us?" he asks.

"I have a theory," she says. "And you're not going to like it. But I need some time."

George stands up. "You take your time. We've been patient for a decade and it brought you to us. Do the work.

You do the work and one way or another, we'll be a little closer to the truth." He shakes Alberta's hand and watches her leave.

Mildred is waiting at the curb. She says to talk to Penny Hodges. "She's doing an internship at the Field Museum in Chicago this term. Talk to her. Before you see anyone else."

Alberta pulls away, making it a few blocks to an intersection where she sits so long someone honks for her to move. She turns the corner and parks. She'd seen what these two parents did with their lives after losing their only child. They rebuilt. They had another kid. They found happiness again. All things she can't yet imagine for her brother's family.

CHAPTER 13

Jun 7 - Was she always this way? So caustic? I remember her laughing. Everything was a joke. Nothing mattered. Nothing was serious. Until that last summer when she snapped at everything. No laughing. I should have paid better attention. What am I saying? I was a kid!

A knock on the cottage door delivers Dan Vogel. In their youth, Dan was the honorary fifth brother. They'd lost touch until he had kids and brought them out to the lake. The two families became fast friends, spending summers next door to each other. Then, as will happen when kids turn into teenagers, everyone started going their own way again. It was the cycle of lake life.

Penn gives him a big hug after which he chastises her for being too skinny.

"Don't you start in on me, too," she says. "I'm not about to fade away so just shut up."

"Yes ma'am," he says. "Bobby's down putting in the dock."

"How is he? How are the babies?"

"Babies? Five and six. And Susan's two boys are five and seven. Just wait until they all show up. Hellions all." He looks over Penn's shoulder. Evelyn works a jigsaw puzzle in the front room. "It's weird she's here. How's she doing?"

"Is that Danny?" Evelyn calls. "Don't just stand there, get in here."

Dan walks over to the table, a tall man, lean, thick head of hair. He picks up a puzzle piece, studies the scene for a second and puts it in its place. "You don't look like you're dying," he says.

"I'm so glad you didn't turn out like your father and grandfather. Big fat bald men. Look at your hair. You can thank your mother for that. How is Marilyn anyway?"

"She's good. Hip bothers her and her knee acts up."

"I bet she still can't play bridge worth shit."

"I wouldn't know about that."

"You can't believe I recognized you, can you? I'm not like Carl. I have lots of clear thoughts, don't I, Penny? Your poor father was a mess. Years. A complete mess. Your poor mother." She places a puzzle piece, smacking it with satisfaction. "I'm sure she's got some of Matthew's leftover beer in there if you want one."

"Mom, they're not leftovers. That would mean they've been in there for years."

Evelyn winks at Dan. "So gullible." Her gaze spills out the window. "What a little oddball collection we had out here. Everybody always getting jumbled up, confused about who belonged where. But then you probably don't know what I'm talking about."

"We all knew a hell of a lot more than you thought," Penn says "Betsy Fry and Marty Wagner? We knew."

Dan laughs. "And did Betsy and Bill really think their voices didn't carry across the water from their pontoon when they were talking about getting a divorce?"

"That's not what happened at all," Evelyn scoffs. "It wasn't Betsy and Marty. It was the other way around.

Gladys Wagner was in bed with Bill, and he had some other woman in town, too. Why do you think Betsy got a new car every year? Betsy actually thanked Gladys when Bill gave her that powder blue Lincoln Mark something or other. White leather seats. That's what they were fighting about at Vogels that Sunday. Betsy and Gladys."

Every thought eventually came back to that last day. The last party. The last argument. The last everything good.

Evelyn tries to get a puzzle piece to fit, forcing it in place. "It was Wagners who finally split. Merci and Al built that cottage. Gladys lost it in the divorce. Broke that old woman's heart. And don't forget the good dentist next door. You remember Carl Vogel. He was doing his hygienists."

"Mom! Stop!" Penn glances to Dan, apologizing.

Dan shrugs like it doesn't matter. "Don't worry about it. It isn't anything I haven't already heard."

"Went through those girls like candy," Evelyn says. "Got one of them pregnant and the practice went down the tubes. You only think you saw what was happening out here. We had lots of secrets out here. Lots of secrets."

"Mom! Stop!"

"I remember all those Vogels fighting over who was going to inherit the cottage when Gert and Mason kicked the bucket. One of them had legal issues."

Dan laughs. "That was Uncle Lou. Embezzlement. Went to jail." Changing the subject, he asks if she remembered how Al Monroe sank his pontoon when he coated the thing in fiberglass.

"Latest and greatest thing, my ass," Evelyn quips.

"And remember the Lovely Laura?" Penn asks.

"Laura the Beautiful," Dan corrects her.

Evelyn says that girl dropped out of college and moved to a commune outside San Francisco. "Fried her brain on drugs. And let's see. Merci cheated at cards, had half a dozen DUIs under her belt, and Gladys married to that racist bigot who cheated her out of house and home. Poor Greg. Gay as a spring breeze that one. Persona non-grata. And such a handsome man. What a waste."

"Did I know that? Did you know?" Penn asks Dan.

He shrugged. "Everybody knew. Or at least guessed."

Penn walks him to the door. Dan hugs her, the kind meant to be quick release, but Penn holds on. She needs to feel arms around her, and he obliges with a full bear hug, whispering she'll get through it, to call if she needs anything.

Evelyn grumbles from the next room. "Goddammit, Carl. Stop screwing around on your wife. You should be ashamed of yourself!"

"Good luck with that," Dan says. "I know how it goes. You'll see. Just when you think they've lost it for good, these coherent thoughts emerge out of nowhere. And just as fast, the crazy is back." He smiles the smile of someone who knows there's nothing he can do to help. "Oh," he adds loudly enough for Evelyn to hear. "Carl never fathered any illegitimate children."

"So you say," Evelyn hollers.

Without discussion, Dan and his son put both docks in the water that day, mow both yards, and launch Penn's pontoon. Dan had, over the years, become the brother she never had.

At dusk, Penn stands on the patio looking to the freshly mown lawn and only then realizes Dan had taken her kayak off the rack and hauled it to the beach. Her first instinct was to do what she always did once the weather warmed, paddle around the lake: Clockwise in the evening, counterclockwise in the morning. On hot days, she'd take the pontoon out into deeper water and swim. But today, she can't paddle. She has Evelyn. Tomorrow will be the same, and the next day as well. She can't leave her mother untended. The unused kayak is but one of many disappointments. The daily swims, long walks, day trips to art fairs and fruit stands, will all be set aside. Penn's life now belongs to her mother.

Penn hears music coming from inside. Billie Holiday's *I'll Be Seeing You*. For reasons she can't yet comprehend, her knees go a little weak. The old Hi-Fi upstairs had, over the years, become just another piece of furniture with a surface prone to collecting clutter. Like it, the records it held were from another time. She never played them. Never looked at them. She told herself it was because Matthew didn't like jazz. There was more to it. The music was from another life. A life packed away out of sight. For thirty years.

She goes inside, Billie's voice more resonant now, and slowly climbs the steps to the living room. Evelyn stands at the Hi-Fi, shoulders slumped, head drooped, magazines and record albums strewn at her feet.

Evelyn hears her daughter and carefully lifts the stylus from the record. The room falls silent. "You don't see it slip away, ya know," she says almost too quietly to be heard. "It just does. And then one day, it's gone. And you don't really miss it. Not at first. You're too busy.

Distracted. By everything. Half empty cereal bowls, ironing, baking for some stupid bake sale, shoe shopping, cooking meal after meal after meal. Diapers. Another kid. More diapers. You disappear, really. Just vanish. Everything you loved about yourself, your life, just disappears."

Evelyn turns toward Penn, glaring at her. "What are you doing with these?"

"The records? You left them here, Mom. When you moved back to town."

"Did not!" Evelyn disappears into her room, slamming the door.

Penn sits on the floor at the Hi-Fi gathering the albums: John Coltrane, Monk, Brubeck, Sarah Vaughan, Miles Davis, Charlie Parker. She'd always known their music, it was familiar, but never thought to think why or how.

Evelyn creeps up behind Penn and shoves her hard. "They're not yours!" she shouts and kicks the albums aside. One of them, John Coltrane - *Giant Steps*, catches her eye. Evelyn reaches down for it but starts to lose her balance and plops against the wall, sliding to the floor. Her rage dissipates as she holds the Coltrane cover. "January 1, 1960," she says. She looks at Penn with quieter eyes and hands it to her. It had never been opened. "Came out in January 1960. Your father bought it." She runs her hand over the other covers. "It's the last one." Her eyes drift across the room. "Do you remember the music?" she asks. "Do you remember?" Her gaze lingers near the fireplace, as if someone is there.

Penn struggles to remember life before loss. "You used to put on jazz for Dad when he came home from work," she says. "In town. Something quiet. And . . ." Penn smiles, surprised at images sifting through her head of her parents holding each other, arms wrapped, bodies swaying. "You used to dance together," she says, smiling. "In the living room at home. And right here. I remember. You'd twirl and laugh."

Evelyn's body relaxes, her gaze slips out a window. "Club DeLisa. The 'Harlem of Chicago' they called it. Our first date," she sighs. "He picked me up at my dorm and he drove me and another couple into the city. I was terrified. No, thrilled. Never been so," her face lit up, "alive."

Penn listens, wanting to ask questions but she knows interrupting will likely break the thread. She'd never heard any of this before.

"Club DeLisa on State and Garfield," Evelyn says, her arm raised, her finger pointing as if walking down the street. "The Chicago Theatre. The Green Mill cocktail lounge. He knew all the jazz clubs. He was so fascinating then. I called him my magic man. We were special then. Our lives were going to be so special." A sneer slides over Evelyn's face. "Good never lasts. It isn't made to. Nobody told us."

Evelyn tries to get up but slumps with the effort. Penn hoists her by the armpits and helps her into bed. "Sarah Vaughn," Evelyn says once she's situated. "Live at the Blue Note. Put that one on." When Penn can't find it, she figures it must have been at the house in town or lost in one of Evelyn's moves. A lot of things disappeared over the years, a collection of records the least of them.

Later that night, listening to some Charlie Parker, Penn writes in her journal.

Jun 8 - How could I have forgotten they were once in love? The silence of memory forgot the music of life - - Whatever the hell that means. She was so dialed in today. Maybe it was the music. A trigger. They were estranged for so long – I forgot they were ever in love.

The next afternoon, Penn finds Evelyn curled up on the bed, writhing in pain. The sheet is covered in pine needles and leaf debris. She administers two doses of Roxy and an Ativan. Glancing out the window, she sees record jackets scattered on the ground outside. Retrieving them, she finds all the records broken. Penn puts it all in the garbage can. It feels like picking up bones of someone she loved.

CHAPTER 14

Jun 15 - Does it make me a horrible person that I resent her when she has a good day? That I'm disappointed when she bounces back from a bad one? That I just want all this to be over?

Penn tucks a petunia into the soil around the geraniums in the flowerpots on the patio. A yelp sounds from inside, almost animal, unrecognizable. Evelyn is on the landing curled up in a ball writhing in agony, her sounds guttural, gasping. Penn climbs over her to get the Roxy from the bedroom and administers a full load. The pain does not dissipate. She gives another dose and calls Hospice. It takes the nurse an hour to arrive. By then, Penn has maneuvered Evelyn upstairs to bed, still writhing, her sounds reduced to a mewing kind of whine, weak but persistent. All the nurse can do is put the call in for a doctor, who takes another hour to show up. All the while Evelyn is in agony. Penn stands in the corner watching the doctor give Evelyn an injection. Finally, Evelyn's body goes limp, and her head rolls so askew it looks disconnected. Penn walks out.

She waits in the living room, exhausted. With a consoling voice, the doctor says it wouldn't be long now.

She wants to ask how long was not long. Minutes? Hours?

"I gave her something to relieve the spasm. It may happen again. I'll put the medication on her schedule so you'll have it if it does."

"I don't understand," Penn blurts. The doctor misunderstood her anxiety.

"This is just part of the process. Once this begins, well, it may only be a few weeks now. Maybe less. I'm sorry, but it is too difficult to say for sure."

Weeks. Not minutes. Not hours. Weeks. Roughly translated: Months.

"Would you like a pastor visit? We have a very nice fellow if you don't have someone of your own."

Penn is abrupt. "That won't be necessary." There is no more discussion. The doctor leaves.

Evelyn used to send Penny and her brothers to Sunday school during the school year. It wasn't that she was a believer. She thought it might ground them. When they hadn't shown up the fall after Tyler died, Rev. Owen heard Evelyn was living apart from her family, that she refused to leave the cottage and come back to town. He attempted to counsel them. With the whole Hodges clan gathered at the cottage, Evelyn told the Rev. Owen, without hesitation, she'd never believed in God. Not in Christ or the Virgin Mary. Not Noah or Moses. None of it. "Your God," she said leaning into him, cocking her head, "does not comfort me. And heaven? How do I believe in that when I can still feel my body. He's right next to me. So how could he be in any heaven when he exists right here in hell with me?" She looked at Dick to make him understand. She was not emotional. She simply stated facts. "I have to stay here. Ty is still here, and he won't understand why everybody left him. He'd be all alone. I have to stay."

It was the first time she'd vocalized a reason for abandoning her family. She was, as she always had, putting Tyler first.

Rev. Owen assured Evelyn she'd feel differently in time. "God can take our pain away if you let Him. Let's pray together." He reached for hands. None rose to his.

"You don't understand, Jack," Evelyn told him. "You can pray all you want. Nobody's listening, cause God's doing whatever the hell he wants."

The nurse hands Penn a parcel of maximum absorbency Depends on her way out the door. Penn holds them by the corner, trying to control her disgust.

Evelyn sleeps straight through the rest of the afternoon and night, allowing Penn what should have been uninterrupted sleep. Still, she wakes listening to the monitor, to her mother's breathing. Once back to sleep, she sleeps in until nine. Evelyn is still out cold, breathing shallow, mouth gaping open, skin sagging unnaturally. *Just die already.* Penn allows herself these little whims. No guilt. Just brutal honesty.

> Jun 17 - Ron called today. He's mad at me, too, for taking her in. He was actually offended. What the hell? You're on your own, Penny. That's what he said. As if I haven't always been on my own. I hate that they still call me Penny.

As a child, Penn believed adults knew what they were doing. They were different from kids. They acted -

like adults. They didn't snipe at each other, or shove each other just to prove superiority. Adults didn't taunt someone just to get a rise out of them. They were in control of their emotions. It's what gave them the right to say *stop crying, whining, pestering, fighting. Stop it! Right now!*

Not until Jim dismissed her over the phone with *Don't be stupid, Penny* and Ron yelled *You're on your own, Penny* did she understand the power of a name to invoke such helplessness and anger, such smallness. Having lived so long without interaction with her brothers, without their condescension and ire, she believed she was impervious to it. She was wrong.

It's like they're children again, even her mother, without an adult in the room.

Penn stands at the kitchen counter making a sandwich when a wet Depends splats the floor of the landing. "What the hell is this? A Goddamn diaper?" Penn utters a single obscenity.

"Why won't the boys come out here? What kind of sons won't visit their dying mother? Selfish stupid boys! Never hear word one from them! Nothing! You'd think Tyler at least would come see his mother!"

"He's dead, Mom! He's dead!" The words fly out, streaming regret in their wake.

Silence follows. Penn looks up to the landing at her mother, barefoot in her nightgown.

Evelyn's response was quiet. Dispassionate. "You didn't used to be a mean girl."

A few days later, Evelyn, in a frenzy, twists the bathroom faucets off as hard as she can and shouted. "Don't let them in! Lock the back door! Hurry,

Goddammit! I'M NOT LEAVING!" Whatever else she's shouting is unintelligible.

The fall after Tyler died, Dick hauled the ski boat away in October, Evelyn cussing him out from the doorway. In late November, Dick took the kids to the cottage to dislodge their mother. What was already a bleak day grew worse as Evelyn watched him and Jim, in the sleet, haul the pontoon up onto shore and cover it. The dock would just have to take its chances over the winter.

Evelyn watched Penny, Mark and Ronny carry the canoe, dingy and the little sailboat up the hill into the storeroom. She couldn't stop them, not all of them, and they were breaking her heart, each one for being part of this extraction. They were all aligned against her.

Dick sent the boys home, reminding Jim to drive carefully, telling Ron and Mark to behave. Jim had only had his license a couple of months.

It was strategic on Dick's part, to include Penny, whether it was good for the girl or not. He'd hoped Evelyn would cooperate if Penny was there. It worked. Evelyn stood staring out to the lake. She'd already taken what she wanted, put it away in a safe place knowing Dick would never notice Ty's flip-flops weren't there or his swimsuit, or his jeans and the tee-shirt he loved so much, the red one.

When Penny finished packing up the sheets and towels, she found her dad in the boys' room cleaning out Tyler's shelf, putting his clothes in paper sacks. He found the rusty penknife rolled up in a sock in the back.

When she said Ty stole it on her birthday, he handed it to her. He told her to take the sacks to the car. "Then go for a walk or something," he said. "Just till I finish up here and bring your mother out."

"It's raining. And it's cold."

"Please," he shouted. Collecting himself, he told her to take an umbrella. Or sit in the car. "Just don't come back in here. Do you understand?"

She didn't but said she did.

Penny sat in the car until she got bored. The rain stopped. She got out. Without intending to, she found herself at the marsh, standing on the edge, where the boys had been laid out. If it had been four months earlier, she'd have thought the woodland spirits had led her there, but that was a childish belief. She was no longer a child. She was something else altogether. Neither child or adult, like the trees and bushes around her, she was stripped bare.

She stepped backward, tripping, falling into a bush, where she found a metal button dangling by red thread. It had *Levi Strauss* stamped into it. She tucked it in her pocket with the penknife. A stiff breeze rushed through trees overhead, branches rubbing, squeaking a warning. A chill sent her running back to the car.

In the cottage, Dick turned off the well pump, flipped the main breaker, and attached a hose to the water heater, draining it into the hole in the floor. Emerging, he found Evelyn blocking his way to the sink, so he went to the bathroom, turning on the shower and sink faucets. She followed, pushing her way through, turning them off. He went upstairs, turning on the sink faucets. She followed him and turned them off. He went back downstairs, locked himself in the bathroom and ran the shower until the pipes began to clatter and spit, then run dry. Evelyn was in the storeroom, trying to figure out how to turn it all back on.

Dick poured anti-freeze in the kitchen sink. He went into the storeroom, pushed Evelyn aside, flipped the main power off again, and padlocked the cabinet, putting the key in his pocket. She blocked his way to the bathroom again, so he went back upstairs and poured anti-freeze in that sink. Throughout this tango, there were no words spoken until he told her it was time to come home.

Penny stepped through the door upstairs, tears streaming down her face, pain finding its way out. She opened the drawer under her cubby and took out the cigar box with the owl skull, snakeskin, heart-shaped stone, scraps of that rag rug. She put the penknife and steel button in, closed the lid and put it in the drawer, but the drawer wouldn't budge. She jiggled it. She got mad and swore at it. She screamed at it and kicked it, sobbing. Angry. "Damn it! Damn it! God damn it!"

Evelyn watched from the stairs, her face showing no expression.

Dick gathered Penny in his arms and held her until her body calmed and the sobs subsided. When he let go, he gave the drawer a solid nudge on one side and it slid into place.

Until then, the changes to her family hadn't fully registered, as if the second half of the summer had only been an aberration and things would return to normal over winter or at the latest, by summer. Penny watched her mother walk out without looking back, a woman sleepwalking into the back seat of the car. Penny followed, the cottage door closing behind her with a thud. She looked, saw the key turning in the lock, the twist of her father's wrist so deliberate, the sound so sharp and clean, her childhood sealed away in a vault. Going forward, life would continue in an unknowable landscape, the future bearing no resemblance to the past.

Penny climbed in the front seat. Like her mother, she stared out the window all the way to town, hands in tight fists, tears sliding down her cheeks.

When Evelyn lost Tyler, everyone else became irrelevant. Dick, on the other hand, the one who'd always existed on the fringes of his family, changed. Losing one of his children taught him how to love the rest of them. He suddenly saw them. He looked each of them in the eye every day and asked them to tell him something about their day. Anything. And he took to hugging them. He needed it, whether they did or not.

In Evelyn's absence, meals had been eaten on tray tables in front of the television. Upon her return in November, she set the table at five o'clock as she used to: seven places. She filled the table with food, poured milk into all the glasses, and waited, silently, for her family to gather. Like trained seals, they each took their seats. The spare place setting went unchallenged for all of a week before the boys, in unison, made their move. Mark picked up the plate and silverware. Jim reached over and drank the milk. Ron removed the extra chair. Evelyn glared in disbelief, demanding they put everything back. She screamed for Mark to put Tyler's plate back on the table, and he screamed back.

"He's dead! Tyler's dead! I'm not sitting at that goddamn table with a goddamn imaginary kid!" He threw the plate to the wall where it shattered, shards ricocheting everywhere. He slammed the door jam on his way out. The meal continued in silence.

Though Evelyn never divorced Dick, she never returned to the marriage. She existed in the same house every winter, present, but absent. She'd emotionally left all of them, the boys especially. They should have heard Tyler get out of bed that night. They should have stopped him. And after Tyler died, watching the boys became excruciating. In every move they made, she saw Tyler. No matter what the boys did, especially if they had the audacity to have fun, she turned away. She got good at turning away from her boys. Especially Mark. Every time she looked at Mark, she wanted him to be Ty, and he knew it.

It was early March the next spring when Penny went with her mom and dad to open the cottage. Dick turned the pump on and inspected the pipes for leaks. Finding none, he turned on the pump. The pipes groaned and spat thick orange sludge from every faucet, smelling of antifreeze.

Evelyn opened all the windows. She hauled in the canvas totes of bedding and towels, several sacks of groceries, and two suitcases. It was a familiar routine, but unlike other years, the boys were not there to haul the dinghy and canoe and sailboat to shore. They were not there to uncover the pontoon or push it into the lake. All these things remained as they'd been left the season before, put away not on a warm September afternoon as they should have been, but during a biting cold day with sleet stinging their cheeks. The dock, left in place all winter, appeared unharmed by the season's ice.

Seeking escape from the snapping static between her silent parents, Penny headed into the woods. She needed her ancient apple tree, to see its buds, to sit within the caress of its crooked branches, to find something familiar and untouched by grief. What she found was a wide scrape carved through her woods, piles of ragged tree trunks, and scrub lining a muddy road. Her woods as she knew them were gone. Following the grated gash, she discovered the trees around the marsh were clear-cut, nothing but stumps. Huge mounds of sand and debris filled in half the marsh. Her woods were an open wound.

A sickening rage made her want to throw up, and she ran to the car climbed in the back seat and huddled there, waiting for her parents.

Evelyn stepped outside to clear a fallen branch from the patio. Her heart stuck in her throat when she saw someone small sitting on Tyler's step, third from the top, where he used to sit when he was a toddler. It was a dog, sitting as quietly as if he belonged there. Dick watched from inside as Evelyn approached it. The dog turned to her, jumped up and ran to her, leaning into her, whining at her feet like he'd been waiting for her. Matted black and white fur covered his long, short-legged body. Suddenly, nothing else mattered to her. She carried the dog into the bathtub, apologizing for leaving him alone all winter as if it was Tyler come back to her.

Dick walked out without saying goodbye.

No one saw her feed the dog ground beef and rice or watch it push the door open to the boys' bedroom and jump onto Tyler's bed. No one saw Evelyn climb in next to him and sleep there. She named him Rabbit.

Evelyn was the only one at the lake so early in the spring except for the Stems. It was too cold, too bleak for summer people. Daffodils hadn't even come up yet. Walking Rabbit along the road, Evelyn ran into Edith sweeping pinecones from the path to their mailbox. It seemed a ridiculous exercise in futility, but then so was hand trimming grass and weeds from the base of the mailbox on the gravel road in the middle of the woods. Evelyn seemed to startle poor Edith who jumped a little and sputtered a precarious greeting when Rabbit darted toward her.

Edith invited Evelyn into the house, a hollow gesture. Velma, peering from the kitchen window, would not have allowed it. And Evelyn was no more interested in socializing than Velma was, leaving poor Edith on her own. A tap on the window drew Edith back inside.

Further down the road, Walter approached in his car on his way home from the high school. He stopped and rolled down his window to speak to Evelyn. She confirmed to him that she was alone and expected to remain so, and if he saw Rabbit running about, he was not to call the dog pound. "He's my dog. You can just leave him be. He won't bother you." He mentioned some issues he'd had with Mark in school. She cut him off cold. "Talk to his father. And put on your damn hat. That bald head makes you look naked!" This was the extent of their interaction for the entire season.

Rabbit came back to town with her in the fall and went out to the lake with her every spring. She loved that dog. He'd lift his face to her and rest his head on her leg. She'd coo to it and comfort it and say *good boy, what a good boy you are*. Rabbit followed her everywhere. He sat at her feet under the table. He cried whenever she left the house without him. He was Evelyn's dog and had little to do with the rest of them. No one ever said as much, but they all knew she believed it was Tyler.

CHAPTER 15

The day after meeting with Mildred and George, Alberta heads out to Chicago to the Field Museum. She's an hour into the two-hour drive before it dawns on her she should have called ahead. There was no reason to assume Penny would be available.

Waiting under the T. Rex in the massive central gallery, Alberta hears the high-pitched chattering of voices draw closer then watches as a teacher corrals a heard of young children out of one corridor and into another, silencing them with one word: Gather. The chorus instantly quells, replaced by the patter of feet on polished stone.

A young woman in jeans and a white oxford shirt approaches Alberta with a confident stride. "Penny Hodges," she says with an outstretched hand.

Introducing herself simply as Alberta Higgins from Pennsylvania, Alberta says she wants to talk about Spirit Lake, but and could tell by Penny's response she'd been misunderstood. With great enthusiasm, Penny starts explaining her work on natural habitat destruction and restoration. It's what had earned her the Field internship.

On the way to the cafeteria, she tells Alberta about how filling in the marsh at Spirit Lake ten years ago had upset the ecosystem of not just that lake, but the entire chain. Lake levels were drastically affected. The deepest spot in Spirit Lake went from twenty feet to fifteen.

"You're awfully young to have accomplished so much already."

"I'm focused. That helps. I'm surprised my paper caught the eye of Penn State."

Alberta lets the assumption ride momentarily. She buys two coffees and a couple donuts. They settle at a small table off to the back of the cavernous hall. Sitting down, she finally tells Penny she's there to talk about Tyler and Peter. About the drowning.

"I don't understand. You're not from Penn State?"

"No. I'm sorry. I'm not. Please. I only have a few questions. I've already spoken with Mildred and George."

"I still don't understand," Penny protests. "What business is it of yours? And why now?"

"Just a couple of things. Please?"

Penny leans back in the chair and crosses her arms.

Alberta feels insensitive about eating a donut, but she's hungry. "What can you tell me about the day before the boys drowned?"

Penny doesn't answer. She takes a sip of coffee.

Alberta waits, finishing the donut slowly. If she gives Penny some room, maybe she'll open up. Nothing draws people out like silence.

"I don't know what you want to know," Penny finally says. "I don't see how it has anything to do with anything."

Alberta asks about the older boys at the lake, what they were like and Penny rattles off little snapshots. Greg Wagner was gorgeous and kind. Steve Fry was always pissed off. Dan Vogel was a good guy. When asked about the men at the lake, Penny runs through all the fathers, who was around and who wasn't. She doesn't elaborate.

Alberta asks about Walter Stem. "You haven't mentioned him."

"He's the only one from the lake we ever saw in town. Walter was the high school principal."

"What was that like?"

Penny says Mr. Stem had treated her brother, Mark, better than he needed to. "Mark was always skipping class. He threw food in the cafeteria. He punctured all the kick balls in the gym. But Mr. Stem refused to suspend him. No one else would have given him so many chances."

"Did you have interactions with him?"

"I was on an academic team in high school. We competed for a science medal. Mr. Stem picked the three us up at home at five in the morning and drove us to regionals and again to the state finals. We made it to state two years running. He drove us every time."

"So, he was a good guy."

"Yeah. Weird as hell, but a good guy. Nitpicky. Skinny as shit but his clothes were, well, like they were incapable of wrinkling. Always perfect. Same gray suit every day. White shirt. Striped tie. His shoes were always shined."

"That's a lot of detail."

"He was a detail guy. Never smiled. I never saw him smile. And, it's not that he was ugly or anything, but, I don't know. He wasn't the kind of guy you'd look twice at. Just sort of blended in. Except for that dome. How did he get it so . . . shiny? I didn't know he was bald until I saw him in the hall at school. Always wore that hat at the lake."

"Except at the marsh that morning."

"What?"

"He wasn't wearing a hat when the boys were found. At the marsh. That morning."

Penny's eyes go wide open, her expression falling somewhere between grief and rage.

"Sorry," Alberta says. "I suppose not much about that morning is anything you want to remember."

"Did he ever say anything to you about the accident? About Tyler or your friend Peter?"

"No." Penny pushes the coffee and donut aside.

"What else can you tell me about him. Sounds like you spent a lot of time with him."

Penny's eyes wander the cafeteria. Alberta waits patiently. "Not really," Penny finally says. She pinches a bite of her donut. "Peter and I went over there that morning."

"Where? What morning?"

Penny looks up. "The morning before he drowned. That's what you're asking me, isn't it? Eastmans went to early Mass. Peter came over after. He had a bird's egg he wanted to show Mr. Stem. Found it on the ground, probably dropped by a cowbird. He couldn't identify it. He wanted to ask Mr. Stem."

Alberta asks about the Stem house.

"I'd never been inside before. It looked like a clown decorated it. Red walls. Green table. Yellow chairs. Even the dishes were all different colors. And the refrigerator? Hot pink. And I don't think Mrs. Stem wanted us there. Velma. She was a . . ." Penny searched for the right word. ". . . a pointed person. Eyes always squeezed tight. They weren't like the rest of the lake crowd. Kept to themselves."

"Did you talk with Walter that morning?"

"He wasn't there, so we left. Took the back path between Spring Lake and the marsh."

"The back path?"

"Through the woods. It bypassed all the cottages and the road. We stopped for a minute at Spring Lake."

"The small one? With the channel to Spirit?"

"Yeah. A two-acre lake. At least it used to be. It was the lifeblood of the entire chain of lakes. A deep spring. 75 feet deep. Crystal clear and cold. No beach. No docks. No cottages. Fed by a network of springs until they filled in the marsh and built the road. The old men, Al Monroe and Mason Vogel, just called it the spring, not a lake, and swore there were hundred-year-old sturgeon lurking in its depths. I remember staring into it that morning, looking for one of those monster fish. Ever see one? A sturgeon?"

"Can't say I have, no."

"We'd all heard a boy drowned back there before World War II and that he was eaten by a sturgeon. Wasn't true of course."

Alberta interrupts her. "Sammy Conner."

"I don't know. The family used to live in the Eastman's cottage." She says kids would sit on the shore at night, tell ghost stories and watch for the drowned boy to appear. "The mist never let us down, sifting and sliding across the surface, fish rising and stirring the water. I was certain we'd have seen him if only old lady Stem hadn't always chased us off. She didn't like kids at the spring after dark." She sips coffee, holding the Styrofoam cup, staring at it. "You suppose kids stand in the woods at night and try to conjure up ghosts of my brother and Peter?"

Alberta finishes her coffee. "Did Tyler spend much time with Walter?"

Penny says all the boys did at some point or another. It was Walter's way.

Alberta asks if Peter spent time with him, if he'd ever said anything about Walter.

"How to be a man." Penny half chuckles.

Alberta doesn't.

Penny says all the boys used to say it. Mr. Stem's big thing was *do this to be a man. Do that to be a man*. It was like a big joke at the lake. *Be a man*. The boys said it all the time. Making fun.

"How was he teaching the boys, Peter specifically, to be a man?"

"I don't know. He had the other boys chop wood. Fix motors. Guy stuff."

"That doesn't sound like Peter."

"It wasn't. But he did it for Mr. Stem. I think he didn't want to disappoint him. But Peter wouldn't kill anything. He'd catch fish, but then he'd let them go. If the hook wasn't in too deep."

"So, he liked spending time with Walter."

"Yeah. But . . ."

"What?"

"Peter asked me if I thought keeping secrets made a person strong."

"Why do you think he asked that?"

She shrugs and says she didn't know, then says she thought everybody had secrets. "It's just human nature, don't you think? I had a secret hiding place. I'm sure my brothers had their secrets."

"What kind of secrets?"

Penny rolls her eyes. "If I knew that they wouldn't be secrets, would they?"

Alberta asks if she thought maybe her brothers had gone to the marsh that night or if it was just Tyler and Peter.

"They'd have said so if they did."

"Were Tyler and Peter friends?"

"Not really."

"Did they like each other?"

"Not really."

"Did they ever have any fights or arguments?"

"No. Look. Peter was above such things, and Tyler wasn't a fighter. He was the guy who stood on the sidelines giving the blow by blow."

Penny says she had to get back to work, but Alberta asks her about Peter again. Penny is silent, sullen. The lunch crowd filters in, high-pitched voices of kids, teachers, and mothers. Eventually, Penny smiles. "Peter was always asking questions like why do we get goose bumps? Why is one sunrise pink and another one yellow? And my all-time favorite: Did I ever wonder why we like the smell of our own farts but can't stand anyone else's?"

Alberta breaks out in a laugh that is too loud, too much for the moment, but the thought grabs hold of her, if only for an instant, and it feels good to laugh, to let loose. Like a rogue wave, the moment passes. In the wake of it, she asks if Penny thought the drownings were an accident. Again, Penny goes silent.

"Penny," she asks again. "Do you believe it was an accident?"

Penny looks away, not at anything in particular, not her hands, or the table; not at the hordes of screeching children spilling in; not at the trusses of the ceiling.

Alberta doesn't press further. The silence between them drowns out the commotion around them until she says she's taken up enough of Penny's time, adding that the Eastmans were proud of her.

"I don't need you to tell me that," Penny says, annoyed.

Alberta's chair screeches across the floor as she gets up. "Can you tell me how to get in touch with your brothers?" It's a simple question, one that should have resulted in a couple of phone numbers. But Penny's one-word response, without elaboration, rouses Alberta's curiosity.

"No."

"No, you can't, or no, you won't?"

Penny doesn't answer. Alberta lets it go.

"She won't talk to you. My mother. None of them will." Penny looks up.

"Why's that?"

"My family barely functions. My mother lost her mind after she lost my brother. My father does his best, but he's not quite right either. Losing Tyler destroyed us. Dredging it back up? I don't see how that's going to serve any purpose. Except to piss a lot of people off."

"Oh, I'm used to that. Pissing people off."

"Yeah. I can see that."

Alberta walks away. Penny calls after her. "She'll be at the cottage."

CHAPTER 16

Penny sits at the table long after Alberta leaves. She couldn't have told the woman about Peter, about who he was. The thoughts flooding her mind at the asking of it were impossible to express to a stranger. To anyone. Toad in a box. Acorns in the cavity of a maple tree. Hawk feather. Owl skull. Garter snakes. Giant beetles. Tiny red mites. Red mushrooms. Red leaves. Red sassafras seedpods. Yellow slime mold. Lichen. Moss in bloom. Bullheads. Perch. Sunfish. Minnows. Night crawlers. Crickets. Night peeping tree frogs. Cicadas. Owl pellets. Full moon. Sun rise. Thunderstorm. Rain. Wind. Lightning. Clear water. Muck. Cattails. Mud. Screams. Tears. But she couldn't say any of these things. It was too personal.

The memory of the morning the boys were found rises in slow motion, her mind dissecting each action, revelation, scream. The men crowding round, then stepping back, looking away. Women on the path sobbing, holding onto each other, to their daughters.

The night before, she'd been lying in her sleeping cubby, her heavy curtain pulled tight to block light from the hall. Both her windows were open wide to fend off the mugginess, the kind that sits heavy before a storm.

A fight on the beach earlier quarantined all the kids to their cottages except for Danny, who played cards in the living room with her brothers. They were quiet except for the occasional outburst, someone winning or cheating, getting shoved to the floor followed by laughter. Penny caught a glimpse of a full moon through the trees as Patti Page singing the Tennessee Waltz drifted from next door at Vogels'. The party had been going since late afternoon. It happened that way most weekends, but never on a Sunday.

The wind picked up. The music next door stopped. Penny saw Al and Merci Monroe walk through the back yard and watched Betsy Fry making her way alone. She heard her parents outside arguing, but she couldn't make out the words. They came inside, sent Danny home, and told the boys to go to bed. The place went silent except for the boys muttering in their room. Evelyn shouted at them to shut up and go to sleep. The muttering stopped. All Penny could hear was the wind, like waves of surf through high branches, snapping twigs onto the cars out back. Acorns skittered off the roof. Sharp shadows swept the road. She dozed off watching a handful of leaves lift into the air, swirling high in some magical dance, sliding about, lifting, falling, lifting again.

She woke later, the light so bright she thought it was morning, but it was just the moon shining full on her face. Chilled, she drew the sheet back up. She would later wonder if something else woke her, if maybe she heard Tyler padding by, or maybe the door clicking closed. She would decide it had just been the moon or the chill because if it had been Ty, she'd have seen him walking to the road. She'd have said something to him. Stopped him. Gone with him. Told one of the other boys. Things would have been different. She might still have believed in magic the next day. But the woodland spirits let her down. They did not wake her in time or warn her of danger. They let her sleep, the deepest of all betrayals.

Penny woke again that night, this time to thunder rumbling in the distance. A storm moving in. The moon was gone. She heard her mother close the window in the boys' room, the one by Tyler's bed. Thunder broke loud. Lightning struck close. Penny cranked her window closed, the squeaking loud enough to let her mother know it was taken care of. Evelyn told her to go back to sleep.

Lulled by sheets of rain washing the roof, Penny fell back to sleep.

It wasn't light yet when Mildred Eastman's knocking at the door woke her. Her father was already up. He had to get back into town to work. He normally went home on Sunday evening, but he'd stayed over. All the men stayed over.

Mildred tried to be quiet, asking Dick if Peter was there, if they'd seen him, if they knew where he was. Penny opened her cubby curtain and said he hadn't been by. The boys crawled out of bed and leaned in their doorway in a sleepy stupor. She asked them, but they shrugged. Evelyn came out, tying her robe. She said something to Ty. When he didn't answer, she sent Jimmy to check the bathroom downstairs.

Sitting in the museum cafeteria surrounded by busloads of kids all talking and laughing, Penny hears none of them. She grips her chair as if she'd fly off it if she didn't hang on. She remembers that last moment when her family was still intact. The last moment before fear set in, before the end began, before the tears and screaming and blaming. The last moment without doubt. It wasn't the moment when Jim hollered up that Ty wasn't in the bathroom and they realized he was gone as well at Peter, because if Peter and Tyler were together, they were fine, probably fishing off the dock. The last moment came when they weren't on the docks, and they did not come when George called out for Peter, and Dick called for Tyler. That was when the end began.

Dawn broke the horizon as Dick rallied the neighborhood, sending Jimmy and Ron to wake everyone. He organized the search sending Vogels to the marsh, Wagners into the woods, and Frys to Spring Lake. He and Mark would search the shore.

Betsy Fry and Laura gathered all the girls, taking them to their cottage.

Penny refused, waiting outside, still in her pajamas.

Her mother and Mildred stood on the road. Gert and Merci stood together under the trees, water dripping from the night's rain. They were the grandmothers of Spirit Marsh Road. They knew this panic. They knew what might come next. One of them spoke but two words. *Not again.* Gladys Wagner paced back and forth, crying.

Voices of men and boys calling out carried from all directions.

Penny stood apart, air cool on her skin. It was the silence of the women that frightened her the most. It was unnatural.

The calls grew fainter with distance.

Marilyn Vogel grabbed Penny and hugged her so tight the girl couldn't breathe. Penny broke free.

Merci wondered aloud if anyone had told Velma and Edith. Then came a whistle from the marsh followed by shouts through the woods. Evelyn and Mildred bolted toward the whistle, toward the marsh, feet faltering on the muddy path.

Walter Stem was deep in the cattails when Mason, Carl and Danny got there. He'd called out that he found them, and Carl blew the whistle. Danny plowed into the water. The other men and boys converged on the marsh. Mark was told to stay on shore while the Hodges, Frys, Wagners, and George all charged into the water and weeds, slipping in the mud and muck, water flying, bodies surging forward in pandemonium.

Al Monroe did his best to hold back Evelyn and Mildred, neither of them fully aware of reality yet.

Penny tried to push past them, but Mark yanked her, held her to the tree line. She tried to pull free, but he hung on tight. She caught a glimpse of something heavy being carried out of the water. Mark turned, put her in a neck hold so she couldn't see, but she heard her dad's cries *No No No No No* and saw him shove his way to the mud. Mark held tight to his sister, struggling to shield her from seeing what he saw.

Evelyn yanked free of Al's grip but just stood watching, in shock.

Penny did not see another body carried from the water, naked, face down, draped in weeds. She did not see George rip off his shirt and throw it over his son as the men placed Peter's naked body on the muddy bank. She did not see George kneel next to him, frantically wiping his face to rid it of debris, revealing a gaping wound, Peter's nose mostly gone. She heard George moaning but did not see him wipe his son's head to find raggedy earlobes mostly gnawed off. Somebody said it was snapping turtles. Penny didn't know what they meant.

Mildred broke free of Al, ran to her son, nearly falling on top of his body before George yanked her back, refusing to let her look at him. She fought him off and reached to lift her boy into her arms, but his body was unyielding, arms unbending, his mouth agape, his eyes wide open, a ragged hole where his nose should have been. "Do something!" she screamed. "Somebody do something! Help him!" But the men did not move. They stood still. Silent.

By then, the other women and girls heard the commotion and came crowding behind them. Al did his best to impede their approach.

The men stepped clear of the first body and Evelyn saw Tyler reaching for her, and bolted to him, falling to the mud, pushing Dick out of the way, grasping Tyler's hand, but it was stiff and cold, his arm, though lifted, unyielding. She retracted as if stung, refusing to look at his face. She began shouting, her eyes casting about wildly, searching. "It's not him! He's not here! Tyler! Tyler!" Dick tried to lift her to her feet, but she threw him off, rising on her own, shouting at everyone, incensed that they just stood there, staring. "Keep looking for him!"

Ronny lurched away and threw up.

The men looked away.

Women and girls on the path kept asking if the boys were OK.

Caught up in the excitement, one of the girls giggled, and was stopped cold by a sharp slap.

Al Monroe hoisted Penny from Mark's arms and carried her away.

Walter's attention fell to Steven, their eyes locking in silent confrontation. When Steven took a breath to speak,

Walter asked him about his black eye. Everyone except the grieving parents turned to Steven, taking in for the first time a bruise blooming on his swollen cheek.

"Did you have anything to do with this?" his father asked, agitated and frightened. "Is this where you were last night?"

"What?" Steven asked in shock. "What? No! No of course not!" He stepped backward and tripped over his own feet and hit the ground.

Walter went to him and offered a hand up. Steven stared at it, then looked into Walter's eyes, the dead calm eyes he knew so well. Taking Walter's hand was a silent transaction.

"I should have seen it coming," Walter said. "Peter was disappointed the older boys wouldn't take him frogging."

Mildred and George didn't hear the exchange, too deep in shock and grief.

Jim agreed, saying Tyler was the same way.

Mason told the women to gather the girls and younger boys, to get them back in their cottages. Merci helped Mildred back to her place. Gert tried to help Evelyn but Evelyn walked away alone, eyes dead ahead, face in a contortion of silent anguish. Carl gathered Danny and the other boys, herding them up the path, leaving George and Dick to grieve in peace. Walter, Bill and Marty stood silent sentry. Carl called the sheriff.

Al tried to get Penny to go inside but she refused. She saw the women walk out of the woods, crying, looking at her like they'd never done before, like she they were afraid of her. When Jim and Ronny crossed the road toward her, Penny asked how bad they were hurt. Al didn't have time to cut Jim off before he blurted it out. "You stupid shit. They're dead!"

"Are not!" But even she knew then it was true and her whole body convulsed into sobbing. She saw her mother and called to her, but Evelyn ignored her.

Penny tried to run to her but Al grabbed her. Held her tight.

Penny was not allowed to see the boys' bodies. Her memory of Tyler and Peter would always be of whole, intact boys. Her brothers would not be so lucky. They'd seen them both fresh from the water, covered in mud, bone protruding where fingers should have been, ragged flesh where ears should have been, Peter without a nose, Tyler's arm bent at that impossible angle from his shoulder, leeches attached everywhere. The vision would follow each of them through their lives. None of them would ever be able to imagine their little brother whole again without catching a glimpse of the damage. Mark's grip was all that protected Penny from that memory. He instinctively had not let go of her.

Penny would only remember peripherals of the day, the stench of acrid swamp muck. Sloshing of wet feet. Wet clothes dripping. The strange lack of voices, save Mildred's moans, Georges sobs, and her mother shouting. Her mother walking away.

When Sheriff Bates arrived, everyone who'd been part of finding the boys were asked to reconvene at the marsh. Al told Penny to go find Merci, to stay with her. She didn't. As soon as Al, Jim, Danny, Ron, Mark, Steve and Carl disappeared down the path, Penny followed, hiding behind a bush, listening, still unable to see beyond the men to the bodies.

The sheriff was upset the scene had been trampled, erasing any kind of evidence that might have led to an explanation. He asked the boys if they knew anything about it, if they'd heard the victims planning anything. He asked if any of them had been along, urging them to admit they were there. "Accidents happen," he said. "We only want to know what happened here." But the boys all insisted they hadn't been with them. He asked if they two boys had done this before, gone off on their own.

"Not that we ever knew," Jim said.

"Probably frogging," Bill Fry said. "Trying to grow up too fast. That's all. Just trying to keep up with the big kids."

As to why the bodies had been found deep in the marsh, so far from shore, somebody suggested there might have been a struggle that kept putting them deeper and deeper into the weeds, into the deep water. Or maybe the storm pushed them to where they were found. There was a lot of wind overnight. Bates said he'd had to move a branch from the road to get there. "A couple trees came down in town."

Danny said the bruises on Tyler's arm and leg were probably from the fight the day before when Steve Fry flung him halfway across the yard.

Ronny said it seemed logical that Peter was naked. "He was so skinny his swimming trunks were always falling off in the water. Makes sense his shorts might come off in a struggle."

"Once," George said glaring at him. "They did that once."

"I guess Tyler's shoulder could have been dislocated if Peter panicked and yanked on it real hard," Carl said. "I mean don't you think Tyler was probably trying to save him?"

Sheriff Bates asked if maybe they'd gotten into a fight, his tone sounding as if such a thing was perfectly natural.

"Tyler hated the wind!" Penny jumped from the bush, screaming at the men standing in the mud. Instinctively, they bunched together, blocking the draped bodies from her view. "And Peter didn't want to kill a frog and eat its legs."

But Penny was only ten. Sheriff Bates wouldn't listen.

"And they both knew how to swim!" Screaming through her tears, she tried to tell the men they were all wrong. But she was gathered up by Al Monroe yet again and carried away, away from the two dead bodies lying in the mud, the cattails bent and broken all around. She tried to explain that neither of the boys was likely to start a fight or hurt the other one, so none of it made sense.

"Things happen," Al said, carrying her until she became too heavy. He stopped, put her down, and took her shoulders in hand, his eyes searching hers for recognition. "Things happen." It was all he could say. It wasn't enough. He took her by the hand into the cottage, where she sat with Gert Vogel, who held her tight, who cooed and tried to console her and never once said everything would be fine because it would have been a lie.

Penny had not heard about the predation, presumably by snapping turtles. She didn't hear that Peter's penis, testicles, nose, and an ear had been gnawed off or that Ty was missing the tips off a couple of fingers and one ear.

Based on facial bruising, Peter may have had a broken nose, but with so little tissue left, it was tough to tell.

Someone pulled a pillowcase from the water, from deep in the cattails. Someone said you couldn't go frogging without a pillowcase to put them in. It seemed all the proof any of them needed to conclude they'd gone frogging together on their own as young boys will. The pieces fell into place.

The bodies were loaded into the ambulance late morning. From her window, Penny watched George walk away. The rest of the men stood and older boys off to the side, hashing it over, boiling the incident down to simple phrases. *They were just frogging, poor kids. That Eastman boy must have gone in too far. Tyler must have tried to save him. Damn shame. Yup, a goddamn shame.*

Penny bolted out the door, screaming again that they were all wrong. "Peter would never hunt a frog to kill it. Tyler would never go out in a storm." She ran out to them, tried to tell them, yelling all the things she knew, and again she was carried away, carried back inside, this time by her father who glared at her, his eyes wider than she'd ever seen, his mouth twisted tight. "You stay inside with Gert. And be quiet. You hear me?"

Her tears poured out. "But Daddy . . ."

"There's enough going on without you getting in the middle of it. Stay out of it. I need you to behave."

"But Daddy!"

"Be quiet!"

"But Daddy," she shouted, her hands reaching desperately for his. He grabbed her shoulders and squeezed so tight it hurt.

"Shut up!" he shouted.

Father and daughter both stunned to silence, it seemed he might apologize and take her in his arms, but he didn't. He turned away. When the door shut behind him, Gert reached for Penny, but she climbed into her cubby and pulled the curtain closed.

After the ambulance drove out, George and Mildred Eastman gathered Peter's books, his collections of lichen and leaves, cicada hulls, and snakeskins. They loaded the canoe onto the car, the one thing that still held any value to them. They released his tadpoles to the swamp where they'd found his body. They prayed. They left. They wouldn't be back.

The next day, Sheriff Bates called the Eastman's with his official findings leaving the message with George's brother. George had no interest in further conversation with the sheriff or anyone associated with Spirit Lake.

The sheriff told the Hodges family directly, stopping at their house in town. He stood in their living room and told them the drownings were accidental. No one was at fault. He offered condolences and left.

Dick went outside, staring motionless at Lake Michigan.

Evelyn went to their bedroom and slammed the door.

Jim, Ronny and Mark disappeared into Tyler and Mark's bedroom.

Penny sat on the couch feeling more alone than she knew was possible. She went up and sat on the top step listening to her brothers through the door. They were trying to figure it out, deciding whether it seemed logical or not that Tyler and Peter would team up, being the youngest kids, and go to the marsh to catch frogs. Of course, they would do it to show up the bigger kids. Of course, they wouldn't back out because of weather. They had to prove they were tough. And they said Peter had never seen how they maneuvered slow and steady in the muck, so it was reasonable that he'd slip and get scared and get all tangled up. And, of course Ty would go in after him. And Peter was scrawny, but he could easily have yanked too hard on Tyler if he thought he was drowning, and they both just got tangled in the weeds, and if Peter kept fighting in a panic to keep from going under, well, it all made sense. The way they figured it, all the injuries were explained away as the result of two frantic little kids fighting for their lives.

Mark blew up. "What the hell was he thinking? Stupid little shit."

Jim told him to shut up.

"No. Nobody's saying it. But it's true, isn't it?"

"I said shut up."

"No goddamn it. He had no business going out there on his own. He knows how tricky that swamp is. He knows it! It's his own goddamn fault!"

Penny heard something hit the wall and shatter, and Mark bolted out of the bedroom almost falling over her as he charged down the stairs.

The last thing she heard Jim say was something about a closed casket. He swore to find every last snapping turtle and string it up. She still didn't understand.

There would be no vengeful turtle hunting, or frogging, or water skiing. There would be no more summers at the lake.

The straw hat that Peter admired so was stuffed away in Penny's drawer. Somewhere over the years, it disappeared.

CHAPTER 17

It's close to five when Alberta knocks on Evelyn's door at the cottage, the back door upstairs, then the front door downstairs. She's exhausted after the drive to Chicago and back. She's cold. She's hungry. But she's determined. From the patio she can see Evelyn upstairs, peering out, refusing.

Alberta turns, taking in the lake, so quiet, no docks in the water yet, still piled in the grass. The house next door towers over the Hodges's small place. On the other side, an old bungalow, unchanged from the photos she's seen, save what looked to be a new roof and aluminum siding. She's about to leave when she hears someone coming down the steps.

Dick shouts from the last step. "What the hell do you think you're doing?"

"Nice place here." Alberta is deliberately nonchalant. *People don't think straight when they're irritated. Rattle that cage,* her father used to tell her. Her dad had been a detective. When she was a teenager, she liked thinking of him as a glamorous spy. He sometimes took her along on benign stakeouts, talking about spy craft. He died when she was in law school.

"My daughter called me," Dick says. "Nobody wants you around stirring things up. You have no right."

"You must be Dick Hodges."

"Yes. I am. And you don't belong here."

Alberta follows Dick's eyes to the upstairs window. Evelyn steps back, out of sight.

"I just need to ask a couple of questions, Dick."

"Who the hell are you?"

"I'm an assistant district attorney. I'm looking into this case as part of another investigation. That's all I can tell you."

"My boy's been dead for ten years. There is no case. You need to leave. Or do I need to call the sheriff?"

"Sheriff's office was my first stop."

Dick looks inside. Evelyn is downstairs now, standing at the window with a blank stare.

"Leave," Dick demands. "Now."

"Mr. Hodges, I'm looking into the death of your son and the Eastman boy. I wanted you to know. I've already spoken with Mildred and George."

"I heard."

Alberta speaks with the kind of authority that comes with expectation of compliance. "I want to talk to you, your wife, and your boys. I'd appreciate it if you could get them here on Saturday. Can you do that for me, Mr. Hodges? Can you help me here? I'd like to talk to your family before I speak with everyone else. It won't take long."

Dick shakes his head.

"Saturday," she reiterates as she heads up the side steps. She's had enough for one day.

Sitting in the same booth at the tavern, she orders the same meal she ordered the two previous days: steak, charred, and three shots of rye. Tucker walks over with a plate of perch and a salad, placing it in front of Alberta.

She smiles and realizes it's the first time she'd done so since arriving in Michigan except for when she found a vase of fresh daffodils in her cabin.

Alberta hadn't taken notice of Tucker except to recognize him as the proprietor. He has a charming smile, the kind people in hospitality hone to perfection, one that invites yet keeps a distance. Something about him makes her think of an old pair of moccasins she used to have, well-worn and comfortable. Maybe it's his faded jeans, tucked in flannel shirt, and suede Hush Puppies. By the gray lacing through his dense blond hair, she guesses he's fiftyish, maybe younger. His eyes look younger.

He slides in across from her, bending his long, lean frame, arms folded in front of him. He smells of soap as if he's just showered, or maybe it's his laundry detergent. Whatever it is, she likes it. Looking across the table at him, at his pale eyes lock on hers, she feels a slight ripple, something unusual for her. She writes it off to her state of emotional vulnerability. She quickly averts her eyes, pulling the salad closer, carefully stabbing a cherry tomato.

"You look tired. Hard day?" He speaks like they're old friends.

"Horatio", right?"

"Nobody gets away with calling me Horatio. Tucker. This is my place."

"Alberta Higgins."

"You've been in town three days. You think I don't know your name?" He smiles a little and leans back. "So, are you a Bert or a Bertie?"

"Alberta."

"Right. I have to ask," he says. "What's with the charred meat? And the Rye? You clearly don't like either of them."

She pops another tomato, its sweetness filling her mouth. "Channeling my dad. A detective. Had a strict routine when he was on a case, especially a tough one." She tries the fish and smiles wide. "Got any good bourbon back there?"

"Absolutely." Tucker waves to the woman sitting at the end of the bar. The bartender sets two beers on her tray, and she drifts through the bar dropping the beers at one table, picking up glasses from another, dropping a check at another, finally landing at Tucker's booth.

"What can I do for you two?" In her mid-thirties, Colleen's denim shirt is tied at her waist over a tight white tank top barely controlling generous mounds of breast.

"A beer for me," Tucker says, "and a Crown Royal for Alberta."

"Manhattan," Alberta says. "Two cherries."

"Thanks, Hun," Colleen says with a grin. "I'm Colleen. You let me know if he gives you any trouble, ya hear?"

Alberta stirs her salad and smiles. Again. "This is a good salad. On a plate. Small pieces. Fresh. Not drowning in dressing."

"We try," Tucker says.

She likes that there are easy silences between them, yet still she feels the need to *fill the void* and smiles. He knows how to draw people out the same way her father used to. It was one of his ploys as a detective. *Silence is the strongest device in your toolbox. Wait them out. People can't stand a void.*

"A lot of Michigan State fans around here, I guess?" She points to a wall of paraphernalia surrounding an MSU football jersey. Tucker brushes her off with a grunt. "Oh," she says. "Now, I know there's a story. Whose shirt? Someone around here play for them?"

"All four years."

"You?"

"So, what about that has you so surprised? That I played football or that I went to college?"

She feels her cheeks flush. He's right on both counts. "You must have been good, playing your freshman year. Ever think about going pro?"

"Korea. Came home. Bounced around. Landed back here."

"Guys like you get married. The ones who come back home. High school sweethearts."

He doesn't take the bait.

"What was your major? At State."

"Why?"

"Curious."

"You think how did I end up running a bar with all that education." He can't help but see she's stumbling for words. "No, I get it. I graduated with a degree in journalism. Haven't written a word for anyone. Helps me look at the world and listen to people without preconceived expectations." He drinks some beer, watching his words settle in. "When my dad said he was ready to sell this place, I came back and took it over. Almost fifteen years now."

She compliments him on the perch and makes no further attempt to engage him in conversation. Still, he stays, leaning back, his gaze wandering the bar, observing arrivals and departures, occasionally lifting his hand in acknowledgement of someone looking his way.

"What's with you and dead boys?" He doesn't look at her until after he speaks.

Alberta fumbles her knife and fork, startled.

"I figured by the way you operate," he says, "you like things direct."

Another smile. "I do." She takes one last bite. She wipes her mouth. "I can tell you want to have a conversation, but it has been a really long day. I'd like to rain check it."

Tucker taps the table and grins. "You got it, Bert." He gets up and tells her dinner is on the house. "For the inconvenience on account of the cook refuses to burn any more meat for you."

Alberta arrives at her cabin, steps out of her shoes, and sprawls on the bed. Her mind teams with too much information. Exhaustion wins out and she dozes off, waking to the phone ringing. Only then did she see the note propped on the nightstand about Michael trying to reach her.

"Michael," she says. "Sorry. I just saw the note." She hears someone take a breath but no words follow. Her throat tightens. "So, the coroner released Alby's body?"

"It's time to come home, Bert." Neither Alberta nor her brother are prone to extended conversations. He tells her the funeral is Thursday. She asks how Tommy is coping, the answer to which was a single word. Not. She asks how Erin is doing? He doesn't answer at all. After neither of them say a word for what seems like a very long time, she says she loves him and will head out first thing in the morning. Michael hangs up first.

Alberta pulls out Alby's picture, touching it gently. She weeps. She tries to hang onto his sweetness but is drawn to the image of his tarped body on the riverbank.

She finally sleeps again and dreams she is reading to Alby in his bed, but he sinks into the mattress, disappearing. She wakes up. 4:30, an hour when reason fades and illusion takes over, when questions without answers haunt.

Unable to get back to sleep, she showers, packs, and hits the road in the dark. The long straight highway is illuminated only so far as her headlights reach. She knows where it leads, but can only see what is immediately in front of her. In much the same sense, she can't see past her suspicions to any conclusion.

The Stem house in Bucks County led her to the house on Spring Lake with its peculiar colors and unnatural rot. Edith's reaction to the jean jacket being on the wrong hook led her to possible blood evidence. There were deaths of more young boys. Drownings all. Proximity. History. It was everything and nothing. With another five hours in front of her, she pulls off for gas and buys a tall cup of burnt coffee. She fidgets with the radio until she finds a clear signal, turns it up, and heads out again as the sun breaches the horizon. Her focus shifts to the Conner boy, wondering if he was Walter's first victim and if something about his death triggered the others. Sammy Conner is one piece in an intricate puzzle, a piece she had yet to place.

CHAPTER 18

Jun 21 - I should be having a party today.

Penn is a loner. Whether it is her natural state of being, or a result of the way her life unfolded was something she hadn't contemplated until she found herself alone on Summer Solstice. There were a handful of friends from U of M who used to come out to the lake every summer on the solstice. They'd spend the day on the pontoon, eating too much, drinking too much. She misses that. She doesn't particularly miss the people, having no urge to call any of them, confide in them, lean on them. They aren't those kind of friends. She doesn't have friends like that. Penn's relationship with her co-workers, as it was with friends in college, is based on common interests, little else. She has never been in the habit of sharing her story, her feelings. She can't recall ever comforting anyone in crisis.

She has Dan Vogel, but he's more like a brother and they only interact at the lake.

She has Mildred, but considering the nature of Evelyn's state of mind and all it stirs up, she doesn't want to infect Mildred with whatever sickness seems to be seeping into her own bones.

As a child, Penn wasn't invited to slumber parties or birthday parties unless the whole class was included. Maybe it was because friendships are forged over summers and she was stuck at the lake with girls she couldn't stomach and who in turn, snubbed her. It could have been because Peter set the bar too high for anyone to meet. He was fascinating, observant, thoughtful, funny. Losing him broke her. Losing her mother to grief broke her. Losing her brothers to whatever it was that drove them away broke her. Watching her father try to fill all the holes in their lives broke her.

Mildred and George saved her, drew her out, opened her to possibility. Matthew saved her, showed her she could love and be loved, even if her way of expressing it was thin. Then she lost him, leaving her with a daughter whose father had been the hugger, the teaser, the anchor, things Penn was never good at. The hole left by his death seemed at the time, and over the years, insurmountable. By not sharing this latest challenge with Andi, Penn thought she was keeping her safe from the drama, from dark truths.

Listening to music drift across the lake, someone's beach party, she thinks about calling Andi. Inviting her out. Maybe, it would be good for both of them. Then Evelyn screams obscenities from the upstairs window. "Stop them! Somebody stop them! Fucking bastards! Stop them!" Again, she screams. A garbage truck revs outside as it turns around and rumbles away. "Stop them, Goddammit!"

Penn gets upstairs just as Evelyn falls out of bed, thudding to the floor, still screaming. Penn tries to help her up, but Evelyn pushes her away.

When Penn grabs the anxiety meds, Evelyn knocks them out of her hand, pills flying all over the room. Evelyn tries to stand, grabbing the covers off the bed. Her legs crumble. She slumps back to the floor, her face twisted, mouth open wide, a convulsive silent agony. Penn doses her with Roxy but Evelyn spits it out.

Penn runs down to the fridge for the med box. Of the six medications, she can't remember which one is for psychosis. She runs back upstairs, crushes an Ativan in some water, and uses the Roxy dropper to shoot it into her mother's gaping mouth. Evelyn yowls and cries. "They've come to tear us apart!"

It takes ten minutes, but the raving woman on the floor finally settles down. Penn gets her back into bed.

> Jul 1 - I never imagined losing the boys would only be the beginning of the deconstruction of our lives. Then we lost the woods. And the marsh. And the springs.

After the boys died, a developer purchased the marsh property. The two track behind the cottages was widened and extended through the woods. At the same time, another road was being carved back beyond the back path. Bulldozers and chainsaws scored the summer with a cacophony of destruction. Trucks rumbled in and out all day with their loads of fill. In the process, they destroyed the spring system. The water level in Spring Lake dropped. The channel became a small stream. Spirit Lake grew shallower, warmer, and the algae blooms became a frequent danger to swimmers and aquatic life. The lake district was annexed into the township, bringing water and sewer service. Taxes went up. Big new houses sprang up where the marsh had been. Property values went up. Taxes went up again. More of the small summer places were sold and torn down, replaced with large year-round houses.

Taxes went up again. Within a few short years, nothing about the lake was familiar save the tavern and a handful of cottages. Even Miller's Grocery, Bait & Tackle closed when a chain store moved in. The Vogel and Hodges cottages were all that remained of the original enclave. Bill and Marty saw to that.

CHAPTER 19

Jul 6 - Was it freedom? Or passive abandonment. We were in and out the door all day. Nobody watching us - hours on end - day after day.

Until Tyler's last summer, life at the lake was a world of open doors. Kids came and went generating a constant stream of activity in and out of every cottage. Kids fended for themselves at lunchtime. Mothers could be found lounging, napping, playing cards, sunbathing.

Evelyn took her naps every afternoon, an internal alarm clock waking her at five. Lake dinners were simple. Boiled hotdogs, sloppy joes, or a can of beef stew. Occasionally if Jim would man the charcoal grill, they'd have burgers and beans.

But something changed that last year. Evelyn changed. It started over the winter.

She began a new routine. Breakfast became mandatory. Eggs. Bacon. Milk. She packed lunches. She did not take naps. She cleaned. Fanatically. Clothes were pressed. Sheets were changed weekly. Pillowcases and sheets were ironed. Dinner menus became more diverse. While she had become the consummate homemaker, she found no joy in her tasks. They were carried out by compulsion. And everyone learned the hard way to stay out of her way. Nothing was worth riling her, and it took very little to do it. This behavior persisted into the summer at the cottage.

She revoked kitchen privileges. Lunch was at noon. Dinner was at six. Be there or don't eat. Evelyn went to bed before her children each evening, closing her door on them with every expectation of it staying closed. Yet nearly each night, after the kids settled into their bunks, there would be footsteps heading downstairs, and a few choice last words inevitably came through her door to her eldest. "For chrissake, Jimmy, go back to bed!"

At fifteen, Jim Hodges sat on the cusp of adulthood yet already felt the burden of responsibility, some strange urgency pushing him to keep track of things, a self-ordained superintendent in charge of maintaining order. He'd taken to getting up nearly as soon as he laid down to check the storeroom to see if the life jackets were on their pegs, the fishing poles on the rack, the canoe paddles hung up, and the skis leaning against the wall and not lying on damp concrete. Occasionally, he would go so far as to venture out into the night to ascertain if the motors were covered. It may have been a reflection of his mother's behavior or something he'd been prone to all his life, yet the results of his behavior, all the lake gear accounted for and kept in shape, earned him praise from his father.

The boys began each summer with crew cuts that by July were grown out and bleached out. Both Mark and Tyler were towheads even before they got in the sun. By mid-summer, their hair was almost white. They were furry creatures, the fluff on their arms and legs glowing in sunlight. They both had bushy eyebrows and pale blue eyes, but Mark's weren't as striking as Tyler's. Mark's dimples weren't as distinctive as Tyler's. His wit wasn't as quick. His grin not as inviting. It was like Mark was the first draft, and Tyler was the new and improved version.

Ronny was thirteen that summer and an inch and a half taller than Jim. His angular build, like Jim's, was all muscle. He had their dad's dark eyes and sullen expression. The freckles across his nose and cheeks multiplied throughout the summer. Where his family was concerned, he lived in a constant state of disinterest. He had, in recent months, taken the brunt of their mother's agitations. His proclivity to occupy the couch engrossed in a book, a half-eaten sandwich on the table, an empty bag of potato chips on the floor, never used to bother her, but suddenly it made him an easy target. "Why can't you be more like your brother? Clean up this mess. If you're just going to sit around all day, do it someplace else. Take it outside."

Mark, on the other hand, was good at staying out of Evelyn's sites, spending most of his day on the lake sailing the little flat top Sunfish, paddling the canoe, or skiing. At least once a summer, a group of the boys would attempt to swim the perimeter of the lake going swim-raft to swim-raft, some of them making it only halfway before hitching a boat ride back. Mark made it all the way around for the first time on the fourth of July.

Tyler could be found just about anywhere. When he wasn't trying to keep up with his brothers, he'd watch Betsy Fry paint her toenails. He'd fetch drinks for Laura the Beautiful, clean water skis with Greg, or ride to the store with Mason.

With her fourth mug of coffee in hand, Penn looks in on Evelyn, sleeping. She'd had an episode at six that morning. Penn stares out over the lake thinking how she could never have let her daughter out of her sight all day.

She kept an eye on Andi all the time, where she was, what she was up to. Was she on the water with Dan's kids, on the dock, in the woods? Did she have sunscreen and wear her flip-flops on the splintery dock boards?

The day started clear and warm, but a storm was sliding in fast. They came on like that out there. Little warning. Wind stirs the curtains and Penn hears something downstairs that raises goose bumps on her arms, like the sound of Tyler saying pleeeeese, drawing it out the way he used to. She steps slowly down the stairs feeling an odd sense of expectation, as if time is shifting and she's a child again.

She sees the front door swing a few inches, its hinges crying out. Pleeeese. Penn steps to the doorway looking out to the roiling lake believing for an instant she might see herself bouncing amid the whitecaps in the canoe with Tyler.

The Hodges' canoe was dull, dented aluminum. Penny and Ty paddled across the lake that summer. Didn't mean to go all the way. Just headed out, found a rhythm synchronizing their strokes. Next thing they knew, they were at the channel to Miller Lake, slipping under the low bridge, ducking like fools when a car passed over their heads.

Slipping back into the sunshine was like entering a secret, sacred place. No cottages. No people. Just woods surrounding the pond, edged in cattails and aquatic arrowhead. Clear, shallow waters revealed thick grasses swaying just below the surface like some breeze ran through them. They slowed sliding through lily pads, hairy stems parting for their passage.

They paddled gently, exploring weedy shallows. Tyler took off his canvas life jacket. "Can't drown. It's shallow," he whispered. "Rubs my arms raw." Penny took off her vest. Two muskrats swam to shore through a narrow passage through the weeds. Penny steered to mounds of grass and sticks topped with caked mud, goose nests full of eggs. Penny watched a kingfisher dive from a high branch straight down into the water. Tyler pointed to the egret flying to a perch in the bare reaches of a dead tree. A row of painted turtles slipped off a log. A sandhill crane flew over so close they could hear feathers. It landed a few yards away on shore and folded down onto a nest, disappearing except for the red patch on its head, its long beak pointing straight at them. It became a moment elongated in time, tattooed on Penny's heart.

They hadn't noticed the sky growing overcast until a large dark shadow passed under them and Tyler grabbed the sides of the canoe. It rose several yards away, turning to look at them. The largest snapping turtle they'd ever seen. It began to drizzle.

Penn closes the front door feeling the oppressive weight of memory. She'd spent her life second-guessing every decision she made that day in the canoe, how she should have headed home before the rain started, how she shouldn't have headed straight across instead of following the shoreline. She was in back, steering. Ty was in front trying to be the power, both life preservers at their feet. They weren't halfway across when the wind hit them from the side, the chop whipping into whitecaps. Penny knew to turn into the wind or they'd capsize. Doing her best J-stroke she dug deep but wasn't strong enough. The canoe started to tip. She told Tyler to try harder and watched him put his whole body into it, feet braced hard to the sides for leverage, his body powering down with every stroke. When the wind began thrashing them about, they stopped paddling just to hang on. Penny kept hollering "Hang on! Hang on!" Then the hard rain hit. So cold. Pelting them. It rained so hard she couldn't see shore and didn't hear the powerboat coming until it was suddenly there, and Jim was yanking her out of the canoe. Ronny hoisted Tyler and pushed them both to the floor of the Lyman. Mark grabbed the rope, and they sped off with the canoe bouncing behind them. Penny looked over the rail as they neared shore and saw her mother standing on the dock, drenched. The instant the Lyman hit the dock, Evelyn grabbed Tyler, Jim tied the Lyman, and Ronny yanked the canoe to shore. Lightning sliced the sky. Thunder cracked as they all ran to the cottage, slid inside, and slammed the door. Standing there, sopping wet, catching their breath, their mother offered no urgent hugging, no reprimands. When she spoke, her voice was measured and subdued. "Good work," she said. "Good work out there." Then she went to retrieve towels.

Standing together that day in the wake of rescue was the last time Penn remembered feeling like a family. Less than a month later, they were all at Tyler's funeral.

Penny's first funeral. July 21st, 1960. A Thursday. Nobody told her to grab her raincoat or umbrella. Nobody paid any attention to her.

The church was packed. Ty's scout troop was there with all their parents. People from the neighborhood were there. Teachers and their husbands. Only six from the lake came. Al and Merci brought Greg. Gert and Mason brought Danny.

It was a closed casket. Penny hadn't seen inside. She hadn't seen Tyler since the night before he died when she went to bed after the boys didn't let her play cards. All the time the minister was talking from his pulpit, Penny kept staring at the casket, wondering if Ty was really in it. She wondered if he could breathe in it, if it was dark, if he was scared. She knew better, but in her heart, he was still alive, alone in that box and it hit her that she would never see him again. With one painful gasp, she began to sob, her wails echoing off the vaulted ceiling. Her father wrapped her into his lap where she buried her head in his neck, limp in his arms. She could feel the shuddering of his chest, his gasps, and his warm tears on the back of her neck.

Years later, whenever she hears the hiss of tires on wet pavement, she thinks back to the rainy ride to the cemetery, the whole family in the big black car, sitting across from each other. No one spoke. As they rode through town, cars slowed down and pulled over to the curb. Penny asked why they weren't pulling over, too. Her father told her to keep still.

No one warned her she'd have to watch her brother's casket lowered into the ground. She couldn't breathe, like they were burying her. Her therapist would later trace her panic attacks to that experience. To the closed casket, unable to see Tyler one last time.

Over the next few days after the funeral, Penny was frantic to remember Ty's voice. She could remember things he said, but not his voice saying them. For as many stare downs as they had, she couldn't see his eyes either, so she took one of the photo albums to her room, stashing it under her bed. She pulled it out a lot the first weeks, stared at his face, cried herself to sleep. She could remember things Tyler did, the way he took such big bites of food and passed the bread plate with both hands instead of one, the way he fumbled the deck of cards when he tried to shuffle. She had these memories, but details were gone. Her heart broke a little more with each new realization of loss. She didn't understand and thought she was the only one who couldn't recall all of Tyler. Maybe she hadn't loved him well enough or paid enough attention. Unwilling to expose her failing to anyone else, she kept it to herself.

Talking about Ty was easy right after he died. Before the funeral, all they could do at home was talk about him, how he wanted to try the slalom ski and he probably would have gotten up the first time. He was a natural at baseball but couldn't throw a football yet because his hands were too small. He loved books and read earlier than the rest of them and was probably the smartest of the five of them. Five. They'd been whittled down to four. Tyler didn't like fizzy drinks. He laughed all the time. He loved hunting for night crawlers to fish with but hated baiting his hook with them. He snored and kicked in his sleep. Before the funeral, they said things like *I miss Ty*, and *I wish Ty were here to see this* and *Ty would have laughed his head off at that*. Once he was in the ground, they started to avoid talking about him. It wasn't a decision, it just happened. And the not talking about him became as awkward as talking about him, so they all just stopped talking.

All the days between the night he died and the funeral, Evelyn fixed his favorite foods. Hotdogs, spaghetti with meatballs, meatloaf and mashed potatoes, pot roast, pancakes. But after the funeral, they didn't see any of those things again. She couldn't bring herself to make them. She couldn't bring herself to do a lot of things.

CHAPTER 20

July 11 - On our best days, we live in the moment as if past and future have no power over us. No judgment. Then we both revert to our worst selves and I just want her to die.

Evelyn seems almost to be in recovery, though Penn knows better.

While Penn makes sandwiches, her mother gets the plates and drinks gathered up as she did in the old days, packing enough for seven, not two. She takes the old plaid thermos off the shelf and carries it to the pantry looking for something she can't find, pulling all the cleaning supplies to the floor, grumbling, "Goddamn your father."

Penn collects everything and they head down to the pontoon. Evelyn insists she does not need the wheelchair, yet clings to Penn's arm hard enough to nearly break it. She's exhausted by the effort and lays down on the back bench in the sun.

The lake is placid. Not a breath of air. They cruise to the middle, cut the motor. Evelyn asks for the thermos.

"We didn't bring it."

"Stop trying to . . ." Words fail. Evelyn struggles to stand. "Slam dog all every day!" She reaches for the gate like she's going to step right off the deck. Penn takes her arm, but her mother yanks away. Penn throws her arms around her, sits her down and gives her a pill and some Vernor's ginger ale. ". . . run my life!" Evelyn's words spill and sputter. "Can't blame me! Your father's Goddamned heart attack."

"Where'd that come from?"

Evelyn loses the thought. "What?"

Penn slides a table up and out of the console, propping it on foldout legs.

"Where'd that come from?" Evelyn asks.

"What?"

"Why the hell did we drag those damn TV trays out here if that table was there?"

"This is a new boat. Not the old one."

"When did we get a new boat?"

A ski boat circles the far end of the lake, its whine skimming across the water. Penn sits behind her mother watching her take an occasional nibble of sandwich.

"And Ronny?" Evelyn says in the middle of an imaginary conversation. "Married three times. Always her fault. Never his. And Mark? Don't get me started. Everything wrong with his life is my fault. I failed him. Ruined summer. His life. He's twenty. Needs to figure out how to live his own damn life."

Penn could let it go but doesn't. "You chose a dead kid over your live ones, Mom. How do you think that made us feel? And Mark is fifty-two."

Penn watches her mother's head droop slightly, but the words kept coming, a strong voice emanating from a wilted shell.

"When I came home, did they ever help out? Even ask? No. Bitch bitch bitch…" She's hung up on the word until it fades away along with the thought.

Penn gives the cord on the motor a hard yank. It comes to life with a rumbling putter.

Evelyn grins. "I'm dying. You should be nice to me." Her gaze floats away, her mind with it.

They are tied at the dock the next time Evelyn speaks. "You got caught in the middle. We did the best we could."

Penn softens. "Were you and Dad ever happy? I mean. . ."

Evelyn snaps. "Grief does things. That's all you need to know."

"But wouldn't you both have been better, happier, if you'd stayed with us instead of spending so much time out here alone?"

"Happier?" Evelyn winces and rubs her side. "We were never going to be happy." She bends over in pain. Penn reaches in her pocket for the Roxy, putting a drop under her mother's tongue before going up for the wheelchair.

The next morning Evelyn is unusually clear-headed. She wants to play cards. All Penn knows is rummy, and it goes well for a few minutes until Evelyn lays down her cards as if she's playing bridge. When Penn doesn't know what to do, Evelyn barks at her. "Damn it, Gladys, if you're not even going to try, why bother?"

"Gladys isn't here, Mom. We're playing gin rummy."

"Well, why'd you lay down like you're playing bridge then?"

Penn smiles. "I didn't. You did."

Evelyn scatters the cards. The game is over.

Two in the morning finds Penn sitting on the dock dangling her feet in the inky water. Evelyn is asleep after two doses of Roxy. The pain has become an entity in its own right with intention, arriving after good days as if to say *Not so fast. You're dying, remember?*

It was easier in the beginning when the two of them were still estranged. It's more difficult now they've started picking at the scars. Evelyn's eyes had once scanned the room when the pain took hold, looking at anything but her daughter. Now one glance between them said it all: whether the pain was a five or a nine, whether the fear was a two or ten. Tonight had been a seven and ten. Penn asked her what she was actually afraid of. Was it more pain, or dying? Dying would end the pain. Isn't it what she wanted? Isn't it what she'd wanted all the years since Tyler died? To end the pain? Evelyn chuckled at the quandary, then squeezed Penn's arm as another wave took hold and Penn gave her a second dose.

In the still air of the summer night, Penn prays to her non-existent god for an end to her mother's life. Only a few weeks earlier, she'd hoped for an expeditious death for entirely selfish reasons, to be done with it, to get her own life back. Now it is more about her mother, about setting her free.

Rhythmic calls of tree peepers surround her. Penn lays back, looking to the stars. The big dipper hangs directly over the cottage now. The boink of a bullfrog brings her upright. It croaks again. Then another. She grins wide. Nature will out. The marsh had been filled in for decades destroying the bullfrog's habitat. A new spring, or maybe the old one fighting its way back, started bubbling up in front of Dan's place the year before, slowly gnawing away at the ground around his dock. She'd seen the first cattails that summer. Apparently, so had the frogs. They're back. Given enough time, they and the spring will probably take over all of Dan's lakefront and hers. How joyous, she thinks. Rebirth. Recovery.

CHAPTER 21

July 15 - 3:30 AM One dose tonight. She's asleep but I'm wide awake. It's so quiet out. So still. Like living in a diorama or a vacuum or like none of this is real - it's all just time out of time where nothing registers.

Penn wakes to the sounds of children laughing and splashing. The sound of joy. From the window, she can barely see her mother perched in her wheelchair on the pontoon in the shade of the bimini awning as a handful of little boys splash in the water with inner tubes and floaties, their parents standing waist-deep with them. Dan and his wife Carla are in lawn chairs under the willow, watching their four grandbabies. A sweet *Grammy! Grammy!* rises above the other voices with a comforting reply "I'm right here, Joshy. I see you."

Penn throws on some clothes and wanders down. Evelyn shouts out that it was about time she got up.

"Great, isn't it?" Dan says quietly.

"Like when Andi and our two were little," Carla says.

"Is your mom around?" Penn asks Dan.

He says the kids were too much crazy for her.

"Does she know about Evelyn?"

"Yeah. One more reason not to come out, maybe."

One of the men in the water calls out, asking when Andi is coming out. Penn waves and shrugs.

She grows pensive. "Was it ever like this?" She asks Dan. "I mean . . . never mind."

"When we were kids?" Dan asks. He squints and glances up and down the shoreline. "I don't know. What those kids out in the water perceive and what we see here on shore, entirely different. I think they love it out here. Thirty years from now? They may tell me it was nothing short of hell, swimming in this mucky lake, sunburns and mosquitoes. They fight over who is going to sleep by the window every night. They argue over board games and complain about being bored." He laughs. "They're kids. I could be scarring them for life bringing the out here."

Penn's expression doesn't change. "Look," he says. "It was what we made it. Maybe freedom isn't all it's cracked up to be, but I think we made the best of it. It couldn't have been all bad or I wouldn't have tried so hard to give my kids and grandkids a taste of what I had as a kid. You, too. You had Andi out here all the time. If it was as horrible as you seem to remember it, you never would have renovated the place."

"Maybe I was renovating the memory," Penn mumbles.

Dan laughs out loud. "Too deep for me for such a glorious summer day."

Evelyn shouts, pointing a stern finger at one of Dan's grandkids. "Ronny, you stop picking on your little brother!" She looks at Dan. "Dick! When in the hell are you going to mow this yard? Rake the potatoes. Raking, raking, raking, raking."

Penn lowers her head and closes her eyes.

Dan doesn't miss a beat. "You bet, Dear. I'll get right on that." He looks at Penn with such compassion she almost cries. "That one is Mark," he says picking out each kid. "That one seems to be me and that one is Jimmy."

"Welcome to my world."

"She's right about one thing. I am about to mow the lawn."

"You don't have to do that."

"Bad night?" Carla asks.

"I'm losing my mind."

Carla asks if the boys have been out yet. "I'm sure you could use the help. She's their mother, too." She saunters onto the dock.

Penn looks up with a twisted smile.

"My dad got stuck in the past, too," Dan says. "He forgot he was married."

Penn laughs. "He always did have a tough time remembering that as I recall."

"Why do you think Mom divorced him?"

For the longest time, Penn sits quietly bathing in the sounds of summer. The drone of a ski boat carries from the far side of the lake. A screen door smacks somewhere. Two jet skis whine, chasing each other from one shore to the other. She watches as one of the little boys tries to throw a frisbee without success. The oldest boy, only eight, retrieves it and shows his little brother how to do it, then swims out to retrieve it when the toss goes too far.

"Why couldn't that last day we all had together have been a good one? Why did it have to be one of the worst?" Penn asks.

"Was it? One of the worst?"

"Don't you remember? Everybody fighting. Ronny fought with my dad over that damn ski. And the fight over who got to go skiing with Wagner's new boat. And the raft war?"

"You mean when Steve Fry threw Tyler halfway across the yard?"

"That was a different fight later in the day."

"No, I heard it started on the rafts. Look. The last of anything is going to take on greater significance. There's every possibility it wasn't any better or worse than any other day. Raft wars aren't anything I'd let my kids do but they were a blast. You were one hell of a defender as I recall."

"Me?"

"Knocked my ass off without mercy. Lots of times. You can't tell me it wasn't fun. And you took to water skiing with such fearlessness."

"Jim and Ronny pissed and moaned every time they had to take me out."

"Who wouldn't. You were not a pleasant kid."

"Me?"

"Seriously? You were bossy and mopey and generally a pain in the ass most of the time."

"Thanks for the enlightenment." Penn punches Dan on the arm.

"You were a little sister," he says with a grin. "You couldn't help it."

He looks out over the lake and back at Penn, takes a breath to speak but hesitates. "I came out here the summer before my senior year at State. Must have been '67. Hadn't been out much since . . ." He winces. "Not since '60."

Penn eyed him over her sunglasses.

"My cousin EJ and his wife were spending the summer out here. Teachers. What other profession gives you three months off? Anyway, their boys must have been seven or eight, maybe younger. His wife hated it here. Complained about the heat, the bugs, made EJ get her a window air conditioner." Dan opens a beer from a small cooler at his feet. "Their boys were brats. Still are."

One of the grandkids calls out from the water for Dan to come swim with them. "I'll take you skiing later, how's that?" Cheers go up all round.

Penn lets the tranquility of the moment seep into her bones. Evelyn is content and quiet. The kids are happy. Adults are happy. No one is drunk. It is a kind of joy she remembered from when Andi was young, and she suddenly misses her daughter and Matthew so much it hurts.

"So, that summer," Dan says, "when Eric Junior was here. They were in town for a couple of days. I came out because he'd screwed up the boats. He didn't know jack shit about motors. Your mom was here like always. Inside. Out of sight." He takes another long draw of beer.

"What is it, Daniel?" Penn asks.

"Wasn't anybody around, but your dock was littered with those orange life preservers. Remember those huge puffy things? And all your boats were in the water. It creeped me out."

"Do you happen to remember the date?" He shakes his head.

Evelyn stirs, talking to no one in particular. "Where are those boys? Time to come in for lunch."

"This is what waits for you, ya know. When she's gone," Dan says nodding toward Evelyn. "This new batch of kids. Another go at it. Gotta get Andi on the ball, get her some kids out here, too. Let the past go. This is the future.

It's all good, Penn." His gentle smile is reassuring. "Why don't you go somewhere? We're here all day. I'll keep an eye on her. Leave."

Penn looks at him, almost in shock.

"Go somewhere," Dan reiterates. "Anywhere."

After a moment's hesitation, Penn gets up and hands him the morphine. "Half a dropper under her tongue."

"Go," he says, over a cacophony of splashing and screaming children, giggles and laughter.

Penn mutters under her breath. "It was never like this when we were kids."

Pulling into a farm stand, Penn parks but doesn't get out of the car, preoccupied with what Dan said. She'd seen what he was talking about. The summer she turned sixteen. She borrowed a friend's car and came out to the cottage on her own.

The pontoon, the Lyman and the dingy were all tied to the dock where four puffy orange life vests and jackets were strewn haphazardly, their canvas straps splayed out. The canoe was up on the sand, paddles in the grass. Beach towels draped the railings of the pontoon. A narrow slalom ski straddled a corner of the dock. Two fatter skis with red boots leaned on the canoe. A yellow and white towrope lay coiled in the grass.

At first glance, it was not a static scene but a place merely taking a breath. It was the silence that first drew the chill. No one careened off the dock into the lake, swimming to a floating water ski, slipping a foot into the rubber sleeve, threading a tow line through their grip as the Lyman puttered away, the thumbs up and the whine of the outboard, a beautiful young boy exploding out of the water, spray flying off his body, skimming across the surface with exuberance. Tyler wasn't in the dingy splashing oars to water, pulling one in one direction and the other in the opposite, attempting and accomplishing a spin.

Penny had the sense something was horribly off when she went inside that day to find seven toothbrushes in a glass on the bathroom sink. The bunk beds were all made except for Tyler's, and under his bed, a pair of small rubber flip flops, one upside down, the other askew next to it.

Downstairs, she saw the cards on the side table, Tyler's game of solitaire, as if left unfinished years earlier. On the counter, a box of Trix and one cereal bowl, the red one, Tyler's favorite. She looked to her mother standing silent in the kitchen, a woman pretending not to see her daughter, not to let anyone's presence interrupt the reliving of that day, the last day her family was still intact.

Penny left the cottage that afternoon without speaking to her mother. Driving home she was obsessed with imagining her mother setting every element in place, how she must have draped the towels so carefully to make them look as though kids had thrown them, how she knew which ski to put where, what knot Jim used to tie the boat to the cleat, what she must have thought before doing it and then after, wondering if she thought it brought Tyler back to her or if it was nothing more than self-imposed torture. In any case, Penny promised herself not to visit on the anniversary of Ty's death ever again.

A woman from the farm stand steps over to Penn's car window asking if she's OK. Startled, Penn starts the car and drives off. She's just realized what day it is. July 17. Forty years to the day that Ty and Peter died.

CHAPTER 22

Alberta's first stop back in Pennsylvania, even before she checks in with her brother, is to see Edith again. She pulls up in front of the house unprepared for what she sees, siding pelted by eggs, broken shells cemented on windows by crusty yolks, *child killer* sprayed on the garage door, garbage strewn about the yard. Several clean casserole dishes line the top step.

She sees Edith peer through a curtain. "Please, Edith. Can we talk?"

The door opens slightly, Edith standing behind it so as not to be seen. "Do you have any food?" she whispers. "I'm starving."

"Please. Can I come in?"

The door opens a little wider.

"Crimes of the husband and all," Edith says, still not showing herself. "No one brings casseroles for that."

As Alberta squeezes inside, Edith quickly closes the door. "I couldn't go to the store," she says. "I can't leave."

A foul odor overwhelms Alberta in the tight confines of the vestibule. It seems Edith hasn't bathed since she saw her last. When Alberta offers to go to the store, Edith darts into the kitchen.

Stepping into the living room, Alberta is surprised to see the books have not been put away, and the couch and chair are covered with piles of clothes.

"Laundry?" Alberta asks, carving out a place to sit.

Edith brings her a sheet of paper. "Packing," she says. "I'm going home."

"This might not be the best time for that."

"I'm not coming back," Edith says. "Nothin' will be the same there. I don't have a place any more. But may as well go back where I came from." She sits down next to Alberta and picks up a sweater that has slipped to the floor. "They arrested him, you know. Said he killed that boy. He should never have talked to them. This is what he gets for giving a little boy a ride on a rainy night."

"Does he know you're leaving him?"

"How would he know? I haven't seen him. He hasn't called. The paper said he won't get a lawyer. How could a newspaper know something I don't even know about my own husband?"

Edith hands her the sheet of paper, wrinkled and worn, typed and organized by department, a grocery list. Food for a week: Three pork chops, one pound of ground chuck, one pound of beef liver, a two-pound chuck roast, one two-pound roasting chicken and one pound of bacon, one gallon milk, one pound of butter, one dozen eggs, one loaf white bread, one can peas, carrots, green beans, lima beans and three cans of corn. The only fresh produce was an onion.

"All of this?" Alberta asks.

Edith looks as if the question makes no sense. "It's the list. Seven days. We have gravy bread the day after the pot roast." She speaks quietly, eyes fading a little. "Peas and gravy bread for dinner on Saturday. Chicken broth on Monday from the Sunday carcass. I shop on Saturdays. I couldn't go Saturday. They took his car Saturday."

Alberta thinks back to the pristine kitchen her first time there, the empty cupboards, the lack of food. "You had the casseroles. At least that was something to tide you over."

Edith's expression is almost as peculiar as her response. "I ate from them once."

"Then what?"

"I threw them out."

"Why would you do that?"

"Leftovers aren't allowed."

"Edith, when was the last time you ate?"

"Sunday."

"It's Wednesday."

Alberta watches Edith begin to rock back and forth slowly, hands in her lap working the corner of her sweater. Only then does Alberta realize it's the same one she had on Saturday. Edith's gaze drifts again. Her mouth rises to a vague half-smile. "I've gone longer."

Alberta's thoughts go to images of the festering Stem house on Spring Lake. "I've seen the house," she says, trying to make a connection with this damaged woman. "You were right. You told me the colors were bad. You were right. It must have been awful living there. In Michigan."

Edith leans back, her hands coming to a rest. She talks slowly this time, far less animated than their previous meeting. "It wasn't so bad. I liked having the neighbor boys around doing chores, learning from Walter. I used to make lemonade for them and fix them lunch. I remember Timmy liked egg salad, but Kevin Wagner wouldn't touch it. Peter liked potato chips and sweet pickles, but Danny and Tyler preferred Cheetos and dill pickles. Then Peter and Tyler died, and it all changed. Nobody needed him anymore. The other boys were too grown up to come by." Tears fill her eyes again. "That little boy who died? He reminds me of little Peter Eastman. Sweet boy. So sad," she sighs. "He died, too." There is a long pause. Edith looks at the grocery list. "We didn't buy those special things again after."

"What changed?"

"There weren't any more boys. It was just me, Walter and Velma."

"And your daughter."

"Gone." Edith sits slump-shouldered, her gaze hung up on a stack of blouses. "That was the one thing that made me sad to leave there when we did. It had been so quiet at the lake for years. But then we were starting to get kids again. Two little boys came out to the Vogel cottage and I thought maybe we'd have them visiting with Walter, like the old days. But it didn't happen. And Velma was pushing Walter all that summer to leave."

"Why do you suppose she did that?"

Edith starts working the edge of her sweater again. "He got passed over for the superintendent's job? I don't know. I never knew what that woman was thinking."

"I want to ask you about Peter and Tyler. Do you remember anything about the night they died? Or the next morning, when they were found?"

"I can make some tea," Edith says without making eye contact. "Would you like some tea? I still have some in the cupboard."

"No. Thank you, though," Alberta says. "Do you remember anything?"

"I remember Debra wasn't home. Her bed hadn't been slept in."

"I don't blame her for running off. Her grandmother was a relentless, horrible, controlling . . . Vel-ma," she says with contempt.

Edith stops talking. Alberta waits patiently.

"That morning," Edith finally says, "when the boys were found in the marsh? Velma beat Walter. With a fireplace poker."

"She what? Why?"

"She hit him and hit him and hit him and he just took it." She lifts a purple blouse with bright yellow dots and drops it to the floor. "He saw me. I was on the stairs. And he just told me, so gentle, real quiet like, to go back to my room. Everything is fine, he said. Not to worry, he said. Then he said in his quiet voice to Velma, that's enough, Mother, and she dropped the poker."

Alberta makes no effort to hide her amazement. "Why would she do that?"

"I told you. Velma Stem was bloody crazy."

"Edith?" Alberta hesitates, then lets it rip. "Do you think your husband had anything to do with Tyler and Peter's deaths?"

Edith turns abruptly. "What do you mean? Of course not!" As quickly as her voice rises, it falls, her composure forced. "He'd never hurt those boys," she says, softly. "That was an accident." She looks to the floor, cocking her head to such a degree it seemed to Alberta it might just twist off. "And he didn't hurt this one either. His whole life has been devoted to young people. And all that's ruined. My life is ruined. You should go now. Go!" Edith shoves the coffee table out of her way and stumbles to the door, her hands in tight fists. "Please. Just leave me alone."

Alberta has one more question. "Edith, where was the jean jacket the morning the boys were found?"

Edith's eyes grow cold. "Why would I remember that?"

"But, you do remember. Don't you?" She walks over to Edith. "Just like you told me about the jacket this time."

Edith looks to the floor for a moment, then straight at Alberta. "It was wet. Hanging on the right hook, but it was soaking wet. And I saw that it was missing a button and I was taking it down to mend it when Velma told me to leave it alone. Real quiet like. That's where Walter got it from. That quiet voice. It was worse than her yelling. I never touched it again. The jacket. Never. Button never did get mended."

Alberta's silence, her stillness, seems to completely unnerve Edith.

"What does it mean?" Edith asks. A kind of fear sweeps her face. "What does it mean?"

Edith leans on the wall.

Alberta opens the front door wanting to tell this tortured woman she's right to go home to England, to reconnect with family, to try to salvage what was left of her life. Instead, she tells Edith not to leave town. Edith says nothing, hiding once again behind the door.

Alberta is already at her car when Edith calls out. "My grocery list! You said you'd take my grocery list." Edith lays it on the porch and closes the door. Alberta retrieves it, Edith watching from behind the curtain.

Alberta drives away, wondering why a captive doesn't flee the moment they realize the cage door is open.

Back at the office, she tells one of the women to do the shopping, stressing not to vary from the list in any way. "Pack it all in a box. Take it to the porch. Ring the bell and leave. Don't engage."

When the staffer delivers the food, she finds an envelope taped to the door with money for the bill, correct to within a quarter.

CHAPTER 23

The morning Tyler and Peter's bodies were found in the marsh, Edith woke early. It was barely light. Walter's side of the bed had not been slept in. She heard distant calling outside and went to the window. Listening carefully, she couldn't make out names. She glanced in to see Debra's bed had not been slept in. At the bottom of the stairs she almost tripped over a mop and a bucket full of dirty water. It didn't belong there. It wasn't Thursday. Velma always mopped floors on Thursday and never before breakfast.

Velma sat at the kitchen table, her hands folded in front of her. She said nothing when Edith came in asking where Walter and Debra were. When Edith started to step outside, Velma shouted in the most piercing tone. "Close that door!"

Edith complied and set about making a pot of coffee, careful not to disturb the room's unnatural stillness. Tilting the percolator under the faucet, she ran the water slowly so it wouldn't splash. She opened the cupboard door, retrieving the coffee tin, placing it on a towel to dampen the sound. She scooped the coffee and filled the percolator basket without tapping the rim as she normally would. She snapped the top of the percolator into place as quietly as possible, Velma's audible exhale a sign it had not been quiet enough. Waiting for it to perk, Edith saw the wet jacket and scuffed down the steps to the landing to look at it.

Velma, her back to Edith, told her in the quiet voice to leave it be.

Edith obeyed, taking a position near the perking coffee. With the last sputter, she poured two cups, placing one in front of Velma before sitting down across from her.

Velma did not drink. She did not move. She stared into her coffee and remained silent. Edith drank hers and got up to refill it.

"Sit. Down."

Edith did as told. What could have been an hour went by before Walter came through the back door, his clothes soaked, stinking of swamp. Edith noticed a scratch across his face and asked how he'd gotten it. He looked at her, then to his mother. "It must have been a cattail."

"They can be sharp," Velma said. "Unforgiving."

In a voice far too calm for the news it delivered, Walter said two boys had drowned in the marsh overnight. When he said it was Tyler and Peter, Edith screamed and began to cry. She charged for the door but Walter grabbed her arm hard. She tried to pull away.

"I need to go to their mothers, to console them. I can help."

"They don't need your interventions or pity," Velma said. "Your only concern right now is that your daughter has been out all night."

Edith ran to her room, closed the door, and sobbed into her pillow so as not to be heard. Velma's shouting drew her back out. Halfway down the steps, she saw Walter cowering on the floor, Velma hitting him with the poker again and again, shouting.

"Bad boy! You are a very, very bad boy!" Walter did not fight back, just took the beating.

"Stop it!" Edith screamed, charging toward them. One look from Velma and Edith froze.

"Go back to your room," Walter said so softly Edith hardly recognized his voice. "It's all right," he said. Velma glared at Edith, her grip still tight on the poker. "That's enough, Mother," he said, and Velma dropped the poker.

Edith walked slowly back to her room and closed the door. She sat on her bed, hands in her lap, rocking back and forth, trying not to scream. Her thumbs worked a worn edge of her nightgown.

Debra eventually made it home that evening. Walter grilled her on her whereabouts. She said she'd spent the night with a friend from school, delivering the lie he would believe for reasons having more to do with apathy than trust. A car picked her up for school the next morning. That's the last they saw of her. Walter later found an envelope in his office at school. *Don't come looking for me - Debra.*

Edith, having seen Velma beating Walter, concluded Velma was, and probably always had been, smack out of her mind. Her insanity had been Walter's secret, the source of their constant tension. She thought of Debra as the brave one. She got out.

Where Edith had once obeyed Velma's every edict, going forward, she gave her a wide berth. Edith began to exert herself. She went to school functions. She stood next to her husband at sports events. People saw he had a wife. They were enamored of her accent. She enjoyed being out of the house. Away from Velma. Whether it was her actions that precipitated the promotion or not, Walter became principal of the largest high school in the district.

Edith recalls these things after Alberta leaves the house. She convinces herself Walter is the victim. He'd been a victim all his life under Velma's rule. She understands it is her job now to make everything neat again, organized. The house has to be spotless for when the police let her husband come home.

She takes a bath and washes her hair, then stands in the bedroom for the longest time trying to figure out what to wear. Velma always laid out Edith's clothes. Every day. Edith did the best she could while Velma was in the hospital, enduring her criticisms for always wearing the wrong thing. But now that Velma was dead, unable to judge her, the choices seem even more difficult. Now it is up to Edith herself to make decisions. Taking all the clothes from the living room back to the bedroom, she sorts through until she found the dullest colors she owns, three shades of blue, and puts them on. A skirt, a blouse, and a sweater.

In the kitchen, she puts dishes back in the cupboard. She puts Walter's books back where they belong, all the science fiction paperbacks, none of which Edith had ever seen him read. She dusts and vacuums. She puts away the cans of vegetables from the delivery, labels forward, in alphabetical order, careful not to let any of them touch. She puts the pork chops in one refrigerator drawer, the chicken in another, all the beef on a shelf. Though she is hungry, only when her tasks are accomplished does she cook dinner. Liver and onions. Edith detests liver, but she cooks it. It is Wednesday. Wednesday is liver and onions night, and if Walter is let out, she knows he'll be expecting it. She eats her portion and leaves the rest. When Walter does not show up, she throws it away.

CHAPTER 24

Tired from lack of sleep, the long drive to Pennsylvania and her visit with Edith, Alberta has one more stop before going home. At 3:30 in the afternoon, she sits at a table in the county jail. Walter's arrest had been made on the thinnest of evidence. A witness saw Alby get into his car. He had no alibi and the blood type on the jacket matched Alby's. He'd been denied bail for his own protection. People tend to take justice into their own hands when children are violated and killed.

Walter is escorted in. He sits down directly across from her, head high, posture straight. He wears clothes issued by the jail for prisoners: A wrinkled gray shirt tucked into gray trousers, both of which are too large for his thin frame. He presents himself, however, as if he's in a suit and tie. He folds his hands in front of him on the table. Alberta studies him, looking for any break in the façade.

"You were at the house when they came for me," he says. "You understand I've been told not to talk about the case."

"I'm Assistant District Attorney Alberta Higgins."

"A relation to Albert Higgins."

Alberta does her best to not show any expression. "Yes. But I'm not here to talk about this case. I'd like to talk with you about Spirit Lake, Mr. Stem."

His expression shifts, almost imperceptibly. "I don't understand."

"What can you tell me about the boys at the lake? The ones you took under your wing."

"Can you be more specific?" he asks.

The exchange so far is almost conversational except for the absence of any tangible emotion on either part.

"Anything that comes to mind. Let's focus on the summer of 1960."

"The drowning in the marsh. That's what you want to talk about."

"In some regards, yes."

"In all regards, it was a tragedy. Bright boys. A deep loss for the families."

Though his words seem sincere, Alberta can detect no empathy from him. "You were close to Peter Eastman?"

"As close as I was to any of them."

"You were there when the boys were found."

"I don't care to talk about that. I've tried to put those images out of my mind. It was nothing I would wish on anyone. Tragic."

"It wasn't the first time a young boy drowned in Spirit Lake, was it?"

"It didn't occur in Spirit Lake proper," he corrects her. "It was in the marsh."

"I see. My mistake. Let's talk about Samuel Conner."

"I don't like to think about that, either."

"Yes, but let's talk about it for a minute." Alberta feigns compassion. "You were a teenager then. Lived alone out there all winter and then in the spring all these kids descend on you."

"I challenge your word choice," he says, mildly condescending. "They did not descend. They arrived and I was happy to see them. It was lonely out there, as you say, in the winter."

"Tell me about Sammy."

Walter does not hesitate, speaking with an air of indifference. "I don't remember him that well. He was so much younger than me. It was the Conners' first summer, maybe their second, so we hadn't had time to get to know them well. They built a couple of years after Vogels and Monroes. If I am remembering correctly."

"I read in the newspaper account that all the boys were skinny dipping the night it happened."

"Yes. Someone should have stopped us. If we had been in the lake, it might have ended differently. But we were in the spring. It was so deep. Cold."

"I see. Would have been different in shallow water. How did you think it happened?"

Walter does not avert his eyes from hers. "I don't care to talk about it."

She is careful to mimic his blank expression. "Please."

He slowly blinks.

She waits.

"We were roughhousing. Dunking. When we all got out of the water, the young Conner boy wasn't among us. We thought maybe he'd gotten out and gone home or was hiding in the woods. As a trick." Walter's demeanor never changes. He relays events absent inflection. "We called out. When he wasn't at the cottage everyone started to search. All night. Men at the water, women and children searching the woods and shoreline, calling out. He could have been too afraid to come out for causing such a fuss."

"It sounds frightening."

He does not respond.

Alberta sits without speaking for a moment, watching Walter, who waits for another question. His eyes hold hers in an unrelenting grip until he finally smiles a little and shifts his gaze to his hands, the hands that have not moved the entire time.

"Did you find Sammy's body, Walter?"

This startles him, and he looks at her almost in disbelief. She perks, thinks she's on to something.

"Strangers don't often call me by my first name."

"I'm sorry." Her hopes fall. "Mr. Stem."

"My father found it. I retrieved it."

"That must have been traumatic for you," Alberta adds.

"Is that what you came here to ask me? Was finding a young boy's body traumatic for me? Was finding two more dead boys years later traumatic? I assure you it was." His angry words seem appropriate yet carry no corresponding emotion.

"I believe that's all I need right now, Mr. Stem." He stands when she stands, a polite gesture. "Are they treating you well?" she asks.

"I have no complaints," he says.

Alberta leaves the jail confident that Walter Stem is involved in all four deaths.

CHAPTER 25

1938. The morning after Sammy Conner went missing, men from all around the lake joined the search. Late in the day, Walter's father, Eugene, came home from a job he'd been on for weeks, furious to find strangers traipsing over his property. Shotgun in hand, he demanded they all leave. If the boy was dead, the spring would give him up when it was damn good and ready to. No one argued. They all left.

By appearance alone, Eugene Stem was threatening. His face bore the remnants of blows delivered throughout his childhood, pockmarks of illness and acne, and a scar from a bramble patch that ripped his cheek running from a neighbor's hen house. There were disproportions about him as if he'd been concocted from scrap parts. He seemed to be all chest and no gut with massive arms and lanky, slightly bowed legs. His head sat on his shoulders like whoever built him forgot to give him a neck. He'd survived the trenches of WWI having been shot twice, once in the leg, the other bullet grazing his head, leaving a rutted striped scar above his right ear where the hair refused to grow back. No one would mistake Eugene Stem for anything but the violent man he was.

Sammy's body emerged three days later, hung up on one of the pilings under Stem's landing, a six-foot platform jutting out over the narrow channel.

Eugene was the first to see the bloated, naked body and hollered to Walter, all of fourteen, who peered over the edge of the embankment and dropped to his knees. "Pull it out," Eugene demanded, throwing a coil of rope at Walter's feet. Walter gasped.

Walter paced the landing and the bank trying not to throw up, trying to wish himself anywhere but there, trying to figure out how to get the body out without actually touching it. Knowing full well his father watched his every move and expression, he fought back his revulsion and worked the problem.

He secured one end of the rope to a post and took it into the water with him. Sliding down the bank a few feet from the body, he lost his footing, slipped, and went into the water face first. Clinging to the rope, he found footing in the cold clay, frigid spring water flowing about his chest. He pulled himself under the landing, bracing his back against one of the pilings. Sammy's body, hung up on the other piling, rocked in the water face down, his head leaning against the mud of the bank like a pillow. It crossed Walter's mind to just pry him loose and let him drift into Spirit Lake.

Eugene stomped the boards above Walter's head. "What's taking so long?"

The cold water stung as he gathered the rope. He knew he had to wrap it around the body under the arms and tie it off. He had to touch it. Feel the cold skin. Walter braced his feet firmly against the piling and the slick clay bank for support. It took every nerve he had to reach under Sammy's body with the rope. He gagged. One of his feet slid, and he automatically reached out, accidentally grabbing Sammy's arm. He instantly let go but not fast enough. The corpse dislodged from the piling and flopped against him, wrapping around him as if seeking shelter, as if Sammy were alive, thankful for rescue. Walter threw up as he tied the body off and pushed it free face down drifting out from under the landing where it rolled belly up, an arm rising and falling, waving. At Walter.

Walter panicked and scrambled out of the water using the rope to pull himself up the bank, repeatedly slipping in the clay, his hands bleeding from rope splinters. Collapsing to the grass, he tried to catch his breath, to pull himself together, to not cry or scream or charge at his father, jump on his chest until every rib was broken, his heart and lungs crushed.

"Finish it!" Eugene yelled.

Walter stood up on shaky legs and tried pulling the body up the bank, but his arms failed him. Eugene pushed him aside. With one swift yank, Sammy Conner's white, bloated body flopped onto the grass, eyes open, mouth agape. Even in that state, it was clearly Sammy, the diminutive, shy little boy who was always running to catch up. Walter threw up again. Eugene turned his back and walked away.

CHAPTER 26

Aunties take a peculiar place in grieving families. Even friends who know how close Alberta was to Alby seem to focus on her brother and his wife. Alby was their child, not hers, and oh, the pain of losing a child. How will they ever survive? Her grief could not, should not, compare, and she doesn't do or say anything to draw attention to her own broken heart, a term used too often for inconsequential disappointments. But this loss, one of the only two children she would ever hold as newborns, one of two boys she expected to watch grow up, raise families of their own - this loss cracked her heart to the core. She didn't know anything could hurt so deeply. Losing her parents hadn't even been as painful. She had her brother Michael to help her through that. Together they identified the bodies after their car wreck. Together they made funeral arrangements. Together they greeted their parents' lifelong friends at the visitation, consoling them, listening to stories. Together they tried to remember names of distant relatives arriving to pay respects to two people they hadn't seen in years. But this time, Michael has his wife. He has to console his remaining son. He has his hands full. And Alberta doesn't fit into the picture.

At the visitation, Alberta is on task running interference when mothers sob on Erin's shoulder, not out of grief for her but terrified to think it might ever happen to them. Erin is strong, she's holding up, but Alberta has noticed medication on her nightstand.

Alberta leaves Michael's that night exhausted but too preoccupied to sleep. Though nearly midnight, she throws a load of laundry in the wash. She stares into her closet, wondering what to wear to Alby's funeral the next day. Most of her wardrobe is black and gray, so that isn't the issue. They're all work clothes. Suits. How could she wear a work suit to bury him? She pulls a sweater out of a drawer. A green one. A turtleneck. She takes a pendant out of her jewelry box. A silver crescent moon, one she bought at Fels Planetarium in Philadelphia the year before when she took Alby and Tommy into the city. She'd worn it the last time she was with Alby.

Alberta meets with her boss early the next morning, before Alby's funeral. DA Groves is an exacting man hiding behind a perpetually rumpled suit. His tie always has a spot on it. His shoes always need polishing. He's short with small hands and a receding hairline. He smokes too much and rarely smiles. A man easily underestimated by strangers, he is highly respected by his peers, judges, and the people who work for him.

Alberta lays out everything she knows so far about the case and where she thinks it's going. He listens, but she can tell he's not onboard.

"Look," he says, "I hear what you're saying about the boys in Michigan, but if you're trying to put together a pattern, how does Alby fit in? You say Stem knew those boys in Michigan. Interacted with them on a regular basis. There isn't any connection like that here. You said it yourself. A man like that doesn't just suddenly pick some kid at random off the street. And the timing doesn't fit.

Twenty-two years between the first two incidents? Then ten years between then and now?"

"His mother was the only thing holding him back. She died. Maybe . . ."

"According to you, that jean jacket is part of his M.O., so there had to be premeditation. He would have worn it knowing what he was planning to do, who his target was, where they'd be. Albert's case looks like a crime of convenience. Some sicko taking advantage of an easy target. We're holding Stem, but I seriously don't think we have a case. I need you on this. I need you working."

"I am working."

"You're chasing the wind. Those were accidents. We have a homicide. I need your head in the game. Here, Higgins. One more week," he says. "Then, I need you back." He let out a long sigh. "But right now? You have a funeral to attend. Go. Be with your family."

The day after the funeral, Alberta stops at her brother's before heading back to Michigan. Michael argues with her to stay, to work the case at home, but she leaves anyway. "What if I need you here?" he asks. "I need you. Does that matter at all?"

"I'm following this thing to the end. I'm doing it for you. For Alby."

"Don't kid yourself. You're doing it for you."

It's only 45 degrees when she arrives in Michigan. She stops at Anglers for dinner, hoping to run into Tucker. She wants to absorb some of whatever it is that makes him so comfortable, but he isn't there. She orders a basket of perch and a Manhattan, sits in her corner booth, and eats in silence. Colleen tries to spark a conversation but can tell it's a dead end.

Returning to the cabin, Alberta sees it's been cleaned, the bed made with fresh sheets, clean towels on the rack, and another vase of fresh daffodils on the table. Exhausted in mind and body, she changes into her flannel pajamas and crawls into bed.

Lying there wanting nothing more than sleep, she realizes she hadn't spent any time with Tommy. She hadn't gone to his room. Talked with him. Asked how he was doing. She hardly remembered seeing him. She calls Michael, waking him up.

"I made it. Back to Michigan."

"OK."

She hesitates. "I didn't spend any time with Tommy."

"I know." There is no empathy in his tone.

"I'll make it up to him."

"Yes. You will."

Michael hangs up.

Sleep comes quickly, but fitfully.

CHAPTER 27

Saturday morning, upstairs in the Hodges' cottage, Alberta tries to collect her thoughts, pushing down a seething undercurrent of rage toward Walter Stem; toward Dick and Evelyn Hodges for being so complacent when their son died; toward her boss for doubting her; toward life in all its unfairness.

Down at the beach, Evelyn sits in a chair, a blanket wrapped around her shoulders. Dick and the boys wait under the window on the patio smoking cigarettes, the smoke curling up, their muffled voices indiscernible. The two younger men glance about as if something was about to pounce on them. Alberta doesn't yet know which one of the sons hasn't come.

She what their boy suffered. Did they wonder if fear had time to take hold in the moments before death or if some God saved him that horror? How had these people been able to live the past ten years, waking each day to the grief, brushing their teeth, buttering toast; Dick watching vats of milk curdle into cottage cheese every day at the creamery; Evelyn walking into a cottage knowing Tyler would never be there? What miraculous element in each of them held them together, if not to each other, then at least within themselves, when all Alberta wants to do is stand in a gale, unravel completely, and let the winds carry her bits away?

Alberta looks about the room, trying to imagine five kids running through in pajamas, fresh from the bathtub, wet hair, smelling of soap. That was her favorite time of day when Michael's boys were little. They'd be sleepy after a day of bicycles and tricycles and running with the dog. They'd cuddle next to her on the couch and watch TV, or she'd read to them. At some point in its history, she thinks, this cottage must have known love. It had to have held laughter within its walls, or maybe she's projecting her life onto it, something she knows she has to stop doing.

She'd seen Alby in a dream that morning, as if he was with her, never gone. He was petting her dog, the one she mourned for years, still mourns, and in seeing the dog knew Alby was dead, too. Still, she clung to the moment as one does in a dream when the dreamer is aware. She listened so carefully as he spoke, but could no longer recall the inconsequential words, yet the lilt of his voice lingered with her still. The yearning to hear it again, now, mid-day, feels cruelly potent. Did they still hear their boy? Did Tyler still haunt them, or had memory of him thinned over the years? The thought of Alby thinning, her grief thinning with it, steeled her nerve. Pain had always fed her. Gave her strength. She looks again at the men below, these men who'd given up, accepted without question, who'd not fought for the truth, finding safety in denial. No more. She was going to crack them open, peel away their souls, and show them the truth. Where they had been cowards, she is a warrior. She would take no prisoners.

She calls through the window to the men. "Jim? Are you down there? How about you start us off."

Dick says he'll go first. "Then, I'll let you know if you're talking to my boys or not."

"I want to see Jim, then Ron, or is that Mark? Then you. I'll talk to Evelyn when she's ready." Alberta closes the window ending the debate.

She flips her notepad to a fresh page as Jim scuffs slowly up the steps. A little over six feet, his hair is light brown and too long, his bushy mustache disproportionate to his weak chin. At twenty-five, he is an overgrown boy pretending to be a man. He sits down across from Alberta with a thud of indifference. His hands fidget as he speaks, his answers brief and vague.

Alberta's greatest flaw is impatience, something she'd wrestled with throughout her career. *You have to let them get there on their own* her dad used to tell her. The rest of his advice also rattled through her thoughts. *Let the story go where it goes. No leading it. Assumptions are often wrong and can easily blind a person to the truth.* But Alberta is working from one very specific assumption: Walter Stem is a murderer. And she needs it to be right.

She tells Jim to run through the last day as he remembers it, the day before Tyler drowned. Jim starts talking the way someone does when they don't have anything interesting to say, listing things without the connective tissue of emotion. He'd had breakfast. He washed the dock. He hauled out the life jackets and lake gear. He took Mark and Ronny skiing.

"What was Tyler up to at this point?"

"In the dingy, seeing how fast he could spin it."

"And a fight in the afternoon?" she asks. "Something that got you all grounded. How'd it start?"

"I don't know. I was out on the lake in Wagner's boat. I heard it started on the rafts when Tyler said something he shouldn't have said to Steve."

"Like what?"

Jim squirms. "Called him something."

Alberta waits.

"Ty didn't entirely understand what he was saying, but he knew enough not to be surprised when Steve nailed him. Called him Limp Dick."

Alberta cocked her head. "Why would he say that?"

"He heard us call him that. One of the girls down the road used to give the older boys handjobs. It's what she called him. Steve could never get it up."

"Who was the girl?" When he says Debra Stem, the hairs on her neck rise. "How old was she?"

"Fifteen, maybe. Don't really know. Spooky chick."

"How so?"

He shrugs.

"What can you tell me about the Stems?"

"I don't know. Walter taught me how to re-rig the steering on the Lyman, our ski boat."

"You called him Walter, not Mr. Stem?"

"Only at the lake. Nowhere else. Never in school."

"I see."

"I was eight, maybe nine the summer he let me take a small trolling motor apart in a shed at their place. He explained every piece I took off it, what it did. Then he made me put it back together by myself. It took the whole summer, a lot of taking it apart and trying again, but I finally got the motor back together and running. I'm a mechanic now, probably because of him."

"You and Walter Stem got along?"

"I suppose. What does it matter?"

Alberta wears an innocuous smile. "It doesn't." She tells him to walk through his steps the morning the boys went missing.

He says he went into Frys' back door. "My dad wanted everyone over at our place to organize a search." Called out and fell on his ass when Laura walked into the kitchen in a long tee shirt and nothing else, her hair looking like she'd just crawled out of bed.

"I don't understand," Alberta says. "You fell?"

Jim thinks. "I guess my feet were muddy."

"Why muddy?"

"It stormed the night before. Everything was wet." He pauses. "I slipped on something," he finally says. "On Frys' porch. Stepped on something slippery. Wet. Clothes, I think. I went down hard. Got mud on my jeans. Most of it was dry, but I was sitting on something wet. Shoes. Wet sneakers. Yeah. Steve's shoes."

"Why do you say they were his?"

"He has huge ass feet. His shoes were like boats."

"So, their floor was muddy even before anyone went out to look for the boys?"

Jim shrugs.

"Do you think Steve Fry was capable of doing any serious damage to anyone?"

"Steve? He was a bully and a pain in the ass, but no, not really. I remember he caught hell from his dad that morning. Bill walked in and cussed Laura out for prancing around in front of me half-naked. I tell him what's going on, to meet at our place, and just as I leave, Steve walks into the kitchen. He's got a black eye, and I see Bill smack the hell out of him. I don't know why."

"Did that happen a lot? Bill hitting Steve?"

"Let's just say it wasn't unusual."

"Meaning?"

"Shit. His dad was never around and when he was, it was like Steve was just a pain in his ass. You asked about Stem. He was probably more of a dad to Steve than Bill ever was. I mean, I'd be over there, to Stem's, once in a while, but Steve, when he was little? He was always over there."

"How little are we talking?"

"Hell, I don't know. Second, maybe third grade. Then it just stopped." Jim glances out the window. "The rest of us ended up over there when we got in trouble for something and our mothers were too fed up to deal with us. But Steve refused. And he was always in trouble. Picking fights. Mouthing off."

"So, Walter Stem was the disciplinarian around here when your dads were gone all week."

"Yeah."

"Were you ever in trouble with him, disciplined by Walter Stem?"

"Of course. We all were at one time or another."

"How so?"

"He'd work our asses off splitting wood, mowing, gardening for his mother."

"That was punishment?"

"It is when you're a kid."

Alberta smiled. "Any chance Bill gave Steve the black eye?"

Jim doesn't hesitate. "No. It was never more than a hard slap, at least as far as I ever knew. Just to get his attention. Could have gotten it that afternoon in the fight at the beach, I guess."

Alberta takes some notes then asks who went to the Stem house that morning, but Jim shrugs again. She asks him to try to remember something. "Who was the first person to call it an accident?"

Jim scowls.

"At the marsh," Alberta says. "In all the confusion. Who was the first person to say accident?"

"I don't know. I don't know who actually said it. We all just thought it. I mean, how could it have been anything else?" It's clear he'd never entertained another possibility.

Alberta is done with him. As Jim hits the stairs, he turns. "There's a good chance we'd have burned the place to the ground without Walter Stem."

By late June of 1960, summer's routine had become monotonous. On one particular Tuesday, like every other day so far that summer, Laura Fry and Linda Wagner, already the color of butterscotch, sunbathed out on a raft, their scratchy transistor radio barely audible on shore. The Wagner girls were inside attempting to fend off boredom with TV game shows, Dr. Pepper and shoestring licorice. Penny was with Evelyn at the house in town doing laundry. Gert and Mason stayed in town for the week. Al was performing a house inspection, something he did occasionally to feel useful. Merci, Gladys, Betsy, and Marilyn played bridge at Vogels', cocktails in hand, fans at their backs. It had been hot all week with little let up at night. Summer had come early and with it, puddling humidity.

All the boys except Peter were playing baseball on a makeshift diamond. With only nine of them, they didn't have teams so much as a rotation system, an outfielder batting as the bases filled. In the middle of an inning, as Mark was about to pitch to Kevin, Peter began pacing the distance from home plate, a boat cushion, to first base, a Frisbee, picking it up and moving it three paces closer in. Steve, being the first baseman, didn't appreciate Peter's interference. He picked up the newly placed Frisbee and put it back where it was originally, yelling at Peter to leave it the hell alone. Peter moved it back, explaining it wasn't regulation distance and how could they play that way. Mark pitched, Kevin hit long and ran to first where Steve was ripping the Frisbee out of Peter's hands, knocking him down in the process, flinging first base into the lake. Kevin sidestepped the ruckus and ran all the bases, ticking Steve off even more. Jim yelled at Steve to go get first base out of the water, and Steve started cussing at Jim. All this occurred without an adult in sight save Walter, who stood just down the way, arms folded, watching. The boys started taunting *Fight! Fight! Fight!* Walter's sharp voice silenced them all.

"Steven. James. The landing. Now."

The boys all looked across the lawn to Walter, standing straight, his Panama hat shading his eyes, white short-sleeved shirt tucked in tight to tan chinos, black canvas shoes. Like a uniform, his clothes never changed.

Walking like convicted felons, Jim and Steve followed Walter toward the channel leaving behind a less rowdy ball game.

Taking the path through the woods at the channel, they emerged onto an expansive well-manicured lawn flowing from the channel's edge to the bright yellow Stem house. A collection of colorful rocking chairs lined the long porch. Two lovely flowerbeds flanked the steps. As the threesome approached the landing, a screen door smacked closed. Velma appeared in a pink and green flowered sundress, hands clasped in front of her, watching from the porch.

Walter led the boys to the red landing. Steve and Jim walked out onto it, keenly aware of the task ahead. Steve dumped two scrub brushes out of a bucket and lowered it into the water with a rope, pulled it up and dumped it all out. Both boys grabbed a scrub brush, got on their knees and started scrubbing, cussing under their breath.

Velma settled into one of the rockers, keeping an eye on the boys. When Edith came outside with two tumblers of Kool Aid, her eyes on the landing, Velma told her to take it back inside. Edith obeyed.

CHAPTER 28

JUL18 - I listen to her some days and it's like some loose string of her soul got caught in a briar bush on the other side. If that thread were to break, everything would unravel.

"Take me down to the dock." Evelyn slowly rises and crosses the room with her walker. Winded by that little exertion, she plops into the wheelchair. "Where's Jimmy? Tell him I want to go out on the boat."

Evelyn had been shrinking all her life, disappearing physically and emotionally, but now she is all of ninety-two pounds. Penn maneuvers the chair out the door, down the side steps and the steps from the patio to the grass. She positions it on the pontoon in the shade of the awning.

"How about a loop around the lake?" Penn asks.

"Absolutely!"

Penn packs her mother tight in her chair with pillows, sets the brake, and yanks the pull cord on the Evinrude. It starts right up.

"I always loved that sound," Evelyn says. "Remember how they'd never let you drive the boat? Not a boy. Must have pissed you off." It is just one of a hundred things her mother said that made Penn realize she'd never actually known her. She slowly backs away from the dock and starts to circle the shoreline.

"Straight across," Evelyn says. "Gun it!"

With the wheelchair firmly secured, Penn pushes to full throttle, and they plow ahead as fast as an awkward pontoon can, wind blowing the hair from their faces. She cuts the motor in the middle, and they drift to a stop.

"Let's go swimming," Evelyn says with a sly grin, making no effort to rise. "Where is everybody?"

"It's Wednesday, Mom. Everyone's gone."

"Used to be crowded every day. Before . . ." the thought dissipates.

They sit in silence, listening to distant cars pass on the east road. A dog barks somewhere. "Rabbit?" Evelyn shouts. "We forgot Rabbit. Rabbit! We'll come get you! Don't swim out! Stay, Rabbit. Stay!" Her eyes scan the shoreline then the thought evaporates, she rests her head against a pillow and sleeps.

Penn tries to imagine being in her early thirties on a pontoon with five kids all running end to end, taking flying leaps into the water, one kid on top of the other, fighting over inner tubes, blood-curdling screams as they gave chase swimming under the deck between the pontoons. Suddenly she's smiling. It had been fun. Playing like wild, mindless squirrels. Play. Something she'd forgotten about.

Evelyn awakens, immediately agitated. Penn starts the motor and heads back to the dock. Evelyn asks where they're going. "Turn around," she says in a panic. So much has changed on the lake, Evelyn doesn't recognize any of it. "You're going the wrong way. Where are we?" She tries to get out of the wheelchair, tugging at the pillows, trying to lift the wheelchair's footplates, but her foot gets stuck between them, and she cries out. Penn grabs her arm and throttles up, cutting the motor with enough inertia to slide onto the sand. She turns to her mother, speaking quietly while she frees her foot. "Look, Evelyn," she urges. "There's your cottage. You're home."

Evelyn calms almost immediately. "Where is everyone?" she asks. "Where'd everybody go?"

"They'll be back. Don't worry." Penn finds it easy now to lie.

"Where's Penny? Probably off with Peter. I'm so glad she found a friend out here."

Still some love left on the bone.

> July 20 - I miss Dad. Maybe he could tell me what the hell she's thinking. I have so many questions these days and there's no one to ask about it. I can't tell if anything she says really happened or if she's just making it up.

The smell of burning paper drifted up to Penn, who shot downstairs and found her mother sitting in front of the fireplace tearing pages from a magazine, crunching them up and tossing in them in, all the while humming Jingle Bells.

Several pages smoldered, too damp to fully ignite. Penn opens the flue, clears the unburned pieces away, pockets the matches, and takes her mother outside. Evelyn sits in the shade of the sugar maple, continuing to tear the magazine page by page, wadding them up, dropping them to the patio, still humming Jingle Bells.

"You used to do Christmas really well," Penn says, trying to distract her. "Decorations everywhere. It used to take Dad 'til March to find all the stuff you put away to make room."

Evelyn keeps tearing pages.

"Remember how you used to make him hang lights around the front porch? And you did all the Christmas shopping, even for yourself, made tins and tins of cookies, and cocoa whenever we came in from the snow."

Evelyn shows no recognition.

"Mom! Damn it! Stop it!" Penn takes the magazine away and goes back inside to turn fans on, clear out the smoke.

Sometime very early in the morning the first Christmas after Tyler died, Evelyn left the house. Dick went after her leaving Jim to make the traditional Christmas pancakes.

Driving through countryside, fresh snow bright under dawning skies, he imagined happy families in all the houses he passed. Christmas trees alight in windows. Tired parents. Excited kids. He used to have that happy family.

He passed wide, deep barren fields interrupted by far tree lines, a vast emptiness, cold, fallow.

He was relieved to see someone had plowed Spirit Marsh Road, probably someone spending the holiday at their cottage. Then he thought about Stems. It was plowed for them, but no farther. He followed a set of tracks to the cottage, parking next to Evelyn's car. Smoke rose from the chimney.

He was hesitant to interfere with her, unsure what state of mind she'd be in. He ventured through the snow down the outside steps, peering in the window. Evelyn stood in the glow of the fireplace, wrapped in a blanket, hanging an ornament on a lone pine bough stuck in a vase. She looked up, saw him, and smiled.

It was cold inside, the fire not enough to cut the chill. "There's coffee in the thermos," she told him. He poured some into a mug, wondering what to do next, what to say, wondering what gave her the right to think she was the only one in pain.

"I won't make it in town," she said without any particular emotion, just a statement of fact.

"And it's easier here?" he said, trying not to lash out. "We're all struggling."

"Remember the year we spent Christmas out here?" A faint smile slid across her face. "You took the day off work to secretly haul all the packages out and open up for the weekend. You set up a tree and we got a sitter so we could decorate it together."

"Yeah," he said, wrapping his arms around her shoulders. "The kids rode sleds down the hill. Tyler was still a baby. How'd we manage that?"

"We just did." Evelyn leaned into her husband. It was the first expression of love between them since long before the accident.

"It's Christmas, Evelyn. The kids need you at home."

"No, they don't. They'll be fine."

"Yes. They do. We all do."

She stepped away, pulling the blanket tighter against his expectations. She was a woman extracted from her life and exiled to limbo. Nothing made sense anymore. There were moments during the day, every day, when she forgot she had children, when she forgot how old she was, when she felt she was barely thirteen wondering if she'd forgotten about a math exam, when she felt old, very old, and everyone she'd ever known was dead and gone. The one thing that always crept in to pull her back was the memory of Tyler, his grin, the shape of his hand in hers, the way he'd melt into her lap when he was tired. Then she'd remember he was dead and the rest of them were alive, waiting on her to take care of them, making demands on her, and she wished them all gone. It wasn't about wishing them harm, it was about making them vanish as if they'd never existed.

"I'm taking you home now," Dick said. He stirred the fire and tossed the two semi-burned logs out in the snow. Collecting the hot coals in the ash hod, he emptied it in the snow as well. He wiped the mugs out with snow. He closed the chimney damper. "If we go now, we can beat the next storm. They say it could be a foot or more." He gathered her coat and the thermos. "Ready," he said.

Evelyn's eyes welled up. "I can't leave him alone on Christmas."

Dick held the coat for her to slip into. "Every Christmas he'd ever remember was in our living room in town. He's right there with his brothers and sister, waiting on us. Waiting on you."

"No" she said. "He's not." Relenting, Evelyn draped the blanket over a chair, pulled on her coat and boots, and walked upstairs and out the door without another word. Dick followed her to town, expecting her to turn around at some point. She didn't.

They arrived home to find the breakfast dishes washed and put away. The aroma of pancakes still hung in the air. In the living room, wearing a new sweatshirt, Mark fed wrappings into the fireplace. They'd opened their gifts on their own. Ron was curled in the big chair, reading a new book. Penny busied herself assembling Barbie furniture she'd bought for herself with money from her dad. Jim sprawled on the couch, staring at the fire. His gift was a card saying they'd go shopping for a used car next week.

Though their mother's entrance brought no grand moment of reunion, it delivered a subtle shift in atmosphere, like an error corrected. Penny retrieved the last two packages from under the tree and gave them to her parents. Dick opened his gloves. Evelyn smiled and opened hers. "It's a sachet," Penny explained. "I made it in girl scouts. Lavender. If you squish it around you can really smell it." Evelyn gave it a squeeze, put it to her nose and took a deep inhale. She thanked her daughter then said she was going to make hot cocoa.

"Can't," Jim said, glaring at her. "Out of milk." An unforgivable crime.

Evelyn retreated to her room. It was the last they saw of her that Christmas. Dick grounded Jim for the rest of the holiday. They didn't go car shopping until spring.

CHAPTER 29

Alberta stretches, waiting for the next interview with the Hodges boys. The screen door smacks below, and someone takes the steps in rapid succession. A young man walks in, thick in the middle with skinny legs and no butt. He goes directly to the couch and sits down. "So," he says. "Here I am."

"Which one are you," she asks.

"Ron. Mark won't be here."

"And why's that?"

"He just won't."

Alberta flips through her notebook and begins. "So, Ron, you were thirteen the summer your little brother died. Makes you twenty-three now."

Ron nods.

She tells him she wants to get a sense of the kids at the lake that summer and asks about Greg Wagner.

"Hell of a water skier. Wagners had the best ski boat, and he was good about taking us out. He never whipped me in the weeds like Jim did."

"Whip you?"

"You know. Speed up and then cut sharp so you're flying so fast you can't hang on anymore and you fly into the marsh which is full of blood sucking leaches. Greg didn't do that. He was a fag but still a good guy."

Alberta glares at him.

She asks if they all knew Greg was a homosexual, and he laughs. He said Tyler was the first one to really notice. "Laura Fry fell water skiing and her bikini top came off, floated away. Everybody in the boat was staring, you know, to get a good look. Greg couldn't have cared less. Tyler said something like *You don't like girls, do you?* I mean, how would he even think to say something like that? And Greg laughs it off saying *No, but your brother's real cute.* We all laughed our asses off, but honestly, I don't think we put it together then. I don't know, we just weren't aware of stuff like that yet."

She asks what he thought about Steve Fry.

Ron shakes his head. "What's to tell? He had an inferiority complex. Probably always will until he tells his dad to go to hell. Bill Fry's an ass."

Alberta makes a note, vocalizing as she writes. "Bill Fry is an ass." She looks up at Ron, trying to imagine him as a teenager, wondering if he'd always been so blunt. "I want to talk about that Sunday," she says. "The day before your brother died."

"Nothing unusual. I remember it stunk right from the start, but like I said. Nothing unusual. I got in a fight with my dad. Somebody at work gave him a slalom ski, and he brought it out with him Saturday. He handed it to me with this big grin like it was something special. It was still in the hall on Sunday, so my mom told me to take it outside."

"And, you hopped to it." Alberta half grins.

"Right. I left it there. Then my dad hands it to me and says to take it down to the lake and try it out, and I just walked away, left him there holding that damn ski. Christ, everything we had was secondhand. The Lyman was old. The motor on the Lyman was old. Every boat we had, except the dinghy that he built, was second or third hand. It was embarrassing. Even the cars were both second hand.

Never bought anything new. Mom yelled at me to get a job and buy my own damn ski if it was so important. Now, how in the hell was I going to get a summer job when I was only thirteen and stuck at the lake all damn summer?"

"You didn't like it out here much, did you?"

Ron resituates himself and grumbles something.

"Well?" she asks.

"What does that have to do with anything?"

"Nothing. Just out of curiosity, what happened to the ski?"

"Dad put it in the trashcan out back. It was gone later on."

"Somebody took it. Somebody not too proud to have an old ski somebody threw out."

Ron hangs his head for a moment. His knee starts to bounce.

"OK." Alberta leafs back to her notes from Penny.

"Walter Stem was your principal. Did you ever have any problems with him?"

"Used to creep us out that he monitored the showers. Walking the locker room after gym or swim practice. Standing at the office doorway watching the shower entrance. If he wasn't in his office or patrolling the halls, he was in the locker room. I swear it. That man was everywhere."

"Why do you think he did that? Hung out in the locker room?"

"We were hormonal boys. How else you going to keep us in check?"

Alberta asks him to elaborate.

"You know. Fights and stuff. And if somebody wasn't on us, we'd be late for our next class."

"What else do you remember about Walter, out here, at the lake? I heard he kept a pretty tight rein on you boys."

"He tried to make me work like the others, but I flat out refused. No way I was going to chop his damn wood." His knee stops. "And I didn't give a shit about rebuilding motors or painting his chairs. I could never figure out why the rest of them did that shit. What was he going to do if they refused?"

Alberta hesitates. "So, what did you do?"

"I read books."

Alberta perks a bit.

"I was nine or ten when my mom dropped me at their door. We'd probably been driving her nuts, and she had to split us up, or I'd done something to piss her off. Anyway, she took me to Stems'. Velma, the old lady, let me in. Freaky old woman. Walter told me to go out to the landing so I walked through the house, across the grass and I see the bucket and scrub brush and I swore there was no way in hell I was washing his damn landing, and I go out there, and there's a book in the bucket. I remember picking it up and looking back, but no one was there. I sat down and spent the whole day reading it. THE MARTIAN CHRONICLES. Walter introduced me to Ray Bradbury. Science fiction. By the end of the summer, I was reading Philip K. Dick and Kurt Vonnegut. I read books. All the time I was over there. I read."

Alberta cocks her head and lets out a little laugh. "You read books? No hard labor?"

"Yeah. I teach English. At my old junior high."

She changes gears and asks him what he thought happened to Tyler and Peter.

After a moment, he says he thinks Tyler probably dared Peter. "It had to be a dare or Ty would never have gone out in the wind like that. He hated wind. Freaked him out. It had to be a dare."

"So, you believe they went there together on purpose."

Ronny looks puzzled. "Well, yeah."

"And you're certain they were alone. None of the other boys went along. You didn't go with him."

"What the hell! No, I didn't go with them! We'd been frogging two, maybe three times that summer. Ty made a huge ass fuss every time because he couldn't go yet. We didn't have a lot of rules, but that was one of the biggest. No frogging at night till you're ten. Are we done here?"

Alberta nods and Ron goes downstairs leaving her with the sense Walter Stem had a profound impact on Ron and Jim's life choices. A tiny tendril of doubt begins weaving its way into everything she wants to believe about Walter.

CHAPTER 30

Alberta hears Dick come up the steps. He pauses on the first landing. She hears a heavy sigh and more footsteps heading up. Together, they watch Jim and Ron push the pontoon into the water. Dick says he'd give anything to listen to what they were talking about.

Alberta surveys Dick. He looks old for fifty, gray already taken over. His coloring isn't good. Too pallid. Their silence echoed with all things unsaid. Alberta could have apologized for what she was doing, but that would serve no purpose. She wasn't there to ingratiate herself into their lives. She was there to get information and get out. "Are you ready to begin, Mr. Hodges?"

"Dick." Without turning around, he asks who she is. Exactly.

"I'm an assistant district attorney for Bucks County, Pennsylvania. Do you want to sit down?"

"What are you doing here? In Michigan."

"Let's just get to it, shall we?"

Dick begins what seems like a well-rehearsed list of events. "I was in the kitchen drinking coffee the morning before the boys . . ." He stumbles a bit but continues. ". . . Sunday. The day before they died. Penny came in to say she was eating at Peter's. The older three boys were still in bed. Tyler was playing solitaire in the corner. I don't know where my wife was. I was tired. A machine broke down and had us running behind at the creamery all week. I only came out on weekends." He continues with his litany of events dispassionately, as if ticking off a list. "Sometimes Friday night, usually Saturday morning. Evelyn called that week to harp on the kids. She was having a tough time. It was a rough summer. She. . ." He stops talking and looks out to the lake. His speech slows. "They could be a mob, shouting, shoving. I should have gone out right after work Friday, but I didn't even get home until after eight, and I was too damn tired." He glances back to Alberta, expecting understanding but sees only indifference. "I didn't make it out until middle of the day Saturday. I had to mow in town. Anyway, so Sunday morning, Ronny blew a gasket."

"About the ski."

"He told you, eh? Well, can't say I blamed him. I'm a working stiff. We could barely afford this place, but everyone else out here had money to burn. The best new gear every year. Bill and Marty always competing with the latest and greatest boats, cars. I couldn't do that. The pressure got to Ronny. Always feeling second-class. Some kids can deal with stuff like that. He couldn't. That afternoon Marty buzzed the shoreline in his new boat, blew an air horn, making us all look. He came in so fast and hard his wake had all our boats bouncing against the docks. The older Fry girl was rocked off her air mattress. Swamped the canoe tossing his daughters in the water. Carl and Mason from next door headed down to the dock. I followed."

"They were the dentists?"

"Yeah. Carl took over the practice a couple years later. Anyway, everybody headed down to check out Marty's new toy. It all went haywire the moment Marty tossed the boat key to Greg, relinquishing control to a fifteen-year-old kid."

"Greg Wagner."

"Yeah. All the kids were clamoring to go first, and it was up to Greg to choose the water skiers for the inaugural run. He took Laura, Jimmy, and Mark leaving poor Steve Fry on the dock holding his ski."

"It sounds like you paid attention," Alberta says. "To the kids."

"Of course."

"It's just that I get the impression they were left on their own a lot."

"I watched. When I was here, I watched things."

"Wasn't it Steve who started a fight later?"

"I'm not sure I'd say that. Kids were crowding the dock, pushing to get in front. They all ended up in the water, it turned into a raft war, with a lot of muck slinging and shoving."

"Raft war?"

"We had two swim rafts anchored off our shore. Kids would break off into two groups, and they'd try to knock off the raft keeper. Like Capture the Flag. It was usually harmless, but this one got nasty fast. They got rough, hitting, shoving, dunking, screaming. I remember Mildred on the end of the dock yelling for Peter, yelling at us, like we could do anything about it. It was always better to let that kind of thing wind itself down. Marty finally had enough and blew his air horn."

Dick's gaze wanders the room as he talks. "When they all climbed out of the water, there were bloody shins, rug burns from the rafts, bruises. Some of the girls were crying. Greg pulled back in with the ski boat and Marty took the boat key."

Alberta listens without writing anything down. She hasn't asked him to tell him about the day. He just volunteered. He seemed to need to tell it.

"Like I said, I usually went back to town Sunday night, but that day, we all started drinking early. We ended up at Vogels. The kids were left to their own devices." He sneered a little, something Alberta read as a touch of self-loathing, but she couldn't be sure. "We started drinking ourselves into oblivion. All except Mildred and George. I think they took Peter and sought sanctuary in their cottage." His eyes fall to the floor then to Alberta. "They weren't drinkers." He looks back to the window, watching the pontoon cruise the shoreline.

Dick says all the boys started pulling together wood for a bonfire. We normally only did one the first weekend and the last. But they wanted a fire. I watched from the patio. They were piling branches into a teepee, then someone got pushed into it, and it fell apart. And I swear they were all at each other's throat like a pack of coyotes. All us dads charged down there. I yanked one of my kids out by the nape of the neck. Mark, I think. Marty pulled one of his boys out, and suddenly, from the middle of it, Tyler went flying out, flinging through the air like a rag doll. I remember he landed hard, rolled to a stop, and just laid there and didn't move. I ran over to him, thinking he was really hurt, but he pushed himself up, cussing a blue streak. I didn't know he knew half those words. We sent all the kids to their respective cottages and told them to stay there. Inside. Out of sight. We went back to our drinking, feeling entitled to a good buzz after all that. Later on, Gladys and Betsy got in an argument. Give them enough booze, and it was inevitable."

"Gladys Wagner and Betsy Fry."

"Yeah."

"You stayed over that night?"

"Yeah. I was tired. A little loaded."

"You normally went back to town on Sunday evening."

"Yeah. But like I said . . ."

"Yeah, I understand that. I suppose everyone pretty much knew everybody's schedule around here. Who came and went and when."

"I suppose. Carl and I usually went back Sunday night. So did Bill. Sometimes Marty would stick around."

"Carl Vogel, Bill Fry and Marty Wagner, right?"

"Yeah. Mondays were tough enough without driving from here."

"I see. But the party next door at the Vogels' kept you all here that Sunday night."

"Yeah."

"Who all was at the party?"

"Everybody."

"So, the Stems. Velma, Walter and Edith?"

"No. Everybody but them. They didn't do that. Oh, and Bill Fry. He was around earlier in the day but left."

"Was it a loud party? Would you have been able to hear it down the road at the Stems' place?"

"No and no. We were all out front. And we weren't rowdy or loud. If you're back at the spring by their place, you can't hear anything. Lots of pines back there. Natural buffer."

Alberta writes something and underlines it. "Why would Mildred Eastman come knocking on your door looking for her son at 5:30 in the morning?"

"She thought Peter might be with us."

"Did your daughter spend a lot of time with Peter Eastman?"

"I couldn't say really. I wasn't around during the week. When I was here, she didn't see him that much. Well, yeah she did. I guess. I don't know."

"Did you see who flung your son out of that fight at the wood pile?"

"Steve Fry."

"Would you say Tyler was injured by the incident?"

"No, I wouldn't say injured. Bruised, maybe."

"Steve's father, Bill, must have seen it. Did he get involved?"

"No. Bill wasn't there. He'd left by then. While the kids were skiing, maybe after. I don't know."

"OK. I see." Alberta flipped through some pages. "Sure you wouldn't rather sit, Dick?"

"I'm good."

"Did Tyler spend a lot of time with Peter?"

"I don't think so."

"So, not while you were around."

"Right."

"Would you say they were friends?"

"No."

"If not friends, would you say they didn't like each other?"

"No."

"Would Tyler have ever hurt Peter?"

Dick spins around. "No. He would not have intentionally hurt anyone. That's not who he was."

"How was it Tyler was out all night, and you didn't know it?"

Dick turns back to the window without answering.

"You were sleeping it off."

"Yeah."

"I know this is going to be difficult, but, I need you to think about the marsh that morning. The boys are being pulled from the water. There's a lot of confusion. Lots of talking."

"No talking." Dick turned back to Alberta and melted into a chair. "Nobody said anything."

"So, who first suggested the boys had been frogging?"

Dick looks to the ceiling, trying to remember. "I don't know."

"Did you agree? That they'd been frogging?"

"I don't know."

"You didn't agree?"

"I don't know!" Dick sits down, gripping his knees.

Alberta sits across from him. "Who pulled your boy out of the water?"

"I don't know."

"Who pulled Peter out?"

"I don't know." Dick takes a deep breath. "All I remember is seeing my boy in the mud. I . . ."

A vice grips Alberta's chest and will not release. She, too, took a long deep breath, trying to erase the image of Alby's body at the river. "OK, Dick. Just a few more questions." Alberta gives them both a moment to settle out. "Did your sons spend time with Walter Stem?"

"Walter? Yes. Evelyn told me they did. It was never on weekends. Not when I was around."

"Did they ever talk about Walter?"

"Not really. I can't imagine how crazy it would have been out here without him to keep a lid on things. He took the boys in. Taught them about motors and stuff. I didn't spend time with him, but he always had a good word about the boys when we'd run into each other on the beach or at school functions."

"That's right. They knew him from school, too."

"Yes."

"Had they ever said anything negative about the man?"

"Not that I recall."

"I understand he drove your daughter all over the state for science fairs?"

"I couldn't do it. Her mother wouldn't do it. He came through for her."

"It seems above and beyond. Why do you suppose he did that for Penny? For you, really."

Dick shrugs.

Alberta takes more notes, but only to give Dick a moment's respite before she goes back to difficult territory. "Did you speak with anyone that day, after the sheriff left?"

"What do you mean?"

"Did the neighbors stay with you, console you?"

"No. Marty came by, but I didn't want to talk to him."

"Anyone else?"

"Yeah. Bill did. He was a real pain in the ass."

"So, Bill left the day before but came back?"

“Yeah.”

“Why do you say he was a pain in the ass?’

“Wouldn’t leave. Just hung in the door saying what a horrible accident it was. Such an accident. Such a god damn horrible . . .” Dick stops talking. He seems to be having difficulty catching his breath. “We left as soon as they took the boys, the bodies, away. Sheriff Bates said to stay, but he was taking too long talking to Marty. I finally piled everybody in the car and stopped over there on our way out. Found Bates, Marty and Bill sitting in easy chairs, talking like nothing happened.”

“How’s that?”

“Smiling. They were smiling. Startled the hell out of them when I yelled at them.”

“What did you say to them?”

“Hell if I know. Probably cussed them out. And I said we were leaving.” Dick tried to compose himself. “Look. I’ve tried real hard to go along here. Penny said you wanted everybody’s take on the day. I’ve done that, but I’ve had enough. What the hell is all this about?”

“I’m going to be asking a lot of questions in the next few days. I’ll let you and your wife know my findings. Look. I wouldn’t be doing this if . . .”

“Right,” Dick says, getting up. “You want to talk to my wife? You’re going to have to go to her.”

“Yeah. I’ve heard that.”

Dick walks out the back door. Alberta hears a car door slam, wheels spitting gravel, and someone driving off.

Alberta pulls out some black and white photos from the case file. She finds one showing the boys’ bodies lying in the mud, their eyes open, ears missing, a black blotch on one where the nose was missing. She stares at the picture long and hard, forcing the image of her nephew's crime scene out of her head. Do the work, as George Eastman said, but nothing is falling into place. All anyone had done so far was make her doubt her assumptions.

CHAPTER 31

Alberta steps onto the sandy strip of shore behind Evelyn. The day has finally warmed, and the blanket Evelyn was wrapped in is folded at her feet.

"You waiting for permission or what?" Evelyn waves her forward.

Alberta sits in a folding chair next to her.

"Here's my terms," Evelyn says without making eye contact. "I don't want to hear any of your theories. I don't want to talk about the night my boy died. I won't talk about what happened afterward. I don't really have anything to say to you."

Looking at this hardened woman, Alberta wonders if she'd ever had soft edges, if she'd ever lived easily in the world or if some aspect of this was always present, simply magnified by grief. She thinks about her brother Michael, trying hard to remember how he managed disappointment when they were kids, wondering if that would have any effect on his recovery now. She'd always been the stronger one. Maybe the weak ones, the ones used to giving in to pain instead of building a fortress against it, are more likely to recover completely.

"I only have a few questions, Mrs. Hodges. About what it was like out here before the accident. How you all got along with the fathers gone most of the time."

"Walter Stem. That's how we all got along. He was the only thing that kept all those boys in line. You're right.

For most of the summer, they were fatherless bastards. All of them."

"Doesn't sound like an ideal situation."

"Do you have children?"

"No."

"Lucky you." Evelyn's expression reveals no contempt or regret. She speaks quietly, slowly, like reminiscing between old friends. "Motherhood isn't for everybody. You think there were a lot of kids out here? Our house in town. A neighborhood with four times the kids. I brought mine out here to even the odds a little. On our block alone there were twenty houses. Twenty mothers. Seventy children. Seventy! Now imagine the next street over and the next. They all looked the same. Children everywhere! And at least there isn't any traffic out here. They could play wherever they wanted to."

Evelyn glances to the boys on the pontoon. They're rounding the far side of the lake. Alberta watches minnows peck the surface near shore. A robin yanks a worm in the grass. Alberta waits for Evelyn.

"Walter would take the boys fishing when they were old enough. Sounded like a good idea, so I let him take Jimmy. Welcomed the break. I had a six-year-old, a toddler, one still in diapers, and another on the way. Taking one off my hands was a huge help. All the moms let their boys go with Walter. They sort of took their turns with him. I don't know what all they did over there, but they always came home with sunburned backs and shoulders boasting it was a sign of manhood. Any Johnson or Evinrude misbehaving, and the boys fought to fix it. You should have seen them. A wad of boys huddled around a motor up on a rack. And if they couldn't fix it or needed a part, Walter stepped in and helped. He was a godsend."

"What about Velma?"

"His mother? Watched things like a hawk."

"So I've heard."

"I wondered what the hell she thought was going to happen. I'd collect one of my boys, and she'd see me and sort of smile. We'd engage in some small talk. And as soon as I'd walk off with my boy, she'd go inside. I always figured it had something to do with that boy who drowned in the spring. I'm sure she worried another boy might fall in. It made me feel safe."

"Safe?" Alberta asks.

"Yeah. She saw everything. What could happen with somebody watching so close?"

"And Edith?"

"Poor, poor English Edith. Living under Velma's thumb. Married to Mr. Perfect."

Alberta thanks her for her time and leaves. She starts to say she's sorry for Evelyn's loss, but had recently become aware of how hollow it sounds, especially from strangers.

Alberta retreats to the tavern, telling herself it has nothing to do with Tucker, yet she's disappointed when he is nowhere in sight. She tosses her satchel on the bench in the corner booth. Colleen brings her a glass of water and leaves a menu.

Alberta pulls out a stack of 8 X 10 glossy black and white photos. Tucker appears and sits down across from her with two ice teas. He glances at the top picture, the bodies of Tyler and Peter on the shore, and pushes them all aside. He asks if she's hungry. "It's nearly two. I know you haven't eaten anything today, have you? If I order you a burger, does it have to be charred on the outside and bloody inside? Cause he can do that."

"Medium with cheese, no onion. Chips, not fries. And a beer."

He hollers to Colleen, who nods and hollers to the cook who repeats the order through the pass-through. Alberta can't help but laugh.

"So, Bert, I hear you're stirring things up pretty good over there," Tucker says. "Evelyn told Marilyn you were coming, Marilyn told Betsy, Betsy told Bill. Bill told Marty. Small world around here."

She cocks her head and smiles. She likes that he calls her Bert and the way he talks, straight forward and honest, his face relaxed, his body resting so comfortably across from her.

"He comes in here. Marty Wagner. Gets himself a snootful every few days around five and goes home. He tore down Monroe's cottage and the Eastman place a few years back. Put up that monstrosity. You can see it from here. Full-time residents. Most everyone is year-round out here now. Guess people can't afford second homes anymore. One's enough taxes for anybody."

"He still owns a construction company, doesn't he?"

"Why are you asking a question you already know the answer to?"

Alberta shrugged. "It's what I do." Her gaze falls out to the lake.

Tucker drinks half his tea in one long draw. "Just cleaned out the walk-in," he says as if to explain his thirst.

"Tell me about Steve Fry."

"Idiot kid," Tucker says. "Was seventeen the year those boys drowned." Tucker takes the top photo and turns it over. "I remember because he kept coming in here all summer expecting me to serve him, and I'd remind him he was just seventeen. Sometimes I gave him a beer just to shut him up. Used to come in with the Stem girl sometimes."

"Debra?"

"Yeah. Debra. Scary chick."

"Did you know what she was up to?"

Tucker admits he knew she was giving blowjobs in the parking lot. "Looked a lot older than she was. Steve caught her at it one night. Got in a big argument with her, then the guy she was doing got in the middle of it and man, it could have been a shit fest. Steve picked the wrong guy to punch. I broke it up but not before he laid Steve out cold. I didn't see Debra again after that. Didn't see any more of Steve after that either. His dad sent him away to some school. One of those military academies."

"Really."

"Yeah. I felt bad for the kid, but it had to be better than living with his old man. A real piece of work, that one."

Alberta asks about the marsh. Tucker says it was filled in after the boys drowned. He sifts through the photos and pulls one out of a group of men and a boy. Tucker looks at it and sighs. "Wow. 1938. That's me. I was twelve or thirteen years old. My dad, everybody. They were looking for the boy who drowned in Spring Lake. There weren't as many cottages out here back then. Everybody knew everybody. When somebody said missing kid, everybody came to look. It took three days for the body to pop back up. What do you have this picture for?"

Alberta looks at it. "You were a cutie."

"I still am." He grins and rises to leave. "Saturday," he said. "Stuff to do."

From what Alberta gathers, the day the boys died would have been unremarkable if it hadn't ended the way it did. Yet, in hindsight, under scrutiny, everything became suspect.

Alberta sits in the small cabin that evening. No television or radio. Nights are long without diversion, just her thoughts, none of them good, none of them sufficient to quell the angst of loss, the fear of failure. She peruses the bookshelf and pulls a copy of "The Man in the Gray Flannel Suit". She takes it to bed, slips under covers, pillows stacked behind her, trying to believe she can slip into the book as easily. She'd read it in college when it first came out, left an impression of marriage, work, and success in America after the war. It makes her think of classmates who died, boys she'd known since her first day of grade school, boy's she'd cheered on at football games, dated, kissed. Boys who barely had time to be men.

She puts the book down and pours three fingers of bourbon into a glass, not the rye, but good bourbon, the kind that goes down smooth and warm. She hopes it might help her sleep. It's a solitary pursuit, chasing after a truth no one else accepts. Minutes begin to melt, her mind finally captured by sleep.

CHAPTER 32

Jul 28 - I can't do this much longer.

"Lock the goddamn door! Your brothers are coming!" Evelyn leans on the door downstairs looking out beyond the patio, over the grass to the shoreline. Behind her, Penn rinses their breakfast dishes and looks outside. No one's there.

Agitated, Evelyn shouts, fumbling with a little bronze dog, banging it on the door handle. "What's wrong with you? Lock it! Fast, goddamn it!"

Penn walks over, takes the figurine away, and turns the deadbolt.

Evelyn scuffles toward the steps, missing them, ending up in the bathroom. "Upstairs. Hurry!" She turns on the cold water and sits on the toilet seat, muttering indecipherable words.

Penn approaches slowly. She tells Evelyn the doors are locked tight. She turns off the water. She helps her mother upstairs, back to bed.

"Damn kids," Evelyn says as her eyelids droop.

As incongruous as her mother's actions seemed, Penn is beginning to decipher some of it, this episode in particular. That last summer had gotten off to a bad start. No one in the household seemed to get along. Ronny and Mark didn't want to be there. Jim was bossing everybody around. There'd been a knock-down fight over who could drive the Lyman one morning leading Evelyn to take lake privileges away from all of them at the same time. No boats. No swimming. No using anyone else's boats. In retaliation, all five of the Hodges brood parked themselves in the cottage where they pestered each other. Incessantly. They wrestled. They knocked things over. A vase full of dead flowers broke spilling stinky water on a rug, after which Evelyn had unbolted to the door, opened it, and pointed outside. She hadn't yelled at them. Hadn't said a word. It was a silent instruction to leave. They did. And Penn distinctly remembered the click of the deadbolt as she, the last of them, stepped outside.

Penn adjusted the sheets when Evelyn grabbed her wrist and glared at her. "Call your father. Get his ass out here before I ..." She lets go and the words fade away.

> Aug 1 - She's calling for Rabbit again. I don't have the heart to tell her one more time that he's dead. Dad's dead. Tyler's dead. The closer she gets to death, the less she notices the living.

"Let Rabbit in," Evelyn calls out. "He's scratching at the door."

It's three in the morning. The scratching is in the wall. Penn lies awake. Waiting to hear if she needs to administer Roxy or not. Then comes the thud of Evelyn's body hitting the floor. Confused and terrified, Evelyn lashes out at her daughter, kicks her, hits her, cries and screams with what little voice is left to her. Penn gets a syringe and the Haldol from the Hospice kit. Only half the Haldol makes it into Evelyn's mouth, but once it's in, Evelyn settles down within a few minutes.

The next night Evelyn wakes up screaming that Tyler is in the room, soaking wet, his flesh hanging off his bones, reaching out to her. Even when Penn turns on the light, Evelyn still cringes at the foot of the bed, crying out to the doorway, sobbing, trying to scratch her eyes out. Again Penn administers Haldol.

There is no greater sense of isolation than sitting in a room in the middle of the night watching the drugs knock her mother out cold. There is no relief or satisfaction or concern beyond just wanting the quiet of it, beyond wanting it to all be over.

Penn wants her father. She wants him to sit with her. He doesn't have to comfort her or console her. He'd never been any good at that. He did everything else, all the required basics of parenting, but he was never any good at finding the right words. Even his hugs, the ones he insisted on every day in the months after Tyler died, weren't exactly out of love, but desperation. Sometimes he'd hold on so tight she'd have to pull free of him. Even so, she longed for his presence, for the man he was before the heart attacks, before he lost his will to live, before the DA from Pennsylvania upended their lives, before Walter Stem became synonymous with hell.

His first heart attack was a warning. The second one should have killed him, but somehow, he survived, his body more resilient than his spirit. Penny left grad school and moved in to take care of him.

Evelyn was living there then, having abandoned the cottage and taken over Jim's bedroom, Tyler's old room. She kept to herself. She fixed her own food and ate alone. She did not contribute to her husband's care or speak to the doctors. She sat with her husband toward the end but never made eye contact with him that Penn could see.

Penn's observation of this detachment without the ability to comprehend it deepened the divide between her and her mother. Only in tending Evelyn did she begin to understand.

In the months it took her father to die, Penny watched him shrink and fade. He stopped walking the hall, too out of breath. He stopped going to bed, choosing to sleep in his recliner. He stopped eating. He stopped talking. He stopped looking at her, his gaze always falling just to the side.

He rallied at the end, as if suddenly awakened. He smiled and asked for a chicken sandwich. With pickles and chips. He asked for and read the newspaper. He asked about the cottage and told Penny to be sure to keep it in the family. *Someday it won't break your heart to be there.* He asked her about her work, how she was coming along with her Master's, and apologized for taking her away from it. "Get back to it," he said. "Work is the best thing." He took her hand. "Never tell your brothers. Never tell them what we . . ." Then, like watching a wax mask melt, Penny saw the stroke take his last words. His whole body slumped. His eyes slid from hers. He died a few days later.

CHAPTER 33

Sunday morning Alberta sits in Gert and Mason Vogel's living room drinking sweet iced tea with Mason and Gert. It's a cozy room with a picture window overlooking the lawn to the lake. Mason is a huge bald man who wheezes with every breath. Gert looks every bit of seventy, skin leathered from too much sun. Alberta tries not to stare, but can't keep her eyes off Gert's lips outlined in bright red beyond the natural lip line, color oozing into vertical crevices.

She asks Mason for a rundown on the residents, who was there the weekend the boys died, how long the party on Sunday lasted, where all the kids had been during the party. Mason is cooperative but of little use. Yes, there'd been a party but the whole summer was like that. He confirms Merci and Al Monroe, Marty and Gladys Wagner, Evelyn and Dick Hodges and Betsy Fry were there. As far as the kids, "Only God himself knew what they did half the time." He has nothing new to offer on anyone.

"Stems were never around for drinks and parties then," Alberta says.

Mason starts in on Walter, saying he should have ended up a criminal the way his father treated him and his mother. "Hard to believe he turned out to be the man he is. Principal. School superintendent somewhere out east? He did all right.

Gert chimes in. "I don't know what went on in that house, but I'm damn sure it wasn't pretty. I'd see Velma sometimes and I'd swear she looked scared. I don't know any other way to put it. She just looked scared of Eugene. Even when he wasn't around."

"Eugene?"

"Walter's father."

"I'd hear things sometimes from the Stem house," Mason says, his face cast downward. "When I was fishing back on the spring. Could never make out the words, but Eugene would be hollering. There were screams sometimes. Velma. I was so ashamed. Didn't do a damn thing about it. Their business. Not mine."

In the extended silence, Alberta is preoccupied with what she would have done in the same situation. It would be easy to believe she'd have stepped up, done something. But maybe she would have kept silent, like they did. It's what people do. Stay out of things.

Alberta breaks the silence asking if the house had always been yellow.

"Yellow?" Gert gasps. "You mean yellow and red and every other color? That happened after Eugene passed. She was a different woman after he passed. Different as day and night. Tell her about the house before she painted it, Dear."

Mason says he'd only seen inside once and only for a minute. He'd walked over to see if Velma was OK when the power had gone out when Eugene was on one of his trips. "Walter was just a baby. The house was white then. One coat at best. But nothing inside. Just wood. Floors, walls, ceiling. That striped wainscoting wood. Flat board counter"

“And tell him about the day he came and dragged her away, Honey. Sick man. That Eugene was a sick man, but then he came from sick people.”

“Not dragged away. Don’t exaggerate. And that other business is nothing but old gossip.”

“Just the same. They weren’t right in the head, those people.”

Alberta sits back, watching and listening as they unspool their thoughts. Gert says she’d invited Velma over for drinks one evening because Velma and little Walter were alone so much of the time. Eugene traveled for work. “We wanted to get her out of that house. Al and Merci were here, too, with a couple of their kids. Carl was about Walter’s age. They'd run around together. We were all having a heck of a time, laughing about something, I don’t know what, when we hear this voice from up behind us, by the road. It was Eugene and he demanded she go with him. Mason called up to him, inviting him for a drink, but Eugene called out again. Velma put her glass down, reached for Walter, and without a word, got up and went to him. And she looked scared.”

Mason says it was the saddest thing he’d ever seen. “Al and I stood up, but we didn’t stop him. We were no match for a man like Stem. Not Eugene Stem.”

“How so?” Alberta asks.

“There are stories,” Gert says. “Horrible, horrible stories.”

Mason gives her a look, the one that says stop talking.

“Some of it’s just wives’ tales,” Mason says. “But not all. My father was out there the day they found Eugene in the chicken coop, head shaved, sores all over it. The old

Stem farm. Two fields over. I was a little kid but I remember him and the other men talking about it. Two dead in the house. One of the deputies and another man killed outside. A couple of them wounded."

"I don't understand," Alberta says.

"A dead boy," Gert says. "Frozen to death. They found him by the Stem farm. God only knows how many bodies are buried out there. They found dead children."

"Gert! Stop that."

"What?"

"There were family graves," Mason says. "A couple of their kids died. Doctor couldn't save the first so they didn't let him look at the next one. That's what I heard anyway. They were queer folk. Kept to themselves. That always makes people nervous, you know? Eugene's daddy had a history of shooting at anyone who came out there, so the sheriff took backup when he went to ask questions about the frozen boy."

"Tell him about the house, Mason."

Mason says he'd heard it was filthy beyond human imagining. "That's what Eugene came from. You don't wash stain like that out of your life. You just don't."

Another silence falls over the room. Alberta wonders how many generations a stain like that endures. She asks how old Walter would have been the night Eugene hauled him and Velma away from their house. Mason and Gert look at each other and answer in unison. "Seven. Like Carl."

Alberta's mind reels. Seven. She takes a deep breath, letting it out slowly. "Tell me about Walter as a boy."

"Like a little weasel," Gert says. "Skin and bones and he had his mother's pointy features, too many teeth for such a small mouth, and he must have needed glasses because he was always squinting. Grew out of that scrawniness though. By the time he hit puberty, he was filled out, wasn't he, Dear? Strong as an ox. A quiet boy. I never went by that place that he wasn't working at something, chopping wood, mowing, trimming things, washing windows, washing the dock."

"Washing the dock?"

"You mean the landing," Alberta says for clarification.

"Yes. the landing. Every day," Mason says. "On his knees with a scrub brush."

"And he was so polite," Gert says. "Yes, Ma'am. Please and thank you. Smart, too. Nothing like his father."

Alberta asks if it bothered them that Walter spent so much time with their grandson and the other lake boys.

"Who better to keep an eye on the boys than a school principal?" Mason says. "Better they be at his place working than sitting in the woods smoking and drinking. Which I'm certain they did, too."

Marilyn comes in through the back with a sack of groceries. She calls out from the kitchen, asking who's there. Mason tells her and to just stay where she was. She doesn't. "I can tell you about that day," she says, insinuating herself into the conversation. "Have they told you about the party we had over here?"

Alberta doesn't have time to answer before Marilyn goes into her carefully prepared story. "We started drinking way before he even tied up to the dock. Marty and his fancy-schmancy new fiberglass boat. It was the reason for the party, not that we ever needed one."

Gert argues that it hadn't started until later in the day.

"Like I was saying," Marilyn continues, ignoring her mother-in-law. "It all started with Greg Wagner. He started it."

"So, you didn't think too much of Greg Wagner?" They are all three silent. "You must have some opinion," she insists.

Marilyn says he was probably a very nice boy, but she'd seen him on more than one occasion riding around the lake with half-naked boys in his boat. "Now, why would he have any reason for that? Unless he was . . ."

Mason tells her to shut up.

"All I'm saying is, the way he was. . ."

Mason insists. "I'm telling you, Marilyn. Shut your mouth."

"All I'm saying. . ."

Gert cuts her off. "He's a homosexual! Was back then, probably still is now. Doesn't make him a bad person."

"What if he was experimenting with all our boys?" Marilyn shouts. "Nobody ever said it but can we really be sure? Can we? And to up and leave his family like he did. Had to be something else going on there, you can be sure of that."

Mason glares at her and she stops talking.

Alberta asks about Steven Fry.

Mason says there'd been a fight between the boys that day, and Steve seemed to be in the middle of it. "He flung one of the boys across the yard."

"Tyler Hodges," Alberta says.

"Yes. Tyler. But it could just as easily been any one of them. I'm sure Tyler was just the closest one. Steven had lots of issues."

Alberta isn't taking notes and Marilyn points at the pad, her eyes wide and furious. "You take this down, Goddammit! It's important." Alberta puts pen to paper and pretends to write while Marilyn prattles on. "All the kids were told to go home and stay home. Then Marty and Carl came back up here, and Mason put a stack of records on the HiFi. Then, Betsy grabs Marty and starts dancing with him. And Gladys got into it with Betsy over that damn powder blue Lincoln. Betsy had the gall to thank Gladys for screwing her husband – thanked her for that car!"

Alberta can't keep any of the names straight, but she's getting a pretty good picture.

Mason barks at Marilyn to shut up, but she keeps on.

"That mess settles down and Dick gets mad at Evelyn because she's six sheets to the wind."

"And how is it you remember all this so clearly?" Alberta asks. "Can you tell me about any of your other parties that summer? Were all your parties so memorable?"

Marilyn slams her hand on the hutch. "I've thought about that day nearly every day for ten years trying to figure out what happened that day, where we all failed those boys, how they ended up dead while we all drank ourselves into a stupor! You bet your ass I remember it clearly! I hope I never forget that day. Because if I do, it could happen again." She glared at her in-laws. "We're all at fault. Every last one of us." She charges out of the cottage slamming the back screen door. An instant later, she comes back in demanding Alberta leave Evelyn Hodges alone. "You hear me?" She purses her lips, either out of anger or fighting back a fit of tears. "You can't possibly know what she's gone through. What you're doing here? It's wrong. It's just wrong!" She leaves again and drives off, spraying gravel in her wake.

Mason slowly rolls his head. "Don't worry about her. Doesn't take much to get her started."

The room seems unnaturally quiet in Marilyn's absence.

Alberta shows Gert and Mason a photo of the search party from 1938. Gert sighs.

"Are you going to throw all our sorrows in our faces, Miss Higgins?" She hands it to Mason and looks away. "The Conners were our best friends. We're the ones who convinced them to build out here so our kids could have summers together. They. . ." she pauses, catching her breath. "We didn't see them anymore after that. Not a lick."

Alberta asks if they can identify anyone in the picture, and they run through all they can remember. "Long time ago," Mason says. "Over thirty years." He glances at Gert, his eyes widening, his breath coming in fits and starts. She says it's time Alberta left. Her husband is worn out.

Before Alberta walks out, Mason assures her that Greg was a good kid. "He never gave any of them a moment's hesitation. And Steve Fry, well, he was just one of those boys who never found his way. If he was a danger to anyone, it was just to himself."

Starting her car, something catches Alberta's eye. Evelyn is in her bedroom window. Watching.

CHAPTER 34

After Vogels', Alberta heads to Anglers.

"Perch or a burger?" Tucker asks, then orders for her, hollering through to the kitchen. "One cheeseburger, medium. Hold the . . ."

"Yeah. I see her," says the cook. "Hold the onions. Chips. Slaw."

Alberta settles into her booth, reviewing her notes, amending them. When Tucker brings her food, a booming voice comes from across the room. A man resembling Mason Vogel but younger storms over to the booth.

"Stay the hell away from my parents! They both have heart conditions!"

Tucker steps away with a sly glance to Alberta. "You want anything, Carl?" he says.

"No, Tucker, I don't want anything!"

"OK. OK. Just asking. Christ." He walks off, turning back with a grin. "You're sure now, Carl. Cause we could rustle something up for you."

Carl glares at him. "Nothing! I want nothing!"

Tucker shrugs, knowing full well it will tick Carl off.

"Carl Vogel," Alberta says as if pleased to see him. "You saved me a trip. Thanks."

"What the hell do you think you're doing?"

"Well, I'm about to eat a late lunch. Take a seat if you like."

Carl remains standing. "You need to stop all these questions."

"I don't understand why everyone's so resistant. I'd think you'd all want to know the truth. Please," she says, motioning to the bench. "Have a seat. Sure you don't want some lunch? A beer?"

"No!"

"You know, I'm real curious about what you can tell me about Greg Wagner. I mean your wife said . . ."

"Yeah, I heard what my wife said. You can't listen to a word out of that woman's mouth. Nobody knew back then he was light in his loafers, no matter what she says. And his father? Marty was mad as hell when it got out later on."

"You know," Carl says, opening his eyes extra wide. "Greg didn't leave. Marty kicked him out. You think maybe he knew something we didn't know? Is that what this is all about? Was Marilyn right? Was he involved? You know, what Marilyn was saying. I never saw anything funny. But maybe he was, I don't know, recruiting. Maybe she was right. You know how they are."

"No, Mr. Vogel. I don't. How are they?"

Tucker delivers the burger and a beer. "Sure I can't get you anything, Carl?"

"No, goddamnit. Fuck off!"

Alberta takes a big bite of burger, juice dripping down her chin. She wipes her face and drinks some beer.

"Look," Carl says, finally sitting down. "I don't know what you're trying to peddle around here, but we aren't buying. It's time you just pack up your little roadshow and go." Carl looks down at the photo of the search party from 1938. "This is it! This is the photo you showed my parents? Why the hell would you show this to my mother of all people?"

Alberta looks through her notes. "You were, uh, here it is. You were thirteen when the Conner boy drowned. You went skinny-dipping with all the boys that night, right? Whose idea was that?"

"What? How am I supposed to remember a thing like that?"

"Oh, you have to remember. A young boy, the son of your mother's best friend dies right in front of you. You'd remember a thing like that."

Carl glares at her.

"Your brother Eric was there, too." Alberta says.

"Yeah, and at least half a dozen others."

"Eight others."

"What?"

"It was you and your brother Ed, fourteen and sixteen? Arthur and Bryan Monroe, sixteen and fifteen. All the Conner boys. Patrick, Julian, Paul, and little Samuel. Fourteen, twelve, nine, and seven respectively."

"And Walter," Carl adds. "Walter Stem was there."

"Ah. Walter. Thanks. He's the ninth. He was fourteen. Do you think it was his idea to go skinny dipping?"

Carl says again he didn't know whose idea it was. "What's this all about anyway? Asking about a kid who died decades ago."

"What do you remember about the morning the boys went missing? Peter Eastman and Tyler Hodges." She eats a potato chip, crunching loudly.

"In what sense? We heard something was wrong."

"How did you hear?"

"I don't know. Somebody pounded on the door. Said the boys were missing. We all met up at Hodges' and Dick directed the search. Sent me, my dad, and my son to the marsh."

"Your son, Daniel. He was eleven at the time? He helped look for the boys?"

"Thirteen. Danny was thirteen." Carl closes his eyes as he explains how they'd started at the lake edge of the marsh and had just started working their way to the back.

"Were you calling out for the boys?"

"Everybody was. It's all you could hear, calling from the woods, from the lake. We were calling their names."

"And when you got to the back of the marsh?"

"Walter was plowing through the weeds when we got there. I blew the whistle. Dick and George showed up, then the others."

Alberta asks how deep in the cattails the bodies had been, if the weeds were broken or bent, if there was a clear view of the bodies from the shoreline, but Carl can't say.

"Walter was plowing through it all by the time we got there and then everyone seemed to be in the weeds. They were in the deep part. The boys. It gets pretty deep in the middle. You can't, well you couldn't see that from shore. People thought it was all shallow. It wasn't."

Alberta pulls another photo from the stack, the scene at the marsh.

"That's me," Carl says, and he named all the others.

"Why do you suppose Walter Stem wasn't looking for the boys in Spring Lake behind his house? Or maybe in the channel? Why do you suppose he was looking in the marsh?"

"How the hell should I know?"

Alberta shrugs and puts the photographs away. She takes a bite of her pickle spear. "Mmm. Good pickle. Walter was pretty broken up when the boys died?"

"We didn't see any more of him that summer. No one saw him again until school started." Carl is quiet for a moment, contemplative. "Peter was that summer's boy."

"That summer's boy? What do you mean?"

"Walter took on all the boys when they were young. Peter was just the latest. I think he felt sorry for the kid. He was kind of a pipsqueak. Peter's dad was a professor or something. If he wasn't working on that broken-down wreck of a cottage, he was at Notre Dame. Even over the summer. That's where he taught. He was gone, oh, I'd say three or four days out of the week."

"You were all gone all week, you fathers, weren't you?" Alberta asked.

"Not all of us. Not all the time."

"Who got to the marsh first that morning, Steve Fry or Greg Wagner?" Carl can't remember and slides up out of the booth. Alberta takes another bite of her burger knowing her apparent indifference pisses Carl off.

"Like I said. I don't know why you're asking all these questions, but you need to leave my parents alone." He starts to walk away.

Alberta swallows fast. "Just one more thing," she says. "Was your boy home in bed that night?"

Carl stops and turns. "Danny? Yes. Of course."

"And you're sure of that. Because the Hodges and Eastmans thought their boys were home in bed, too. Maybe it wasn't just Tyler and Peter at the marsh. Maybe all the boys were there and something went wrong. Do you think the boys could be hiding anything?"

Carl heaves a sigh, annoyed. "If there was any more to it, I'd have heard about it. You can't have that many kids hide something that big for all these years without spilling it." He turns to the door and takes a couple steps before Alberta calls out.

"Who was at your cottage in '67? Somebody with little boys?"

Again, he stops and turns. "Three years ago? How the hell would I know? Unless it was my brother's kid. I know Eric Junior came out one summer. EJ, Janet, and the boys."

"Young boys?"

"Yeah. And as far as my boy, on the night those two boys died? You'd have to talk to my wife about that. I'm sure she checked on the kids when she came to bed."

He makes it almost to the door before Alberta lets go with one final volley.

"Mr. Vogel. We both know your wife was too drunk to know if her kids were in bed or not."

Carl pounds the door open on his way out of the bar. Colleen and the cook follow shortly after and Tucker locks up. He takes two fresh drafts to Alberta. "We close at two on Sundays."

"But it's nearly three," she says, suddenly aware they are alone. "I should go." He gives no indication he agrees.

She finishes her lunch as Tucker talks about his parents losing the bar before the war then getting it back after. It isn't a particularly interesting story, but she likes the way he tells it, with heart.

"Well, Miss Higgins. What do you do when you're not chasing ghosts?"

Over another beer, she tells him about her job as an assistant prosecuting attorney, how the system actually works sometimes, but is just as likely to fail miserably.

They begin an ambling conversation, one thing leading to a tangent leading to another unrelated topic. They compare his growing up in a tiny town with all twelve grades in one school to her growing up in Philadelphia.

"And you never used your journalism degree," she says with a hint of admonishment.

"I use those skills every day. It's all about finding the truth. Just like you," he says. "In your job. You can't go into a case prejudging things. You have to look for the truth."

Alberta rolls her eyes. Prejudging is exactly what she's doing. "It's usually all laid out before I ever go near it. If somebody else didn't think the defendant was guilty, I wouldn't be pursuing it."

"So, what you're doing here. It's different. Why are you here?"

When she doesn't answer, he gets up for another draft. "From what you say then, the idea that a trial is a vehicle to arrive at the truth is a lie. Want to try a dark beer?"

"No. Thanks. Just a Carling, please. And I wouldn't go that far. A trial is battle. Innocent or guilty is dependent on the talents of the legal teams, the facts they have to work with, and the money they have at their disposal."

From across the room, she watches him top off his draft. "And you're comfortable working in a rigged system," he says opening her bottle and pouring it into a glass."

"It's the only one we have."

"Fair enough," he says. "Guess I better keep my nose clean." He sits back down, sliding her beer in front of her. "Have you ever been wrong?"

The question surprises her, yet her response is immediate. "I've lost, but I've never been wrong."

Years of standing behind the bar listening to drunken confessions has trained him to withhold reaction. Though he is certain she was delusional, he shows no sign of it. He drops the topic. "In another life, I think I'd write movie scripts. *Bob, Carol, Ted & Alice, The Italian Job, Easy Rider.* It's been a good year for movies."

"Did you see Butch Cassidy and the Sundance Kid? I loved that."

"That bicycle scene? What was that? And two far-too-handsome, clever, funny men cracking jokes when you know they're criminals about to get gunned down? True Grit. That was good storytelling."

"You've seen a lot of movies. I don't have time."

"Movies are the perfect escapism, aren't they? Reading can take you into another world, but movies do it in two hours, transport you to some other life then drop you right back where you live. What could be better?"

It suddenly seems ridiculous that she hadn't carved out more time to see a movie occasionally, or to do anything fun, other than playing with her brother's boys on Sunday afternoons. Alberta suddenly winces and presses a fist to her breastbone. Tucker has done what no movie could have. He'd taken her out of her life for a while, but she just slammed back into it.

Without any obvious concern, Tucker asks if it's acid or anxiety.

"The latter," she says. She wants to talk about Alby, about all the sweet things he did, the silly stuff he said, but she'd probably start crying and doesn't want to do that.

Tucker takes away the plate and glasses, returning with water and two fresh beers, which makes her smile a little. "You trying to get me drunk? On beer? Next time try bourbon. Much faster and doesn't make me have to pee so much."

"Is that an invitation?"

She gets up and heads to the ladies room. When she returns to the table, Tucker is looking at the photos again. He puts them away as she sits down, all except for the picture of Walter as a young boy. "You're going to hear some strange stuff about the Stems if you ask enough people," he says. "Most of it will be myth. Some of it, well, it'll be true. Walter's grandmother and mine were sisters. I can tell you the truth part if you're interested."

Alberta takes a long drink of water. The tightness in her chest has eased. The alcohol is beginning to register, not so much a buzz as an easy unraveling. She settles into the corner of her bench, feet up.

"It starts way back in the 1800s with Washington Stem," he says. "Strange man, ugly as sin. Showed up from out of nowhere in 1889. Bought a large, boggy tract of land with an old house and barn not far from here. He drove a buckboard all over picking up cast-off stuff, everybody's junk. Some, he fixed and sold. Some he just threw out back. One day he cleaned himself up and went calling on his neighbor, a widower with two spinster daughters."

"Your grandmother's house?"

"Yeah. His willingness to marry my grandmother's sister in spite of her hair-trigger temper was a relief to her father. That much is true. But the rest of it? It gets pretty wild. Supposedly on his trips around the county collecting junk, he kidnapped young women and held them captive at the farm. They had babies, some say four, some stories put it up around a dozen." Tucker's eyes go wide in mock horror. "All died by sheer neglect, filth or ritualistic murder." Tucker leans back and grins.

Alberta sips her beer, clearly not believing a word of it.

"When a young boy was found frozen to death by the road, a posse was put together to storm the house. Wilma and Washington were killed when they bolted out of the house shooting at the men."

Alberta grins. "Butch Cassidy style?"

"Exactly," he says. "The property was all overgrown, the house pure squalor. An infant was found in a drawer nearly encased in his own excrement." Tucker takes a long, deep draw of beer. "A boy, as ugly as his father, was found half-frozen to death in the chicken coop."

"Eugene."

"Yup. That's the myth."

Alberta grins. "It's a good one. The truth?"

"Well, according to my grandmother, Washington was a quiet man who didn't much care for people. All that junk he couldn't sell, chairs, tables, old farm equipment, he piled it together for fencing to keep in the cow and pigs. Personally, I think it was ingenious. Anyway, the true story, not that crazy shit? He showed up at their house when Grandmother was around seventeen. Washington said he'd met her older sister Wilma in town and he needed a wife if she'd have him. Now, Wilma was no looker, and she had peculiar ways about her. She married him and moved out to Stem's place. They didn't want visitors. I heard Great Granddad went out there once, but the place was such a shambles he refused to go back. And Wilma had gone feral, whatever that meant. He said good riddance and never spoke her name again. My grandmother would go out there every few years to see if her sister was still alive or not."

"So, what about all the dead babies," Alberta asks. "At least a dozen, was it?"

"People fear what they don't understand. You don't come to town for church, you don't shoot the breeze at the feed store, you don't shop at the dry goods store, people talk. The only time anybody saw Washington was when he'd bring a hog in to sell. They had a monthly order of staples delivered to a tree in the woods. Left money in a sack on a string. It was probably one of the stupid delivery boys who snuck onto the property and saw the graves."

"They were real?"

"Wilma had a son who was born wrong in the head. My grandmother saw the boy once, said he was a sweet creature, had Washington's big chest, but something wasn't quite right about his eyes. She said he was always smiling. He died young. Buried out by the barn with two other siblings, babies that didn't make it. My grandmother called it bad seed. All three graves were marked and encircled with stones. No mysteries."

"And Eugene?"

"Eugene was a late-in-life baby. My grandmother said he seemed sound enough, strong, but she feared for him, growing up out there, no schooling. My grandparents went out once to try to take Eugene away, to raise him in town, give him a chance at a normal life, but Washington ran them off. Bad seed is bad seed and better to let it grow or die where it falls. That's what Granddad said about it."

"So, no wild shootout."

"Oh, definitely a shootout. A boy had been found frozen to death not too far from the Stem farm. He'd gone missing a few days earlier. The sheriff and a few men went out to talk to Washington. Somebody in the group shouted at the house, accused them of kidnapping and killing the boy. Somebody saw a rifle pointing out a window and he shot at the house. Somebody inside shot back and set it all off. Washington and Wilma were killed defending themselves from a bunch of angry men. And yes, Eugene was found in the chicken coop with a shotgun in his hands, shaking in the cold. He was thirteen. The parents of the dead boy later admitted they'd whipped him for his own good a few too many times until he finally had enough and ran off. Died of exposure."

"Oh my God," Alberta says. "Then, it was all for nothing?"

"Yeah. They weren't doing anybody any harm out there. But people just couldn't let them be."

Tucker stops talking, turning his glass around and around, the quiet scraping the only sound.

"So," Alberta asks, "no baby in a drawer encased in ..."

Tucker shakes his head. "Wilma was a hoarder," he says. "Nothing but paths through piles of junk, crap Washington picked up along the road or at a dump. Everyone assumed she was a bad person. She wasn't. She was just a little off the mark. My grandparents took

Eugene in, but he ran, refusing to live anywhere but that filthy house."

"Do you know what condition he was in? Eugene when they found him?"

"Well," Tucker looks to the ceiling, trying to recall. "Shaved head, bites all over his body. I remember my grandmother didn't want him in her house until they doused him in gasoline and scrubbed him down. Lice, scabies and whatever."

Alberta winced. "That had to be painful. I heard he had open wounds."

Defending his grandmother, he asserted she was just trying to get him clean.

"I'm sure she was doing her best."

"A bunch of town people cleaned out the house, made it livable. Eugene basically raised himself after that with the help of my grandparents and some do-good church ladies. He never went to school, but he kept the house clean, washed his clothes, took care of the chickens, the cow and pigs. He was land wealthy but ignorant as a rock. The county gnawed away at the acreage for taxes every year. Eugene sold the animals and enlisted for World War I. Came back home to find his house just a pile of ash. House, barn, chicken coup. Sold the farmland and built a house over there on what land he had left around Spring and Spirit lakes. About fifteen acres. I only met the man once. By then, Walter was in the picture."

"So, Walter is your cousin."

"Second cousins."

"Ah. I'm always confused on that stuff."

"We were actually in school together. I had no idea we were related 'til my grandmother told me the stories, so of course I had to go digging around in matters that were none of my business. I went over to the house. I wanted to tell Walter we were cousins, but I had no more than knocked on the door when Eugene ran me off, cussing me out, telling me to stay the hell away. Can't say I blame him. He just didn't trust people. Especially any of Wilma's family."

Tucker stopped talking. His gaze fell to the empty bar. "I always felt sorry for Walter."

"Because of Eugene?"

"That, but he didn't have much of a life out of the house either. Eugene shaved his head. Walter came to school with a shaved head. We all got used to it, but he got beat up over it more than once."

Alberta remembers the school photo of Walter with little but a shadow of hair. She'd thought at the time is was unusual. "Did you know Walter's mother?"

"Velma? Was years before I ever met her. I was too afraid of Eugene to go out there again. He was a welder, I think. Learned it in the army. Used to go out on jobs that kept him away for weeks. I can still see Walter's face in the window upstairs that day. Avoided him in school after that. Was ashamed of myself." He leans back, his gaze drifting about the bar. "It was years before I got to know him at all. He used to come in here in the summer, have a couple beers. Always two. Never three," he says, tapping the table. "He'd bring Tyler Hodges in with him sometimes. Funny kid. Was just a little shit, but that kid . . . Ty was something else. He could make the grumpiest old fart laugh. Didn't see Walter in here much after the boys died."

Tucker has about run out of words and glances around the bar, the room growing dim as the sun goes down. "I don't know how the hell he did it, but Walter survived, made a life for himself. He was always getting good grades. Quiet kid. Neat. Skinny as shit and private. I guess his Mathers genes finally came through. Our grandmothers were Mathers. Sturdy stock."

Their glasses empty, Alberta and Tucker sit in silence. He's done with his story, and she's still absorbing it. She came to Michigan wanting to find some dark history, some predilection toward violence, but instead realizes Tucker could be right. Walter was a good man who found his way out of a tough upbringing.

"How about I walk you home?" Tucker looks at her with raised eyebrows. Only then does she realize how much she's had to drink. For an instant, she imagines him groping her nether reaches, their mouths locked in a sloppy kiss. It has been years since such a thought occurred to her.

"I believe I'm fine on my own, thanks." But the words come out with less clarity than intended. Somewhere during his story, she'd finished her fourth beer.

"Yeah," he says. "I'm walking you home."

The evening air revives her senses and the half-mile walk along the shoreline sobers her up a little. All talked out, it's a silent saunter to the Travel Court. Tucker unlocks the cabin door for her, steps in to turn on a light, and steps back outside.

"I get the feeling this is not your first time walking a drunk woman to her cabin," she says.

"Good night, Alberta Higgins." Tucker smiles and walks away without a glance back. If he had, he'd have seen her watching from the doorway. Waiting.

When Eugene's parents were killed, and it was clear he would not leave the farm, church people descended with buckets and disinfectant. They held their noses as they emptied closets and chests and cupboards, taking everything to the burn pile. The ladies scoured floors and walls. The men burned all the furniture, mattresses and bedding. Women brought Eugene new dishes and curtains and fresh clothes. They gave him a bed, a table and a chair.

Through their efforts, the church ladies believed they'd civilized Eugene. The proof was in the manner in which he kept the farmhouse. He'd taken to cleanliness with a vengeance. The proof was in his silence, a seething animosity they mistook for respect. The proof was in the ever-growing woodpile, an indication of budding self-sufficiency. They couldn't have known Eugene had been splitting kindling since he was five, sawing trees since he was nine, beaten if his output had not satisfied his father. The proof was in his willingness to passively listen when their food deliveries were accompanied by lengthy bible readings, when he watched them the way he'd watch an ant carry the carcass of a beetle into a hole, curious but unengaged. They spoke in quiet tones unfamiliar to him with gentle cadence and stillness of body. They were not women or even people. They were the rabbit in the yard eating clover before he shot it.

CHAPTER 35

Alberta has spoken with enough people to know she hasn't found what she came looking for. She's found more. And less.

The morning after Carl accosted her in the tavern, after her long talk with Tucker, Alberta finds her car parked out front of the cabin with the keys on the seat. It takes a minute for it to register that Tucker must have brought it to her and she begins to berate herself for what could have happened the night before if he'd turned around, if he'd made a move, if he'd spent the night with her. She realizes how emotionally compromised she is. It can't happen again. She has to be more cautious.

She drives to town and knocks on Merci Monroe's door. It's been raining. It's chilly. She waits on the stoop under an awning for a good five minutes, all the while hearing a woman telling her to hold her horses. When the door finally opens, a diminutive woman with curly white hair smiles at her, steps aside and lets Alberta in. "Let's get this over with," she says cheerily.

Merci offers her a glass of bourbon, apologizing that she didn't have any rye. "Word's out on you."

Alberta smiles, saying it's too early in the day, but Merci pours one shot each and puts the glasses on the kitchen table.

Merci is a striking woman, obviously beautiful in younger years. Alberta notices a group of photos on a wall in the next room and wanders over to them. "Handsome family."

Merci explains who they all are, lingering on a portrait of Al. "Passed three years ago," she says, kissing her fingertips and touching his photo. "This is Greggy, just as handsome as his grandfather. And here's Gladys with her new husband. Good man. She did good this time."

They sit at the kitchen table. Merci throws back her shot. Alberta follows suit. Merci starts talking the way a lonely old woman does when no one visits anymore. Alberta asks why she didn't live at the lake. Merci compliments her on cutting to the quick of a matter. "My husband got confused once in a while. Little strokes, you know? He let Marty – that's Gladys's first good for nothing husband. Not that the new one is good for nothing. He's a sweetie."

"Merci?"

"Why don't I live at the lake? I'm getting to that. Marty ran the construction company Al started. Al eventually turned the business over to him. Should have sold it to him but instead, we got a cut each month but they got shorter and shorter. How could we know he was bleeding it dry? Who'd even think such a thing? Well, when Al passed, Marty tells me business has been bad for a long time, just didn't want to bother Al with it. He said I didn't have a pot to piss in. I just thanked God Al never found out. It would've killed him."

"Marty said he'd buy the cottage from me. Gladys assured me they'd never tear it down. Assured her brothers they'd still be welcome whenever they wanted to come out. Not that it mattered. Neither of them ever brought their families out."

"Why's that?"

"They were already teenagers when we built out here. They'd be up before dawn, out on the lake fishing. They'd come in and I'd feed them. They'd go out again, to the woods, to the swamp, to the spring, out swimming, paddling around. Sometimes I didn't see them all day until it was time for dinner.

"Then that little Conner boy drowned back in '38, and that was it. My boys didn't want to be there anymore. It did something to them. Like maybe it was their fault. Nobody should have to learn about death that way. The Conners were real nice people. Only had a year or two out there before their youngest drowned. Then they just stopped going. Took over twenty years to finally sell the place. I heard the parents died. I think one of the kids sold it to the Eastmans. Fixed it up real nice."

"How did it happen? The Conner drowning. I've heard some of it, but what do you think happened?"

"Oh, sad thing, very sad thing. All the boys were skinny-dipping in the spring and Sammy drowned. Awful thing. My Gladys used to babysit for them in town sometimes. She was a wreck the rest of that year. Just couldn't get her head around it." Merci fiddles with her shot glass. "Didn't babysit for them after that."

"Do you remember anything about him?"

"Sammy? He was their youngest, that's all I remember."

"You were telling me about Marty buying the cottage from you."

"I told Gladys from the get-go he was no good. Married him anyway. Gladys kept insisting nothing would change when they bought me out. Well, it did! He lowballed me on the price. Then he bought the Conner place . . ."

"The Eastman cottage?"

"Yes. Conner. Eastman. Right next to ours. He bought that through the business as an investment just before he ran the business into the ground. No more crews. No more equipment. Sold the warehouse. Sold the Conner cottage for a loss. Then he filed for divorce! And all that was left was the house in town and my cottage. His cottage. Gladys kept the place in town."

Merci's voice gets pitchy. "The ink on the divorce papers wasn't even dry when he bought back the Conner place for peanuts and bulldozed both cottages."

"From who? Who would buy a cottage then turn around and sell it back?"

"Well, that is a question, isn't it? If you're asking me, was it a shady deal, I say yes. Absolutely. Can I prove it? Of course not."

"So, he bankrupted one company and started another?"

"Yes, he did. Son of a bitch. It was all a scam, but Gladys wouldn't even look into it because of her affair with Bill Fry. Convinced her she wouldn't get a dime of alimony if she fought him. Next thing you know he puts up that monstrosity of a house and moved into it! Have you seen his new wife? She's a child! She's not even thirty!

"You know my Al built all those cottages. He was such a good builder. Ours and Vogel's. Then the Conner place and Fry's. Built the last one on spec after the war. Dick and Evelyn got it for a song. Al couldn't stomach debt and he'd carried that place for two years. Marty would never have done that. He'd have sat on it forever, jacking up the price every damn year." Merci runs out of words.

It's still raining. Alberta hears the patter through the open window over the sink, and the occasional big drop smacking a trash can lid.

Merci starts back up, more reflective, subdued. "Jane and Calvin Conner broke up after they lost their youngest. Lots of parents can't take the stress. It's amazing Evelyn and Dick have made it this far, but I don't suppose they're really together, are they? I don't know what I'd have done if we lost any of our kids." She starts to pour two more shots, but Alberta stops her. "You go ahead if you want. I'm at my limit."

"Now that's not true. You're a three-shot woman."

"Word's out on me, eh?"

Merci laughs and rattles on about who could be considered alcoholics and who just drank too much. "Marilyn Vogel, Carl's wife? She was an alcoholic. Woke up to a tall tumbler of wine every morning. Called it fruit juice. Couldn't get going without it. But she always managed to make breakfast, lunch and dinner for their kids and any others who showed up at the door. We all did that. Fed whoever came through the door. She stopped drinking a while back. Just stopped and that was that.

"Gert and Mason have a daughter and another son, too. Eric and his wife have a couple kids. You know how some families just can't seem to spend any time together without landing in a big messy argument? That's them. Eric and the sister couldn't stand the fact that . . ."

"Merci," Alberta interrupts. "Can we get back to my questions?"

"You've been asking everybody about the drownings in the swamp. I guess that's what you want to know. I saw Steven Fry manhandle little Tyler the day before. Flew him to Timbuktu. Damn near hit a tree. He had issues. Steven Fry had anger issues."

"I understand your son-in-law had issues with your grandson."

Merci's eyes narrow. "You're talking about the apron thing, aren't you?"

"Apron thing?" Alberta was lost.

"Well, I never saw it. He only had his card games when Al and I weren't around."

She stops talking suddenly. "Where was I?"

"The apron thing."

"Oh yeah. Supposedly Marty made Greg dress up in an apron and serve them their drinks. I don't know if I believe it or not. But like I said. Marty was a shit head. Broke Gladys's heart when Greg left home, but I have to say it was for the best. Everybody thinks Marty kicked him out. Not true. Greg left on his own. He's good to his grandmother, that boy. Calls me regularly. Came back to town for his grandfather's funeral. He's out in Colorado now working with runaways. Just finished his Master's degree. It's more than I can say for his siblings. The girls are brats, and Kevin is no better."

"Bill Fry." It isn't a question so much as a new topic.

"You mean my daughter and that Romeo? Marty was gone a lot. Marty was a shit." Merci smiled at Alberta. "I may have said that already. Bill Fry could be quite the charmer. I didn't blame Gladys for anything except believing he'd ever leave Betsy. I mean really. Seven kids between them and she thought he was going to marry her?

I told her to keep it simple but she had to go and fall in love with him. Broke her heart when Betsy showed up with that powder blue Lincoln. That's how we always knew when Betsy was tired of Bill's latest fling. She'd make him buy her a new car."

Alberta stays for another half hour as Merci runs through a litany of familial complaints. None of it is relevant to the case, but it never hurts to listen. She finally asks if Merci knew if all her grandchildren were in their beds the night Tyler and Peter drowned. Merci assures her they were. "I heard that storm coming and I closed all the windows. Checked every bed. Counted heads. I like a house full of sleeping children. Beats a houseful of wide awake ones."

When it seems she has just about run out of steam, Alberta asks about Eugene and Velma Stem. "I know they lived at the lake full-time and they just had the one boy, Walter."

Merci revs up again. She says something was always strange about Eugene and Velma. "He was a silent man and she was pleasant enough, but something was always a little off. In the beginning, she'd come by for coffee. Even drop in for a drink with us. But only when Eugene was out on a job. He'd leave her out there for weeks at a time all alone with that little boy."

Alberta tells her Eugene was a welder. "Intermittent work."

"That would explain it. You see? I didn't even know that. We knew nothing about them. We were just getting to know Velma a little when Eugene retrieved her one evening and that was the end of that."

"Retrieved? You mean the Vogel thing."

"Hauled her off. There were weeks when we wouldn't see her at all. If she was outside when we walked up, she'd go inside. She had this gash on the side of her head once, like she was missing a chunk of scalp. If you ask me, he probably beat her. I suppose we should have done something, but back then you just let things be. They always kept the place up nice. We all appreciated that."

"What about the skinny dipping? Back in '38. Whose idea was it?"

"When the Conner boy drowned? Whose idea? They were boys, weren't they? It could have been any of them."

"Do you remember who found the body?"

"Well, if I remember right, it showed up in the channel a few days later. I guess it was the Stems who found him."

Alberta excuses herself, saying she has places to go and people to see but Merci isn't finished. "You asked about Eugene and Velma Stem," she says. "The Velma Stem before Eugene died and the Velma after he died were two different women. If you put them side by side, you wouldn't even think they were related."

"How's that?"

"It was right after Eugene died. Walter was off fighting. England, I think. The war. We didn't even know Eugene died, but we were out to get something from the cottage. Don't even remember what now. I remember it was off-season. No one around. We saw smoke through the woods and went over to see her standing in her yard, stuff piled everywhere, I mean everywhere, and this huge blazing fire in the middle of the yard. She was burning clothes, curtains, rugs, furniture! And it wasn't just his clothes. All hers, too. All those nasty brown and gray dresses.

"You remember the color of her clothes?"

"Never told you this, did I? Black lace-up shoes. Black tights. Long sleeved dresses buttoned all the way up. Even in summer. Long hair tied back. Not a lick of makeup. That was Velma before her husband died.

"Al helped her haul an old easy chair out of the house and drag it onto the fire on top of a mostly burnt mattress. Don't know how she managed that on her own." Merci grows more animated. "She was throwing stuff onto that fire like a crazy woman, like she was releasing it all to hell or something. We left her there. You know, I don't remember now if we even went to the cottage after that. I think we just went straight home. Oh. It was late winter because, in the spring, Al and I were the first to show up. You can't imagine how shocked we were. She'd cut down a couple of the huge pines in front of her place."

"The Stem place?"

"Yeah. You could actually see it from the road. And there were men there painting the house yellow. Bright yellow! She saw us and ran out hollering, all happy like I'd never seen her before, wearing this electric green blouse and hot pink pants and she told us to stop over for a visit. Well, later on we did. And she came to the door in a sleeveless flowered dress, red open-toed sandals, and make up. She didn't even look like the same woman. I remember like it was yesterday. Tons of makeup. Too much blush, red lipstick and blue eye shadow! Her hair was cropped as short as a man's. She served us cocktails from a fully stocked bar and toured us through the house. We'd never been in it before. Seriously. Never. She had everything painted in the most god-awful colors. Even painted the landing on the channel. Bright red." She leans back and shakes her head. "Bright red," she says again, quietly.

Merci is clearly spent and Alberta stands. "This has been delightful, Merci. Absolutely delightful. Thanks for your time."

Merci doesn't get up. "Think I'll give my Greggy a call."

"Sounds like a fine idea." Alberta slips on her coat and steps out.

Merci calls after her. "You leave Evelyn out of all this mess. She can't handle any more pain."

CHAPTER 36

Aug 17 - Who can ever say they got what they expected out of life? I don't know what I expected really. I'm not sure I ever had high - make that any - expectations. Just kept putting one foot in front of the other. Don't know what I'd be without George and Mildred. I'd have never found any ambition on my own I don't think. I wonder what Mom's expectations were that she felt so disappointed? She lost a child. But she had four others. And a husband. What more did she expect?

So many moments pass by as inconsequential as the shadow of a drifting cloud. When Penn walks up from the lake one evening in late August, she stops outside the kitchen window, watching her mother standing at the kitchen counter, drenched in the amber glow of sunset. Evelyn hums, repeating the same three notes as she stirs piles of Cheerios on the counter.

Penn opens the door and Evelyn spins around, waving her arms slowly in the air. "Ronny's dancing!" She wobbles and almost falls.

Penn guides her to a chair. "In the street!" Evelyn shouts, trying to shove Penn away. Finally in the rocker, Evelyn sits, working her hands, like kneading bread or knitting, both things her mother never did. They won't keep still. And like her hands, her mind spits out random words and sounds, none of it making sense until she demands a spoon. Penn brings her one. Evelyn grabs a magazine and tries writing with the spoon. "Eggs, vodka," she says. When the spoon falls from her grasp, so does the intention and Evelyn finally calms, humming again, new notes, but still only three.

All summer, Penn has watched her mother go in and out of lucidity, but things are declining fast now. Evelyn's mind is almost always misfiring, sending indecipherable messages her words can no longer untangle. It reminds Penn of her garden in Ann Arbor, the overgrown conglomeration of perennials she hasn't gotten around to thinning out. Left to their own devices, daisies crowded out sundrops that had overtaken a once-great sea of coral bells. Individual Japanese iris had begun growing among the foxglove and salvia. The poor peonies had to push through ever-increasing roots of false dragonhead. All semblance of what had once been an orderly arrangement was gone now. The garden was simply a jumble of peculiar textures and colors, weeds and grass, their seedy stalks waving in the breeze, everything out of context.

Tears stream down Penn's face. She sits on the landing behind the rocker and lets them flow. No matter what had come between them over the years, love held on, and the ache of it won't let go.

She does not yet know it will be the last time Evelyn will negotiate the stairs, the last Penn will see her mother stand at the kitchen counter.

Penn takes the untouched bowl of oatmeal away. A Hospice nurse, yet another they haven't seen before, arrives. "Boys everywhere," Evelyn mutters. "Mice. Little biting ants." Sometimes her mouth keeps moving, but no words come out. "And the girl," she says. "Always starting something."

The nurse sits next to her and slips the oxygen meter on her finger.

"Me, Mom. That girl was me."

Evelyn squints at her, then relaxes, her mind wandering again.

"Men yelling at him all day." The nurse wraps her arm with the blood pressure cuff, and Evelyn complains it's too tight and slaps the woman's hands. "Out here, his kids. Shoving, shoving, shoving!" She waves her arms around. The nurse groans and starts the cuff inflation again. "He stayed away. Only me. Me, me, me, me . . ."

"Were we so horrible?" Penn asks as if she expects a real answer.

Evelyn glares at Penn, searching for something, then looks at the nurse and cocks her head, sneering. She asks for a drink as the nurse removes the cuff and takes out a measuring tape.

Penn pours a small glass of Vernor's and hands it to her mother, who takes one sip and intentionally drops it to the floor. "Vodka," she demands. Penn grabs a towel from the bathroom and cleans it up.

The nurse asks Penn how the pain has been.

Evelyn snaps. "It's my pain, not hers. It's been shitty! That's how the pain's been! She wants me to suffer!"

The nurse looks at the med log Penn keeps. "Mrs. Hodges, this is your daughter. She doesn't want you to suffer."

Evelyn spits. "Bastards. Other kids loved each other. Not mine. Nasty. All the time. Head bashing. Bashing their little heads." In slow, deliberate syllables, Evelyn speaks directly at Penn. "Should have wrung your necks." She yanks the oxygen monitor off and throws it across the room.

The nurse averts her gaze.

Penn goes downstairs.

The nurse helps Evelyn to bed and comes down to Penn. She reminds Penn not to take anything to heart, that confessions of the dying are just the mind losing touch, like in a dream. But she doesn't know the family. These confessions are no dream.

"You can increase her morphine drops," she says. "Up to three doses in any four-hour period. Wait fifteen minutes between each until she feels relief. And be sure to keep up with the senna and liquids. This stuff will stop her up if you don't."

Watching the nurse leave, all Penn can think about was her mother's words. *Should have wrung your necks.* Evelyn didn't love her children. Evelyn didn't love *her*.

Penn comes close to leaving Evelyn alone but stays. At two in the morning a single word came blaring from the monitor. "Drugs!"

Penn gives her mother the bottle of Roxy and goes back to bed, slamming her door and yelling through it. "Do it yourself!"

> AUG 19 - We are organic beings subject to the laws of nature. A person can only hold so much poison in their soul before it works its way to the surface.

Penn wakes early, or more to the point, just decides to stop trying to sleep. She looks in on her mother. Evelyn lay stiff as a board, fists clenching the sheet. The Roxy bottle is on the floor, open in a dried puddle.

"I didn't want to wake you," Evelyn says. "You need your sleep."

Penn quickly pulls another bottle from the med pack and doses her, this time sitting on the bed, touching her mother's white knuckles. "Ten minutes. We need to give it ten minutes."

Evelyn's jaw is in a vice grip. Her brow tight. Her eyes frantic. "What are you afraid it will do? Kill me?"

Penn gives her another dropper. Evelyn's face relaxes a bit. Then a bit more. Her grip loosens.

"I'm sorry, Mom. Really."

"Don't leave me." Her voice is weak. "Please. Don't leave me."

CHAPTER 37

Alberta drives around the lake after leaving Merci. The rain has quit. The day is getting steamy with temperatures expected to hit eighty. In May, that feels hot. She is beginning to get a feel for the lake boys, for what their summers must have been like, none of them choosing their exile, all of them struggling with a sort of captivity. And was it really so different for the parents? Living two lives. Spending summers cooped up with a clutch of people, relationships borne of proximity. Husbands gone more than not, their lives barely upended, going to work, sleeping in town in their homes, a solitude taken for granted. Wives left to fend for themselves, outnumbered by rambunctious children, grateful to return to winter lives back in town with activities, civic and social, reunited with real friends. No wonder they drank themselves to sleep.

On Spirit Marsh Road, a name that no longer held any topographical meaning, Alberta pulls into the driveway of the biggest house, Marty's three-story *monstrosity*, as Merci called it. A young woman is putting a baby into a car seat in a Buick. A toddler dances at her feet. She looks up at Alberta with a beauty queen smile, automatic and insincere. Alberta, still sitting in her car, asks if Marty is home.

"And you are?" the pretty young woman asks, still smiling.

"Doesn't matter. Is he here?" Alberta is pleased watching the girl's smile disintegrate. She doesn't trust people who smile, and this one was clearly adept at using her looks to get anything she wanted. Marty walks outside. Alberta watches him kiss his wife and buckle the toddler in the front seat. Alberta has anticipated they'd be a ridiculously mismatched pair, but the woman looked mature for her age, and Marty looked young for forty-eight. She was arm candy for sure, but he made it work. They were actually a handsome couple.

As his wife pulls away, Marty saunters to Alberta's car. "I don't have anything to say to you."

"Oh, you might be surprised. It won't take long, Mr. Wagner." Marty stands too close to let Alberta get out of the car. "Marty. It's only a few questions."

"So, ask."

"I prefer to sit inside if you don't mind. Mosquitoes are out already." She smacks one as it lands on her arm. Marty backs off and walks into the house. Alberta follows.

The kitchen is massive and open to the living area with a full view of the lakefront. Marty grabs a beer from the fridge and situates himself on a barstool at a marble-topped island with a bar sink in it. He does not offer Alberta a beer or indicate she should sit. "Nobody knows what the hell you're doing here," he says. "Or what gives you the right to ask all these questions. Who the hell are you anyway?"

"My name is Alberta Higgins, Mr. Wagner. And this is an official investigation." Alberta pulls out a stool on the other side of the island. "Mind if I sit?"

"Would it matter?"

"Pretty simple stuff. What did you see the night Tyler Hodges and Peter Eastman died?"

"The thing is, I heard you're a prosecutor. Prosecutors don't investigate."

"Hmm. Curious. What did you see that night?"

"What do you mean, what did I see? Nothing."

"You and Gladys were in bed. Sleeping."

"Yes."

"When did you leave the party down at Vogels'?"

"Hell if I know."

"Who was the first person aside from family that you saw the next morning?"

"What do you mean?"

Alberta lets out a long, rattling sigh. "Are you going to make me repeat every question because that would make this take much longer than it needs to. Try to remember that morning. Someone let you know something was wrong, something happened. Tell me how that morning in particular unfolded."

"I heard Millie Eastman calling for her boy. It was weird because it was still dark out."

"Millie? I haven't heard anyone call her that."

"Mildred sounds too stuffy. She looked more like a Millie to me."

"Were you having an affair with Millie?"

"What do you mean by that?"

Alberta cocked her head and grinned.

"No," Marty said. "I was not having an affair with Mildred Eastman."

"OK. I'm going to ask you a lot of questions. Don't think too much. Just tell me the first thing that comes into your mind."

Marty takes a draw of beer and cracks his neck. "Let's get this over with."

“Who was the first person you saw that morning?”

“I’d say Millie. Mildred. I saw her walking down the road calling for Peter. Then I heard Ronny Hodges next door hollering that the boys were missing.”

“What did you do that morning after you heard the news?”

“I went to the Hodges house.”

“Where were you that morning? Where were you sent to look for the boys?”

“Dick sent me and my boys to look in the woods.”

“Who found the bodies?”

“I heard Walter found them.”

“How did you know they’d been found?”

“The whistle. We heard a whistle.”

“What was said?”

“When?”

“When you followed the whistle to the marsh.”

“I don’t remember.”

“Who went in after the bodies?”

“We all did.”

“Did you see anything unusual?”

“Two drowned kids was unusual.”

“What did you hear? What was said?”

“His face is gone.”

This stops Alberta. Marty says he’d seen worse in the war, but that, at the marsh, it nearly turned his stomach.

“What else did you hear?”

“He’s naked.”

“What else?”

Marty starts to take another swig but stops. He speaks deliberately. “Jesus Christ. Something ate his dick.” He takes the drink.

Alberta keeps drilling. "What else was said?"

"They must have been frogging."

"Who said that?"

"I don't know. That's enough of this shit."

"Think. Who said they must have been frogging?"

"I don't know."

"Was it a boy or a man?"

"A man." Marty looks up, startled by his response. "It was a man. Walter maybe. Or Bill."

"Bill Fry?"

Marty nods.

"What was George's reaction?"

"The professor? He was all over his boy. So was Dick."

"How did Walter Stem act the rest of the summer?"

"Didn't see him after that."

"Was that unusual?"

"Yeah. No. I don't know. I hardly ever saw him." Marty said Walter was always doing stuff with the boys. "Then he kind of stopped."

"Did anyone else change behavior the rest of the summer?"

"Anyone? Everyone. Two kids died."

"Did you go to Tyler's funeral?"

"No."

"Did you go to Peter's funeral?"

"No."

"Describe your relationship with Walter Stem."

"Nonexistent."

"Did you ever have anything to do with Walter away from the lake?"

"Christ almighty! Enough with this shit. I feel like I'm on a witness stand. But then, you are a prosecutor." He finishes his beer and gets another.

"Did you ever run into Walter away from the lake?"

"No. Well, at the school when our team played his. We didn't talk."

"Where was Steve Fry?"

"When?"

"When you were all searching."

"I don't know."

"Was he at the marsh?"

"Probably. Yeah. He was in the water, pulling one of the boys out."

"Then, he was one of the first ones in if he was pulling one of the boys out?"

"I suppose."

"But Dick sent the Frys way over to Spring Lake. How would he have been one of the first to go in if he was the farthest away?"

"How the hell should I know? Maybe he wasn't. It was kind of crazy. Everybody was everywhere."

"When did you know your son, Greg, was a homosexual?"

Marty slams his bear on the counter. "None of your goddamn business."

"Did you ever hit your son, Mr. Wagner?"

"Only when he needed it."

"Do you have any reason to believe Greg would have lashed out at others as a result of your actions?"

"This is bullshit. What you're getting at?"

"When Greg was a teenager, did you really make him wear an apron and wait on you and your poker buddies?"

"Look! He never did a damn thing to those boys. I don't care what anybody says."

Alberta got what she came for. "I don't believe I suggested he did." Alberta gets up, takes a wine glass from a nearby rack, and fills it with tap water. She drinks it all and puts the glass in the sink.

"We're done here," Marty says.

"Yes, we are. That wasn't so bad, was it?" Alberta turns to leave. "I'll show myself out. Oh. One more thing. Who filled in the marsh?"

Marty doesn't answer.

"It's a simple question. Who filled in the swamp?"

"Velma, I think. She did it. Before she sold it."

Standing in the doorway, Alberta smiles at Marty. "I see. And, if I go looking at the registrar of deeds office, that's what I'll find?"

Marty stands up, puts his hands in his pockets, looking Alberta dead in the eyes. "I think we both know you've already been there."

Alberta shrugs and goes out, finding Bill Fry waiting for her.

"Just who the hell are you?" Bill demands.

Alberta gets in her car. "I really want to talk to you. Mr. Fry, right? Really, I do."

"You see, the thing is," Bill says, "no one seems to know anything about you." He motions to Marty for confirmation. "And that makes me very uncomfortable."

"Where is your son, Mr. Fry?"

"Steve? What did he do now?"

Alberta says nothing.

"Look," Bill says. "He's on probation. He's got a job somewhere up north. What the hell do you want him for? Inside," Bill says. "Come on. We can talk inside."

"I do want to talk to you," Alberta says. "Tomorrow. I've had enough for today." She drives away, giving Bill time to stew. She wants both Bill and Betsy uneasy.

CHAPTER 38

The next morning, standing at the screen door of Bill and Betsy's house, Alberta overhears Bill coaching his wife. "Simple answers. Better yet, just don't talk. And . . ." Alberta makes her presence known with a knock. Bill stops abruptly and lets her in.

Entering the Fry house is like walking into an *Architectural Digest* magazine spread. Beautiful but heartless. Betsy smiles, greeting Alberta with the pseudo-graciousness of an old friend come to visit. Like the house, she is beautiful yet lacks any hint of warmth. She is impeccably dressed and at fifty-two has held her figure nicely. While her hair looks rich and thick, her skin, shiny with some hyper-emollient lotion, bares the ravages of too many summers in the sun. Still, her features have a timeless quality, thanks in part to a touch of work somewhere along the line, indicated by the taught line of flesh between her ears and mouth. Compared to Bill, she's the fountain of youth. His skin is a withered field of freckles flowing in and out of a web if wrinkles.

Betsy leads the way through to the front room, a showcase in pale blue and white with a large glass and chrome dining table on one end, surrounded by white upholstered chairs, and adorned with a massive silk flower arrangement. Betsy indicates they all sit in any of the large white leather chairs overlooking the lake.

Betsy asks if Alberta wants something a drink, a cup of coffee, a pop.

Alberta tells her to just make herself comfortable then jumps right into the muck of things. "Bill, I've been curious. Why do you suppose the swamp was filled in?"

Bill answers immediately with an authoritative cadence. "Liability. It was Velma's land. A hazard. She was damn lucky neither of those families sued her when those boys died."

"And you advised her? Suggested she fill it in?"

"No," Bill says. "Never talked to her about it."

"Certain about that?"

He shrugs.

Betsy jumps in, saying Marty did it. "Declared bankruptcy. Dumped his wife. Married that prom queen and bang. Bought that land and started building down there." Bill grabs her knee, squeezing. "Well, he did!"

"You have anything to do with that deal, Bill?"

Bill's words carry no expression. "I did some legal work for Marty's company. I'm not at liberty to . . ."

"Yes. Not at liberty," Alberta says. She asks if Bill knew who Marty's silent partner might have been, but Bill says again he is not at liberty to say.

"That's what you came here to talk about?"

"No," Alberta says. "I'm sure you know why I'm here."

Betsy tries to say she hadn't really heard much except that there'd been questions about the two boys who drowned ten years ago but Bill jumps in, talking over her. "I don't believe you're acting in any official capacity."

Alberta's expression doesn't change. She looks Bill dead in the eyes without speaking.

"We're not going to talk to you. In fact, I'd like you to leave," he says.

Alberta doesn't budge.

"Now," he says, standing up. "I'd like you to leave now."

Betsy's eyes dart between the two.

"Sit down, Bill," Alberta says with a strong note of condescension. "It's either me or somebody else. Either way, somebody's going to ask you about these deaths. Let's just get it over with."

Bill sits back down and shifts into lawyer-to-lawyer-help-any-way-I-can BS mode. "I'd like to help, but I don't see that we have anything you need here."

"That's not exactly true, is it?" Alberta speaks slowly. "You know as much as anyone out here. You were here all that week, before it happened. You stayed over that Sunday night instead of going back into town, didn't you? And seems to me . . ." She fumbles through some notes, but only for show. "Bill, you were at the party down at Gert and Mason's."

"Oh, he never made it over to Vogels'," Betsy quips.

Bill looks away.

"Yes," Alberta says. "I guess that's what I heard. And Betsy, you got into it pretty good with Gladys?"

Bill and Betsy both sit up a little straighter.

Alberta looks up at them and smiles. "Well," she says. "I guess that is a bit off topic, isn't it?" She's beginning to have fun. "Let's talk about the morning the two boys were found dead in the marsh. You were awakened by Mildred Eastman calling for her son."

"No," Betsy interrupts. "I didn't wake up until Jimmy knocked on our door."

Bill grabs her knee again.

Betsy glances to the floor.

Alberta insists she just has a few questions, routine housekeeping stuff. "You know what I mean, counselor."

Bill says he does corporate law. "For Hamilton Manufacturing. I don't know much about …"

"I see, well then." Alberta interrupts. "It's all in the details, does that work better for you?"

Bill rolls his eyes.

"The morning the boys were missing," she asks, "who was the first person you saw that morning?"

"Jimmy Hodges," Betsy says again. Bill agrees.

"I heard he took a tumble when he saw your daughter in her nightshirt. How do you think that happened?" Alberta lifts a large photo of Laura from an end table. "I can see she was knock down gorgeous. I guess he literally fell for her."

"I don't know anything about that," Bill says, taking back the photo.

"But you were right there. You must have seen how it happened."

Betsy looks to Bill who gives her a condescending half grin.

Alberta asks what they did that morning after they heard the news.

Betsy explains that she'd gotten dressed in a hurry and stuck close to Evelyn and Mildred. "I wanted to be there for them. I told Laura to corral all the girls and get them inside. We didn't need them getting all hysterical."

Bill says he headed over to Spring Lake to look. "As Dick suggested. It was his idea we look over there."

"Was Steve with you? Your son? Steven?"

"Of course he was," Betsy snipes.

"Yes," Bill says quickly. "Steve was with me. We were searching the spring and the channel."

"You're certain. He was with you when you were searching the spring and the channel."

"Yes. I just said that."

"Well," Alberta says, "this is what I don't understand, because from what I can tell, there were a lot of trees between the channel and the marsh."

"What's your point?" Bill asks.

"It seems to me that it would have been virtually impossible to hear a whistle from the marsh. I believe Carl blew a whistle when he found the boys. That was the signal to everyone. Now, there are five cottages and a lot of trees between the marsh and the spring. How did you know the boys had been found way over there?"

"We heard somebody yell it out, I guess. Maybe Marty or Greg. They were searching the woods."

"And Steve was with you at this point?'

Bill says again he was.

"Who found the bodies?"

"Vogels. Walter."

"When you got there, Bill, who was already in the water?"

Bill looks up to the ceiling, thinking. "Walter, Carl, Dick maybe. Greg, I think."

"Wasn't your son in the water when you got there, Bill?" Alberta leafs through her notes and reads out loud. "Mason and Marty both said … uh, here it is. Steve Fry was one of the first in the water. He pulled Tyler Hodges to shore. Is that right? Because the official report didn't say that."

Bill's expression is difficult to read, somewhere between anger and outright fear. "I don't remember."

"You saw it, didn't you? The official report?"

"I don't remember."

"But you basically wrote the thing."

"I did not," Bill snaps.

"Says right here you were the sheriff's primary source."

"I don't remember anything but confusion. A lot going on all at once. We were all pretty upset."

Alberta starts to write, muttering. "A lot going on all at once. We were all pretty upset." She looks up to Bill. "Do you remember what was said? In all the confusion, as the boys were being pulled out of the water?"

"Of course not. I don't remember," Bill says.

"Fair enough. Betsy, how much time did Steven spend with Walter Stem when he was a little boy?"

"What the hell does that have to do with anything?" Bill gripes.

"Please answer the question, Mrs. Fry."

"Well, he spent a lot of time with him. He was seven when Timmy was born. Laura was a toddler. I had my hands full and I suppose Steve just got lost in the shuffle."

"What did they do together?"

"Do?" Betsy looked befuddled.

"Yes. What was your son doing all day with Walter?"

"I don't know. Why would I know that? Bill? What is she asking me this for?"

Bill heaved a sigh and told Alberta to find another line of questions.

"Did they spend a lot of time alone, Betsy? Walter and Steven?"

"I suppose so. Well, no. I mean, Velma and his wife were always there."

"Bill, did it bother you that your son spent so much time with another man?"

"I don't know where you're going with this," Bill said. "I worked a lot. He was a handful. Every hour he spent with Stem was an hour my wife could breathe."

"Did spending time with Walter help Steven? I mean, did he stop acting out, or whatever he did?"

"Nothing helped that kid," Bill grumbles. "Still treated me like shit. I finally put my foot down and said he couldn't go to Stem's anymore. Privilege revoked."

"How was he after that, Betsy?"

"I don't know. He was nine by then. Out the door in the morning with the other boys. Didn't see him all day."

"Bill, where was Steven the night the boys went missing?" Betsy's eyes open wide. She looks quickly to Bill.

"Was he home?" Alberta asks.

"Of course," Betsy says, trying to sound believable.

"When was the last time you saw him that night?"

Betsy doesn't answer.

"Listen here!" Bill shouts. "I've heard all the questions you're asking everyone! You're trying to make everybody think something criminal happened to those boys. If that's what you're saying, I put money on Greg Wagner. He's a homo, you know. We all knew it."

"Yeah," Alberta says. "I've heard that."

Betsy chimes in. "Who knows what that pervert did to those boys. Always taking those little boys skiing, helping lift those half-naked bodies into the boat." Bill grabs her hand this time and squeezes.

"Calm down, Darling. Take a breath."

"Mrs. Fry," Alberta asks. "Is there any reason you might have a grudge against Gladys and Marty Wagner? Some reason you might want to get Greg in trouble to get even with them?"

"You mean because Bill here was screwing Gladys?" Bill shoots her a hard look. No effect. "Honey, Gladys was only one in a long line of women my husband screwed. She just happened to be the most inconvenient for me. But I got my powder blue Lincoln because of Gladys. I think I even thanked her for it."

"You got that car because you threatened to divorce him, isn't that right? And you were going to take Laura and leave the boys with him?"

Betsy laughs. "You can't believe everything Merci Malone says. She's a crazy old drunk."

"What does any of that have to do with anything?" Bill barks.

Alberta grins. "Nothing. You people out here just fascinate me, that's all."

"I suppose," Betsy says, "you're going to tell everyone about Laura's abortion."

Bill shouts at her to shut up.

Alberta looks at them with discernable disgust. "Let's try this again. Where was your son that night."

Betsy says very softly that she doesn't know. "He wasn't in his room."

"He was," Bill says.

Alberta continues drilling. "Let's go back to the marsh. There's a lot of confusion. Somebody's carrying two dead boys to the muddy shore. Women are crowding the woods. Mothers, fathers, grieving over their dead sons' bodies. Did no one have an explanation for why the boys might have been in the swamp that night in a storm? Did no one offer up any ideas to these grief-stricken parents?"

"Yeah," Bill says. "Uh, I think someone said they'd probably been frogging."

"Who said that? Was it a man or a boy? Or was it one of the women? Or a girl, maybe?"

"No. I don't know."

"Was it you, Mr. Fry? Did you come up with that supposition?"

Bill squirms. "It might have been. Seemed obvious. I mean, why else would they have been there?" He composes himself. "Don't forget the pillowcase. That explained it. You need a pillowcase to go frogging. Standard issue stuff."

Alberta's brain skids to a full stop.

"Standard issue," he says again, driving home the point. "You put the frogs in a pillowcase. Why have one if you're not catching frogs?"

"Who found the pillowcase?"

"An officer," Bill says. "It was in the water. In the weeds. We didn't see it at first."

Alberta starts ruminating aloud. "In all that sloshing around, no one saw it. But it was there later. When the . . ." She pulls out the police report searching for reference to the pillowcase. "Here. Found it."

"I told you."

"Yes. You did. Whose was it?"

Bill looks at her, shrugging.

"Mr. Fry, did no one ask who was missing a pillowcase?"

Bill leans forward looking at her hard. "What are you trying to say?"

"I don't know, really. Just seems convenient that the one piece of evidence that proves your theory…"

"My theory? Everyone thought the same thing."

"But it strikes me as a little peculiar how everyone decided those boys had an accident. The Eastman boy had a broken nose. He was naked. The Hodges boy had a dislocated shoulder. Can you tell me what made your son, Steven, so angry the day before that he threw Tyler Hodges halfway across your front yard?"

Betsy bolts upright, her hands shaking.

Bill snaps at Alberta. "What are you trying to say? Our son had nothing to do with killing those boys."

Alberta gives Bill a moment to realize the words he's chosen. "Mr. Fry, I didn't suggest he did. Why would you think anyone killed those boys? Says in this report, the one you helped write, that it was an accident."

Betsy looks to Bill in a panic.

"It's all right, Mrs. Fry. You should sit back down. You bring up a good point, Bill. Did anyone, when you were all trying to piece together events that might have led to the deaths, did anyone suggest that some of the pieces just didn't fit right? Let's take them one at a time."

Alberta makes her points, one by one, carefully taking in the expressions they elicit from both Bill and Betsy. "Peter Eastman. Seven years old. Eighty-two pounds. Tyler Hodges. Eight. A hundred pounds. An athletic boy. Strong. On his best day, could Peter have ever pulled Tyler's arm out of its socket? And how did Peter break his nose?" She didn't give them a chance to answer. "And here's where this theory really throws me. Looking at these photos," she reaches into her satchel and pulls three out, "that water is shallow. I know there were a lot of weeds and reeds and cattail and such. But even if Peter fought like hell, all Tyler had to do was walk in and help him stand up. The water wouldn't have even been up to his armpits. Yet they were found way out in the middle, in deep water. And why didn't Tyler have his flashlight? And what's the point of catching frogs if no one's awake to cook them? I gotta tell you. Not much of this makes any sense to me. Why did your seventeen-year-old son beat up an eight-year-old kid the day before that kid turned up dead? And where was your son that night?"

Betsy starts to cry. "I don't know! I don't know how those boys died! I don't know!" Tears pour out.

"Betsy! Just shut up!" Bill yells.

Alberta continues as if there has been no outburst. "Looking at the sheriff's notes from that next day, Bill, it looks like you did a lot of the talking for everybody. Makes sense, I suppose. Being a lawyer. Seems you were the one who concocted the story, how it had been accidental, no one else involved. Just two boys being boys. You tied it all up nice and neat in good lawyerly fashion. Almost as if you had something to hide. Only Steve wasn't searching with you that morning. He was at the marsh. Almost like he knew where they'd be. Why did he come home all muddy that night, Bill? So muddy Jimmy Hodges slipped on the wet, muddy clothes in the morning."

Betsy looks at her husband in shock. She could barely speak. "You think he . . . those boys . . . Steve had something … you think he … Is that why you sent him to Madison?”

"Betsy! Shut up!"

She runs from the room. A door slams down the hall.

Alberta is finished. She's gotten what she came for, proof Bill always suspected it was no accident. She steps out of their lovely, large, beautifully decorated house.

Bill white knuckles the doorknob. "You do anything you can for your kids. Anything. You won't find one shred of evidence against my boy."

"Mr. Fry, you're absolutely right. Your son Steven was an angry boy. Maybe it was because his father was fucking the neighbor's wife, and God only knows who else. Maybe because his mother was a money-grubbing bitch. Maybe there's more to it than that. I don't know. What I do know is that your son was in a fight at the tavern across the lake that night trying to defend Debra Stem. Tucker kept him there until he cooled off, which happened to be most of the night. Drove him home himself just before dawn. Dropped him off up the road. Didn't want to get stuck in the washout. Tucker watched him slip and fall and get up covered in mud. That's why your son was wet and muddy when he got home. Not marsh muck. Road mud."

Bill stands in the doorway watching Alberta get in her car.

She backs up and turns to drive off, stopping to deliver one last blow. "Steven wasn't home all night because he heard you and your wife arguing over whether or not you were going to stop fucking Arleen Miller."

Alberta pulls away with Bill hollering after her. "Then what is this all about? You fucking bitch! What the fuck is this all about?"

CHAPTER 39

Aug 25 - Summer came so early this year. Seems like it's been here forever. It should be fall. She should have died by now. I should feel some sort of guilt writing that, I know. But I don't. I suppose it will set in later. Maybe not. What in the hell does that say about me?

A Hospice nurse finishes her exam and packs up. "There's significant decline," she tells Penn. "Have the Depends been helpful?"

"She's been making it to the bathroom OK."

"Well, I'm leaving you with more Depends and ointment. She'll be stationary more now and could be prone to bedsores. You'll need to keep her clean. How often are you bathing her?"

"She's been doing that herself. And I won't be applying any ointment. You have aides for that, don't you?"

The nurse smiles. "I'll set you up on a schedule for daily aide visits. That should do it for now. Here is your extra Roxanol, more anti-anxiety meds. Remember to keep up with the senna tablets. These opiates will stop her …"

Penn interrupts. "Yes, I know the drill."

The nurse says she's only doing her job. "I need to know you understand how compromised she is."

"I do understand. Believe me."

"Push the liquids. I'd like to review the comfort pack with you in case she gets psychotic . . ."

The nurse gathers her things to leave, like all the rest, having covered everything on her checklist.

Following that visit, an aide arrived every other day to bathe Evelyn, change her bed, wash her hair, trim her nails, whatever needed to be done. It was rarely the same woman two times in a row. Most were nice enough, performing their tasks with a modicum of respect and kindness, a difficult thing in the face of Evelyn's slaps and outbursts. She didn't like to be touched. One woman in particular regarded Penn as if she should have been doing these things for her mother instead of hiring it out. Penn had her taken out of rotation.

Penn is good at living alone. She fills her free time without effort and rarely gets lonely. Even though Andi is off on her own, Penn can sense her daughter, wherever she is, as certain as she can sense her own existence. And she still feels Matthew, though in a deeper place, a room in the back of memory where he still putters on his tall ship model, the one he never finished. Her only issue with being alone is maneuvering around the silence of it. The lack of another body stirring next to her, no one breathing, no one turning the page of a book, padding through the house, locking the door and turning off lights. Something about Evelyn lying in the next room, her breathing so tenuous, reminds her of all she's lost. The weight of silence made heavier.

The summer after Mathew died, Penn took the double bed out of their room at the cottage and replaced it with a new twin, a bed he'd never slept in. She told herself she'd done it because it was a small room, and the small frame freed up more space, but it was more than that. It was an invitation for him to leave. Or a request. She wasn't sure which. She sometimes felt his presence in bed with her at the Ann Arbor house, and that was fine. He didn't die there. Memories there were full of comings and goings, quick dinners, long lazy Sundays, Andi bounding in and waking them, her small body climbing over them after a dream or running from thunder or the moon watching from her window. Those memories, Penn welcomed. He was always whole there.

It was at the lake in the last few months of his illness that Matthew began to vanish by increments, his face growing thinner, his wit slower, his hands weaker. This is the Matthew she wanted to banish. They'd made love for the last time in that double bed. Though they knew each other's bodies by heart, this time, their intertwining took them to a place they'd never been before, where time had no dominion, where corporeal bodies vanished, a place without words or thought, where all that existed was love.

With her mother dying in the next room, Penn wants Mathew back. She wants to feel him next to her in their old bed. Instead, reaching over with her foot to what would have been his side of the bed, she confronts a knotty pine wall. It seems particularly cruel that Evelyn can conjure Tyler from the dead, but Penn can't manifest Matthew, now that she so desperately needs him.

September brings rapid change. It becomes more and more difficult for Evelyn to string words together. She has less eye contact, and what little there is carries no recognition. Hearing thumping in Evelyn's room, Penn finds her mother on the floor wrestling with the pillow, pushing her arm into it, saying that her blouse shrank. Penn extricates her, helps her on with her robe, gets her into the wheelchair, and takes her to the living room.

"Penny's in the fridge," Evelyn says.

Trying to make sense of chaos, Penn retrieves a cold Vernor's, putting it in a kid's sippy cup. It seems to calm Evelyn for a time, so Penn curls up across the room with a book she's been trying to read, but the words don't stick no matter how many times she reads them. Her mind isn't willing to take in anything beyond making it through another day. When she looks up from the page, she sees Evelyn, teeth clenched, eyes squeezed tight. Three doses of Roxy later, the pain persists. It takes another two hours for a doctor to show up. A new one, a woman. She helps get Evelyn back in bed and listens carefully to her gut.

"Is she eating?"

"Please," Penn says. "The Roxanol isn't working. She needs relief."

The doctor gives Evelyn an injection and listens again to her belly. "Very little bowel sound. But if she's not eating, that could explain it." Evelyn's body melts into the sheets, her head falling to the side, her mouth hanging open. Penn thinks she's died.

"This should hold her over till the morning. I'll get a pump installed. The cocktail of meds should curtail the worst of the pain. It will have a button to administer each dose. There's no issue of overdosing. She will be out of it more now."

The doctor continues, but Penn isn't listening. She knows the drill. The doctor leaves. There is nothing for Penn but silence laced with anger and regret.

Sept 25 - I live inside a heartbeat, like my life is only as brief. I see this room as it was when I was two and as it is now and see what comes next. Andi with a family, then it's empty again, dark, damp. And I see through to the next people and to the next time it's empty, until it's dozed over. The lake dries up. It isn't just my life spinning away, it's the planet moving toward its next iteration. Our extinction. When the sun has its way with us and wipes the planet clean. Inside that heartbeat, the space between one and the next is interminable - just waiting for her pain to ease.

"Bake me!" Evelyn shouts the next morning, rolling on her side, clutching her stomach.

Penn watches from the hall as a young man screws a piece of monitoring equipment onto a stand next to Evelyn's bed then gets down on his hands and knees to find a wall outlet.

"Ketchup!" Evelyn screeches, her legs shifting under the covers. "K-K-K-K-K-K." Like a broken record, she is stuck on the sound until the needle jumps to another groove.

He plugs in the unit and leaves. Two nurses step in to hook up the med pump. One takes hold of Evelyn's arm while the other inserts the I.V.

Evelyn continues her incoherent rant, looking to the ceiling. "Raining in here!" The nurse pushes the button and Evelyn settles.

"Beetles," Evelyn mutters. "Dick. Beetles."

With Evelyn freshly sedated, one of the nurses goes to wash her hands. The other, one Penn hasn't seen before, gazes at her with patronizing eyes. "Korsakoff," the nurse says. "Rough stuff." She thumbs through some pages in the back of the file. "I see some atherosclerosis in here, too. But with her history of alcoholism, this is the Korsakoff psychosis. The distended belly, jaundice, the puffy fingertips. Cardiomyopathy. Liver failure. Between the pancreatitis, gastritis, and cirrhosis, the pain will only get worse. Her kidneys will be shutting down soon. We're nearing the end."

"What alcoholism? I don't understand," Penn says. "She's got cancer."

The other nurse shoots back into the room, grabbing the file. "Karen! Stop talking!" She flips to the first page, showing Karen the red NON-DISCLOSURE stamp. "We need to go. Now!" Dodging Penn's questions as they pack up, Karen disappears out the door in a hurry.

Penn yells after them. "Did my mother ever have cancer?" After a long silence, the nurse answers. "I am not breaking any confidences by saying your mother does not have cancer."

The nurse gives Penn a moment to gather her thoughts.

"Twenty-four-hour care," Penn demands. "Starting tomorrow. I don't care how you do it. Make it happen. I need to get out of here."

The nurse says she'll take care of it. "I'm sorry you had to find out this way."

Penn tries to knit together the remnants of her life while everything she thought she knew disintegrates. She looks at her mother. Her mother, the alcoholic, who's hidden in plain sight all her life, who's let her assume she had cancer. The woman who thought the best way to get through to her kids was head bashing. Never hugs. Or kindness. Or love. Her mother, who is so drugged out she does not flinch when Penn slams the door.

> Sept 27 - Midnight - We are all deeply flawed individuals. All we can hope for in this life is someone to look past those flaws and accept us for who we are. How in the hell do I look past this?

Escaping her mother, leaving her in the hands of a stranger, should have felt good. It didn't. On the highway the next morning, Penn flies in and out of traffic, passing everyone, needing the greatest distance possible in the least amount of time. She's running from lies, from the cottage her mother is contaminating.

For two hours, one word hammers her brain. Alcoholic. It explained her mother's secrecy, isolation, and anger. Alcoholic. The word turned her mother's life from a tragedy into a choice. Alcoholic. No matter how many times she says it, Penn can't wrap her head around it. My mother, the alcoholic. Whatever pity she'd ever had for the woman dissipated with those words. Given the option of choosing family over booze, her mother chose booze. And Penn wonders how she'd missed it all those years, why she hadn't noticed the drinking was obsessive. More than at any other point in their strained relationship, she now feels she never knew her mother, and she wonders if the woman had always resented her children, held them in contempt. Was there ever love? The emptiness of revelation makes her gut squirm. She pulls into her driveway in Ann Arbor, ready to break. She hasn't noticed Andi's car parked out front.

As Penn steps through her back door, she sees Andi, who feigns being caught in the act of theft. "I'm stealing your food processor," she chirps. "Cooking for a hoard this weekend." One good look at her mother, her strained face, and Andi envelopes her, pulling her close, holding her tight. "I love you, Mom."

Penn begins to cry, but the tears stop as fast as they began. Anger won't let pain break through. She can't bear her anger spilling onto her daughter who is giving a dinner party, who has friends, who is happy. "I need to be alone," is all she has to say. Andi knows better than to argue and leaves, yet on her way out the door, she turns. "You always act like you're alone. You keep cutting me out? Maybe one day you will be." Andi leaves her mother standing slump-shouldered in the middle of the kitchen.

Penn sits at her dining room table in the dark, remembering the incessant arguing throughout her childhood, the quiet kind the kids weren't supposed to hear. But her parents' bedroom was next to hers. She heard. It was muffled, but she heard a pill bottle hit the wall once. She heard Evelyn say over and over it wasn't her fault. It seemed to quiet down the winter before Tyler died. Not as much fighting. But Evelyn began obsessing about housework insisting everything was fine.

Penn remembers coming home from school one day to find her mother standing at the stove in a daze while a pan boiled over. She called her dad at work. He came home and told Penny to take a long walk, but she could hear the yelling from the driveway and something crashing, and she went back in. They both told her to leave. She didn't. She was afraid the way a kid is afraid but doesn't yet understand why. Her mother disappeared up the stairs, and her dad shouted at Penny, his hands in fists. "I told you to take a walk. I mean it! Go!" Penny ran outside.

Even in her own bed in Ann Arbor, far from the cottage, Penn startles awake, sitting up with the impulse to administer Roxy. She is on her feet, stubbing her toe on the nightstand before she realizes where she is. It takes a moment to get her bearings, and yet again, sleep eludes her and she pulls out her surrogate therapist, the journal, spewing an incoherent rant only to tear the pages out the next morning.

Over the course of the next couple days, Penn tends her overgrown garden. It isn't a large garden as she spent too much time at the cottage every summer to mess with a large plot, but it was pretty when it was kept up. This year it had been ignored. She deadheads and trims. She plans to dig and transplant. She hoists bag after bag of mulch from the car to the wheelbarrow, too many at a time to manage without tipping. She hauls them to the shrubs along the driveway, to the hasta patch at the front porch and into the garden, spreading it all by hand on her knees until her back and shoulders are about to give out. She goes to bed physically exhausted.

As sometimes happens, Penn wakes in the early hours with an epiphany as if someone has just explained to her the inexplicable. Normally these episodes were welcome. Not this time. It suddenly occurs to her Evelyn's alcoholism was, in fact, not a surprise, but something Penn had chosen not to see. In this realization, she is forced to accept she's done little more than feign attention - for years. Of all the times she stopped by the apartment, she couldn't recall an instance when she wasn't relieved with her mother's refusal to open the door. She'd heard the slurring, the fumbling. She'd known. Or did she? It could easily just be the hour screwing with her head.

Her cheeks flush with embarrassment, wondering how many people had seen through her ruse. As horrible a person as her mother had been, she was no better, visiting for the sake of being able to say she had, taking Christmas dinner to be able to say she tried, checking on her out of some guilt-borne sense of responsibility having nothing to do with love or even caring. Resentment grows by keeping distance, and they were both well practiced at pulling away.

And now Penn and Evelyn had become prisoners in the present as well as the past, Evelyn floating between the two with ease. Lying in bed, a sliver of moon eyeing her, judging her, Penn realizes how superior she'd felt to her mother, to her brothers.

She was the one who stepped up to tend their dad after his heart attacks and made the funeral arrangements when he died. When Evelyn refused to drive after an accident, it was Penn who found her an apartment within walking distance of a store and downtown. It was Penn who found a buyer for the house. It was Penn who set up Evelyn's finances, put her on a monthly allowance, found her a job. It was Penn who moved Evelyn to a cheaper apartment after Evelyn couldn't hold a job anymore. How noble. How selfless. How much a fraud she was.

All these things were little more than a desperate attempt to hang on to any thread connecting her to that fragile childhood, those first ten years when she had a family. The others had found ways to move on and away while she clung to the cottage and the lake for dear life, her entire identity wrapped up in it. Matthew tried to tell her as much before he begrudgingly agreed to buy the unkempt cottage from her mother, before he agreed to spend every summer there, before he agreed to put on a new roof and redo the wiring and plumbing and remodel the kitchen. He wanted to put in new windows, but Penn refused, only willing to go so far for fear of cutting out the heart out of the shrine. That's what Matthew called it once. Only once. Penn didn't speak to him for nearly two weeks, banning him from setting foot there: Just as her mother had banned her and everyone else.

Thunder rumbles in the distance. A gust of wind buffets the house. Tears fill Penn's eyes as she finally understands she has become her mother, equally tormented, stuck in the past. She begins to cry, a full-throated sobbing, something she had not done since Matthew died. It feels good. Cathartic. Loud and wet and convulsive. The storm hits full force. Hail pounds the house, her sobs reverberating with each burst of thunder. The storm passes. And in its wake, Penn falls back to sleep and dreams she's floating high above Spirit Lake clutching a heavy rock to her stomach. She holds on to it tighter and tighter until suddenly she lets it go, and watches it fall through the mist until it plunges into the water, the splash barely audible as she floats gently upward, unburdened. She sleeps through till morning, packs clean clothes, and drives back to the lake.

Penn arrives to find her mother shockingly gaunt. Evelyn's gaze seems slower to move from one thing to another. She'd stopped eating the day Penn left. She slept more with fewer stretches of wakefulness. She sees Penn and asks to look at the lake, but she isn't strong enough to sit in the wheelchair. She falls back to sleep before disappointment has time to register.

The caregiver leaves just as a doctor arrives to explain what comes next, but Penn already knows the drill. There will be Hospice people in and out now until the end.

Sept 29 - I should not have left.

For five months, Penn has waited for her mother's death, on the bad days sometimes hoped for it. Only now does she realize the foolishness of her indifference. Only now does she begin to fathom the finality of it, when it is conceivable their last words to each other, understood by both, have already been spoken. She had dreaded taking her mother in. Now, she feels an urgent sense of losing time with her, of losing something that mattered, something she will miss. It was all too cliché.

October brings a cold snap. The furnace kicks on. Wind whips the trees clean. Evelyn wakes late morning, asking for a sandwich. It makes Penn think of her father right before his last stroke. Penn goes through the motions of making a chicken sandwich and brings it to her. Evelyn's already dozed off again. Penn eats it bedside while she peruses the summer's journal entries, adding a brief note to mark the succession of last days.

Oct 1 - Why is she hanging on so hard? I used to think life was tenuous, fragile. Watching this woman cling to it, I think life is one stubborn force.

After lunch, Penn dusts the dresser, unaware Evelyn's eyes following her every move.

"Dusting the bunks?" Evelyn asks in almost a whisper. The dresser stands where Jim, Ronny, and Mark used to sleep.

The softness of her mother's voice washes over Penn. She turns to look at her, at eyes that hold recognition, at a smile that holds love.

"You were the easy one," Evelyn says, her eyes gentle. "I worried when you lost Peter."

"You mean Tyler?"

"No." Evelyn says, and she begins to fade, her words streaming from some distant place. "You were so alone."

A single tear slides down Evelyn's face. She pushes the button. Her face glazes over.

"Mom?"

Evelyn retreats back to the void, leaving Penn yearning for more. It was the first time anyone had shown compassion for her over the loss of the boys. No one consoled her when it happened. No one asked her how she was. No one ever said they understood why she was so sad and angry and lost. Not her father. Certainly not her mother. Now, out of nowhere, Evelyn decides to care? It is too much.

Penn bolts outside, slamming the door behind her, and starts walking the road, the one that used to be a simple two-track but was now wide and paved. She passes the two big houses where the three cottages once stood, one of them Peter's. She charges past the place where the back path used to be, now a paved road leading over to the filled marsh and big houses. She wants a do-over. As much as she loves Andi and Matthew, and teaching, she'd give it all up for a do-over, to get Tyler and Peter back, to see her mom succeed with her sobriety, to have her dad a few more years, to have her brothers grow into decent human beings, to have the life that was stolen so long ago. Stumbling over her own feet, she falls to the pavement, in the middle of the road, and lays there, the ache in her gut more painful than the ankle she's twisted.

Slowly rising to her feet, she suddenly feels the cold, realizing she's gone out without a jacket. She hobbles back to the cottage, cold, sore, and angry.

Penn builds a fire downstairs and sits wrapped in a blanket with an ice pack on her ankle. She calls Andi, suddenly panicked with an irrational fear that even thinking about erasing her from this world could have somehow triggered a response from the universe, an accident, or some irreparable harm to her. It hadn't. Andi answers, her first words full of love and concern. "How are you holding up?"

From there, the conversation travels an uncharted course through reflections on the final hours before death, choosing between two fellowships in the fall, a man Andi had just met who might show promise, the garden in Ann Arbor, car repairs, and a new recipe for wilted kale with apples and sage sausage.

All summer, throughout the ordeal with Evelyn, Penn had purposely avoided talking with her daughter, believing it was better to keep Andi separate from the toxic family drama. She'd carefully protected Andi from it all her life. Why burden her with it now? Yet hanging up the phone, after nearly an hour, she realizes talking with her was a helpful distraction. A tonic. It got her out of her own head. More than that, she hopes it gave her daughter a sense of inclusion. Going forward, Penn would do her best to fix whatever distance she may have inadvertently put between them. She didn't want Andi to have to learn at her mother's deathbed she was loved.

In the morning, an aide stops by to bathe Evelyn. As she finishes securing the diaper, Evelyn mumbles, her words falling untethered to thought. "I put the boulders out. But my bike is wet."

The woman smiles, pulls the covers back up, and leaves the room. Evelyn starts to hum Jingle Bells. Her expression deadpan, her physical being limp and still, contrary to the buoyancy of the song.

The humming stops. "Dally dog," her mother whispered. "Dog og og og og." Her eyes slowly wander without focus, then close. The sheet rises as her frail body begins to arch. Penn pushes the pain pump and watches the sheet lower, the body underneath melting into stillness.

Penn pulls on her sweats and goes outside, leaving the aide to watch over Evelyn. Standing at water's edge, she zips her fleece up to her neck and crosses her arms against the chill. Wind from the north stirs whitecaps across the lake. All the docks except hers and Dan's are dismantled, stacked up on the beach, and strapped down, pontoon boats pulled up, encased in tarps. She didn't have the heart to dismantle the beach so long as Evelyn was still aware. It could wait. Dan said he'd be out by month's end to do them both. If Evelyn was still around by then, nothing was going to matter to her anymore. He'd bring his son to help and Penn said she'd cook a mess of perch for them.

Penn likes a clean shoreline, an uninterrupted ribbon of sediment between the grass and water. She knelt down and looked into the soup. No longer the clear water of summer, it was full of decaying matter floating just below surface and on top, like rafts of sewage to the untrained eye. In the air, the smell of sulfur. The lake was turning over. It was a natural process that came with colder temperatures in the fall, warm surface water cooling and sinking down through the cool middle layer, the cold oxygen-depleted waters of the bottom rising, bringing with them the gases and decayed vegetation built up over the summer. Turnover mixed fresh oxygen into the lake, replenishing deep waters, releasing sulfurous fumes, making it possible for fish to return to the depths for winter. It was messy, but it was healthy. It was necessary for the lake to survive.

Penn's world, like the lake, is turning over.

CHAPTER 40

Alberta leaves Bill and Betsy Fry, certain she's set them straight, certain the drowning of Tyler and Peter was no accident. She pulls up to the cabin to find a car parked out front and a hefty man with graying hair standing at her door open.

"Sheriff Bates," he says. "We need to talk."

Another car pulls up. An old man climbs out, slowly shuffles past them, dropping to a chair inside, breathless. "Doctor Patrick Leary," he says to Alberta, who's now picking sweatpants up off the floor and the bra off the bathroom doorknob. "Coroner. Retired."

"You've been busy, Miss Higgins," Bates says.

"I know who you both are." Alberta sits in one of four chairs at the table, taking her notepad out, flipping to a page with a list of questions. "OK. Let's do this. You need anything, Dr. Leary?" Leary shakes his head and waves a hand but she gets him a glass of water just the same, talking all the while. "You both had to know there was more to it than two kids messing around and accidentally drowning. One boy naked. One maimed. Both bruised. Their bodies hidden in the middle of a marsh. Strikes me as worth at least the contemplation of an assault of some kind."

"Nobody thought it was anything more than it was," Bates grumbles.

"Mr. Bates . . ."

"Sheriff Bates," he interrupts.

Alberta gives him a little smile, correcting herself. "Sheriff, did you ever try to find out whether it was Evelyn Hodges or Mildred Eastman who was missing a pillowcase?"

"Irrelevant."

Alberta makes a note.

"Did you investigate at all? I'm looking at a mighty thin report."

Bates leans forward, arms resting on his knees. "Look. I talked to everyone I needed to. I was there. You weren't. What you're suggesting doesn't happen around here."

"And what am I suggesting?"

Bates leaned back again, throwing up his hands. "You tell me."

Leary speaks up. "I did my job. Those snapping turtles didn't help matters. Gnawing off what they did. A little closer to shore and the possums would have made short work of 'em. They'll eat every last thing. Hair, bone, teeth. And those leeches. Never seen so many at one time. Disgusting. And I don't say that lightly."

Alberta squirms a bit. "When exactly was the pillowcase found?"

"What? I don't know. Later."

"Later," Alberta mumbles as she writes.

"Dr. Leary, what about the bruises on the back of Tyler's neck and shoulders, like he'd been gripped, held tight. By hands larger than a child's?"

Leary wheezes. "Ever seen one of those really big snapping turtles, Miss Higgins? Scary creatures. The ones that chewed off their body parts were big ones." He holds up a closed fist. "Head this big. Those little boys, in the water, in the dark, wind howling around them? I guarantee if they saw one of those things in the water or half a dozen other scary critters, they'd scramble. They'd get caught up in roots and cattails. They'd lose their bearings in a heartbeat. Maybe the Eastman boy headed to deeper water. Maybe the Hodges boy died in shallow water and the wind blew him back out to the middle later that night. So many scenarios and every damn one of them feasible, but that's not my job. I just present the facts." Thrusting a thumb at Bates, he says it was up to him to figure it out. "As for the size of those bruises? Subjective. They could have been fighting. Or Peter was panicked and tried to take Tyler down with him. As I said. Not my job."

"Same for the ankle and wrist bruising, then?"

Leary says it was consistent with the boys tugging on each other.

She asks about the fragment of bark found imbedded in Peter's cheek.

Leary says it was likely acquired when they brought the body out of the water face down before turning him over.

Bates mentions a log on shore that had been shoved out of the way.

"Did you check the log for blood?"

Bates says no. Alberta makes a check mark on her notes. Bates rolls his eyes.

"All the bruises on your diagrams," Alberta asks. "You marked them all, Dr. Leary? You're sure?"

Leary glares at her. "Of course."

Alberta pulls the autopsy diagrams for both boys then sifts through the files for two photographs. "Here," she says, pulling her chair closer to Leary. "How's the light? Can you see well enough?" She opens a curtain wider, flooding his chair with sunshine. She hands him the photos. "This is Tyler's body. It's easy to see the bruises on his ankle and wrist. Just the left ankle and left wrist."

Leary agrees.

"And this body diagram shows those bruises."

Leary agrees and Bates reminds him the boy had been thrown in such a manner earlier in the day by an older boy.

Alberta tells him to hang on to that thought, then shows Leary the photo of Peter's bruising, identical to Tyler's.

Leary agrees. "Yes," he says.

She hands him Peter's body diagram. "Dr. Leary," she asks, "would you show me those bruises on your diagram here? I can't seem to find them."

Leary grumbles and points. "Are you blind? Right there." When he takes a closer look, he realizes there are no such notes. "I don't understand. I don't make mistakes like that."

"Is the rest of this your handwriting, Dr. Leary? I mean, it looks like it, but there are a few things that look a little off to me."

Without studying it closely, Leary says of course it's his writing. "I don't know how I, I, well, what does it matter? It doesn't change anything."

Alberta fights to contain her anger. "Let me show you another photograph, Dr. Leary." She pulls a photo of Alby's naked body on an autopsy slab. "Do these bruises look familiar? Ankle, wrist. Upper back and neck?" Leary only glances and looks away. "Look closely." She makes him take the photo.

Leary studies it, looks over to Bates, and hands it back.

"What I want to know is really very simple, Sheriff Bates. What was your motivation to lie?"

"What's that supposed to mean?"

Alberta sighs. "I get it. Bill and Marty were pretty convincing. Pretty damn scared I bet. Worried about their boys. Nobody but his own father thought Greg Wagner could hurt anyone, and then just because he's a homosexual. And Steven Fry? Nasty piece of work, wasn't he? And no alibi? Missing all night. And the bruises on Peter looked just like the bruises on Tyler, and everyone saw Steven put those bruises there. What are the odds one of those fathers put that pillowcase in the marsh to be found later?"

"You're out of your mind," Bates says. "Somebody would have seen that happen."

"Why did Bill send Steven away? To Madison, was it? Enrolled him that week. Summer school."

Bates looks up fast, eyes wide. "I have no idea what you're talking about."

"Madison," Alberta repeats. "The Military school. You have anything to do with that?"

Bates leans back and takes a deep breath, seething. "You don't have kids, do you?"

"No. I don't."

"Then you don't know how far a parent will go to protect them."

Leary gasps, glaring at Bates. "Carson?"

"We're not talking about your kids here, Mr. Bates," Alberta says.

"No. We're talking about an entire community. They're all my kids. And I took care of things. Quietly. Whatever happened to those boys, I'm certain it wasn't intentional. Things just got out of hand. We sent Steven away. And everyone woke up the next day and the next feeling safe."

"And you woke up with a bright and shiny future in real estate. I've seen where you live, Mr. Bates. Pretty upscale house for a law enforcement officer. Lovely landscaping. Four-car garage? Who needs a garage that big?" Bates cocks his head and purses his lips. Alberta continues. "You've made quite a nice living out here buying and selling property, haven't you? Bill made sure it all looked legit. Must have been lucrative being Marty Wagner's silent partner when he started up the new construction company from the ashes of Al Monroe's old business, the one Marty embezzled to death." Bates shifts in his chair. "You were pretty smart, picking up that marsh for next to nothing. I bet Velma Stem was happy to get rid of it at any price. And you filled it in and sat on it until Marty was ready to make his move. And he built those huge luxury homes down there with their big dock for their nice new boats. Too bad the lake got so shallow." Alberta sits still looking at Bates with utter contempt. "I'd say those boys dying was a pretty good deal for you."

"Now wait just a fucking minute!"

Leary gasps. "I wasn't in on anything illegal. Just what are you getting at here?"

"I'm saying, Dr. Leary, that the sheriff here altered your autopsy of Peter Eastman. He forged the diagram page, deleting the ankle and wrist bruising, knowing if anyone took a closer look, they'd assume Steven Fry was involved."

Leary looks at Bates who refuses to make eye contact.

"Did you honestly ever think it was all an accident?" Bates remains silent. "See, I don't think you're a bad guy. Seriously. I think you got caught up in something and thought you were doing the right thing. Am I right? Tell me how you envisioned it, how you came to think a seventeen-year-old kid killed two little boys. Just map it out for me."

Bates cocks his head at Alberta. "I'm not playing your little game."

Alberta glares at him. "You never believed it was an accident. Did you?"

"Not entirely," Bates says. He looks to Leary and then to Alberta. "I took care of it."

Leary's mouth falls open, incensed. "You took care of it? What did you do?"

"I was just thinking of Steve Fry," Alberta says. How does a kid live his life knowing his own father thinks he killed two little kids? That's got to mess his head, don't you think? I wonder if anything will change for him now."

"What does that mean? I'm not going to press charges against him now."

"Oh. You haven't heard from Bill yet. Steven was nowhere near the marsh that night. He was with Tucker at Anglers." She waits for reality to nick the bone.

Bates freezes. "So, what are you saying? It was one of the other boys? Greg Wagner?"

Alberta stares at Bates and slowly shakes her head. "There it is. The question you should have asked ten years ago. Tell me, Dr. Leary. You're pretty damn old. Were you by any chance the coroner for the Conner boy's death back in 1938?"

Leary glares at Alberta. "I'm pretty god damned certain you know I was. What's that got to do with the price of beans?"

"Beans? Really? Dr. Leary, you seem to have a history of making the facts fit the story."

Dr. Leary stands up too fast and falls back into the chair.

"I just can't see your angle yet," Alberta says. "If I look a little deeper, Dr. Leary, am I going to find out you came into a large unexplained sum of money right after you signed your coroner's report? Either of them? Or are you just incompetent?"

"You can spout your bullshit all you want," Leary wheezes. "You don't know what the hell you're talking about!" Dr. Leary tries to get up again but can't manage it. "Goddammit, Bates, help me out of this chair!"

Alberta stands over the men like an impenetrable wall. "Did you ever wonder why Walter Stem was at the swamp before sunrise, before anyone had even told him the boys were missing?"

"Someone told the Stems," Bates says.

"Who? I didn't see that in your report."

"Somebody."

"I see." She puts the autopsy photo of Alby back on the table. "Do you know where Walter Stem was the night Tyler and Peter were killed?"

"They weren't killed," Bates insists.

Alberta sees something begin to register in their faces. She pushes Alby's photo to the edge of the table.

"Bucks County, Pennsylvania. Two weeks ago. You know who lives in Bucks County, Pennsylvania, Sheriff?" Bates says nothing. Leary looks at Alberta with what seems pity.

Alberta opens the door. Sunlight streams in. "If you gentlemen would excuse me," Alberta says, "you need to leave."

Bates gives Leary a hoist up out of the chair and steps outside. Leary, catching his breath, speaks in a low, consoling voice. "Miss Higgins, I am sincerely sorry for the loss of your boy." He can see he's startled her. "I can read reports, too. Soon as you showed up, I went looking for why a woman would come here out of nowhere and start stirring up things that are of no concern to her. I did my job back in 1960. I did my job back in 1938. You're grasping at straws here. I guess you desperately need to make sense of a thing that just doesn't make any sense at all. I don't believe Bates here forged any report. It was my mistake. Unintentional. I'm not perfect. Walter Stem is a good man. He was up for the school superintendent's job here. Somebody else got it. Why he decided to leave is anybody's guess. A change of scenery. A fresh start. Who the hell knows? I know he left with a damn good recommendation." He starts to get breathless and wheezes as he gasps. "You're only seeing what you want to see, need to see, Miss Higgins. I can't fault you. I believe I'd do the same in your shoes. But you're not going to find the answer to what happened to your boy here. Go home to your family. Leave us to our own."

Alberta watches the men drive away. She is suddenly sure of nothing and feels emptier than she's ever felt. She walks into Angler's tavern hungry and weary. Tucker isn't around and her booth is occupied.

"Have a seat," Colleen says from the end of the bar. "They'll be gone soon."

Alberta sits down a couple stools away. "Colleen, isn't it?"

"Yeah. How long you in town for?" She takes a long draw on the tail end of a cigarette and crushes it into a full ashtray.

"I don't know. A few more days. Depends."

"I see you over there with Tuck. Getting along good with him, are ya?"

Alberta half smiles without answering.

"He's a good one. Good boss. Ya always know where ya stand with him."

Again, Alberta holds back.

"Free agent, that one."

This catches Alberta's attention and Colleen doesn't miss it. "Yeah, he was married for a while. Some girl he met in Atlanta. He wrote for a newspaper down there. Decided to come back here. She lasted about a year. Maybe less." Colleen digs the last cigarette from her pack and lights up. "Long time ago now." She glances to the mirror behind the bar in time to catch the people leave Alberta's booth. "Give me a minute. I'll clean it up for ya."

Alberta slides into her booth seat as Colleen takes one last swipe of the table with a damp bar rag. "Yeah," Colleen says. "She didn't want to be married to a bar. Or Tuck, I guess. Only way to see him is to hang out here every night. I don't think we were her kind of people." She wipes down the ketchup bottle. "She hated me. Whoa, she hated me!"

"Are you married," Alberta asks.

"Divorced. Twice. Two boys. One by each. Teenagers now."

"How do you manage . . . ?"

"Ha! Almost scarier to leave them on their own now than when they were little! I work the hours I want. Their dads step up. Can't stand the women they married, but can't have everything I guess, can we?" She picks up the dirty dishes she'd put on the next table. "Perch plate and a salad?"

"Sure."

"To drink?"

"Ice tea."

"Sweet?"

"No."

"Okeydokey." Colleen disappears into the kitchen.

CHAPTER 41

Alberta uses the bar phone to make some calls. By 7:00 that evening, she's parked behind Evelyn Hodges's cottage. Three other cars are already there.

Dick meets her at the door, sullen, and shows her in. In the living room, Mildred sits opposite Evelyn, both of them silent. George is at the window, his eyes quickly shifting from the lake as she enters.

Alberta thanks the Eastmans for driving up from South Bend on such short notice, Evelyn for letting them meet at the cottage, and Dick for showing up.

"I wanted you to hear this before I take it to the district attorney tomorrow. I'm certain when he sees what I have, he'll reopen your case."

Dick protests. "Why? Why reopen it?"

"If it gets to the truth," George says, "then she should move forward."

"I'm afraid it goes beyond your boys," Alberta starts. "George," you said that Peter wouldn't have gone out that night if he didn't feel safe. You thought he had to have gone with someone he trusted."

"Yes. I still believe that."

"A young boy, just seven years old, was recently drowned in Pennsylvania." She hesitates, wanting to tell them and not wanting to at the same time, suddenly second guessing herself. Whether it's their grief infiltrating her own or just her own grief rising, she feels her breath come up short. "He was murdered. The last anyone saw of him he was getting in the car of someone he trusted. The bruising on his wrist and ankle indicates he was thrown. Other bruises indicate he struggled, was likely held under water."

Mildred asks what that has to do with their boys?

"The bruising pattern matches those on Tyler."

"Wait a minute," George says.

"What are you saying?" Dick asks.

"I'm saying the boy in Pennsylvania was thrown into a river in the same manner your boys were thrown into the marsh."

Dick hollers. "What the hell . . ."

"So, what are you saying?" George asks, his face flushed. "No one was thrown! They struggled."

"Sheriff Bates and Bill Fry believed Steven Fry was involved, that it was an accident, but Steven was somehow responsible. That's why he was sent away to military school."

Dick shouts at her. "He what? What the hell?"

Alberta continues. "But Steven was nowhere near the marsh that night. And the autopsy diagrams. They were inaccurate. By error or forgery, I don't know. Maybe to cover it up."

"Cover what up?" Mildred interjects.

"So, what are you saying?" George asks again.

What she says next should register with them, she thinks, she hopes. It should answer all their questions, ring true, set things straight. "Walter Stem," Alberta says. "Walter Stem."

Mildred's eyes narrow. "What about him?"

"He is the prime suspect in Pennsylvania. He's the last person to see the latest victim alive. He's now the prime suspect in the death of your boys as well as the drowning of Sammy Conner back in 1938."

"Wait a fucking minute," Dick shouts. "You're trying to say our boys were murdered?"

"This is what you've been doing?" Mildred is aghast. "Weaving some insane story that Walter Stem killed our boys? I don't believe it."

Alberta tells them no one told the Stems the boys were missing. "How is it he was already in the marsh and …"

George interrupts. "We don't need to hear any more."

Mildred gets up. Her ire dissipates, her tone is almost conciliatory. "I think I understand what you're doing now," she says. "You don't have a good enough case against him in Pennsylvania, do you? You need a conviction here, or at least a status change on this case, something to implicate him, to show a pattern. Isn't that what you're doing?"

"Yes," Alberta says. "His proximity to the deaths of three other boys the same age under the same circumstances . . ."

"What do you mean three?" George asks.

"Another boy drowned swimming with Walter in 1938." She's overplayed her hand. She's lost them.

"No more of this bullshit," George says. "I don't want anything to do with this." He turns to leave but stops. "You've used us. Horribly. To suit your own needs. Shame on you. Shame on you!" George takes Mildred by the arm to leave.

"Wait," Alberta says. "Please. One question. Mildred, Evelyn, which one of you was missing a pillowcase? Whose pillowcase was found in the marsh?"

George and Mildred walk out without answering.

Dick and Evelyn remain. Silent.

Alberta waits for their reaction.

Dick talks quietly, rationally, without emotion. "I don't see what good it will do to break it all open, spread this horror story of yours all over the papers. We'll never have a moment's peace again. But this thing has always bothered me. It never felt right. Do you honestly, I mean in your gut without a doubt, think Stem did this? Do you have a case? Cause it doesn't sound like it to me."

"I have a case."

"What exactly do you think happened?" Dick asks.

Evelyn speaks for the first time. "No."

Dick makes her look at him. "It's time to know the truth, Ev. Let's listen to her."

Alberta takes a long breath to settle her nerves. She wants to get it right. "I think Walter had plans for Peter but Tyler interrupted. Intervened. Whatever happened, I think Tyler was a hero. I believe he was trying to save Peter."

"What do you mean plans for Peter?" Evelyn asks.

Alberta comes out with it directly. "The boy in Pennsylvania was sexually molested."

Evelyn lifts herself to her feet. "I hope you rot in hell." She disappears into her bedroom, slamming the door.

Dick stands slowly, his breathing shallow. "I hope to God you know what you've done. If you put this out, make any of this public, there won't be a parent at this lake or in our school system who won't think that asshole messed with their boy. All of them wondering did he touch my kid? Is that why my kid can't hold a job, or keep a wife, or whatever the hell else he does? Get the fuck out of my house!"

CHAPTER 42

Dick knows it's up to him to tell his kids what the upshot of the investigation is. Driving back to town, he contemplates what effect it will have on them, but he's certain the mere suggestion of violation will change them. It changed him. Nothing physically changed. His son was still dead and buried. But nothing would ever be the same. Every memory of Tyler going forward would be stained by violence, whether it was true or not. He'd never be able to think of his son without thinking of Walter Stem, without imagining Walter's hands holding Tyler under water, without imagining the kind of absolute terror his boy must have endured. Not wanting his kids to suffer the same thoughts, he decides to leave Walter's name out of it. If it was true, if he'd killed them, it would come out soon enough.

Dick sits in his living room staring at the phone in the hall. Choosing words. Picking them carefully for his children. Words that would say only what is necessary. Words that sound strong. Words without pain. Words that do not exist.

He wants them to hear it from him instead of someone else who might sensationalize or twist it. He would say it was just a theory, inconclusive, but they would hear behind the words that he believed Alberta Higgins's story. He would give them the facts and let them do what they could with it. It is all he knows to do.

He calls Jim first, tells him the whole story, including Walter's part. He tells Jim because Jim will know if he or the other boys had ever experienced anything inappropriate with Stem. Dick needs to ask. He needs to know. Jim says no. Not only no, but of course not.

"I don't believe it," Jim insists. "I'd know something like that. They're wrong."

Dick tells him he's not going to tell the others about Walter. "Keep this to yourself," he says. "Have Mark call me when he gets home."

"I'll tell him. But that's not what happened."

Dick hangs up. He's forgotten to say things like I love you and I'm here if you need me.

Jim steps to the kitchen sink and throws up into it. As the eldest, he already feels responsible for losing Tyler. He should have been more alert or sensed something was wrong. Though he was certain Walter had nothing to do with it, the implication it was not an accident has him grappling with who else could have been involved. Steve crosses his mind. It doesn't take long to dismiss it. Even Steve wasn't that screwed up. It had to be someone else. A stranger. Some other asshole at the lake who knew stuff. Somebody, anybody. "Shit. God damn fuckin'shit!"

Across town, Ronny listens to his father's words, to the concise, unemotional yet vague theory of assault. Then he calls Jim. Jim tells him about Walter. Ron says he doesn't believe it. He hangs up, telling himself nothing has changed. It's all conjecture at best. It changes nothing. But it changes everything. He'd never forgiven himself for ignoring the sounds that night when he heard Tyler get up.

He could have stopped whatever happened. But he didn't. He drives over to Jim's.

The more Jim and Ron talk it over, the more they believe there had been no attack. It was an accident. They're certain. When Mark gets home, they tell him everything, but he comes to the opposite conclusion. He's known in his gut from the outset it was never an accident, and he latches onto this version as his new reality. Having never spent one-on-one time as a kid with Walter, he has no reason to doubt Stem's involvement. "Fuckin' tight ass. You guys saw it. Wound so tight, walking the halls, nailin' my ass in school for stupid shit. He's not right in the head. Never was." He looks at his brothers, astonished at their ignorance, their willingness to believe Stem had nothing to do with it. "Seriously? You both can stand there and tell me you honestly don't see it?"

Ron and Jim both look at Mark like he's nuts. Nothing his brothers say changes his mind. No talking him down will settle him. "Walter could not have been involved," Ron insists.

Mark tells them they have their heads up their ass and storms out.

Penny listens to her father's words. She tells him it will be alright. She tells him they'd all find a way to move forward. She tells him she loves him. She thinks she hears him crying as he hangs up. She's already heard the news, the entire theory, from Mildred. Mildred had been gentle in her delivery. "Walter Stem may have been involved. Another boy has drowned where he lives now. There is no way to know unless Walter confesses. We love you. You're welcome here any time."

Dick sits in his easy chair. He hasn't moved since he fell into it after talking to his kids. He can't remember what he said to them. Did he say he believed Stem was involved or not? Did he say anything to help them process it? Did he just spew it out or was he careful? As if waking from some dream, he realizes the room is dark. He's alone. The rage floods over him and he sobs, hands clenching the arms of his chair, heart pounding against his chest, he sobs. The phone rings. And rings. He yells at it to stop. Screams. It stops. And rings again and again. This time he charges from his chair, grabs the receiver, about to shout *I can't help anybody!* when he thinks it might be one of his kids, and he pulls himself together. The voice on the end of the line is at first unfamiliar, a garbling, until he recognizes the incoherent slurring. It's Evelyn. And she's drunk.

"I'm done with it," she seems to say. "All of it."

Dick falls into the ensuing silence. When she was that drunk, nothing he said made a difference.

"He's here," she mutters. "He's on the road. He's watching me." Dick asks who. "Tyler!" she blurts. "He needs me. I have to help him. He needs my help." These may or may not be her words. It's just what he can make of them. He hears a clunk, the phone dropping, then shouting, indecipherable ranting from across the room. Small things clatter to the floor followed by a heavy thump and high-pitched wailing. He slides down the wall and listens, tears streaming down his face. She mumbles something he can't make out until she says it over and over again, each time louder. "I killed him. I killed him. I killed my boy!" Dick calls out her name to get her to come back to the phone, but all he hears is stumbling and then nothing until the scraping, like a drawer opening and then a crash to the floor, and he recognizes the tinny sound of silverware clashing. More silence. Bare skin, maybe a foot, squeaks against linoleum and another thunking, a crack, and he remembers the loose cabinet door and thinks she's fallen against it. Silence. She speaks, her voice weak as if carried by a last gasp. "He's all alone out there, Dick. He's so alone." The last silence is unbreakable.

The thoughts occurring to Dick as he drives, flying through a four-way stop, are unsettling and at the same time oddly comforting. If she's drinking again, if she's killed herself, would it really be so bad? Just one more tragedy to contend with. Her death would be easier for him than facing another bout of drunken stupors and vodka-induced tirades, all aimed at him for failings real and imagined. They've been estranged for so long. How would it really be any different? She'd at least put an end to her suffering. He comforts himself thinking if she's done it, if he finds her dead body, he'll already be halfway to rationalizing it. Yet even in these thoughts, his foot presses heavy on the gas pedal and he flies through the stop sign at County Line Road and nearly slides into the culvert, turning onto the road to the lake.

He skids in next to Evelyn's car, nearly hitting a tree. The cottage is dark. Time stops for a moment as he sits quietly, the motor idling, his heart calming to a steady beat, he thinks maybe shock setting in. How else could he explain it? *I'm about to find my wife dead on the floor and I'm calm.* He turns the key in the ignition, withdraws it, opens the door, gets out, shuts the door and stands there for a few breaths, slipping the keys into his pocket, pulling them out again in case he needs to unlock the door. His steps toward the cottage are measured and sure, his body merely a vessel conveying his heart and mind. The door is unlocked. He puts the keys into his pocket and steps inside.

Turning on lights as he goes, he hears the repetitious tone from the phone receiver downstairs. He goes down, steps over a lamp on the floor, finds the phone and hangs it up. He sees the kitchen floor strewn with knives and silverware, but no Evelyn. Glancing outside, he catches the fine line of her bare arm draped over the edge of a wicker chair, illuminated by the light from the window. She sits motionless. Breathing. Intact. His chest tightens. He struggles to breathe. He stumbles to the rocker, sits down and waits for it to pass. It always passes. This time feels different.

He moves Evelyn back to town the next morning.

She will not set foot in the cottage again for thirty years.

CHAPTER 43

Wednesday morning, Alberta shows up at the Lake County district attorney's office before it opens. Two women arrive at 8:30. She follows them in. It feels odd that they don't speak to her, like they expected her but are making it clear she's not welcome. One makes coffee, the other checks paper trays in the printer. Alberta finds a chair outside the DA's office and sits surveying the room, a few desks in the middle, walls lined with small offices, not unlike her department. Two more women arrive and settle at their desks. Alberta notes the hierarchy. These two are in suits. The others wear skirts and blouses. One sorts through a stack of files, then delivers them to various offices. Another starts right in typing. Four men walk in, all in suits, each barely offering the women a nod. They glance at Alberta, then at each other. The coffee's done. Everyone gets some. Except Alberta. One of the women makes a fresh pot. The men disappear into offices. A phone rings in the main room, answered and soon followed by a ringing in one of the offices. Three women type away, the tapping sometimes almost synchronous, then shifting, like a river of sound. A woman stands at the copier as it spits out page after page. Alberta sits. Still. It's 9:30 before DA Sterling arrives.

Alberta watches him approach. He's a nondescript man, an everyman, a man one would be hard-pressed to notice in a crowd. Seeing her, he grumbles to his secretary, one of the suited women, who shrugs. Walking past Alberta, he steps into his office, drops his briefcase on the floor, and sits down without once addressing Alberta, much less looking at her.

Alberta stands. "Mr. Sterling, I'm . . ."

"I know who you are."

"It's about those boys . . ." She steps over to his desk.

"I know," he says, clearly annoyed. "Walter Stem."

"If you don't press charges on Walter for the deaths of Peter Eastman and Tyler Hodges, I can't use any of this in the case against him in Pennsylvania."

He smiles and cocks his head. "I am aware of that, Miss Higgins," he says with unadulterated condescension. "However, your case in Pennsylvania is of no concern to me. Present your findings for this case here and let's see where it takes us."

Alberta lays it out slowly, deliberately, certain of the strengths. "First off, they all had reason to lie, make it look like an accident. Marty Wagner was scared to death his queer kid did it, or even more afraid of falling property values if it got out that a child killer was running loose. He'd just built four spec houses by the tavern. How would he sell them? And Bill Fry. He caught Steven sneaking in just before dawn, all muddy. Bill was the first to suspect his own son had something to do with the whole mess. Bates agreed but didn't want to charge a kid with murder and thought the best thing was to keep it quiet and send Steve away. Somewhere safe. Straighten him out. "

Sterling leans back. "Please tell me you have more than conjecture."

"Tyler's lungs were filled with organic material, muck, found in shallow water. Peter's lungs were filled with clear water found twenty-five yards away in the clear spring water in the middle of the marsh. Yet, according to the sheriff's report, they supposedly died together."

"The boy got turned around, went deeper instead of back to shore. Next."

"It can't be coincidence that the bruises on Tyler's right ankle, wrist and upper back match the bruises on the Bucks County boy. And look," she says, spreading out photos. "This shows the bruising on Peter, but the autopsy diagram doesn't. It's been forged. There are differences in the handwriting. It's close, but there are huge discrepancies between . . ."

Sterling interrupts her. "Move on."

"What? This is important. Someone in the coroner's office or maybe even Sheriff Bates tampered with evidence."

"I said move on."

"But. . ."

"You're skating on very thin ice here, Miss Higgins."

"Walter found the bodies but no one told him they were missing."

Sterling interrupts. "I dispute that notion and so will a jury. People were calling all through the woods. He knew the boys better than anyone and his hunch that they were at the marsh paid off."

"But his jean jacket. He wore it the night the Pennsylvania victim died. He has no alibi for that night. There was old blood on the jacket, enough to test. It wasn't a match to Alby Higgins, but it is the same blood type as the Eastman boy. Blood evidence." She winces, chiding herself for saying Alby instead of Albert.

"Blood evidence. And how many people in the country are that particular blood type? Move on."

"Look at these photos," Alberta urges. She spreads the childhood pictures of Sammy, Tyler, Albert, and Walter on his desk. "Look at the physical similarities of the boys. Can't you see it? They are all Walter. Something happened to Walter in that house he grew up in. Something awful, and he's going to keep reliving it with other little boys. These won't be the last. There may even be others we don't know about. Bates should have stopped him years ago! You have to stop him now!" Tears well in her eyes, something she promised herself she'd never do, lose control of her emotions.

"Coincidence," Sterling says, averting his eyes as she wipes her face. "Young boys are more vulnerable than they realize. Trying to keep up with older boys can be dangerous business."

"But Walter Stem's proximity alone to the drowning deaths of four young boys has to mean something."

"Any defense attorney will convince a jury it's just coincidental. He lives around water. He works with children. Here's the bottom line." Sterling speaks with a bite to his tone. "All you've told me is that there is a possibility the Hodges and Eastman boys might have met with more than an accident. You say the autopsy diagram was forged. The missing notation could just as easily be an oversight. Forgery is a very serious allegation. Dr. Leary is retired. You want all his cases scrutinized? Do you have any concept of how that will affect past convictions? And Bates is respected. I'm not going to charge either of them with something I can't prove, ruin their otherwise exemplary careers. They'd lose their retirement benefits."

"Retirement benefits? How can you be so blind? Bates was bribed! He always knew there was more to those deaths but covered it up, for the wrong reasons, but he covered it up."

"Bribed."

"Bill Fry and Marty Wagner paid him off. They thought their boys were involved."

Sterling rolls his head and mutters an obscenity. "You're implicating innocent boys now, Greg Wagner and Steven Fry?"

Alberta's voice gets tighter, higher, argumentative. "I'm not implicating the boys, it's their fathers. I think Bill Fry planted the pillowcase after the fact to protect his son from suspicion, but Walter Stem is the one they should have been looking at."

Sterling crosses his arms. "You've gone too far."

"Bates profited when those marsh houses went up."

"You mean he made a good investment? A lot of people around here have made good money in real estate. Not a crime." Sterling leans forward. "So you're saying you believe foul play, but you've already ruled out the Fry and Wagner boys, hell, all the boys at the lake, and the only person of interest in the deaths of Hodges and Eastman is Walter Stem. Oh, and let's not forget the Conner boy back in the thirties. Your motives here, your bias . . ."

Alberta suddenly realizes her error. All she needed to do was raise suspicion enough to reopen the case. She has gone too far.

"There was no murder," Sterling says. "Walter Stem did not kill anyone, and I hope to hell you people in Pennsylvania drop it before it ruins his life if it hasn't already. You haven't given me any hard evidence. And I'll be damned if I'm going to stir up any more mess than you already have. Just pack it in and go home."

"But Walter Stem is the common denominator!" Alberta pleads. Her voice cracks. "And . . ."

Mr. Sterling stands up, his eyes cast downward to Alberta. "Go home, Miss Higgins. And maybe think about another line of work. I don't think this one suits you."

Alberta looks Sterling in the eye, defiant. "It's the jacket," she says. "It's the key."

"Well, you put that jacket on Walter at the scene and we'll talk," he says.

Alberta walks out berating herself for losing control. She'd let her voice get pitchy. She allowed tears. She blew it.

Lydia Metzger holds the door open for Alberta at the paper. "I already got the call," she says as Alberta walks in. "I'm not supposed to talk to you."

Alberta stops, her mouth hanging open in disbelief.

Lydia mimics the expression, her jaw dropping even lower than Alberta's. Then she huffs. "You don't think he's going to tell me how to run my paper, do you? Let's look at what you got. We'll compare notes. "My father always thought Walter had something to do with it. Right from the start. He knew the other boys weren't involved. He knew Steven Fry was at the Angler all night. Hell. He did more investigating than Bates ever did. And he knew about the kickbacks on the housing project. He knew all of that. But it wasn't enough to print. He'd have lost the paper in a slander suit. Bill Fry may be a shithead, but he's a hell of a lawyer. No winning against him."

"Then, you're not going to run anything either?"

"Me? Of course I am. Your case in Bucks County gives me every right to print it. All of it. Proximity and predisposition. That's all I need. Let the facts speak for themselves."

"They could shut you down."

"They won't. Because they know we're right. Maybe you can't nail his ass in court, but I can sure as hell let everyone know the truth. And that's what we're going to do."

For the next couple of hours, the women weave together what they each know. Lydia has most of her story already written. She'd begun the night after Alberta picked up her files. As soon as Alberta places the photos of the boys next to each other, Lydia knows she has her front page. "This alone tells the story," she says. "This and the bloody jean jacket. Blood gets 'em every time."

Alberta needs to leave. She has a long drive home ahead of her, but she can't quite bring herself to go.

"This was nice," Alberta finally says. "Working together."

"Two women working together, you mean."

"Yeah."

"Don't make a big thing of it. That's what bothers them the most. Act like you belong in the game. Now get out of here. I've got work to do."

Alberta stops at the tavern to say goodbye to Tucker, but he isn't there. By noon she's starting out on her ten-hour trudge back to Pennsylvania. She's due at work the next day.

As she passes through Youngstown, Ohio, Dick Hodges is pulling up in front of Walter Stem's house in Doylestown, Buck's County, Pennsylvania.

CHAPTER 44

Oct 2 - 1 AM - Mom woke up a few times today. Nothing coherent. I used to lie here expecting her to call out in pain. Now I listen to the monitor for her breathing. Now I check to see if she's died in her sleep. She saw me last night. Spoke – didn't make any sense but her eyes seemed to know me.

The med pump keeps Evelyn's pain managed. Penn pushes it regularly. She's surprised to hear Evelyn has pushed it, too. A lot. The nurses record all the attempts, the first indication Evelyn is still somewhere in there. Aware enough to seek relief.

Evelyn doesn't drink or eat any more. No more Vernor's. No more chicken sandwiches. An aide arrives in the morning to change the bed, give Evelyn a wipe down, change her diaper. Evelyn sleeps through it all, waking only once to say she has errands to run. The aide sits with her until noon, giving Penn a break.

Penn takes a walk, intending to stay close, but ends up on the outer road past the marsh subdivision to the county road to the other side of the lake. When she was a kid, they had to circumnavigate the marsh and woods to get there. Now there's a road. Paved. With curbs. With new houses.

Penn has made a career out of looking beneath the surface of things, studying ecosystems. An expert in her field, she's lectured all over the country. She's held symposiums in lake communities on the importance of conservation and the maintenance of a healthy lake system. Too much phosphorous and nitrogen runoff from farmland promotes algae blooms, which in turn choke off other plants. Bacteria feed off that dead plant matter, decomposing it. That excess bacteria uses up the oxygen until fish and other aquatic species can no longer survive. As complicated as an ecosystem is, in many ways, it's also very simple. Throw off the balance, and it's in trouble. Throw it off too much, and there may be no recovery.

Penn can read a lake like no one else. She can gauge the degree of its health or decline by its stratification, its aquatic life, temperature, marshes, insect activity, and water clarity. Yet when it comes to her own life, she's been oblivious to all the indicators. She's seen only what was in front of her without looking any deeper. Only when her mother is dying can she see how deep the waters were. And how the decay was rising.

Penn returns and sends the aide home.

> Oct 3 - Nurse stopped in. Yet another new one. Don't they know the dying need consistency? At least the caregivers do. We've had the same aide all week. That helps. I like her. Jean. She's quiet, gentle. Has a peaceful quality to her. She speaks to me as calmly as she speaks to Mom. I can't believe I miss the yelling. I miss who we should have been. Forty years of ache tends to hollow out a soul, I guess. If one of the other boys had drowned instead of Tyler, would I idealize them as we all did Ty? If it had been Jim, the oldest, would we feel we'd lost our rudder? Would Mom still

have left us to grieve alone? Or maybe Ron or Mark, the middle born. Would we have felt the same searing scar? Or were they somehow more expendable? I can't help but wonder if we collapsed under the weight of Tyler's death because he was the youngest of us, our last chance to get something right. Had he lived, might we have had more generous lives? That's a lot to hang on an eight-year-old kid, responsibility for keeping us all sane, productive, kind. Sometimes I think he could have ended up as screwed up as the rest of us, our family trajectory already off course before he drowned. Other times, I think Tyler was the cotter pin that held the family together. His laugh ended every argument. His silly faces broke every silence. Without him, the wheels fell off. Tyler was perfect, though I know such perfection can only exist in memory, and memory is the purest fiction. The instant time passes, we're rewriting it to fit a narrative. I think we spend the rest of our lives editing based on new observations, flawed perspectives and rampant inaccuracies. The book never gets finished. Then we die and those we leave behind edit us into something they need us to be, something that never existed. Should call the boys but I don't want them here.

Oct 4 - Her skin is changing. I remember from Matthew. Sort of waxy. That skeletal look. I think maybe death is like a sinking ship. If those left behind aren't careful, they get pulled down with it. The strong make it back up. Others swim – or drown – in the wake of it for the rest of their lives. I'm in those waters now, have been all summer, feeling the pull from below, swirling through the debris of history, my childhood brushing against my ankles. Maybe this time it will all sink into deep waters where no turning of the lake can lift it.

Penn brings the wingback from the living room into her mother's room. In the half-light of late afternoon, she watches the irregular breathing, little shudders of a frantic diaphragm followed by long gaps, her ribcage barely expanding. The years seem to compress as the regrets grow, new ones piling onto old. Penn will later recall this as the moment she began to mourn.

CHAPTER 45

Rage propels Dick Hodges down the highway, driving from the early morning hours, heading east to Pennsylvania, to the Bucks County jail. When he hears on the radio Walter has been released, he speeds onto the next exit ramp so fast he slides into a guardrail, scraping his rear fender. When he sees a phone booth at a gas station, he looks up Walter's address. Soon after, Dick Hodges is on Walter Stem's porch.

The front lawn is neatly trimmed, the garage door freshly painted, its epithet erased. Windows and door show no signs of dried and rotten egg. Dick rings the doorbell.

Edith looks through the curtain and opens the door. Her expression is hard to read, but she doesn't seem surprised to see Dick. Without speaking, she leads him through to the kitchen.

Edith points out a window to Walter, in his Panama hat, kneeling on all fours hand-trimming grass at the back fence. She opens the door and steps out of the way for Dick. She watches Walter glance up as the screen creaks. When he sees Dick, there is a kind of resignation on his face. She's seen that expression before, the morning the boys were found in the marsh. The morning Velma beat Walter with the poker. She couldn't put her finger on it then, but thinking about it now, it's almost as if he knew he deserved to be punished. She hadn't thought of it that way before, but now it seems perfectly clear because Walter is looking at Dick, Tyler's father, the same way, and why would he do that? Why would this man be in their house if Alberta hadn't been right about Walter? Why had the jean jacket been moved? Why did Velma ask him every day who he talked to and where he'd been? What did Velma know that Edith did not? Something about seeing Walter look at Dick that way suddenly gives her permission to think all the things she hasn't allowed herself to think.

Dick stands stone still, his breath growing heavier with every step Walter takes toward him.

Halfway across the yard, Walter tells Edith to go to the bedroom. "Everything is fine," he says in his quiet voice. She steps up into the kitchen.

"Dick," Walter says. "It's been a long time." He casually slips his clippers into a tool caddy on the stoop. "Let's go inside, shall we?"

Edith steps around the corner into the hall.

In the kitchen, Dick watches Walter wash his hands, dry them, carefully folding the towel before placing it back on the rack.

"They should never have let you out," Dick says.

Walter brushes his hand along the towel, straightening a uneven end.

Edith goes the bedroom. She pulls a suitcase from under the bed. She can hear clearly the conversation from the kitchen.

Walter asks Dick about the boys and says he'd always thought Penny was a remarkable person. Dick tells him to shut the fuck up.

"You're one unlucky bastard," Dick says. "I mean, it's one hell of a coincidence to be so close by when all those boys died. Four so far? So, you're either the unluckiest bastard on the face of the earth, or you're a monster. Which one are you, Walter? Which one?" Dick's hands clench.

Edith pulls undergarments from a drawer, throwing them in the bag.

Walter remains calm. "I'm not a monster, Dick. I watched over all the boys. Yours included. Kept them safe while you dads were working."

Dick finds the man's composure, the stillness of his body, unsettling.

"Everyone at the lake counted on me," Walter says. "No one ever had a doubt back then, so why now? Just think back. Did I ever cause you doubt, Dick? Ever?"

"What about this new boy?" Dick asks, his heart racing now. "You keep him safe, too?"

"It was drizzling," Walter explains. "He was walking. I gave him a ride. All charges have been dropped, Dick. I was just the last one to see the poor boy alive. They'll find the person responsible, Dick. What happened to your boy so long ago is tragic. I liked Tyler. He was very bright and strong and . . . "

Dick lunges across the room throwing Walter to the floor. "Don't you speak my son's name, you fucking bastard!" Dick's knee presses into Walter's chest, both fists battering Walter's head.

Edith walks down the hall and watches Dick slug Walter in the face, blood splattering the cupboards. Walter isn't fighting back. Something about it feels satisfying to her. She says nothing and goes back to her packing.

Dick stands up and kicks Walter in the gut, in the ribs, in the head. Walter groans and curls up into a ball.

Dick stumbles, grabs his chest, and keels over, falling backward into the hallway.

Only then does Edith call for an ambulance. For Dick.

Dick has his first heart attack in Walter Stem's kitchen.

CHAPTER 46

Having failed to make her case against Walter, Alberta is depleted. It's after midnight when she arrives back in Doylestown and drags herself into her house. She sees the blinking light on her answering machine and hits rewind, listening and deleting the four calls from the office telling her to call in. The last message explains the previous ones. It was her boss, DA Groves. "Dick Hodges had a heart attack this evening after he beat the shit out of Walter Stem. They're both at Memorial Hospital. I want you in my office first thing." Only then does she notice the newspaper's headline: CHARGES DROPPED AGAINST STEM. After eleven days in jail, Walter Stem was a free man.

Alberta calls Angler's Tavern wanting to be comforted by Tucker, to hear his voice, imagine his gentle smile. The bartender answers, putting the phone down while he hollers out. She can hear him say *long distance* and Tucker say he'd take it in his office. As soon as he answers, she hears a click and the sounds of the bar disappear.

"It's Alberta," she says.

"What did you think was going to happen, Bert?" Tucker asks, his tone cold.

"Then you know about Dick?"

Tucker is silent.

"And Walter," she says.

"Whatever this is you're doing," he says, "finish it."

He hangs up.

Alberta calls her brother in the morning to say she's back. He wants to see her, tells her to come over, but she says she has to go into the office. He says fine and hangs up. In that one word, she hears a multitude of complaints. *You're so selfish. You have no sense of family. You've abandoned us. You failed. You're a total shit.* Whether he meant any of these things is irrelevant. It's what she heard.

She walks through the office feeling all eyes on her. Assistant district attorneys, all men, offer condescending smiles. Women, from the receptionist to the secretaries, look at her over their glasses. She goes directly to her boss's office.

He's silent as he closes the door behind her.

"How's Walter?" Alberta asks.

"A broken nose, some eye damage, bruised and fractured ribs. Lucky for you, he isn't pressing charges. Dick Hodges is in stable condition."

Alberta has no response that seems to fit the moment.

"So, what the hell did you say to piss Sterling off so much?"

She feels her diaphragm cramp.

"You had every reason for him to reopen the investigation. Yet he calls me and asks me why the hell I sent an incompetent woman to tell him what his job is."

Remaining calm, she says she didn't say that.

"You were too close to it," he says. "I shouldn't have let you go."

"No one else would have . . ."

"Anyone. Anyone could have handled it better." He's yelling now. "A first-year could have handled it better!"

"I had the case!" She blurts it out, knowing better than to argue when he's on a rant.

"Yeah. And you blew it!" he shouts, pounding his index finger on the desk, glaring at her. "All we needed for our case, this case right here in our jurisdiction, for your nephew . . ." He stops, looking away. "All we needed was for the DA in Michigan to reopen the case there. That's it! And that fiasco in the local paper? You called DA Sterling and the sheriff's office corrupt idiots."

Alberta takes his reprimand, unflinching, speaking with quiet control. "I didn't write it."

"She quoted you!"

"May I go now?" Alberta asks, every muscle in her body tensing.

He waves her off. She isn't but a few steps out of his office when he calls out loud enough for everyone to hear. "Get your head in the game, Higgins. For now? Go home."

A young attorney, a man fresh from the bar exam, walks over to her desk. "For what it's worth," he says, "no one here thought we had enough to get a conviction. Too circumstantial. He was really counting on you."

An immediate *fuck off* slips out of Alberta's mouth.

Arriving home, Alberta sits in her car, staring at her condo, her door just one of a dozen identical doors, a brick wall of doors, and windows, perfectly trimmed shrubs, spotless walkways. She wonders when she became resigned to such conformity. Inside, she mindlessly sorts through a stack of mail. As if anesthetized, she's numb to the angst and pain. She feels no disgrace or animosity. She looks at her performance analytically. She could have been more convincing, held back, focused. As a woman, she'd failed, having cried in front of the DA in Michigan, having shown emotion. If she hadn't, he might have heard her.

Though it isn't yet noon, she opens a bottle of wine and fills a tumbler, fully cognizant that at some wholly inappropriate moment in the future, her emotions will erupt. For now, she is content to hover in limbo.

CHAPTER 47

The phone rings as Penny is on her way out the door to catch the bus to the Field Museum. She almost doesn't answer.

"Penny?"

"Dad? What's . . ."

"I'm in Pennsylvania."

Her mind immediately slams into Walter Stem. "Why are you in Pennsylvania?" He doesn't answer. "Dad? What did you do? You didn't kill him, did you?" She can't believe how easily the words spilled out.

"What? How could you ask such a thing? Who would I kill?"

"I know about Mr. Stem, Dad. Mildred told me. What happened?"

Dick doesn't tell her he damn near beat Walter Stem to death or that her mother is on the verge of suicide. "Just come get me."

She asks why he can't just drive himself.

"You need to come get me. I'm in the hospital but I'll be out in a couple days. I had a minor heart attack"

"You what?"

"I'll explain when you get here."

"But dad, I can't just walk out of the Museum."

"You're an intern," he says. "You can leave whenever you want."

She argues that her mother should do it, or the boys. Dick doesn't respond except to say he's booked Penny on a flight. "You're on the two o'clock out of O'Hare tomorrow afternoon. And I need you to go check on your mother before you leave."

"I don't have a car," Penny gripes, hoping to find any reason to stay as far away from the drama as possible. "I can't just leave."

"Take the train. People understand family emergencies. Please don't argue with me. Go check on your mother. She's at the house in town."

Penny calls her department head at the Field, surprised at his willingness to let her go for however long she needs. She believed to that point she was a valuable part of the team, yet he makes her feel insignificant.

It's pouring rain when she runs from the bus stop into Union Station trying to catch the morning eastbound train. Getting soaked is just one more thing to wreck her day. Missing the train would be the topper, but she gets her ticket with five minutes to spare. Pulling out of the station is like pulling into a car wash, a deluge of rain against the window obscures everything she sees. The morning came on so quickly, she hadn't had time to take in the weight of it all. Above everything else, above the horrific revelation that the boys may have been murdered and that Walter Stem was involved, are two words: Heart attack.

Skies clear just west of Gary. Arriving in Edgewater, Penn walks the six blocks home hoping to make it there before the rain catches up to her. It is clouding up as she lets herself in.

Evelyn is asleep upstairs, a full bottle of sedatives on the nightstand. Penny puts the pills in her pocket. She nudges her mom then hollers at her when there is no response. Evelyn groans and rolls over.

Evelyn wakes later, groggy, dehydrated and hung over. Penny is on the bed next to her reading a book. "I have to throw up," Evelyn says and stumbles to the bathroom just in time. "You know then," she says after the first round of heaving. "You know what that woman turned up, what she thinks happened. She says Walter. . ." She leans against the wall then clutches the toilet again.

Penny watches her mother dry-heave the same way she'd watched roommates in college. With no compassion. The retching subsides. "Did you know Dad's in a hospital in Pennsylvania?"

Another wave hits. More dry heaves. When it's over, Evelyn washes her face and brushes her teeth. "He called last night," she says. "Didn't know he had it in him."

"I'm going to go get him tomorrow."

Evelyn leans on the doorframe, the dresser, and anything else she can reach to get back to bed. "Where are my pills?"

"You need to eat first."

"Where are my goddamn pills?"

Penny holds them up and walks out of the room with them. "Grilled cheese and chicken noodle soup. Then you can have a pill." It's not lost on Penny that she's become the adult in the room.

Penny hears a thud at the front door. Retrieving the paper, its headline hits her hard: STEM SUSPECT IN CHILD MURDER. Subhead: *Father attacks Stem, suffers heart attack.* Lydia Metzger did what Alberta couldn't. She made the case, if only to the public.

After reading it through, something about the jean jacket catches Penn's attention. She makes a cold cheese sandwich and leaves it on her mother's nightstand with one pill. Evelyn is out cold again. Penny drives her mother's car to the cottage.

Until that moment, until she read about the missing button from the jean jacket, she hadn't made up her mind about Walter Stem. It was easier to think there had been no violence involved. It was easier to think things were as they seemed, not just a conglomeration of lies. The cottage door is unlocked.

She hadn't been inside for several years. Somehow it doesn't look any different. But it doesn't feel the same. She rummages through the drawer under her old sleeping cubby pushing through mounds of extra bedding. She digs through one closet, then another. She finally sees a box on the shelf down in the storeroom. Sifting through it, she finds her old cigar box. If she finds what she's looking for, it might not prove anything. Or maybe prove all of it. She wonders if she wants to be the one who confirms beyond a doubt the boys had been murdered. Heart racing, she opens it. The metal button is still there. Stamped with *Levi Strauss*. Red thread. A bit of denim still attached, darkly stained.

She knows then Tyler and Peter have not been lost. They've been stolen. She holds the missing button from Walter's jean jacket and can't get out of the cottage fast enough. Driving back from the lake, Penny screams obscenities at the universe, too enraged to cry. Too enraged to take care of her mother. Too enraged to think straight. She pulls another pill from the bottle and leaves them on the dresser for Evelyn before driving back to

Chicago. She needs to be alone. In her own bed. She gets a speeding ticket just outside Union Pier in Michigan.

Her mind won't stop racing trying to remember the lake years differently, looking for clues, looking for any sign of what was going on all around her. She tries to remember what she'd said to Alberta Higgins in the cafeteria that day. She tries to see Tyler's face, then Peter's but they won't come to her. Everything stews into a deafening static. Arriving home, she takes one of her mother's pills and crawls under the covers, waking an hour before her flight the next afternoon. Again, she finds herself rushing, almost late, on the edge of failing everyone she loves.

In Doylestown, Alberta, sleeps late. She calls her brother to say she'll be over eventually. Just not yet. He doesn't argue. She brings a pot of coffee to her nightstand and crawls back under the covers with a book, but can't manage to get past the first few paragraphs. It feels like forever since her days were predictable, since she played with Alby and Tommy; since she sat at her desk complaining about the workload; since she knew her place in the world. For the moment, she is adrift. No telling how long that moment will last.

It's late afternoon when someone knocks at her front door and Alberta finds Penny Hodges there with an indecipherable expression. "How's your dad," Alberta asks even before inviting her in. In the space between the question and answer, she imagines Dick has died, and she'd have to carry that burden along with the rest of her failings.

"He's fine," Penny says. "I'm driving him home tomorrow."

Relieved, Alberta invites her in, but Penny doesn't budge.

"Here," Penny says and hands her a small box. "I found it in a bush by the marsh. November. After the boys died. Hung up on a bush. The leaves were all gone, so I could see it. It's a match for the jean jacket. It has to be." Then she hands Alberta the newspaper with Lydia's article.

They go into the living room where Alberta reads the paper's account, gritting her teeth. If she'd presented the case so succinctly, maybe Stem would have been held over for trial. She looks at the button and grills Penny on specifics: Why was she at the marsh in November, where exactly did she find it, where had it been since then, why did she suddenly remember and retrieve it.

Satisfied with the answers, Alberta calls her boss. "I can put Walter's jean jacket at Spirit Lake marsh. Penny found the torn button out there that fall." There is no response. "I have it. She brought it. Looks like there's dried blood on it." Still no response. "Did you hear me? I think you should be the one to call Sterling. He won't listen to anything I have to say."

"It's over, Alberta."

"No! This is what Sterling wanted. This puts him there."

Penny overhears and protests. "But it's proof! Isn't it?"

"Who's that?" he says.

Alberta pushes Penny aside and steps as far as the cord lets her. "It's Penny Hodges."

"Shit. Listen. That button proves nothing. It puts the jacket there at some unspecified point in time. The person you'd have testify to finding it was a child at the time, the sister of the victim. They'd rip her up on cross."

Penny draws closer. "What's he saying?"

Alberta glares at her, waving her away.

"Alberta, Walter's blood type is the same as Peter's. There's nothing to say it isn't Walter's blood on the jacket." He gives her a moment to process. "It's over."

Alberta knows she can't speak without exploding.

"Take some time off," he tells her. "We'll talk next week, see where we are."

Penny watches Alberta hang up. "Well?"

"There is a word in my field of work, a word that may as well be a slamming door: Inconclusive." Alberta watches Penny's eyes lose their charge as resignation takes over.

"That's it? They're done?"

"Yeah."

Alberta goes to the kitchen for water, but mostly to calm herself down. "It's probably better you don't tell anyone about this," she hollers to the living room.

"Miss Higgins," Penny says from the doorway. "What if you're wrong?" her eyes well. "What if they're right? They wouldn't let him go if he killed a kid. They wouldn't do that. What if this crusade of yours. . ." she fights back tears " . . . is just one huge ass mistake? What if you're wrong and they're right?"

"They're not," Alberta says, straining not to shout. "And I'm serious. You should probably keep this to yourself. Your family needs to be able to believe it was just an accident. Let them have . . ."

Penny shouts at her. "Have what? After all this, you seriously think any of us can go back to believing it was just an accident! My dad's in the hospital with a heart attack after beating a man to a pulp. Because of you! This. ALL of this is on YOU!"

Alberta looks to the ceiling then to Penny. "It's my job." Opening the front door, she tells Penny to never screw up. "They get all the chances in the world. We get one."

"Who?"

"Men," Alberta says. "And change your name. They're never going to take you seriously calling yourself Penny."

Penny stands on the stoop, her breath slowing, her demeanor calming. She begins to speak softly, like the beginning of a bedtime story. "One night, ten years ago, two little boys snuck out to the marsh late at night to go frogging. They giggled and laughed, dared each other to be the first. Frogs were croaking all around them." Alberta listens and watches Penny turn, taking the steps one by one to her car. "The wind stirred the trees above them, the bushes all around them. They saw a big fat bullfrog on a branch sticking out of the dark waters, in the cattails. One of them shined the flashlight on it." Penny got in the car, closed the door and started it. "The other one stepped in to grab it. But he saw a huge snapping turtle swimming toward him and he plowed through the weeds to get away from it, but not toward shore, to the deeper part."

Driving through the neighborhood, she tells herself the tale as she needs it to be. "He got caught in the roots and the other boy went in to help him. Then he saw the same huge turtle, its gnarly back, its sharp pointed snout and then both boys were in trouble. One tried to help the other, and they ended up deeper and deeper, both getting caught up, both of them drowning. *That* is the story of Tyler and Peter." Tears well. No matter the words, the story is a lie.

Penny loads her dad in his car the next day for the long drive home from Pennsylvania. He sleeps off and on. Even when he's awake, he stares out the window. Not until they're skirting Detroit does he finally speak. "I don't want you to think too much about this." His next words are forced. "I made a mistake."

Penny squeezes the wheel. She sees a tear slide down his face. She's held off as long as she can but finally speaks. "No," she says quietly. "No. I'm not so sure."

"What do you mean?"

She pulls off the road into a rest stop, parks the car and turns it off. Her hands fall limp in her lap.

"Penny? What?"

She looks over to him. "I found the button from the jean jacket. That fall, when we came to get Mom. It was at the marsh. I took it to Higgins, but it wasn't enough. It wasn't enough."

He smiles.

"How can that make you smile?"

"Because it's the hard proof. That's all I've ever wanted. The truth. He's guilty." Penn begins to cry. "Thank you," he says. "Nobody else needs to know. They're not strong enough. You understand?"

"But. . ."

"You're going to live your life. You're going to honor your brother with a life well-lived full of love and accomplishment and . . ." Penny reaches for him and he rakes her into his arms, both of them crying.

Another three hours on the road and they pull into the drive at home. They confirm to each other they will say nothing. Evelyn meets them at the door. Dick envelops her in his arms, something that hasn't happened in over a decade. She does not reciprocate, but he holds on tight before releasing her. Too weak to take the stairs, he makes his way slowly to the den, stopping in the doorway. "Penny. Tell her."

From those two words alone, Evelyn knows the truth.

When the newspaper hits doorsteps, as expected, every parent with a boy who'd ever come in contact with Walter Stem begins looking at their grown sons as if they hold some horrible dark secret. When interviewed for a follow-up story, a few men lie, tell exaggerated stories about Walter watching them in the shower, some saying he touched them. But he hadn't.

Women in the grocery store now look at Evelyn differently. Her son, who had once died in a tragic accident, is now seen as the victim of violence and pedophilia, without regard to whether it is true or not. Evelyn sees it in eyes that no longer avert their gaze with condescending pity, but instead linger on her like an accusation of complicity, as if accidents happen but violence can be prevented.

DA Sterling is forced to re-open the case.

The jean jacket button is deemed inconclusive.

No new evidence is found.

The investigation is closed.

The recall petition falls short of signatures.

Marty Wagner buys the last of the Stem land from Walter and hires a demolition crew to take down the house.

Without a trial in either Michigan or Pennsylvania to prove Walter's guilt, there remains the painful uncertainty as to whether Ty and the other boys died at his hand or not.

Jim chooses to believe Walter had indeed been a good and generous man, and Tyler and Peter died trying to save each other. Yet, the ambiguity surrounding his brother's death, the possibility of brutality, carves a hole in his self-confidence. He finds it difficult to make the simplest decisions.

Ron shoots down anyone accusing Walter of murder, yet going forward, for reasons he can't understand, every little sound in the night wakes him. He takes to patrolling his apartment building at night, even walking the street, looking for some invisible threat.

Mark withdraws into himself. He drinks. He moves away. Yet no matter where he lives, he can't stop imagining what being held underwater must have felt like, how it hurt, how long it took, how hard Tyler must have fought. This manufactured memory becomes an obsession. For the rest of his life, Mark suffers nightmares about drowning. And the anger grows. Not toward Stem, but toward Tyler for putting himself in the situation, for dying, for ruining all their lives.

Penny, Dick, and Evelyn alone know the truth. It becomes the invisible mortar between them, always there but never spoken of. Placing the blame on Walter Stem, however, did not alleviate the blame they'd each placed on themselves. And each other.

CHAPTER 48

October 5 - I don't want them here. I don't want their negativity. Judgmental attitudes. They will never see this time I had with her as the gift it is. In our most vulnerable moments, when we surrendered to them, shared them, that's where we began to understand the other, connect. I can't expect them to get it. I brought a daughter into the world, yet I think my greatest service in this life has been to help people I love transition out of it. It is a privilege. I know this, feel this in my bones, but I can't explain it to anyone who hasn't experienced it, who isn't open to it. Life is a miraculous thing. Mystical. Right up to the quickness of its leaving. Abrupt even when expected. The finality of it so potent, the hollowness –

Penn summons her brothers, angry boys who'd become unhappy men. The four Hodges siblings had not been in one room since their father died nearly thirty years earlier. They hadn't been to the lake since the November after Tyler died when they pulled the boats out of the water. They hadn't stepped inside the cottage since the minister hauled them all out there attempting to reunite the family. It took Evelyn's dying to bring them together.

Ron, having recently been relieved of the latest in a series of wives, arrives first to survey the accuracy of impending death. Yes, she's dying, and yes, it will be soon. With Ron's assessment, Jim shows up alone. Penn watches him pull a wet nap from his pocket and wipe the knob as he closes the back door. He wipes the chair before he sits and opens another packet for his hands before he can pretend to relax. If Penn had been a hugger, she feels certain he'd have refused her embrace.

No one expects Mark to show up or if he's even gotten the messages Ron left at an old number, but he wanders in, a twelve-pack under each arm.

Penn observes in all three a hesitancy to step over the threshold, a reticence having nothing to do with anticipation of grief. Grief would imply love.

Mark's greeting upon seeing Penn: "Shit. You look like hell."

"I know, right?" Ron agrees. "When the hell did you turn into Mom?"

Jim is quick to confirm the observation. It's not meant as a compliment.

Penn is startled by their appearance as well. None of them have aged well. At fifty-three, Mark is weathered with bags under his eyes, his uncombed hair as white as hers. Ron has a paunch and is losing his hair. Jim is as a fat as she is thin.

"It's amazing how much you look like her," Ron reiterates.

Mark puts the beer in the fridge as if he lives there, as if he hadn't disappeared from all their lives decades earlier.

There are no exclamations of fond reunion. Like puzzle pieces from different boxes, the men don't fit. Penn wants them gone before she finds anything recognizable in them. She wants to make clear this event is not an invitation to her life, but says nothing. She doesn't have to. They are all thinking the same thing.

Jim and Mark loiter in the front room, ignoring Penn like a stranger. They have yet to look in on their mother.

Ronny goes in to see Evelyn and comes out in less than a minute saying she wants the window open. Jim says that's ridiculous. It's too cold. Mark's comeback is quick. "What. You worried she's gunna get sick and die?" No one laughs.

Penn returns to her mother's bedside, taking her frail hand. Cool. Soft. Jim follows, hanging in the doorway for a moment before turning away. Penn watches her mother's eyes, so still under thin lids. It is a deep sleep, drug-induced, her body shutting down. Penn had called her brothers to tell them when Dad was failing. But the thing about a protracted illness is there are many moments of crisis, and after a while, people tend not to take them seriously. When Jim and Ron came to see him, Dick perked up. He asked for a sandwich. They left, frustrated not only with Penn for being wrong, but with Dick for not having the courtesy to die while they were there. When he had the stroke, Penn called them again. They didn't come.

She remembered wandering into her dad's room occasionally to see if he was still breathing. It was so shallow, his chest barely lifting, and such a long time between breaths that she and her mother swore more than once he was gone. Then, like a bad joke, he'd take a breath, and they'd count again, out loud. Laughing. Deathbed humor. It took two days after the stroke for his heart to give out.

Evelyn hadn't slept beside her husband in years but laid with him his last night. In the morning, Penn called the boys, and somehow it was her fault they were too late. She didn't understand why the moment of death was so important to them when they hadn't bothered to spend time with him in life?

Evelyn suddenly speaks in a voice that seems too hearty to be real. "Did you see Ty?" she asks with a warm smile.

Penn squeezes her mother's hand. "Hi there."

Evelyn opens her eyes and looks straight into her daughter's. "Where'd he go?"

"I'm sure he's around here somewhere."

Evelyn closes her eyes again, the flickering moment gone. The voices of complaining men carries from the front room, Mark the most belligerent of them. "At least she's finally going to get her wish to be with Ty again."

"You're such a shit." That's Jim.

"He was a little kid. She made him out to be a saint." Mark again.

"You really are an ass, aren't you?" That's Ronny.

"And that goddamned empty chair at the table. What the fuck was that about?" Mark again.

Whatever softening might have occurred between other siblings over the years when age and maturity gained ground over petty rivalries, the Hodges siblings remain frozen in childhood animosities, unable to find comfort in shared memories. The boys still live in the space where pain and anger gnaw at every happiness. In their eyes, it would seem all Penn's happiness was accomplished to spite them. She'd found a way forward into college and a career, into a loving marriage. She had a daughter who loved her. They never looked behind the curtain to see Mildred and George in the wings, substitute parents who rescued Penny from the minefield of family.

Evelyn slowly rolls her head toward the open window and smiles, taking in the cold fresh air. "Get me a Vernor's, Dick," she mutters. "The kids are at it again."

Penn smiles half expecting her father to appear from the hallway with a sweaty aluminum tumbler of Vernor's and Vodka. The nurse steps out, closing the door behind her and urges the brothers to settle down or go outside.

Penn stands up, catching her face in the mirror. She'd always been a full-faced girl, a plump-cheeked woman. In this regard, she bore no resemblance to her mother. And having had this image of herself for nearly her whole life, she is still caught off-guard to see her present visage, narrow faced and thin lipped. Perhaps the boys were right in saying she looked like Evelyn, and she might not have been so offended if they hadn't attached the connotation of something negative, as if all Evelyn's worst traits were built into the physical similarities.

She goes to the front room to the bank of windows overlooking the patio where her brothers stand in the dark, bundled against the cool night, drinking longneck beers. She feels like a little kid again the way she used to watch the men out there drinking and smoking cigars. Now those men are her brothers.

She cranks open a window to tell them she's prepped the fire ring. Mark looks up, his face aglow in the light from the kitchen below. He smiles for the first time since arriving, comes in and grabs a 12-pack. Jim goes down and lights it up. The flames hesitate at first, then careen into the sky with great golden lashes. Ronny hauls chairs down from the patio. Penn joins them, but only after the nurse urges her to.

Penn listens to Ronny talk about the huge ass bonfires they used to have, the massive pyres that lined the lakeshore. The moment feels difficult to navigate. The men who are now drinking beer as their mother lay dying had once been frenetic young boys. Time suddenly feels particularly cruel, having slipped away so fast.

Dan walks over from next door with a 6-pack and a folding chair. "Room for one more?" Though the men haven't seen each other since they were kids, he is welcomed without fanfare. The fire crackles. Dan opens a beer.

"I wouldn't be surprised if Mom thinks Rabbit is on the bed up there with her," Jim says. "Mangiest dog I ever saw."

Opening another beer, Mark starts in on how much he hated the lake as a kid. Dan cuts him off hard.

"Bull shit! You were the craziest one out here. Couldn't sit still. If you weren't skiing, you were rowing that stupid dinghy, sailing, catching frogs, or making us all play tag football or torturing the girls on the raft. What the hell would you have done in town? Town was boring." Jim and Ronny throw bottle caps at Mark, agreeing with Dan. "And if I know you, you'd have found trouble in town. Hell. This lake probably kept you out of jail, my friend!"

They talk about Steve Fry, about being sent to military school, about how his tour in Viet Nam screwed him up even more than he was to start with. They talk about his stint in County for marijuana, and someone says he did two rounds of rehab somewhere. It seems to explain, if not predict, his dying of an overdose. There is nothing more said about him. Nothing about the fight the last day. Nothing about the last summer.

Penn asks how none of them had to go to Nam. Dan says he got a deferment for a bad knee, something he thanked Mark for since it was his tackle that wrecked it in a high school football game. Ronny and Mark had high draft numbers. "Dodged a bullet there," Ron says.

"Lots of them, I suspect," Penn says, earning her a barrage of sticks. "What about you, Jim?" she asks.

Jim grumbles. "Never mind."

"No. Really. How'd you . . ."

Jim cocks his head and glares at her. "Well, from eighteen to twenty-one, I was supporting these two jackoffs. Local draft board let me slide."

Penn isn't going to let it go, but Dan intervenes, cutting the tension by bringing up Debra Stem, how she'd given them their first handjobs.

Mark objects. "Where was I? I mean, come on. Fair is fair!"

"She had the rule," Dan says and starts reciting it when Jim and Ronny join in. "You had to be at least thirteen for a handjob." As Mark grills them on her technique, they turn into hormonal teenagers, laughing out loud, using the grossest terms possible.

"Mom doesn't have cancer." Penn interrupts. She isn't heard. She blurts it out. "Mom never had cancer!" The laughing stops. They all look at her.

"Did you know Mom was an alcoholic," Penn asks, her words strained.

The guys all exchange glances. Ron finally answers. "Of course."

Jim asks what she means by no cancer. It's less a question than an accusation.

Mark kicks her foot. "Well? What the fuck?"

"The cancer was a lie. It's alcoholism."

Jim attacks. "Why would you lie about that?"

Penn shoots to her feet. "I didn't lie! She did!"

Dan reaches up and takes her hand. "Sit down, kid. They don't know shit." She reluctantly sits back down.

Penn says it had to have started after Tyler died, or maybe after their dad attacked Walter.

"You start in on that shit and I'm out of here!" Mark blurts.

No one says anything for the longest time. Sparks waft up as Dan stirs the fire. Walter Stem's name and all he represents are out of bounds.

Ron breaks the silence. "She used to keep a bottle in the pantry. Vodka. Remember? In her orange juice every morning."

Mark grumbles. "In her Vernor's all day long."

Jim says it had nothing to do with Tyler. "She was a drunk long before he ever died. It just got worse after."

Mark says he poured out of her thermos once out on the pontoon thinking it was lemonade. "Vodka. Straight. She slapped me. Hard! Never made that mistake again."

Penn says she didn't remember ever seeing her drunk. Mark stares at her, the contempt in his voice chilling. "That's because you never saw her sober. She was drunk all day. Every day." He throws a branch onto the fire sending more sparks flying out and up. "I need another beer." Dan hands him one.

Penn asks if Dad knew. Jim answers. "Why the fuck do you think he stayed in town all week? Work? He wasn't that important. He could have come out here every night. Hell, it's only twenty miles."

"Don't you remember their fights?" Mark asks. "He'd threaten to divorce her if she didn't stop drinking and she dared him to do it."

"Shut up! She did not!" Penn shouts.

"Of course she didn't see it," Ron says. "Too young." He glares at Penn, shaking his head. "Did you think he measured booze bottles because of us every time he came out here? He used to take her bottle of vodka from the pantry every Sunday night when he left but she just went out and bought another one."

"One?" Dan says, chuckling. "She kept half a dozen in a box in the back room."

"How the hell would you know?" Ron says.

Dan tells them about a rainy afternoon when Tyler was still little. "Hell, I was only eight or nine. You three were upstairs raising holy hell. I found her pouring the last of a bottle into a tall tumbler of pop. She asked me to get her another one from a box under the laundry basket. I did."

More than any behavior they may have seen from their mother, this singular revelation, that Dan knew all along more than they did, is insurmountable.

For as much as there is to say about the past, the present, and all the years in between, they all sit silent. The fire pops and sizzles, flairs up, and settles to a warm even burn until Ron asks if anyone remembers when Greg's dad would bring guys out for poker night and make him wear his mom's apron and fetch their drinks.

"His dad was a shit head," Mark says. "No wonder his wife left him."

A small voice sounds from the shadows. "That's a mean word, Papa." Dan turns and reaches for two little boys.

"Where are your cousins?" Dan looks behind them, spying two more bodies. He waves them forward. "Grandkids if you can believe it. We started early and so did our kids. All boys so far. We brought them out for the weekend." He looks up to his cottage and sees a woman in the window waving back. "My wife doesn't see you, Penn, or she'd be down here. Probably thinks it's man turf."

Something magical comes over Mark, his expression softening, his eyes grinning. He begins telling the little boys that years ago the fires used to be huge, that there were lots of them all along the shore, all around the lake. He creeps closer to the fire, his face aglow. He speaks slowly and softly, with reverence, capturing the boys' attention. "Many moons ago, there were evil spirits that lived at the bottom of the lake. And every fall, all the children around the lake burned giant fires and all us boys would tear off our clothes and dance around the fires naked and yell and shout, and we could hear other kids on the other side of the lake, and all our voices would fill the lake scaring the evil spirits and the next morning, the water would be so dark you couldn't see your hand dipped into it, and the stink of it was horrible. Like roadkill!" The boys, transfixed, do not move. "You smell it? Take a long deep sniff." Noses high, the little boys all begin sniffing. "Smell it? Smell the evil?"

One of the boys looks to his grandfather. "Is he lying?"

Dan bolts to his feet. "Nope!" He yanks off his jacket, then his shirt, and starts to dance around behind the chairs, yipping. Jim follows suit, then Mark and Ron, and the little boys yank off their shirts and the youngest one pulls everything off and runs around naked prompting the other boys to do the same. Penn watches four grown men strip to their boxers and tighty-whities and dance among the naked little boys like they were all children again.

In that single moment of revelry, when her children had finally let go of animosity, Evelyn Hodges dies. Alone.

Penn glances back to the cottage and sees the nurse raise her hand from the window. Penn goes in and the nurse goes out to the patio. She only has to stand still for the men to see her and understand.

Dan gathers up the children and their clothing and herds the shivering little bodies home. The brothers pull on their pants and shirts, step quietly past the nurse, and file into the bedroom. Jim is already in tears. The other two are hesitant at first, but their tears come, and the three of them stand over their mother, fighting with gasps against their unexpected grief. Penn stands in the corner as an observer of pain, not one experiencing it, an immunity born of repeated trips to the edge and back.

It is after midnight when Evelyn's body is taken away. Ronny's down stoking the fire. Jim, Mark, and Penn put on coats and go back out. They start talking about Tyler, as if they'd just lost him, not their mother, how he talked all the time, laughed at everything, cheated at solitaire, and loved that dingy.

They talk about frogging in the marsh, shining them with flashlights, jumping in after them. They talk about how the mothers would get all pissy when they took one of their good pillowcases to carry the frogs in. They agree

Evelyn was the best frog-leg cook. Nobody else could get them just right. Cook them too long and they'd turn to rubber.

Dan joins them, saying the kids are all tucked in, but he can't sleep. "You mentioned those bonfires. Spring and fall." His voice is low, melancholy. "Remember how the adults would call out all our names before they lit it to make sure we were all clear of the pile?"

"That's why they did that?" Mark asks.

Dan laughs and shakes his head. "And we'd all call out. And it was like a competition all round the lake to see who had the biggest fire and made the most noise? You guys weren't here that first fall after the boys drowned. Your mom was. I remember her standing in the window up there. We all saw her. And it was odd, because nobody said anything. Nobody called out names because we would have had to skip calling Tyler and Peter and you guys, and we didn't want to do that. And there weren't any other fires on the lake until after we lit ours. Then, one by one, they started flaring up. And it was so quiet. All anyone could hear was the snapping of the flames and the popping and hissing of wood. Nobody on that whole lake made a sound. It was the last one. There weren't any after that."

Ron stirs the fire, sparks rising high carrying their attention to the sky as clouds part. Suddenly they're illuminated by a full moon. The wind picks up, leafless trees swaying. Penn has had enough, goes to bed and finally cries, not just for her mother, but for all the losses. Her mom. Dad. Tyler. Peter. Matthew. The years.

The brothers scrounge for places to sleep, a couch, a chair, the floor, anywhere but Evelyn's empty hospital bed.

They leave first thing the next morning. Ron says he might like to get together for Christmas. Mark says he might be back next summer to teach Dan's grandkids to waterski. Whether any of it will actually happen is less important than the fact it's even spoken of. None of them offer to pull out the dock or stow the pontoon.

Not long after the last of their cars pulls out, Dan's mother, Marilyn, plows through the door without knocking. She's angry. The extent of Penn's relationship with her over the years has been limited to a wave and exchange of pleasantries on the rare occasion Marilyn came to the lake. Yet here she is demanding Penn sit down and listen. "You kids have it all wrong." She plops down into a chair and points at Penn. "I said, sit down!"

Penn sits. She hasn't seen Marilyn recently and thinks she makes seventy-something look closer to ninety. Maybe it was all those summers in the sun, or the smoking, or the wine.

"Danny told me what you talked about last night," Marilyn said. "About your mother's drinking. You kids don't know shit."

Penn sips coffee and settles into the chair, ready to listen to anything Marilyn needs to say. Death has a way of drawing truths to the surface, like splinters leaving the body.

"Your mother stopped drinking the winter before Tyler and the Eastman boy died. Did you know that?"

Penn shakes her head.

"She didn't have anything to drink that whole summer. At least not until Marty bought that damn boat. That day went every kind of sideways. And your mom slipped. Got lit like the rest of us. And then, well, no need to go there. But she didn't take a drink again for ten years. Ten years she was sober. I like my wine, but I can take it or leave it. For your mom, it was a struggle every day. Every damn day! Raising kids is tough work. Tougher drunk. Tougher still when you're trying to stay sober. She couldn't do both. Not in the wake of losing her boy."

"And the pills," Penn grumbles. "Don't forget the pills."

"Damn doctors. They think a pill can straighten any woman out. She threw the pills away. Cried her ass off when she flushed them. I was right here with her. You have no idea!" she says, pointing her finger. "No idea!"

Penn can see Marilyn is getting breathless.

"Your mother was a hard woman to love, but I loved her. You can fault her all you want for staying out here so much instead of in town, but it was what had to be. I never saw a woman try so hard."

"So hard to what?" Penn asks, more annoyed than hurt.

"Everything!" Marilyn shouts. "She had to try hard at everything. It was like life was a dress that was never going to fit but it was the only one she had. And when your little brother died . . ." Marilyn took a deep breath and closed her eyes the way someone does when they want the world to disappear. "I don't know what the hell your brothers were saying last night, but from that horrible day until the year your father died, she was sober. Ten years!"

Marilyn stops talking and her body sinks into itself like a deflating balloon. With the saddest eyes, she looks at Penn, tears welling. "And that whole last summer except for that one night. Sober. She did the best she could." Marilyn struggles to her feet and waits to catch her breath.

She looks at Penn hard for a moment before sitting back down. "There's more," she says. Her eyes prowl the room seeking absolution for the promise she is about to break. "She didn't have the flu at Christmas."

Two days before Christmas in 1959, Dick caught a ride to work so Evelyn could do some last-minute shopping with the car. Watching him leave, she drew her chenille robe tighter and adjusted the thermostat. Dick kept it at 67. She bumped it to 72. Rummaging in the closet, she collected a pint bottle from a shelf and poured a bit of bourbon in her coffee waiting for the furnace to kick in. The household began to stir. She heard the boys arguing in the bathroom upstairs. She stood at the kitchen window watching snow fall like feathers on a good ten inches of snowpack already on the ground. The blower on the furnace whined, ramping up. A blast of cool air billowed her robe. She stepped back. A plow rumbled and scraped by out front. She poured another mug and another shot before sitting at the kitchen table. Mark shuffled in barefoot and half asleep, his flannel pajamas dragging the floor. He pulled a dish from one cupboard, cereal from another, a spoon from a drawer, milk from the fridge, filled the bowl and sat down, all of this without once looking at his mother. Penny walked in, her fluffy robe tied tight over a flannel nightgown, her shoulders hunched against the chill. Jim and Ronny exploded down the stairs, fully dressed, hollering at Mark to get a move on. They had plans. They needed to get going. Dishes clattered as the boys got cereal and juice, made toast and dared each other to take Devil's Run, the steepest, narrowest sledding path in the ravine. Mark left his half empty bowl on the table and bolted upstairs. Penny made a piece of toast, slathered it with peanut butter and went back up to get dressed. She had plans for the day as well. Evelyn was pouring her third cup of coffee when Tyler wandered in. She fixed him a bowl of cereal and put it in front of him at the table. With her back to him, she slipped another shot of bourbon into her Santa mug. "Hurry up," she told him on her way upstairs. They all had places to be.

Jim hollered up, nagging Mark to hurry. Penny hollered down, nagging Tyler to get dressed. A horn honked from the street. Mark tore out of his bedroom sidestepping Tyler. Jim and Ronny were already out the door when Mark scrambled to pull on his coat and boots. "Hats and gloves," Evelyn called down, knowing they'd forget. Mark grabbed a bunch of gloves from a big basket and left, slamming the door behind him. Penny ran downstairs hollering she was going to be late if they didn't leave soon. Tyler was dressed, finishing soggy cereal. She told him his sweater was on backwards. "I did it on purpose," he said, but he didn't. Evelyn came in, handed him his jacket and hat and slipped into her coat. Penny stood at the door whining about being hot. She unzipped her jacket and took off her hat. "Come on," she said. Evelyn grabbed her purse and keys. The three were out the door, leaving behind a kitchen cluttered with bowls and glasses, cereal boxes, little puddles of milk and a piece of half-eaten toast. Evelyn pulled the car out of the garage through four inches of fresh snow. Penny and Tyler climbed into the front seat.

The day so far was unremarkable in that there was nothing unusual about it.

The snow was coming down harder by the time Evelyn dropped Penny at a friend's house. Intent on heading south a few miles to a model train store, it crossed her mind to go back home, then reconsidered. If she hurried, she could get there and back before the worst of the storm hit, so Evelyn turned onto Lakeshore Drive, a road that hugged the bluff along Lake Michigan. Wind blowing off the lake swirled the snow into a mesmerizing flurry. Tyler sat on the seat beside her fidgeting with his mittens and running through his Christmas list, a recitation she had long grown weary of. Little he wanted would show up under their tree. No new bicycle, no pony, no backyard castle.

The accident began as a simple loss of traction, but Evelyn slammed on the breaks, putting the car into a spin like an amusement park ride, round and round, suspending reality, her hands letting go the wheel, her body flying to the other side of the car, then the sudden jolt when everything came to a halt.

She was dazed when a man pulled her out. She was still in a daze when Tyler was pulled unharmed from the floor under the dash.

She had momentarily forgotten he was with her.

It was only nine in the morning. No one thought to suspect she'd been drinking.

A man on the edge of the road waving off gawking motorists proclaimed it a Christmas miracle. "It was Jesus Christ! Jesus saved them! Thank you, Lord!"

It took a few minutes for Evelyn's head to clear enough to see the car half buried in a snowdrift. Just a few more feet and it would have gone over the thirty-foot drop to the lake. She sobered up fast.

Evelyn did not have the flu over Christmas. She went through self-induced withdrawal.

By the time a new guardrail was installed along the stretch of Lakeshore Drive a week later, Evelyn Hodges was sober and would remain so until the night Tyler drowned.

If the man in the road that December morning was right, and it was all God's doing, then Tyler dying the one night she was drunk again was punishment, a big *I warned you once* from God.

"I promised your mother years ago to keep that confession to myself," Marilyn says. "It's yours now." She stands up, gives Penn a sad look, and walks out mumbling about needing her oxygen.

Once again, Penn is left alone to rearrange her history. There is suddenly an inevitability to Tyler's death, as if nothing could have prevented it, but that would imply fatalism, something Penn doesn't believe in. She wonders if Evelyn ever thought these things, if she resented the snowdrift that saved them from the lake, thinking at least they'd have died together instead of Tyler dying alone. Did she live the rest of her life exiled in a kind of purgatory because of it?

If she were to tell Mildred the story, Mildred would certainly agree with the man in the road and see God's hand in it: Instead of taking Ty at Christmas, they were given a reprieve, one last summer together. But the flip side would mean his death was God's retribution for Evelyn's recklessness. Penn does not accept miracles or retribution. She does not believe in God.

A wave of warmth engulfs Penn's body and with it comes a sense of connection, of knowing, of love. Then come the tears, free-flowing, cleansing. It passes quickly leaving behind memories of her father's embrace, of her mother's laugh, of Matthew and Peter and Tyler, as if in that moment they were all with her and happy. She takes a deep breath and can't help but smile.

The rest of the day passes in a state of grace, unaware of time. Penn does not watch Hospice clear out the sick room, removing the bed, meds, supplies and wheelchair. She calls Andi and Mildred to inform them Evelyn is gone, but does not elaborate or invite condolences. She needs to be alone, to feel the silence. The empty room holds no residual energy or animosity. No ghosts.

Sitting on the window bench, she watches the sun's descent toward a bank of clouds over Spirit Lake contemplating the multitude of misconceptions she's lived with all her life, wondering if this is what her mother used to do, if she bounced through time trying to resurrect the past, and at the same time bury it?

She cranks both casement windows open, one wide, the other long ago having decided it would no longer open more than halfway. A cold breeze sweeps over the water, through the willow's leafless tendrils, across the wide expanse of grass, to the patio, and up to the second story window of the small cottage. It chills her cheek. Catching a faint reflection in a narrow rectangle of windowpane, she appears pale, her features slack and gaunt. Fifty suddenly looks very old.

Dusk begins its slow crawl. The air smells sweet, like rain closing in. The room behind her dims, the room lined with windows on three sides where, as children, Penn and her brothers played cards and watched TV in soft summer pajamas; where they cowered as storms swept the shoreline; where they stood in awe as sunsets blazed across the sky; the room where the past is sometimes louder than the present.

Rain begins, a gentle shower that does little more than wash away dust. She closes both windows, turns on a lamp. Dusk and dawn, like those moments between waking and sleeping, are where sorrow lives. Though it is her mother who's just died, Penn can't stop thinking about the boys: Tyler, her little brother; and Peter, her best friend for eight weeks and two days. Boys who never grew up. Boys who, by their absence, altered the course of so many lives. Even now, forty years later, she holds to a variant of the truth, making up bits, choosing by sheer will which images to carry forward. This way they live on in memory as an amalgamation of what was and what Penn has made of them.

She'd never kept a journal outside of field notes. Writing about her life, her feelings, used to seem self-indulgent. Yet, over the summer, as she struggled to manage her mother's last weeks, the journal became a holding pond for unpredictable emotions. She stares at a blank page. Words that spilled so readily all summer suddenly hold back. She could write about seeing her brothers again, or her mother's death, but she is preoccupied with something else altogether: The beginning of it all.

CHAPTER 49

Relieved to be home, Alberta sleeps for a full fourteen hours. Upon awakening, she transitions to her couch, immobilized. She falls into full wallow mode replete with over-zealous navel-gazing. Would her parents, had they lived, counseled her against pursuing a career in lieu of a family of her own? Was losing them so young what propelled her forward, an attempt to ease the pain with ambition? She'd told herself professional accomplishment was enough, believing her father would have been proud of her, yet no matter her success, it was never enough to ease her mind and heart. Something always tugged at the edges, maybe her mother's spirit, trying to pull her back to the world, back to love.

Tucker crosses her mind. She imagines the embrace she could have felt, the closeness she could have had if only she'd let down her guard, but there was no more possibility there. She would never go back, not after what her presence wrought, the anger, reopening of deep wounds. She does not regret any of what happened except for her failure to prosecute Stem. That alone would have made the rest of it worthwhile. Pushing all that aside, she imagines Tucker on the couch next to her, his voice comforting her, his arm tight around her. He, too, is a failure and she begins to see her life as an empty misuse of years.

Michael shows up at her condo. He lets himself in, finding her on the couch wrapped in a blanket like she used to when they were kids. Their mother would let her do it for as long as she needed, sometimes nearly all day. "Bertie, Bertie, Bertie. Cocooning, I see," he says.

Hearing the term her mother gave for her healing time, never moping or pouting time, breaks down all barriers and Alberta begins to sob, a full-body bawling, tears drenching her face, snot flowing, open-throated wailing. It's wondrous.

He knows better than to try to console her. His wife and son have been sobbing for two weeks. He goes to the kitchen, opens the fridge. "You're out of beer," he announces. "And it smells out here. What the hell was this?" He holds something covered in multi-colored mold.

"Stop picking on me. I'm a mess over here."

"That you are."

He grabs a box of tissues and sits down next to her.

"Stop looking at me."

"Or what?"

Alberta laughs and cries, all her emotions fighting their way out. Yanking a tissue, she blows her nose, then grabs another and another, using them and throwing them to the floor.

"Bert. You smell," Michael says. "Take a shower, get dressed. We'll go get something to eat." Alberta pulls the blanket tighter. "I can't take one more casserole or lasagna," he says. "You know. Funeral food. Had to buy a new freezer for all of it."

She laughs and looks at him for the first time. "I'm lost," she says.

"We all are. You're just catching up. You've just kept too busy to notice you're very, very sad. It's what you do. You hide in work. Then I wait."

"What does that mean?"

"Took you a full year before you grieved Mom and Dad. You buried yourself in law school. Never came up for air. Then I found you. Like this. Immobile. Remember that?"

A long silence falls between them and in his stillness she sees his exhaustion.

"How do you do it?" she asks. "How do you get through the day?"

Michael speaks without looking at her, his eyes glazed. "I wake when I hear my wife crying. If I wake first, I try to let her sleep because if she's awake, she remembers and she cries. I get breakfast for Tommy who doesn't talk much anymore. I take him to school and watch him drag his ass into the building. He tries so hard not to cry but when it hits him, usually when he looks at his mother, it slams him. I mean it just slams him. I figure he's better off there than home. I think. How the hell do I know? I can't go back to work yet. Can't focus for shit. Don't want to leave Erin alone in the house." He turns and looks at his sister. "We're all afraid to laugh. Like it's some betrayal to grief, I guess. And we wait. All we can do is wait for the sadness to let up and even that? What comes then?"

Alberta sees he's about to break.

"It's like all we have left of him right now is this stabbing ache and when we let go of that, what will we have?" He slowly stands up, says he needs some coffee and goes to the kitchen.

Alberta hears the coffee grinder, hears him prowling around the cupboards. She calls out. "Top one to the right of the sink." A cupboard door closes. Water runs. The carafe clicks into place. The lid snaps closed. She waits for him to come back out while it brews. He doesn't. She assumes he's pulling himself together so he can help her pull herself together. He lost a child yet he's here helping her. It should be the other way around but she's not good at the emotional stuff. Never was. She smells the coffee. She hears the coffee maker sputter. It's ready. She waits, wondering if she should go in and check on him or let him be.

"Your boss called me," he says, walking in with two steaming mugs.

"He did not." She can see he's been crying.

"Yup. Said you were screwing up. The worst attorney he'd ever seen."

"Bull shit." She ignores that he's been crying.

Michael smiles.

She blows her nose again, throwing the tissue to the floor with the rest. "What, he called to tell you to tell me I'm fired?"

Michael puts both cups safely on the end table and yanks the blanket. Alberta hangs on tight. He pulls harder. The two grown siblings engage in a tug of war until they both end up on the floor.

"I had him, Michael. I had him and lost him."

"Who we talking about here?"

"Stem," she says, but in the question she sees Tucker, too.

"Ah," he says and turns away. He retrieves both their coffees. "Well, from what I hear, you went above and beyond. Something about having the balls to follow hunches."

"What are you talking about?"

"You're the best he's got, Bertie. Groves wants you back, but he wants you back in one piece. Sane. Personally, I think that's a bit much to expect." He ducks Alberta's swat.

"I can't go back in there. Did he tell you I cried? I cried! I was everything they expect a woman to be. Weak. Sniveling. Whiny."

"Would it surprise you to know they respect you? Groves and that DA in Michigan. You didn't just lose a case." He locks his tired eyes on hers. "You lost Alby. They knew you lost Alby." He watches her eyes fill again and the floodgates release a new wave of tears. "You're human. Live with it."

They sit in silence, calming with every sip of coffee. Her exhaustion feels bone deep, as if grief has entered her marrow and she wonders if it's like a cancer that will eat away at her heart or the opposite, like chemotherapy, something she has to endure to come out on the other side, in full remission. And she wonders what will be left of her, if there will be permanent damage and what it will look like. Will it soften her or make her brittle? She feels a wave of tears well up from her gut, like the stomach flu, something that will overtake her no matter what she does. But this one ebbs and dissipates.

Michael rises and takes his cup to the kitchen. "Go take a shower," he says. "I beg you. Then pack a bag. We've rented a cabin in the Adirondacks. Schroon Lake." He leans against the counter. "Erin needs to be somewhere Alby has never been. She sees him all the time," he says. "At home. She hears him. So we're leaving."

She watches him try to hold himself together.

"Won't be warm enough to swim," he says, "but we can hike our asses off. And cry."

"Hike and cry," she snipes. "Sounds like fun."

"And maybe we'll laugh."

"I'm not . . ."

"Yes. You are."

Once at the lake, Erin makes a point of sending Tommy and Alberta out together with a trail map each day. She knows they are too alike, too stubborn, to reach out to each other, even though they desperately need one another. She hopes time together might soften both of them, well aware Alberta's stoic nature could just as easily harden her son. Her gamble pays off. By the end of the first week, they are more at ease in the world and with each other. They nudge and smile and find connection.

Tommy is the first to say it, the one thing they're all trying like hell not to say: Alby would have loved this. No one cries. They all smile. And something changes. Alby is still with them, but he's not as heavy.

After two weeks of hiking their asses off, they do not return home free of grief, but they all come back knowing better how to live with it.

By the time Walter is released from the hospital, Edith has returned to England.

Their house in Bucks County burns to the ground. Arson. There is talk of using the empty lot for a play park.

After returning to Spring Lake long enough to sell his property to Marty, Walter disappears.

The drowning of two boys in Spirit Lake marsh once again becomes little more than a cautionary tale to parents of young children.

Alberta goes back to work to find her desk occupied by someone she's never met.   DA Groves calls her into a vacant office.

"You've been a victim," he says, closing the door behind them. "Now you know what that means. How it feels. Use it. Use it every day. And do something with this place. Needs some pictures or something. Maybe a plant. Women are good with plants, right?" He hands her a nameplate for the door, looking a little surprised by her lack of recognition. "It was nothing you did or didn't do," he says. "If he's guilty, he'll screw up. And you'll have everything the next guy needs to nail his ass. But in the meantime, I need you here. Welcome back."

He walks out and she lets him get halfway across the room before she speaks. "They knew each other."

"What? Who?'

"Walter Stem and Alby."

She has the full attention of everyone within earshot. "Albert's brother Tommy is in seventh grade at the Junior High where Stem was principal. Played basketball. Tommy and I got to talking last week. Alby had a piano lesson every week. A block away from Doylestown Junior High. He'd go and watch the practice for a while when the lesson was done. He always sat up high by himself. Walter used to sit with him sometimes. Then track started. Same thing. There was a track practice the day before Alby went missing. I imagine Alby trusted Walter. Probably liked him. Liked the attention. Probably told him what he was doing the next day, where he'd be. Then Velma died. And Walter did the very thing she'd kept him from for ten years." She stops for a moment, her eyes scanning the room. "He chose Alby. He knew where he'd be. They knew each other."

Groves slowly bows his head, shifts his jaw, and struggles to get the words out. "We missed it."

"It wouldn't have made a difference," she says. It's tough to admit, but she's come to accept it.

"Still," he says, "for what it's worth, this here, well, this is pattern. This is history of predation. Good instincts."

A woman calls across the room to say there's a call for Alberta. Grove says to put it through to her office.

Standing beside her empty desk, Alberta lifts the receiver proudly saying Assistant District Attorney Alberta Higgins, thinking it's probably her brother checking up on her. Her smile is cut short. She looks out to Groves as she listens, her face registering something seismic. She hangs up as Groves steps into her doorway.

"That was Lydia Metzger," she says, "the editor of the paper in Michigan, the woman who helped me. One of the boys at the lake . . . Steven Frey. He was sent away to military school after the drownings in 1960. . ." She stops, putting all the pieces together. "His parents thought he had something to do with the deaths of the boys, but he didn't." She looks at Grove with a kind of astonishment. "I didn't see it. I never thought . . ."

"What?"

"They all said he was such an angry kid. I should have seen it." She takes a breath, fighting back the sense of failure. "He showed up right after I left. Went to the police to say Walter Stem abused him for two years when he was a kid. The police didn't take him seriously. Said he was high when he told them. It never got passed on to the district attorney."

Groves asks if she wants to go talk to Steven.

Her eyes well up. "A demolition crew did a walk-through of Stem's house last Friday. They found Steven's body." She felt her chest tighten. "It'd been there for maybe a week as far as they could tell. About the same time Stem would have been in town to sign papers selling the place to Marty Wagner. They're calling it a suicide. Drug overdose."

Groves says to make sure they get a copy of the forensics.

"No forensics. Took him out. Knocked it down. He's in the ground. How many others are there, Ben? How many more will there be?"

CHAPTER 50

Walter was seven the first time his father taught him how to be a man, taking him upstairs to the room at the end of the hall, locking the door. Walter never fought back. He lived his life in a place of dark indifference where fathers abuse sons and mothers let it happen; where mothers are beaten and sons are powerless to stop it.

Walter was thirteen when the Conners built their cottage on Spirit Lake next door through the woods. He was fourteen when all the lake boys went skinny dipping, and Sammy Conner drowned, and Eugene made him fetch the dead boy's body from the channel. That was the night Walter Stem, wearing his father's jean jacket, took a rolling pin to his father's skull. "Next time," he told Eugene in his quiet voice, "I'll kill you."

Walter went into his mother's room afterwards to tell her Eugene would not be bothering her anymore. Velma saw the rolling pin, the blood, and ran to find Eugene unconscious but alive.

Velma returned to Walter. She sat with him. She held him. She rocked him. Comforted him. Walter felt vindication in his mother's embrace, and in her consolations, he found forgiveness.

"You didn't know what you were doing," she cried. "You couldn't help yourself. We won't tell anyone."

"He was so scrawny," Walter whimpered. "I just wanted to help him be a man but he didn't understand."

Velma's grip loosened. "What?"

Walter spoke calmly, without inflection. "He screamed at me. It was his fault. He was going to tell. I couldn't let him tell. He just sank."

Walter tried to rise up to look into his mother's eyes, but her grip tightened, not out of consolation but panic. Only then did she realize how she'd failed her son, how her weakness and cowardice had twisted him into something more dangerous than Eugene ever was. She clenched her boy tight enough that he was certain to feel her shudder.

He broke free and ran from the house.

Standing on the silty shoreline of the spring, his mother's words careened through his brain. *You didn't know what you were doing. You couldn't help yourself.* He replayed the night Sammy died. All the lake boys, naked, jumping into the water. How it was so cold. How he sidled up to Sammy in the dark, both of them treading water. Reaching under the surface feeling the slick lean leg. Sliding up higher, finding and fondling. *You couldn't help yourself.* Sammy's yelp and cry was lost amid hollering of other boys and brothers. Sammy's swift kick. The panic and confusion. Gulping air and ducking under, swimming down, reaching up. Grabbing Sammy's ankle, yanking hard. *You didn't know what you were doing.* Pulling him under just to stop his screaming. Lungs stinging, ears hissing, fighting the writhing body, gripping thin arms, pressing feet against bony shoulders. Huge bubbles sifting up along his back, Sammy's body quieting. Pushing it deeper, a limp hand slipping off his foot. Lungs aching, bolting to the surface, gasping. No one yet noticing they were one less. *We won't tell anyone.*

Sammy had screamed. Sammy fought back. Only then did Walter understand he could do the same and he attacked Eugene.

Eugene survived his son's bludgeoning, yet the blows left him addled. It was days before he felt well enough to leave the house, and he bellowed when he couldn't find his jean jacket, the one he wore every day to work, the one he wore every time he assaulted Velma and molested Walter. He only had to see his son's dead stare to understand Walter could make him disappear just as easily as the jacket. The power dynamic shifted.

In September of 1943, a month after Walter shipped out, Velma was on her knees in front of Eugene, her hair tight in his grip when he keeled over and died of a stroke. Velma had him cremated and wore an ugly little grin whenever she walked over the septic tank, having flushed his ashes.

As she dismantled the house, burning all trace of Eugene, she kept only one thing. She'd found his jean jacket on the floor of Walter's closet. She hung it on a coat hook by the back door, keeping it as she kept her vigilance, in plain sight, for twenty-two years until that Monday morning in 1960 when she woke to find it gone.

Heavy rains turned the path to a stream as Walter ran from the marsh in the dark, more like a frightened child than a man. Flashes of frightened faces lit up his brain. The thunder could not mute the cries echoing in his ears. The wind could not sweep away the sensation of flinging small bodies. He could not let go of the yearning to feel tender flesh, denied him by Tyler's interruption. His legs gave out at the road and he fell, ducking behind a tree when a car went by, taillights heading away. Back down the road he saw Steven slip in the mud making his way home.

Cold and soaked, Walter stumbled to his house, falling to his knees at the back stoop when he saw Velma in the window.

She had only to look at her son, a grown man melting in the deluge, the jean jacket on his back, to know she'd failed him again. She called him in, but he didn't rise from the mud and she went to him, her nightgown drenched and clinging. She knelt down to him, rocked him as a child, her embrace yet again offering vindication for his sins.

"They didn't understand," he said.

She pushed him to arm's length. "Who?" she shouted.

Walter looked at her, his face an expression of indifference. "They didn't understand," he said calmly.

Velma recoiled and slapped him hard across the face, a broken fingernail scratching his cheek. "What have you done?" she screamed and hit him again before dragging him inside.

Both of them stood in the hallway dripping mud. Walter, his eyes cast to the floor, said he needed a pillowcase. Velma took his head hard in her hands, pulling his face to hers, demanding he look at her. His eyes were vacant. "Just one," he said, and fear alone propelled her upstairs to pull one from her own bed, muddy footprints in her wake. Handing it to him she noticed the missing button on his jean jacket, one of three she'd sewn on with red thread. She asked how it was torn off and when Walter once again couldn't look at her, she panicked. "You find that button! Do you hear me?" She tore the jacket off him and watched him run back into the woods, not yet knowing the fullness of his crime.

Walter was at the marsh nearly to the deep water, searching for Tyler's body, hoping the button was clenched in his hand or in the fold of his clothes when the beam of a flashlight caught his face and he heard Steven on shore.

"What did you do?" Steven shouted.

Walter turned away, making his way deeper to the bodies. Steven plowed in after him, grabbed Walter's shirt and tugged. Walter, finding footing within the cattails, yanked free, facing Steven with a steely expression. Steven froze. The waters calmed around them.

"I saw you," Walter said in his quiet voice. "On the road just before dawn. I saw you."

"I'll tell them what happens out here," Steven said, his hands shaking. "I'll tell them what you do. I'll tell them."

"No," Walter said. "You won't."

When Peter's naked body filtered through the cattails, Steven surged toward it, to help him, but Walter grabbed his arm, squeezing tight, and with the other hand pushed the body down and away.

"Who do you think they're going to believe?" Walter asked.

Not far down the path, Carl called out for Tyler and Peter. "I found them!" Walter hollered. "They're here!" Steven bolted through the weeds and ran into the woods, emerging only after Carl and Dan were waste deep in the marsh, too preoccupied to notice Steven was already wet before he stumbled in after them.

Somewhere in the commotion, Walter crammed the pillowcase deep into the tangle of roots.

In the convoluted turn of events that followed, Walter was seen as heroic for finding the boys. No questions were asked of him. No accusations placed upon him. And the button, having disappeared, could not point to him. No one noticed him slip the pillowcase into the marsh to be found later.

Walter was unusually buoyant in July of 1967, his step lighter, quicker. Velma couldn't figure it out until she observed him on the road one morning when a young man, maybe in his late twenties, walked up. It was the oldest Vogel boy, Eric Junior. Eric had been the first lake boy Walter took under his wing, teaching him how to manicure a lawn, chop kindling and catch bass.

As the men talked, two young boys, maybe seven or eight, ran up behind Eric. There hadn't been young boys around in years. The thought of a new generation populating the woods set Velma's heart to pounding. She watched the men talk, the boys paying close attention as their father pointed to the woodpile. A woman's voice carried from down the road, and the boys ran off towards it. Eric followed. Walter turned to go back to the house. Velma blocked his path.

"No," she said, and Walter tried to walk past her, but she grabbed him, her arms gripping as tight as she could. "We're moving," she said. "Or I'll tell the world what you are."

A colleague had an old friend in Pennsylvania who wanted to retire. Walter took the position, arriving with high recommendations, greeted by a staff eager to have a man under fifty for a boss. Velma, Walter and Edith moved into a lovely neighborhood in a quiet town. Velma hung the jean jacket on a hook by the back door where she and Walter would see it every day: To Walter, it was a temptation; to Velma, a threat.

CHAPTER 51

Peter liked Mr. Stem. He'd caught the first fish of his life with him. It was a little Sunfish. He threw it back, watched it swim away. Bigger fish came along, and Mr. Stem taught him how to remove the hook, string them, gut and clean them, something Peter lied about to his parents. He didn't want to kill anything. He did it out of respect. Mrs. Stem cooked the fish he caught. Peter liked Mrs. Stem but didn't particularly like the fish. Under Mr. Stem's tutelage, Peter learned how to use a hatchet to split wood into kindling. Mr. Stem said when he grew bigger, he'd be able to handle the ax. He liked Mr. Stem because he was an educator like his parents. Peter liked reading up on a thing in the evening so he'd have something interesting to tell Mr. Stem if he saw him the next day. Mr. Stem listened to him. Mr. Stem was helping him to become a man. *The marsh comes alive at night* Mr. Stem had said. *So much to see and learn.* Mr. Stem said the other boys weren't smart enough to appreciate what he had to teach, that Peter had so much more to offer the world. *You're special.* The last thing Peter wanted to do was disappoint Mr. Stem, so he took the flashlight, pulled on his jacket, and snuck out of the cottage into the windy night to meet Mr. Stem at the marsh.

Tyler hadn't been awakened that night. He hadn't slept. It was the wind. He didn't like it. It was invisible. Unstoppable. He couldn't keep his eyes off the trees bending side to side, their shadows racing back and forth. When he saw a light dancing along the road, someone walking in the dark, he could tell it was Peter by the way he moved. It was a distinctive gate, leaning forward like he was just about to fall over his own feet. Ty waited for Peter's dad to come along, thinking they were on a night foray together, but no one came.

Ty pulled on his pants and tee shirt, walked past Penny's cubby, and reached for the flashlight that was normally on the ledge by the door, but it wasn't there. He looked out. The moon was bright enough, he thought, and he snuck out. Making it just past the car, a gust of wind buffeted his face, and he fought the urge to go back inside. A branch snapped overhead. A twig fell against his back, making him lurch aside, brushing it away in a frenzy. Whether curiosity or concern drove him that night, it was the moon, illuminating the path to the marsh like a ribbon through the woods, that gave him the courage to venture forth. Even after tripping over a fallen branch, he regained his footing and continued on.

Above him, trees rubbed together, creaking, taunting. Bushes along the path seemed to reach for him. Drawing closer to the small clearing on the edge of the marsh, the ribbiting and croaking grew louder but was nearly drowned out by the swishing of the reeds and cattails; by the rattling of bushes and trees all around him; threatening sound surging and ebbing. He thought he heard someone talking, then a higher voice, like Peter maybe. Angry sounds. Then he saw what could have been Peter standing with his back to him, a flashlight shining through the grass between bare legs. Words slid on the wind. *Stop it. Don't. I don't want to,* and Peter appeared to be trying to pull away from someone. What else Tyler saw he wasn't sure, the ambient light being bright and not bright at the same time, edges undefined.

Ty called out. Peter shouted back, calling for help. A figure rose, a tall shadow. What followed happened fast, too fast for either boy to comprehend anything but fear. Peter yelped and went flying through the air, landing with a thud against a log. Tyler charged forth, instinct coursing past reason, pouncing on the shadow, kicking, grabbing, a button yanked and tossed, an arm gripped and tugged, searing pain and vice grip and water and gasping and kicking and lungs stinging and ears hissing and gulping silty water. Choking. Pain. Terror. Stillness.

Forty years after her young son's death, Evelyn Hodges lay in bed in the cottage on Spirit Lake, her face tilted to the window Tyler once peered from as a child. She was not aware of her grown children sitting around a blazing fire talking to each other for the first time in decades. She was drifting into the moment of transition. In her gaze, the cold silent night on the edge of winter, sighed. A breeze rustled bare branches, slowly replenishing them with dewy foliage, returning to their mid-summer canopy. Warm air, heavily scented with moss and pine, drifted in through the now open window. Cicadas and tree peepers and crickets sang out. A hidden moon slipped from behind a cloud to rest in a clear dark sky. Breeze became wind, sailing through the trees, high branches dancing in slow motion, waving to her, to the moon, its full face shining down, illuminating a young boy padding over twigs and gravel to the road. She watched this boy, his steps gentle, his motion effortless. She watched this boy, her son, hesitate at the road's edge and slowly turn back to her. He smiled as he used to, full and honest and comforting, then ran as one does in a dream, weightless, and disappeared into the woods out of sight. Evelyn Hodges slipped away with him.

In the half-light of a full moon or on winter nights when light reflects off lake ice, Penn has sometimes thought the cottage looked like it used to when she was ten, like time had stopped the day the youngest of them died and everything after was just an apparition. She even swore she could still smell the iron in the well water even though the county had long since converted to city water.

She tried to abandon the cottage once, as her mother had, but like an invasive vine whose roots grow stronger when cut, the tendrils reached for her, pulling her back. In spite of all that happened there, or because of it, she now realizes the cottage is the only true home she's ever known.

Any expectation of further reconciliation with her brothers fades. Even with Marilyn's insistence on setting the record straight, Penn has no inclination to share any of it with the boys.

Penn picks up her journal and writes the last entry.

> October 6, 2000 - I know now my mother never forgave herself, and why. But there was enough guilt to haunt us all. I've lived my life preoccupied with Tyler and Peter, boys who never grew up. Always something of them lingers - only a hair's width out of reach. It isn't their presence so much as what their deaths wrought, the interruption of

what should have been. I've imagined Peter as a teenager coming into his own, class valedictorian, following his parents' footsteps into academia. Sometimes he's married to me, and other times I gave him someone better, a lovely woman, much like his mother, and they had nerdy little kids who adored their father. Always had a harder time nailing down Tyler as clearly, but he usually seems to end up in Bozeman Montana with an outdoorsy wife and three daughters, all of them beautiful and centered and happy. And here I sit. Mom just died and everything I believed about her has become a knotted tangle of lies, yet Tyler is the one stealing all my attention. So – I'm left to mourn a woman I never truly knew and only now – when there is no one left to answer – do I finally find the questions.

Penn closes the journal. She pulls on her fleece and a down vest and heads to the beach. Skillfully stepping into her kayak, her foot dips into cold water to shove off. She hasn't paddled all summer. The silence of her stokes, the faint drops of water, settle her soul. Something about seeing windows aglow gives her the kind of calm that follows chaos of lake life, voices quieted after a raucous day. She feels the bone deep memory of love taken for granted, when each day was a given, far too many wasted, held in disdain as brothers pestered and little wars broke out along the shore. Even now, she seems set on disparaging what was in all likelihood a time of amazing freedom and exploration. It all changed when they lost the boys, but before that, it might have been magnificent. She is certain of it and she chooses to carry a better story forward than what might have been. It isn't so much a denial as self-preservation, a healing, it's the story where Walter is a good man. The boys are happy. It's the story that fits into a cigar box tucked in a drawer under a sleeping cubby.

Stars begin to appear, the North Star, Mars and Orion. Drifting in silence, her spirit expands, reaching ever wider. On still waters she sees possibility, maybe even her future, one entirely her own. It's a vision she wants to write about, but in the attempt later, the words will not come. The page will remain blank. She is left only with the emotion of it, the inexplicable sensation of release.

- The End -